# Possession

## The Shadow Walker Chronicles, Book One

## Timothy E. Sizemore

POSSESSION




Edited by Tammy Sayler and Joseph Nassise

Cover Illustration: G&S Cover Design Studio

Chapter Header Illustrations: Whitney Law and Kamraan Allibhaye

To the great men of **C/38 Long Range Surveillance**, A.K.A. **The Lucky 38**. I knew what it meant to stand on the shoulders of giants when I served with you. This story wouldn't be what it is today without your inspiration and leadership. I hope you are well.

**IN ORBE TERRUM NON VISI**

# The Ranger Creed

**R**ecognizing that I volunteered as a Ranger, fully knowing the hazards of my chosen profession, I will always endeavor to uphold the prestige, honor, and high spirit de corps of the Rangers.

**A**cknowledging the fact that a Ranger is a more elite soldier who arrives at the cutting edge of battle by land, sea, or air, I accept the fact that as a Ranger my country expects me to move further, faster, and fight harder than any other soldier.

**N**ever shall I fail my comrades. I will always keep myself mentally alert, physically strong, and morally straight, and I will shoulder more than my share of the task, whatever it may be, one hundred percent and then some.

**G**allantly will I show the world that I am a specially selected and well-trained soldier. My courtesy to superior officers, neatness of dress, and care of equipment shall set the example for others to follow.

**E**nergetically will I meet the enemies of my country. I shall defeat them on the field of battle for I am better trained and will fight with all my might. Surrender is not a Ranger word. I will never leave a fallen comrade to fall into the hands of the enemy and under no circumstances will I ever embarrass my country.

**R**eadily will I display the intestinal fortitude required to fight on to the Ranger objective and complete the mission, though I be the lone survivor.

**Rangers Lead The Way!**

# Chapter 1

"If you know the way broadly, you will see it in all things."
- Miyamoto Musashi -

I've always marveled at how suddenly and completely the world around you can change based on a simple choice, regardless of how small or insignificant the choice may seem.

*Feet set, shoulder-width apart. Right foot back, toes just behind the heel of the left foot. Knees slightly bent. Bend slightly at the hip with arms extended. A solid, comfortable fighting stance.*

Or how, in spite of the most basic and well-thought-out plans, the smallest variable or misinformation can completely upend the world around you. The decisions that are left for you, no matter how simple or complex they may be, can just as easily unravel everything you thought you knew, sending you flying off your feet like a leaf in hurricane winds.

*Hands firm and steady. Fingers of the right hand wrapped firmly around the textured grip of my father's old 1911. Fingers of the left hand wrapped firmly, but loosely around the fingers of the right, providing a steadier platform and shooting base. Thumbs pointed in the direction of the target. The trigger finger extended outside the trigger well.*

Yet in this ever-changing and often chaotic world, it becomes all too easy to be distracted with the bigger picture of events while missing the finer details that often throw the world into chaos in the first place.

*The target is set, unmoving in the distance with a large mound of dirt nearly ten feet tall directly behind it. The front and rear sights are set level to each other and placed at the center of the man-shaped silhouette. My eyes begin to focus, blurring the target and the rear sights in kind.*

Starting from the beginning of basic training, the Army will teach you to "keep your head on a swivel" and to "pay attention to detail." Surely a hard lesson learned by the countless warriors throughout the ages. Is there any wonder why even the best-laid plans can be foiled by a simple explosive, cleverly disguised on the side of the road as a piece of trash?

*My finger on the trigger, my breathing becomes slow, smooth, and steady. I can practically feel the thunder of my heart within my chest as my breath pauses on the exhale. A simple application of force and the trigger is slowly pulled to the rear. The sear breaks, the hammer drops, and the slide lurches back as it sends the expended brass tumbling up and to the right. The solid boom of the .45 ACP round reverberates within my chest as the recoil gently pushes against me.*

But I suppose it's never just one little thing, is it? It always seems like it's the accumulation of multiple minute details that truly defines the bigger picture. A slight shift in the wind, a piece of trash out of place yet unnoticed all combined can play their part. All it would take is a simple step back, opening your eyes and observing all the details within the bigger picture for you to notice the danger before you and to react accordingly.

*The slide lurches forward as it extracts the round from the magazine, feeds it into the chamber and locks it into place. I realign the sights with the target as I take another breath and once again hold on the exhale. A gentle application of force. The sear breaks. The hammer drops.*

So how do you react when it seems like the smallest step or the slightest breath can make the difference between serenity and calamity? How do you live with the consequences of these decisions? When faced with this understanding, is it really any wonder why so many people would rather avoid the events that are unfolding around them? Can you really blame them? Then again, how can you not?

*The final round takes flight as the slide locks to the rear. Keeping eyes on target, I eject the now empty magazine as I seamlessly reach for a fresh one. Feeding the mag into the weapon, I send the slide home. I realign the sights as I hold on the exhale. A gentle application of force. The sear breaks. The hammer drops.*

As an Army Ranger, I was taught to adapt to changing surroundings, and in doing so to overcome in the face of adversity. So how do you do so when everything you know changes? How do you react when reality warps into the realm of fiction, and everything you thought you knew turns out to be a lie? What do you do when a creature of myth and legend reaches out her hand to take yours, offering salvation in the wake of catastrophe and annihilation? Do you take it?

*With a final burst of thunder, the slide of my father's old 1911 locks to the rear.*

––––––––––––

Expelling the last of my ammunition, I found myself no longer held within the confines of my mind, but in the empty firing line at an outdoor shooting range. Dropping my firing stance, I closed my eyes to take in the quiet of the day while the cool North Dakota breeze blew across my cheek like the light caress of a woman's touch. It was still so strange how even here, in the empty hills of the high desert and miles away from civilization, even the MacLean Bottoms firing range felt like it was caught in the eye of a vast hurricane-like storm.

Taking in the smell of cordite with a deep breath, I opened my eyes to the call of a raven breaking the quiet stillness of the world around me. Since my enlistment as an Army Ranger had ended a decade ago, it was ranges like this that I called my church. A now weekly ritual, I came here to escape the ensuing storm so I might make sense of the sudden changes that had befallen my once seemingly simple life.

Since my discharge from military service and the death of my father, it was this sort of ritual that I found to be essential in the daily fight to keep the literal internal demon locked and buried within the confines of my soul. Without this sort of vigilance, I feared that one day, Asmodeus would break the magical bonds of her captivity and once again take control of both my mind, and my body. Lord knows what sort of havoc this "demon of chaos" might unleash if such a day came to pass.

And that was the totality of the war I now fought, each and every day. What were once battles waged in lands far from home, soon became a war fought from within; the battleground becoming the very soul I fought for.

It was a battle fought largely in seclusion, while hiding in plain sight, deep within the rolling hills of central North Dakota. It was a war fought far and away from the watchful eyes of the Thirteen Pyres Society, who would execute me if they found me, and from the terror of the United Magistrate, with whom my family once fought alongside for the sake of mystic supremacy.

This train of thought was broken suddenly by the quick, silent buzz of my phone within my pocket. I holstered my weapon, pulled out my phone, and felt myself frowning as I silently read the email notification that flashed onto the screen.

*Kyle E. Goodwin,*

*On behalf of MCI Institute LLC, I would like to thank you for showing interest in joining The MCI Institute family. After reviewing your application, I regret to inform you…*

"Awesome," I huffed out loud to myself. "Another one." I understood that finding a new job in today's market would not be easy, but the constant flow of rejections was really starting to grate on me. I wasn't out of options though, and I had to remind myself that I came out here to give myself a break from focusing on all that.

I grunted in frustration while I pocketed my phone and walked toward the target, gathering my thoughts along the way. Walking the twenty-five meters it took to get there, I was not disappointed to find that after nearly a full day of shooting, not a single round made it outside the six-inch spread that marked the center of the man-shaped silhouette target.

When I reached the target, I paused for a moment while I inspected my handiwork. In doing so I couldn't help but notice the onset of a slight smile beginning to creep over the normally stern features of my face as I pulled a pen from my pocket and circled the newly formed groupings. "Damn!" I exclaimed to myself. "Why can't everything in life be this simple?"

# Chapter 2

The trip from the shooting range to my apartment in Bismarck wasn't exactly a long one. The gentle hum of the four-cylinder engine inside my little red Toyota pickup along with the chatter of the radio had a way of placing me in a trance that always seemed to make the twenty-minute ride much shorter than it really was. Before I knew it, I was already parked outside my three-story residential apartment building, up the stairs leading to the second floor, and through the metal door leading into my apartment.

As I made my way through the door, I was surprised to see my fiancé covering the twenty-foot span of the living room on her way to greet me. I barely had the opportunity to close the door before I found her slender arms wrapped around the muscular frame of my chest as she drew her body into mine, burying her face into my chest as she did so.

"Good afternoon, honey," came her slightly muffled voice through moans of pleasure, the sort that sends a man's soul soaring to the moon and beyond. "How was the range?"

"It went well. I was practically alone the whole time, and the 1911 ran like a dream as always."

A sea of curly red hair churned away from me and two bright eyes, like emeralds, emerged to meet mine as they rose up from the tide. My heart nearly thundered out of my chest as I slowly took note of the various curves and features that made up her perfectly round face, from her little button nose down to the rosy-red lips framing her marble-white teeth. Her mouth blossomed into that perfect smile, a true living work of art in her own right.

"I love the way you smell after you come home from the range!" she exclaimed through a lazy sigh. "But anyway, I've been rather productive today myself."

"Have you now, how so?"

"Well, the bank called today and they approved the loan for the house we were looking at for Ms. Eldonna, which it sounds like she will pay off right away. Now all we need to do is to make sure the inspectors finish with their business, and she should be able to move in within the next couple of weeks."

"That's outstanding, Amber. I'm really happy for you."

With the sort of kiss that would make Aphrodite envious, she spun on her heels and walked into the living room where she had apparently been doing laundry, her five-foot six-inch frame unapologetically swaying in her gait.

I've always viewed Amber as a warrior in her own right. After graduating from high school, she went right into college to study business and made the dean's list during all four years of study. After her stint in college, she naturally flowed into the realm of real estate and became a seemingly instant success. Of course, her success never came without work. With nearly three-quarters of a realtor's success coming from referrals, she was nearly always away from home attending any social event she could manage. Considering how she wasn't even from Bismarck, this sort of grunt work was even more essential for any amount of success in her new profession.

"So, what is the final say on the price of the house then?" I asked, untying my boots by the door.

"One million seven hundred and fifty thousand dollars," she casually stated, plucking a blue shirt from the pile of clothes on the living room table.

My jaw nearly fell through the floor. "The hell did you just say?"

With a cocky jerk of her head and a glint in her eye, she looked at me with a smile. "You heard me."

With the usual three percent commission that comes with nearly any sale, she would make nearly our typical annual income with this one deal. *Cocky little twerp. She is lucky she's cute.*

Our apartment wasn't anything too grand, but it definitely suited our needs. We had the well-used but orderly kitchenette on the east side, where a half wall separated it from the living room. The south end had a door that led into the bathroom, and on the south side of the living room were the two doors that led to both bedrooms. To the west was the sliding glass door with light blue blinds on either side, which accented the light shining in from the bright summer day.

The living room was pretty modest itself, with a light brown leather couch in the middle. In front of the couch was a solid cherry wood coffee table we'd picked up from a garage sale along the way, which was now covered by a pile of clothes. And of course, we had a basic entertainment center leaning against the kitchen/living room dividing wall. A brown leather La-Z-Boy recliner sat against the south wall between the bedroom doors with a painting of the Eiffel Tower hanging overhead.

After grabbing the cleaning kit for the 1911 from the closet to the right of the door, I casually made my way to the couch where my future wife was folding her clothes. The way she was watching me from the corner of her eye, I could tell that she wasn't fooled by my seemingly innocent and casual approach. When I made it to within a few feet of her, I dropped the cleaning kit to the floor, which landed with an audible thud, and attempted to pounce on her. This prompted her to toss the shirt she was folding into my face. As the shirt unfolded midflight and opened up like a bright blue parachute, my right hand caught the middle of it and tore the shirt from its trajectory, while my left arm wrapped around the contours of her flat stomach. Using my momentum, I found it all too easy to direct the tackle directly into the padded cushion of the couch below.

Landing in a fit of giggles, she wrapped her legs around my waist while grabbing two fist-fulls of my shirt, pulling me into a tender kiss. With moans of pleasure, I pulled away from her and stared once again into those big green eyes as she let go of my shirt and wrapped her arms around the back of my neck.

"That is outstanding, Amber. I am immensely proud of you. I'm glad all that hard work finally started to pay off," I said as I reached up with my right hand, gingerly stroking her cheek with my thumb.

The light that normally shone from deep within her eyes seemed to grow ever brighter as her face blossomed into a smile. Catching herself, she modestly contained her smile and with a nod she closed her eyes and gave a quiet, happy little thank you.

After a moment she opened her eyes and looked deeply into mine, but for only a moment before her smile could no longer be contained and she drew me into another long kiss. As the fires of passion engulfed the inside of my chest, fueled by her loving kiss, a blanket of calm waters cooled the inferno as she pulled my face into her neck and held me in a loving embrace.

I could practically feel myself enveloping her, an easy thing to do considering the half a foot I had on her, and the two hundred and fifteen pounds packed into my heavily muscled frame. In spite of this, our bodies fit together like puzzle pieces perfectly married to form a once-lost picture, only to melt into each other as our very souls intertwined in our embrace. As I relaxed into her and softly kissed the contours of her neck, I was subtly reminded of how utterly different my life would have been without her in it.

Amber and I had known each other since we were practically children. We first met in sixth grade, after her father decided to move her and her brother to our little Wyoming town when he got a job in the nearby coal mines. This was shortly after her mother died. Unable to cope with the death of his wife, as well as the added responsibility of being a single parent, her father turned to alcohol, and the violence at home soon followed. Over the next couple of years, you could see the decay of her living environment slowly growing. It started of course with her clothes, which slowly became worn with age, and then the bruises which increased in frequency and became ever harder to explain away. It took far too long for the authorities to catch wind of what was going on before they finally placed her in foster care, where she remained until graduation.

The one thing I always admired about her was the incredible amount of strength and grace she showed in spite of everything she'd had to endure during those years of loss, abuse, and neglect. No matter how bad everything seemed to be, she always seemed to maintain her ever-positive attitude, and she never once seemed to let the circumstances of her life dim or crush her spirit.

Coming from a broken home myself, it was easy for the two of us to relate to one another, although my circumstances were admittedly far different and much more positive. My father was a police officer for as long as I could remember and had become well respected in the department, gaining both rank and position relatively quickly throughout his career. My mother, however, died of a stroke when I was eleven years old, leaving my father to raise me by himself.

With my father working long hours in his ever-chaotic schedule, it left me with a lot of time and plenty of opportunities to get into trouble, especially after those first couple years after my mother passed away. That was until Amber moved into that little Wyoming town. Although our friendship formed due to our shared backgrounds and interests, it was strengthened through adversity as her life at home slowly began to decay. As her father's alcoholism worsened, so did the abuse; and as the abuse worsened, Amber and I would spend more time together. Over time our bond steadily grew as we continued to rely on each other for support.

After high school, we inevitably lost touch with each other as we went our separate ways. She went off to college, and I ended up joining the Army right after graduation. With multiple combat deployments to both Afghanistan and Iraq, it was nearly impossible to keep in touch with anyone long distance. Our paths didn't cross again until after she graduated from college. She had moved back home, and we saw each other again for the first time while I was visiting during a post-deployment leave. It was like a day hadn't passed.

We lay together on the couch for what seemed like a blissful eternity, relaxed in each other's warm embrace. With a sigh of effort, however, I somehow found the will to push myself up into a seated position.

"Thank you, Amber, for being such an important part of my life," I said as her big green eyes seemed to put me into a trance.

Sitting up, she met my eyes kindly as her face once again broke into a smile. "Kyle, you have always been the one person I could count on, no matter what the circumstances. Without you, I would have lost my way a long time ago."

"Love you, hon." I said, shaking my head, bending over to kiss her.

"I love you too, love, and thank you."

And with that we embarked on the never-ending quest to fold the last of our clothes as we stood together in quiet reminiscence. We soon found ourselves in a timeless waltz oblivious to the stresses and the cares of the world outside our doors. In this dance we shared the rest of the day together, a rarity these days with Amber's ever busy schedule. Our waltz flowed from the folding of the clothes into the sharing of the meal and ended with her cradled in my arms back on the comfort of the couch. As the daylight hours faded into night, we shared our dreams and our visions of the future together but soon drifted into a comfortable silence, alive in each other's loving embrace.

# Chapter 3

The deceptively cool predawn mornings in Mosul, Iraq, always seemed to be just hot enough for me to form little beads of sweat along my brow, especially while packed to the brim with over eighty pounds of gear and prowling along alleyways with a platoon of eager Rangers like a pack of hungry wolves on the hunt for a kill. The green hue of the night vision goggles provided an otherworldly ambiance of the ancient desert city as we passed quietly through the dark of night.

Our mission that morning was like the countless others before it. My platoon was to conduct a raid on an insurgent-held compound in order to kill or capture a high-value target believed to be inside. From there we would high-tail it back to FOB Marez with our prize and hopefully call it a night, only to wake up later the following evening and repeat the process all over again.

Weaving between the brick high-walled compounds and small alleyways, my eager and hungry nine-man squad passed quietly through nearly two blocks of residential neighborhoods before we finally made it to the target building. As we approached the alley way entrance of the ten-foot-high wall surrounding the building, my squad stacked up by the gated door and took a tactical pause as the other squads and sniper teams moved into place. Standing in my place behind my four-man Alpha team, I decided to take this opportunity to move to the head of the stack, passing tired, battle-weary, and sweat-covered young men to see firsthand what we were up against.

Passing Sergeant Ramirez and his team, I couldn't help but glance over to these men and note the mixed emotions woven within the squad. Surprisingly, fear wasn't one of them. For the SAW gunner on the team, it was a look of sly and cunning anticipation, the sort of calm eagerness that only machine gunners seem to possess. Maybe it's the understanding that they are capable of killing at over six hundred and fifty rounds per minute that gives them this sort of confidence. As I passed him, he gave me an ear-to-ear smile of near-manic joy. Come to think of it, Specialist Langston was always a crazy little bastard. Maybe that had something to do with it too.

When I passed Ramirez, he was scanning the rooftops that peered over the courtyard wall on the other side of the alley. "Stay here while I have a look." I whispered.

Ramirez had a look of pure steel. With his rugged Hispanic features, he emanated quiet confidence, but his eyes carried the sharp edge that only years of war and conflict can temper. His response was merely a quick "Roger," followed by a nod before he returned to his task.

For Specialist Albers, it looked like it was business as usual. He was here, he knew what to do, and that was all there was to it. Although there was the anticipation of the fight ahead written on his face, there was a quiet Zen-like quality in him. He gave me a wandering glance as I passed beside him, and as I did, I gave him a wink. With a quiet laugh he simply shook his head and resumed scanning, his weapon at the low ready.

Watson on the other hand was brimming with apprehension. Not that you could blame the guy. Being the first man in a stack can be nerve-racking at times, especially considering that this was his first deployment, and he had only a couple of raids under his belt. Be that as it may, he had already proven himself and I was more than happy to have him on the team. As I passed him, I gave him a quick pat on the shoulder, which seemed to relax him a little bit. With a sigh of relief, he dropped his guard when I took his place in the stack.

By the gated door there was a section of the wall that had crumbled away just low enough for someone to poke their head through. The residence seemed like any of the other homes you would find in the "middle class" suburbs of Mosul. It was a plain two-story rectangular building with a flat roof and a courtyard in its center. Directly on the opposite side of the gate was a hard-packed walkway leading to the back door, which cut the dirt-filled yard in two. The home itself seemed quiet, almost vacant, as it stood before me, ghost-like in the green hue of my night vision goggles.

As I slunk back from my little hole in the wall, it was the quiet that got to me the most. It wasn't that I was worried we had been compromised or anything; the lack of noise and movement indicated to the contrary. For reasons I could not explain, the quiet seemed to create an ambiance of lifelessness. It was as if death himself had descended upon this place and had determined to hungrily lie in wait for the ensuing chaos to come. For a warrior, death is a constant. Death is everywhere. You live to slake death's lust and his hunger for departed souls. I thrived on the knowledge of being his instrument as I drove my force and will into the enemy while plunging his very being into Death's open and eager maw. This time, however, it felt as if death was smiling hungrily down upon *me*.

In this profession, it was natural to feel some semblance of fear. I would even go as far as to say that it wasn't human not to. Every day we were deployed outside the safety of a FOB, or "outside the wire," we were constantly walking a tightrope between life and death. With the never-ending rehearsals and the constant checking and rechecking of equipment, we did all that we could to prevent ourselves and our fellow Rangers from falling off that rope. But the harsh reality of war lies in the fact that the enemy is just as determined to kill you as you are to kill him. No matter how much we trained or how prepared we were to enter the fight, the enemy would still do everything in his power to turn us into rotting corpses left to cook in the hot desert sun.

But this had a different flavor than fear altogether. Instead of the usual tidal wave that would normally try to envelop me in terror, it felt more like a shadow. It was as if this ever-faithful companion of mine was standing over me, silently watching me in quiet contempt while his toothy smile closed into a hungry grin. Yet strangely it didn't feel quite like death himself, but something else entirely.

Forcing these thoughts from my mind, I turned to Watson, who still seemed a little apprehensive about his given situation.

"Slow is smooth, Watson," I said as I placed my hand on his shoulder. "Just like we rehearsed back at the FOB, you got this."

"Roger, Sergeant" was his stern reply as he slowly relaxed.

With that I began to move back to my original place within the stack, and I was once again taken aback by this feeling of being watched by this new, unknown stalker. As I was about to pass Ramirez, my eyes were drawn up to a rooftop on the opposite side of the alley, and what I saw sent a deep, paralyzing chill shooting down my spine. A woman was standing so close to the edge of the roof that her toes were hanging off the ledge. The part of her white robes that didn't cling to her body waved like a flag in strong winds, along with her black hair, which was cut merely a couple of inches past shoulder length. What struck me about this woman, more than anything else, was the expression on her face. Her dark eyes appeared ancient, filled with a cold anger that seemed to burn steadily colder as I stared into them. Her young dark face, although strikingly beautiful, was set in a stern, hard expression. I had only seen her for a mere fraction of a second before I passed Ramirez, his hard mass momentarily blocking my view. Once I moved past him, and her original location on the roof was once again revealed to me, she was no longer there.

I was so startled by what I had seen that I nearly tripped mid stride and had to stop to catch myself. As I scanned the area where I had spotted her, I found myself gasping for breath while fear gripped me tight in its cold grasp, my heart thundering within my chest. Looking to my brothers for some sort of sign they had seen her, I was chilled further to find no indication anyone had noticed her presence. No look of shock or confusion in their faces, or even the slightest clue that they had seen anything at all. Many were scanning the same building where I had seen her, but not a single one had even so much as flinched to suggest the possibility that they had seen anything out of the norm.

Moving into place behind Langston, I was beginning to wonder if I had seen anything at all. With these back-to-back missions, sleep had been hard to come by lately. Was the anticipation of the raid stressing me out more than I thought? Was it possible I had simply hallucinated her? With such a strikingly out-of-place figure, someone would have made some sort of sign or mention of her. Maybe that was it. Maybe I was just seeing things.

Crouching in my fighting stance, M4 at the low ready, I initiated a tactical breathing exercise designed to steady my breathing and heart rate. I began with the inhale. A slow and steady count to four, tongue pressed against the roof of my mouth. At the peak of the inhale, I lightly closed my eyes and held my breath for a steady count to four. With the exhale and yet another count to four, I slowly opened my eyes and scanned the surrounding area. With each breath, I could feel the tension in my shoulders slowly ebb away, my mind focusing into place on this quiet Arabian night.

I continued to visually scan the area, my eyes occasionally wandering to where I had last seen the woman in white. Although she was no longer there, I couldn't help but feel as if I were still enveloped in her deathly shadow. It was as if concealed behind some window or dark corner, her beautifully young yet ancient gaze was still fixed on me, hungrily waiting in quiet anticipation for the meal to come.

A sudden break in radio silence came.

"Viper 1-6, this is Viper 1-4."

"This is Viper 1-6, send it."

"Viper 1-6, over watch in place."

"Viper 1-4, this is Viper 1-6, roger that. Viper 1-1, you are clear to engage."

With a flick of my wrist, I sent the signal to Ramirez to breach the gate and head to the house. With a nod of confirmation, Ramirez sent his team to work, and quiet nudges and hand signals were passed between the men to communicate what they needed to do between them. It wasn't long before Ramirez dropped his guard and grabbed a pair of bolt cutters that were strapped to the top of the assault pack he wore on his back while he moved to the front of the stack. At the gate, he placed the blades of the bolt cutters on the padlock that secured the gate and with a moment's strain, Ramirez broke the lock sending it tumbling to the ground.

But as the lock descended, the colors of the sky changed. The reds, oranges, and yellows of the morning sun cascaded across the sky as if flung through the air by some sort of explosion. The light created the illusion of a burning halo around Ramirez as his team flowed into the courtyard with the sort of grace that can only be honed through countless hours of training. As Langston crossed the threshold of the gate, Ramirez followed close behind, his hands finding his weapon once more.

I followed when Ramirez and his team flowed through the gate, taking Watson's old position, watching Ramirez and his team as they made it safely to the back door of the compound. Just as they stacked up to the door, I led my Bravo team through the gates and into the courtyard to join them. As I made it about halfway through the courtyard, however, the sun finally began to crest the compound, and with it, the silhouettes of several men armed to the teeth with AK-47s and rocket-propelled grenades clear in their intent to kill.

For the briefest of moments, the world around me erupted into chaos as every man with a weapon engaged their respective enemy. Then, in a blink, everything was covered in hues of gray, and the world slowed down nearly to a stop while everything went silent. It was as if I had suddenly walked into a movie that was stuck in slow-motion, where my body, as well as the world around me, was moving agonizingly slowly, but my mind was moving in real time. Try as I might, I simply could not move my body any faster, regardless of how much I strained.

As I looked ahead of me, I could see plumes of fire slowly erupting from rifles like flowers opening in the morning sun. Green and orange tracers filled the sky around me in silent slow-moving streaks as a black swirling mass formed a few feet in front of me. This mass was flat and looked almost like a hole in the ground, but it slowly rotated at its center and grew from a mere couple of inches to an area roughly five feet across. As the mass grew, I noticed something rise out of its center. As it took shape, sheer terror completely engulfed me like a flood when I realized what it was that I was looking at.

As if by some sort of spell, the woman in white rose from the center of the mass, her hair and robes flowing around her in complete disregard for the laws of gravity. With her eyes closed and her arms hugging her chest, she slowly dropped her hands to her sides in her ascent, hands open and palms facing me. Once she reached the apex of her ascent, her ancient eyes opened and stared hungrily into mine like a predator on the prowl.

"It's time to awaken me, Kyle," she hissed with ethereal calm, a cocky half smile stretching across the contours of her face. "How can we right our wrongs if I am bound like this?"

"N-no." The paralyzing terror nearly muted me. Her reaction made me wish I had never said anything at all.

Her eyes formed themselves in a fixture of seething hatred, her face fixing into a scowl. "We will awaken, Kyle." She floated closer to me as she spoke, mere inches from the ground. "And they will burn!"

She lunged, screaming, face-first into me. As she closed the distance between us, her scream became a high-pitched, earsplitting wail that lowered and deepened as she came mere inches from my face. When our faces collided, I found myself sitting in a dark room, covered from the waist down in fabric.

Her scream had become my own and once I realized this, I immediately tried to gather my senses. I was panting uncontrollably, a cold sweat covering nearly every inch of my naked torso. I could hear my heart thundering like a heavy drum in my ears. I struggled to calm down, to catch my breath, frantically searching around when I realized I was safely tucked away within the confines of my bedroom.

I was safe…

Amber sat at the foot of the bed, a mixture of terror and concern widening her eyes, a hand instinctively reaching out to me.

"Are you okay?" Fear threaded her shaky voice.

It took me a moment to register what she had said. "Yeah, I think so" I breathed with a nod.

Visibly relieved, she grasped my hand, moving close to sit next to me at the edge of the bed. "You scared the hell out of me, Kyle. I had no idea what to do. You just started thrashing, and then screaming…"

"I'm sorry, hon, I-"

"No, don't be. Don't ever apologize for something like that. I just didn't know what to do. I've never seen you like that before. Are you sure you're okay?"

"Yeah, I just need a minute to calm down is all. Sorry to scare you, hon, I love you."

"No, really, it's fine. Can you tell me what that was though?" she said, concern thick in her voice. She was closer now, truly troubled by the night terror that had transpired.

"I'll be okay, hon. Just give me a minute to clean up and I'll be right back."

With a worried nod, she reluctantly let go of my hand when I got out of bed and left the bedroom, moving into the bathroom. With a flick of my wrist, the light flickered on, casting a reflection into the mirror above the sink to my left. With a slight squeak from the nozzle, I turned cool water on in the sink and splashed it on my face, washing off the grime the sweat had produced. For a moment I simply stood over the sink, listening to the water as it trickled down. I let the sound of the water calm my mind and ease me into a trance as I gradually slowed my breathing. Finally, after a slow and steady inhale, I held it for a brief pause.

"Spirit bound inside of me, asleep forever you shall be." The only spell that I still practiced, taught to me by my uncle the day Asmodeus killed my father in their failed attempt to exorcise her. I had no true way of knowing if the spell worked since my magic remained dormant, but it was all I had to keep the demon locked away.

Opening my eyes, I stared momentarily into my reflection, and then into the running water below. "How has my life come to this?" I asked myself. The nightmares, as infrequent as they were, had become more and more common lately. Although Asmodeus was still most definitely dormant, it was nights like this that I couldn't help but wonder if I was starting to lose my hold on the demon. *Is she beginning to break her bonds?* I wondered. *Can I hold her back if she does? Furthermore, how am I going to explain any of this to Amber?* I was no stranger to nightmares, but they'd never escalated to anything like a full-blown night terror, not since we'd moved in together anyway. The severity of these dreams always seemed to be suppressed whenever she was around. So up to this point, she'd never experienced one of my night terrors until now. I was able to keep these sorts of concerns to myself as a result. Now that she'd finally experienced one firsthand, however, I was going to have to broach the subject somehow.

At that I turned the water off and dried my face with a towel. "Whatever the case," I said to myself, "she isn't going to be happy."

# Chapter 4

The rhythmic beeping of Amber's morning alarm drew me from my otherwise calm, dreamless sleep. This was certainly a welcome alternative considering the night terror that occurred just a few hours before, though I could still feel its effects weighing down on me. The fatigue of the night's restlessness enveloped me like a weighted blanket, sapping me of my will to move. It seemed to take a bit of effort to open my eyes and stare into the empty darkness of our bedroom ceiling.

With a lazy sigh and contemptuous moan, Amber lifted her head from my chest and rolled to the nightstand on the right side of the bed, promptly silencing the alarm and snapping on the bedside lamp.

"Good morning, husband," she tiredly whispered into my chest as she nuzzled back into me, tracing her fingers along my ribs as she did. "Did you sleep okay?"

"Yeah, I think so." It had taken some time for the adrenaline to wear off before I could calm down enough to sleep. We said little before we lay down again either. We had simply flowed into spooning under the covers, using my biceps as her pillow while she molded herself into me. She formed into me well, like a little puzzle piece falling perfectly into place. I always thought that was the perfect metaphor for our life together.

Amber was my happy little puzzle piece, and I wouldn't want it any other way.

"Good," she said, looking up to me with concern and doubt in her eyes. "I'm happy to hear that." She reached up to caress my face and our lips met in a tender kiss before she promptly rolled into a seated position on the side of the bed. For a moment, she sat there stretching with her arms held over her head, and I couldn't help but admire the picturesque form of her toned muscular back in the lamp light. I absent-mindedly reached out to her, caressing the contours of her mid-back while she stretched which caused her to arch subtly and pause at the touch. Looking over her shoulder with a playful smile, she stood up to walk into the closet, her naked form swaying within her stride.

I could feel my heart pounding in my chest when my libido rampaged despite itself. Damn, if only we had a little more time…

With an effort of will, I tiredly pulled myself out of bed and dressed at the dresser by the bed. Gym shorts and a simple red tank top would do for now. I then moved into the kitchen to make breakfast while Amber got ready for work. Today, it was scrambled eggs with sautéed spinach and cheese mixed in. Simple and easy. I then put a couple of slices of wheat toast into the toaster and made coffee with the French press on the counter while I waited. Once the toast popped out of the toaster, I served everything on two plates: three eggs worth for her and four for me. It was a simple, nearly meditative process that had long been a part of our daily routine, and everything was ready and served on the table just in time for her to step out of the bathroom, dressed and ready to conquer the day.

Her attire was simple, really. She sported a dark gray dress with a navy blazer over a crimson shirt. Her hair hung loosely in tidy, unfrazzled curls that bounced elegantly as she walked. She was usually minimal with her makeup, though she never really needed much anyway. What little she had with her red lipstick and natural freckles made her green eyes explode into gems that captured an aura of power and quiet confidence, while still projecting a friendly and approachable demeanor. Her jewelry was always elegantly simple as well. She wore a silver-banded watch with a blue face on her right wrist and a claddagh on her left ring finger, with the heart facing away from her. She also had a small diamond piercing in her left nostril that she only removed when she was home.

Her expression glistened as she approached the table with a simple "Thanks for breakfast, sweety," before joining me and taking her seat.

"Of course," I said through a mouthful of eggs. "Are you looking at another busy day today?"

"Yeah, I think so. I have some loose-end paperwork to do for Ms. Eldonna, and I might try so schedule another showing later too. What about yourself?"

"Gym and job-hunting mostly. That's about it for now."

"I see…"

We sat in uncomfortable silence for what felt like an eternity, the scrape of silverware all but filling the void between us. It was evident that she had a lot on her mind, and it wasn't hard to discern what it was considering what had transpired the night before.

Finally, she pushed her empty plate aside and slumped over the warm cup of coffee she held in both hands. She sat there for a moment, as if a great weight were pressing down upon her. "About last night, are you sure you're okay?" she asked before lifting her eyes to meet mine.

She wasn't hiding anything from me. I could clearly see the concern and fear in her eyes. She had every reason to be afraid. She was there when the demon presented herself to my father and uncle, before everything spun out of control. She was there for the ritual, the fire, the magic, and the death. She was there for everything, even the moment my uncle taught me the spell that kept the demon locked away inside me. She was there for it all, yet she continued to stay and support me after everything that had happened. She chose to continue to love me despite the risk involved with simply knowing me.

"I'm not sure. To be honest, I'm still trying to sort it out."

She sat patiently for a moment, waiting for me to continue before nodding her head. "Okay."

I could feel a tinge of guilt build up inside me. I knew that I owed her more than that. Communicating even the most difficult subjects typically came easily with us. It was actually one of my favorite aspects of our relationship, but this… this was different. This was something we rarely talked about, and I blamed myself for that. She always gave me the time and the space I needed, and she never judged me whenever I felt ready to open up to her.

"I'm sorry—"

"Don't be, it's okay. You know that I'm here for you when you need to talk."

"I know, it's just that… I'm not sure. I think the stress of finally being done with school and having to find something else now is getting the better of me. The dream last night was about Asmodeus."

She sucked in a quick, quiet breath at that, but she kept it under control. "Okay. Do you have dreams about her often?"

"No, not so much anymore. Not since we started living together."

"I've never seen you like that before. That really scared me."

"I know. It scared me too."

She nodded slowly, fidgeting nervously with her ring. "Do you think… do you think you might be losing control?"

"I don't think so. I haven't had a night terror like that for a long time," I said, trying to sound calmer than I felt. "I think the spell is still holding strong, and I have always tried to maintain it. I'm counting it as a one-off for now."

She shifted nervously in her seat for a moment, and I could see a hint of suspicion in her eyes. "Okay. Is there anything I can do?"

*Look at her, fighting for me still. How did I ever get so lucky?* "I don't know, I don't think so. I think finding a job will help with the stress. I'm going to send out some applications today and see what else I can find."

"Okay, sounds good. Any word on your grades yet?"

"Not yet, I should see them come in by the end of the week."

She seemed to consider that for a moment as she stared trance-like into her coffee. "How would you feel about working in the oil fields?"

"I'm not sure. It's not exactly within my skill set and I hear it requires a lot of time away from home. It sounds like there is a lot of money in it though."

"Well, Ms. Eldonna is trying to expand her company into the Bakken oil fields, and she mentioned that she is looking for some good workers. I can put in a good word for you if you'd like, since I'm going to be speaking with her later today anyway."

"Are you sure that wouldn't cause some sort of conflict of interest?"

"No, not at this point in the process. It should be fine."

I paused to consider that for a moment. We weren't struggling financially. The post-9/11 GI Bill wasn't exactly making me rich, but between that and Amber's income, we managed to stay well within our means. We lived fairly conservatively since we'd moved to Bismarck, so we never had to dip into our savings either, which was sitting at a healthy sum. My father's life insurance policy saw to that. Still, college life presented its own flavor of stress and I had been longing to get back into the work force. If there was an oil company expanding into the area and looking to hire, that could open some interesting doors all on its own.

"Okay, sure. As long as you're sure it's not an issue, I think I would like that."

Her expression blossomed into a relieved smile. "Okay, sounds good. I'll bring it up when I talk to her later."

"Thank you," I said after a pause. I could almost feel a weight being lifted, and a small wave of gratitude taking its place. "I love you."

She answered with a mere smile and nod before glancing at her watch. "I should go," she said as she stood to leave. On her way to the door, she walked behind my chair and embraced me from behind while nuzzling into my neck. "I love you too, honey. Have a nice day." With a kiss on the cheek, she was out the door.

I sat for a brief moment to meditate and digest all of what was said. The sense of relief was palpable. There was still a small tinge of fear left behind, but it felt as if most of my worries trickled away. "We got this," I said out loud. "We got this." After slamming the rest of my coffee, I quickly gathered the dishes into the sink and walked out the door behind her.

The remainder of the day seemed fairly routine. The gym was a little over a block away, so the jog to it proved to be a good warm-up. After crushing a hard leg-day routine with conditioning, the jog back home left me fatigued yet energized and focused. Once I found my momentum, it was always hard for me to stop or slow down, so I was already well into a determined mindset and ready to conquer the day when I got home. After a quick shower, I changed into jeans and a simple orange t-shirt before sliding a silver claddagh onto the ring finger of my left hand, heart pointing away from me. I gathered my backpack, which already had my laptop and a couple of notebooks, and drove to a Barnes and Noble bookstore nearby, where I settled into the store's Starbucks.

After some brief small talk with the flirty college-age barista, I grabbed my coffee and found my usual seat near a back wall that was next to an outlet and plugged in my computer. It was typically quiet in here this early in the day, and the staff had become accustomed to seeing me as I had spent much of my time studying here over the last couple of years. The coffee shop was just to the right of the entrance as you walked in, with about a dozen or so tables scattered throughout. It was modest in size, but the tables were comfortably spaced, and the full-size windows created plenty of warm natural light through most of the day. My little table at the far corner of the lounge was a near-perfect vantage point of the area, which was great for people-watching and was something I often took advantage of.

After logging into the Wi-Fi, I went to work on the sluggish and grueling task of browsing websites, finding and filling out applications, writing and rewriting my résumé, and so on. Time only seemed to drag slower and slower until I finally found some respite in the quiet buzzing of my cell phone.

"Hello," I answered, which probably came out more irritated than it should have. I realized immediately that I should have at least checked to see who was calling me first.

Amber's voice came over the phone. "Cancel your dinner plans for tonight. Ms. Eldonna invited us to The Pirogue at seven."

"Wait, what? She wants us to meet her for dinner?"

"Yeah! I mentioned that you were looking for work when I met with her today and she seemed really interested, so I told her a little bit about you and your background, and now she wants us to join her for dinner so she can meet you."

"So, she wants to meet me for dinner… as a job interview?"

"I mean, I guess so. I know it's a little unorthodox, but it sounds like this could be a big opportunity for you."

"Yeah, okay. That sounds great. So, you said seven o'clock?"

"Yeah, and I know it's an oil field job, but she is kind of a classy lady and it's kind of a classy place, so you should probably dress nice. I have a couple of things I need to wrap up at the office too, so I'll have to meet you guys there."

Glancing down at my watch, I was surprised to see how much time had passed. "Well, it's almost five o'clock. You sure I can't get by on my stunning smile and charming good looks?"

"Well, that works pretty well with me," she said with a giggle "so don't forget to bring that too. What are you doing?"

"I'm at the bookstore filling out applications."

"I know it's kind of short notice. Do you think you can make it?"

"Yeah, I should have a button-up already prepped. I'll see you guys there."

"Great! I'll see you then. I love you!"

"I love you too, hon."

# Chapter 5
## Mosul, Iraq

Three sharp raps on the metal door of my room were all it took to startle me and my roommate, Staff Sergeant Taylor, awake. Before either of us could climb out of our racks the door opened and the dark silhouette of our platoon sergeant appeared within the door, framed by the blinding light of the mid-afternoon sun.

"Nap time is over, gentlemen. We have a mission brief at eighteen hundred for a raid at twenty. I suggest you two get your squads down to chow while you still can if they haven't gone already." And with that the door was closed and the darkness once again enveloped us.

From the other side of the room, Taylor's zombie-like groan came out, sounding as groggy and listless as I felt, while we both pulled ourselves out of our racks. "I got the light" came his voice out of the darkness as I glanced at my alarm clock.

"Damn, eight whole hours. They are spoiling us today, brother."

"What time is it?"

"Fucking thirteen hundo."

"Goddamn it." He flicked on the light and shambled back to his bunk. "Well at least we will be able to get some chow in beforehand."

"Thank God. I'm fucking starving."

"Amen to that, brother."

To say that Taylor and I were close would be an understatement. Although we came from totally different backgrounds with virtually nothing in common, we had been practically joined at the hip since basic training. Like so many Americans at the time, 9/11 had been our war cry. Although he might have had different plans before he joined the Army, we quickly found ourselves marching to the same beat.

Taylor was the oldest of three brothers and came from an upper middle-class family from the suburbs of Atlanta, Georgia. Living the American dream, he was of course a natural athlete all through high school and held a near 4.0 GPA. With that in his favor it was easy for him to find his way into an Ivy League university working toward a degree in law. But that all changed on one September morning when he walked into his morning lecture only to find a room full of students shocked into silence, and a tower burning on the TV screen. He described the walk down to his empty seat as one of the longest walks of his life as he watched the second plane crash into the second tower on live television. He immediately understood that his life would be forever changed. By the end of the year, with only two years of school under his belt, he had orders to attend basic training at Fort Benning, Georgia.

I, on the other hand, had already determined that I would join the Army and was already signed up under the Delayed Entry Program in my senior year of high school when the Twin Towers fell. Like Taylor, I waited until the end of the school year before shipping out to basic, and the beat of the war drums only seemed to get louder as my ship date drew ever closer. When we found ourselves in the same platoon in basic, it was this newly formed patriotic sense of duty and unyielding determination our friendship was forged on.

Those sixteen weeks of hell turned out to be a cakewalk as we were constantly looking out for each other. Learning how to parachute out of perfectly good airplanes in Airborne School was like a vacation in comparison—but RIP, or the Ranger Indoctrination Program, well that was a hell all on its own. No matter how bad things got, however, we always found a way to motivate each other, usually by turning each shitty situation into some sort of competition. When we graduated RIP and found ourselves in Fort Lewis, Washington, with the Second Battalion, 75th Ranger Regiment, we couldn't help but find an irony in the fact that not only were we in the same platoon together, but we somehow managed to find ourselves in the same four-man fire team. It wasn't until after our first deployment together that we found the trend broken when they sent us to Ranger School and he was in the class after me.

As time went on and we found ourselves climbing in both rank and position, we would constantly lean on each other for advice and motivation, pushing each other to improve and to grow. It was a brotherhood in its truest form. We would literally fight, kill, and die for each other if the situation called for it, and being as this was our fourth deployment together, we had plenty of opportunities to prove it.

Walking outside into the scorching Iraqi afternoon sun clad in my pants, undershirt, shower shoes, and nothing else, I glanced back to see him examining the scruff under his chin in a mirror he kept in his wall locker. "Try not to break that mirror while I'm gone there, pretty boy."

"Fuck off, Goodwin. You only wish you could look this good," he responded with nothing more than a sideward glance. That being said, at six feet tall, with blond hair, piercing blue eyes and a bodybuilder's physique, he could have been nicknamed "Pretty Boy" with how many people called him that over the years.

Walking into the Iraqi afternoon sun this time of day was like walking into the seventh circle of hell. Imagine walking into a man-sized furnace set at 130 or even 140 degrees Fahrenheit and closing the door behind you. If you thought a nice breeze would be your saving grace, you would be sadly mistaken. When the wind would blow, it was basically like someone stuffed a hair dryer full of sand and turned it on in your face while you were sitting inside said furnace, just to remind you that God actually hates you. If you can imagine that, then you more or less have your basic Iraqi afternoon in a nutshell, and today was nothing extraordinary.

Fortunately, we weren't packed into a bunch of tents without any sort of heat regulation like many would expect. That may have been the case during the beginning of the war, but as the military began building up their camps into more permanent forward operating bases, otherwise known as FOBs, they also slowly replaced their tents with shipping containers converted into housing units. Each shipping container, or CHU, was sectioned off into three rooms with two soldiers per room. They tended to be a little cozy when you crammed two Rangers with all their gear inside, but they had AC units in each room, so we didn't voice any complaints when we could see the alternative on the other side of the road.

Knocking on my team leader's door, which was right next to mine in the middle of the CHU, I felt the hair on the back of my neck and arms stand up as if my body suddenly became electrically charged. Frozen on the metal porch just outside the door, I could feel a rush of adrenaline as my fight-or-flight mechanisms shifted into full throttle, sending a cacophony of drums thundering in my ears, my heart pumping into overdrive. Suddenly hyper aware, I looked around trying to find the source of whatever the hell it was that set me off. Looking to my right, I saw a line of CHUs, dirt, T-barriers… some guy half in uniform and flip-flops meandering to the showers. To my left, more of the same…

The normally soft click of the metal door into my team leader's room sounded like a thunderous crash in comparison to the norm, but that, it would seem, was what it took to bring me back to my senses. "Afternoon, Sergeant," came Sergeant Locker's tired voice as he appeared out of the dark catacombs that encompassed his and Sergeant Ramirez's room, blinking away the bright afternoon sun all the while.

"Just had our WARNO for tonight, mission brief at eighteen hundred for a raid at twenty. Get your men off to chow if they haven't gone already, and have them suited up for a weapons-and-equipment check no later than sixteen. I want everyone's shit squared away before the brief so we can squeeze in some rehearsals after if possible."

"Roger, Sergeant" was his tired reply. "Yo, Ramirez…" His voice trailed off as I turned to descend from his metal porch.

It was at this moment that the world around me slowed down, as if a switch flipped and everything was suddenly thrown into slow-motion. The desert sun made everything blindingly bright as it was, but everything slowly brightened more while at the same time taking on a crystalline clarity and shine. I could feel my situational awareness heighten and my senses push out all around me when I descended the stairs. Once my foot touched the first step, the hairs on my arms and neck stood up as if suddenly electrically charged. On the second step a shiver cascaded down my spine like a lightning bolt. Suddenly, I was consumed with the feeling that I was not alone in this makeshift alleyway.

Almost in unison, as I planted my foot on the gravel below the patio and pivoted toward my room, the door to my room opened. I was stunned, frozen in place when a strikingly beautiful woman in white robes crossed the threshold of my room and glided down the stairs. There was hardly a breeze, yet her robes clung to her as if pressed into her by a heavy wind. Her long, jet-black hair bobbed about her as if submerged in water. When she reached the bottom of the patio and turned to me, the beautifully Persian features of her face locked in a deathly stare.

"Be wary, there are those who seek to destroy you this day," she all but whispered, her voice silky smooth. Poisonous.

She seemed young, though her eyes were ancient, burning with a fiery wrath and intensity that left me nearly breathless. "What?"

"They mean—"

The door to my room swung open. With a flash, the woman disappeared before my eyes with Taylor energetically descending the stairs.

"Bro, you okay?" came Taylor's concerned voice, and in a jolting blink, he was standing in her place. Just as suddenly as it had changed, everything fell back into its natural order.

"Yeah, I'm good."

"Are you sure? You look like you just saw a ghost."

"Yeah, man, I'm good. I'm just going to grab a water or something," I said, reaching for an excuse to leave.

"Yeah, you should probably do that. Maybe grab something to eat while you are at it too," he said with a skeptical look as I passed him. "I'm going to freshen up."

"Sounds good, man. I'll see you in a bit."

Once back in the CHU, I grabbed a water bottle from a pack we had set up by our door and sat down on my bunk for a moment to gather my thoughts. I took stock of my mind and my body to discern what was amiss. Everything seemed fine though. I was mostly awake and alert. My body ached mildly, but that was likely due to the non-stop work we'd put in lately. I may have been a little tired from just rolling out of bed, but everything else was otherwise fine. But maybe that was it. Maybe I was just a little too tired and a little too fatigued from these non-stop missions, and stepping into the blistering Iraqi heat must have thrown me off for a moment.

After taking a long pull from the bottle, I stood up, set it down, and grabbed my body armor. Whatever the case, I couldn't focus on that now. I had work to do.

# Chapter 6

The engine of my little old Toyota seemed to echo my bewildered excitement when I cranked it over, threw it into gear, and glided into traffic. As old as it was, it was a zippy little thing when it wanted to be, and I piloted it like a guided missile all the way to the apartment. Once there, I took the steps to my apartment two at a time, burst in like a barbarian savage, kicked off my shoes, and strode right into my bedroom.

I'd had a crimson button-up shirt and gray slacks cleaned and pressed a couple of weeks ago in preparation for what already seemed like an unending search for the ever-elusive job interview.

Okay, I'll admit, it seemed a little impatient of me to expect a job interview so soon after getting out of school. Patience had never exactly been my forte though, and at this point, I was just happy to see an absence of moth holes in my clothes since getting them ready.

So, I hurriedly shifted out of my clothes and threw on a white t-shirt, the button-up, and the slacks. I had a rose-gold watch with a brown leather strap that Amber had given me as a gift a couple of years ago, so I grabbed that too. After sliding on a pair of black socks and dress shoes, I shuffled into the bathroom to check myself in front of a full-length mirror we had hanging on the wall and found myself sighing in frustration at what I saw. I had to admit, I looked fairly good if I were cosplaying as a homeless guy playing dress up, but the week-old stubble had to go. After taking off the red shirt and hanging it up on the door, I quickly shaved, redressed, and finally headed out the door.

I paused after turning over my Toyota at the sudden recognition of an encroaching anxiety, and I actually had to chuckle a little at this invisible specter. Truth be told, I've never actually failed a face-to-face interview before, even when there was strong competition stacked against me. I had to recognize that this anxiety was simply due to the fact that I didn't know much about this industry or what to expect from it. Even so, if I managed to walk away from this with a job offer, then I would have to ensure that I would stay flexible with the learning curve and attack it with the utmost aggression. That was nothing I hadn't done before, too easy.

At least, that's what I told myself anyway. That brief moment of reflection didn't aid much in reducing the anxiety, but it was at least enough to steel my nerves a little. So, with the pause, I threw the little truck into gear and drove out of the driveway.

Although Bismarck is the state capital, it isn't a large city by any stretch of the imagination. With a population of only seventy-five thousand, this state capital is surprisingly easy to get around with its winding streets and steep hills. It's certainly a stark contrast from the flat plains of the Red River Valley to the east. The beauty of this little town is only enhanced by the aesthetic of the mighty Missouri River, which separates Bismarck from its neighboring county to the west, and the smaller town of Mandan. Getting lost is hardly an issue either. All you have to do is look for the large skyscraper in the middle of town, which dwarfs everything else in Bismarck. Once you find it, you can pretty much reorient yourself from there. All roads lead to the capital, it seems.

So, naturally, it didn't take long for me to find the place, even with the late rush hour traffic. After I drove north on Third for a few blocks and climbing the steep hill that brought me into the downtown district, another right turn brought me pretty much to their front door. Parking was a chore, as is typical for downtown, but I was early enough to not have to worry about parking in the nearby parking garage.

Even with the large black doors and elegant sign hanging over the entranceway, the brick building that The Pirogue resided in blended well with the surrounding neighborhood. It was easy to miss, but not hard to find if you were looking for it. It wasn't until I got there when I realized, in my excitement, I had actually arrived early. Maybe a little too early, by about thirty minutes. Still, I went in and was warmly greeted by a middle-aged woman, who I assumed was the owner, and was promptly taken to the table that Ms. Eldonna had apparently already reserved for us.

The restaurant was beautifully elegant and was separated into two sections as you walked in. The section to the right, which the hostess led me to, was elevated by two steps and separated itself from the other with a three-foot wall. Although the elevated level only had a row of booths, which lined the main wall on the right-hand side, the main level to the left was adorned with tables of various sizes. The restaurant was dimly lit, which created, at least in my mind, a romantic ambiance that emphasized the brown tones of the décor. Paintings were displayed throughout the restaurant depicting colorful landscapes typically found in the Midwest. The entirety of the restaurant seemed to buzz with its respective occupancy. Well-dressed families and business associates conversed in polite conversation while the professional staff catered to their needs.

I barely wanted to sit down when the hostess delivered me to the booth near the back of the restaurant, as I imagined that simply touching the white tablecloth would probably set my wallet off into a fit of rage. After the hostess politely pissed off my bank account by way of reciting the daily specials, she handed me the menu and left me alone with a promise of a glass of water and the uncomfortable feeling of being in a beautiful establishment that I had no business being inside of. It didn't take long for me to settle in though, and I soon found myself lost in the colorful painting hanging over the table depicting the North Dakota Badlands.

Amber was the first of the two to arrive. I didn't see her until she was already walking down the aisle to our table, but once my attention shifted to her, I couldn't help but notice how the dim lights and light browns in the restaurant seemed to enhance the quiet confidence in her demeanor, and the humble power in her long, elegant stride. I felt as if suddenly entranced by a vision far more profound than the painting that had so recently captured my attention. The very ambiance of the restaurant played with the color of her red curly hair in such a way as to produce a near visible aura around her, and her emerald eyes shone with fierce excitement when her face blossomed into joy at the sight of me.

When she came close, I slid out of the booth and greeted her by way of open arms, to which she replied by flowing into me and putting her arms around me.

"You made it," came her quiet, happy purr.

"Of course." I chuckled. "Thank you for inviting me."

"She just got ahold of me, by the way," she said, pulling away. "It sounds like she might be running behind, but she'll be here soon."

"That's fine," I said, noting the time on my watch, sliding into the booth next to her. "That just means that I have more opportunity to torment you in the meantime." It was only six fifty-five anyway.

"Okay, Kyle, sure," she said, rolling her eyes.

"Here is your water, sir," said the lovely young women who practically came out of nowhere. The little blond ninja, in her early twenties, politely placed the water in front of me.

"Thank you."

"Of course, sir," she said happily. "And welcome to The Pirogue. It's my understanding that you have one more joining you this evening. Is there anything I can get you two while you wait?"

"Just a water for now, is fine," Amber replied politely.

"Very good. I'll be right back with that and to check on you soon," the waitress said before slipping away and into the kitchen in the back.

"To be honest, I thought I was going to be late for a moment too," Amber said as she stared at the menu in front of her. "I had an awful lot of paperwork to do, I wasn't sure if I was going to get everything done in time."

"Did you manage to get everything squared away though?"

"Yes, I did." She turned smiling at me with a wolfish grin. "The inspectors finished early, so I wanted to get a handle on it right away. But all the *T*s are dotted and the *I*s are crossed, and submitted."

"Dang, that's awesome!"

"Yeah, but don't mention anything about it to her when she gets here. It's sort of confidential, so technically, you're not supposed to know about these sorts of details."

"Right, got it. Secrets are my specialty. Do you think I should have put that on my résumé?"

"You're a funny guy," she said with an arched brow.

"And to think you chose this." I chuckled.

The headache was subtle at first, it started as nothing more than a tension in my forehead just between my eyes. I barely even registered it was there as it grew while my eyes tracked to the front door, almost by instinct.

"Hey, Amber, do you have any Ibuprofen or anything?"

"Yeah, I think so. Are you okay?"

"Yeah, I think I have a migraine coming on, though."

"Oh no," she said, reaching into her purse. "Ope, I think I have some right here. Here you go."

"Thanks." I took a small handful of tablets from a travel-size container she pulled from her bag, slamming them with a mouthful of water.

No sooner had I put the cup down than the front doors opened, and a small wave of tension built up in me. As the doors closed, a tall, athletically built woman strode toward us with the confidence and fluidity of a predator. A long red dress clung to every curve of her voluptuous body, and a long, slender, strong right leg peeked out of the front of her dress with the forward motion of her stride. Her dress was sleeveless, showing off the definition of her arms and shoulders, while the low-cut neckline in her dress did more than enough to emphasize her generous bustline. Her silky-smooth brown hair bobbed around her head like a lion's mane while she walked, and it flowed just a few inches past her shoulders.

The buzz within the restaurant seemed to hush as she ascended onto our raised section, and I realized that nearly every eye within the restaurant was fixed on her as she came near. I glanced around, noting a tall waiter with a tray in his hand had stopped in his tracks on his way to a table, and stood peering over the three-foot wall separating the two sections in an awestruck trance.

"There she is. That's her." Amber's voice came in an excited whisper. She sat a little taller next to me, breathing slowly, but high into her chest. Her gaze was transfixed on this newcomer and gleamed as if marveling at a beautiful painting. "That's Ms. Eldonna."

As Ms. Eldonna came closer, I noticed that people started to peer around from inside their booths when she passed them. Although the tension from my migraine was far from overpowering, it slowly increased in intensity when she drew nearer.

Her red lips parted in a smile as she approached our table, and I stepped out of the booth to reach out my hand to shake hers, which stopped her dead in her tracks. "Good evening, Ms. Eldonna. My name is Kyle Goodwin. It's good to meet you."

Genuine surprise shattered her gorgeous smile, and it took her a moment to regain her composure. "It's good to finally meet you too, Mr. Goodwin," she said, recovering her smile. "Amber told me a lot about you."

# Chapter 7

The patrons within the restaurant seemed to uniformly shift their attention away from us and back to their business when we sat down in our booth, the tension from the migraine receding as we did. Amber shifted nervously in her seat, regaining her composure, though she glanced nervously at me for a moment before lowering her head to return to the menu.

"I would like to thank both of you for meeting with me today." Eldonna's curious stare never left me. "I know it probably seems unusual to meet like this for an interview. Unfortunately, my office is still under renovation, being as we are just now moving into the area. With how wonderful Amber has been in handling our business, I would be remiss not to invite her for something so casual as dinner. I hope that is okay, Mr. Goodwin."

"Thank you." Amber blushed, looking up from the menu shyly.

I noted how not only did she dress high class, but the way she articulated her speech indicated that she may have had an expensive education as well. She enunciated everything with a pristine clarity and fluidity that I would have expected from someone used to spending their time around old money, and I thought I could pick out the subtle hint of a Southern accent hidden underneath. Her posture was flawless, projecting a sort of courtly confidence and power. Although the migraine hadn't quite receded entirely, I think it may have been more of a distraction than I thought, because I had just noticed the expensive-looking diamond-studded chain she wore, which came to a point a couple of inches below her throat. It made it difficult for me not to track it with my eyes, or to follow where it was pointing, though I was able to note it in my lower peripheral.

"It's okay, I don't mind at all actually. I always appreciate any opportunity to spend time with my wonderful fiancée, and I appreciate the opportunity to meet with you today too, Ms. Eldonna."

She smiled a little at that. "Please, call me Lillian. May I call you Kyle?"

"Absolutely."

Lillian's sweet smile shifted to my right, and onto the waitress who approached the booth from behind me. "Here is your water miss," she said, placing a glass of water in front of Amber. I could feel the tension of the headache returning, though just before she nearly knocked over an empty wine glass on the table. "Ope, I'm sorry," she said, fumbling to catch it, clumsily returning it to its place.

"It's okay, thank you," Amber said, her eyes shifting nervously between the waitress and Lillian.

Taking a step back from the table, the waitress took a moment to gather herself. "Is there anything I can get for you while you look over the menu, ma'am?" she said referring to Lillian.

"I think I am ready to order if you two are." Lillian stated after ordering a cabernet that I never heard of, nor one I could probably afford anyway. "Don't worry, dinner is on me tonight. It's the least I can do for asking you to meet me so late in the evening, and at such short notice." Her rose red lips parted into a flawless smile, the migraine slightly increasing in intensity as she did so.

Amber perked up at that. "Yes, I am. Thank you very much, Lillian."

The waitress slowly stepped a little closer to the table, opening a notepad she had been carrying, and gingerly pulled a stray hair behind her left ear, all the while staring shyly at Lillian. "Okay, sure. What can I get you?"

It was hard to focus on what everyone was ordering while dealing with the migraine. I took a moment to drink some water and focus on pushing the tension from my mind while the others placed their orders, until it was finally my turn. "I'll take the chicken breast with mixed vegetables and rice, please."

The waitress gingerly nibbled on her lower lip, scribbling on her notepad. "Okay, sounds good. Is there anything else I can get you folks?"

"No, thank you," Lillian responded sweetly.

"Okay," the waitress responded with a flirtatious giggle. "I'll be right back with your order." She scampered back into the kitchen.

As she was leaving, I could feel the tension from the migraine suddenly recede, and I could hear Amber quietly suck in a breath, taking the glass in front of her and slowly sipping her water.

"So anyway, did Amber tell you anything about the job or the sort of work we do?"

"Not too much. She mentioned that you mostly work in the oil fields and that you were looking to expand into the Bakken. I don't recall her mentioning much more than that."

"Indeed," Lillian stated, poised and professional. "Although the energy sector is our primary customer, for the moment, Phoenix Energy Solutions is able to provide an array of gas and propane-powered generators that supply electricity to a diverse clientele, for a variety of uses. In addition to oil and gas, we also set up grid networks to supplement the power grid in parts of Texas, and we even managed to secure contracts with FEMA to supply them with power in areas where electricity is not available, such as when hurricanes destroyed the power grid in Puerto Rico last year."

"Wow, that's really cool," Amber said, absently stroking the bottom of her glass. "Has Phoenix done a lot of work in emergency response?"

"Not yet." Lillian smiled, sweetly. "The company is less than a decade old, so the contract with FEMA is still new. Last year's efforts were, more or less, our debut into that particular market. Things have looked promising since our contributions to FEMA's emergency response efforts significantly aided in reestablishing the desperately needed power grid in Puerto Rico. We've already started negotiating with FEMA in the hopes of expanding upon our contracts with them, and we even produced more generators to aid in those efforts."

"That's incredible!" I said, placing my own glass down. "So, by moving into the Bakken, I'm assuming that you believe the oil is going to come back?"

"Indeed, although it never fully left. Oil prices are rising again, so many of the old companies are reopening some of their pads. Many are even planning to drill again. We have a little bit of competition, so we would like to strike while the iron is hot, so to speak." Lillian's sweet smile returned for a moment, and the tension from the migraine seemed to subtly rise with it. "The basin lead already secured a location to work out of in Killdeer. I don't want to bog you down with too many details right now, but we are looking for someone to act as the lead assistant, to work as the manager of the supply clerk while seeing to the needs of the vehicles and equipment within the facility."

"I see," I said, swallowing down some of the new tension. "So, I would essentially work as the supply and shop manager, while reporting directly to the basin lead?"

"Precisely," Lillian said. A puzzled look crossed her face briefly, and oddly the migraine subsided a little bit more. "Would you mind telling me a little about yourself? Where are you from?"

"Well," I said, staring into my water glass, now held lightly in my right hand. Although my upbringing was overall fairly good, I found it difficult to discuss my home life, or my family in general, since moving to North Dakota. I could feel a new subtle tension building in the center of my chest, drying my throat, not from the migraine, but from the memory of my father's violent death by my hand.

I felt myself pulled away from the memory, though, as Amber gently clasped my left hand under the table. She stared at me lovingly as she did so, as if she knew what I was thinking. She anchored me as she held my hand on my thigh under the table, and I took another sip of water, pushing the memory out of my mind before answering. "I'm originally from Riverton, Wyoming, but I grew up mostly in Gillette. I joined the Army after high school, though, and we moved to North Dakota after I got out a few years ago."

"Riverton," Lillian said thoughtfully. "That's in the Wind River Reservation, right?"

"That's right. My mother was from the reservation, and my father was working there as a police officer at the time."

"I see," Lillian said, flashing her sweet smile again. "Can you tell me a little about them?"

I could feel the tension of the migraine suddenly building again. It came on like a wave, far more intense than at any other period in the night. It brought with it a sense of nausea, and it took a great deal of effort to swallow it down while trying to maintain my composure. Next to me, I could hear Amber suck in a breath, letting it out slowly as she absently placed my hand on her inner thigh. Opening my eyes, I could see Amber staring at Lillian with lustful intent, biting her lower lip while breathing high into her chest. Her trance only seemed to last for a moment, however, as she glanced at me and visibly shook herself out of it in embarrassment, letting go of my hand when she did.

Lillian, on the other hand, was staring at me with the utmost intensity. Her piercing brown eyes shone with a golden aura as she seductively traced her lower lip with a finger and smiled, waiting for me to respond. The clatter of dropped silverware diverted my attention as another patron a few booths in front of me bent down to retrieve it. He was facing away from me, but once he retrieved his silverware, he turned to stare at our booth, his eyes never leaving us as he rose. I realized that he wasn't the only one. The restaurant became eerily quiet as every eye that could be seen had diverted their attention to us.

"Well, like I said, my mother was from the reservation. My father was working in the area as a county sheriff when they met through a mutual friend."

"Is that so?" Lillian's lovingly seductive gaze never left me as she rested her chin on the heel of her left hand. My entire skull throbbed with every beat of my heart.

"Yeah, she passed away when I was about eleven or so, so I don't remember too much about her."

Lillian raised her head abruptly at that, genuine surprise and grief written on her face. "I see. I'm so sorry to hear that. How did she die?"

"It was some kind of stroke. My father found her in our living room. It took quite a toll on him, well… on all of us, really. He found an opening in the Gillette Police Department soon after that, so he took it. I guess he felt the need to leave and start over after she passed away, though he never remarried."

Lillian seemed to visibly wilt a little, dropping her hand to the table with her gaze going solemn and distant, her eyes drifting momentarily down, then focusing back on. "What about your father? Does he still live in Gillette?"

"I'm afraid not. He passed away in 2009, shortly after one of my Iraq deployments."

"I see. How did he die?"

"In a house fire," I said as Amber's hand reached for mine again under the table, squeezing gently. "No one knows how it started, exactly. He was living a little outside of town so it took a while for the fire department to get there. It's been ruled as some kind of accident, but there wasn't anything left of the house after the fire. Nearly everything was completely destroyed."

Lillian sank back into her booth as she took in the story, her solemn gaze filled with grief as she stared at an empty space on the table. The pulsing tension of the migraine receded to nothing more than a mild annoyance as she did, and I could hear the buzz of the restaurant returning as the patrons' attention seemed to return to their tables. A small breath escaped me, the release of tension left my head momentarily swimming. Once I regained myself, I noticed that the staff within the restaurant were only mostly engaged in their work, while they still occasionally glanced at our table, looking away in embarrassment when I met their gazes.

"I'm sorry, I didn't mean to bring up such a painful subject," Lillian said solemnly, as if sensing my confusion. She gradually regained much of her lost poise, sitting upright in her seat again while she absently spun an empty wineglass between her fingers. She stared at me with a questioning look as she did, as if I had been behaving oddly. "Amber mentioned that you were a Ranger in the Army. Can you tell me a little about that?"

"Sure," I said after a momentary pause, meeting her unyielding gaze. "I joined the Army after I graduated high school right after September Eleventh as an infantryman, and I joined the Second Ranger Battalion right after basic training and Airborne School. While I was with them, I deployed a couple of times to Iraq and Afghanistan before getting out of the Army in 2010. During that time, I had worked my way up to team leader, and then later to squad leader, where I was placed in charge of the training and well-being of roughly eight junior Rangers, while also leading them into combat."

"I see, so what made you want to get out of the Army?"

"After my father passed away, I thought it would be a good time to get out and pursue something different." I glanced at Amber, who was staring at me with her loving gaze and encouraging smile. "I also managed to reconnect with Amber around that time, so I wanted to get out to be closer to her."

"That's really sweet," Lillian said, her chin resting again on the heel of her hand, smiling knowingly. "What did you do when you got out?"

"Well," I replied after taking a sip of water. "I thought about going into law enforcement myself, actually, so I worked for a couple of years in the state penitentiary as a corrections officer. It was a good job with rewarding work, but the bureaucracy got to be kind of grating after a while, so I joined the railroad as a train conductor when I found out they were hiring during the last oil boom. I was laid off when the oil prices dropped though, so I went back to school for my bachelor's in business management and dabbled in construction during the off seasons. I just finished my last semester, actually."

I had to admit, the gears shifted within the conversation from there relatively flawlessly. The headache subsided while Lillian poised herself with the utmost professionalism as she dug into the meat of the interview, questioning me in regard to my skills, knowledge, job history and so on. The tone and tenor within the restaurant even began to normalize, for the most part, while the patrons and staff returned to their business as usual, sparing us only the most occasional glance.

Even the waitress managed to snap into her ninja routine, making me nearly jump out of my skin when she returned to our table with a tray full of food. Though she was still evidently charmed by our table, and Lillian in particular, she no longer displayed the shy nervousness she had before. She was confident, cheerful, polite, and professional. She simply dropped off our plates and topped off our drinks with the practiced fluidity and helpful cheer you might expect from someone used to serving a higher class of clientele, before returning back to her other tables: a marked difference from how she behaved just after Lillian arrived.

The interview resumed casually while we ate our meals and Lillian proved to be an engaging host, at no point excluding Amber from the conversation. They would routinely quip and laugh at the occasional inside joke, like lifelong friends. Even so, Lillian seemed no less interested in the content of the interview itself. The whole thing seemed natural in spite of the unorthodox setting.

It was eerie.

It was a complete contrast from before, when the entire restaurant seemed compelled to respond to Lillian and her presence. Nobody seemed to be even remotely bothered by what had happened, nor did anyone seem to take notice of these changes. With the migraine gone as suddenly as it had come, I was even beginning to wonder if I had imagined it. I did my best not to show that I was in any way bothered, but I couldn't help but to wonder, *how could this entire place practically pulse with lust and desire toward Lillian only to suddenly transition to what seems like business as usual? Did the medication Amber gave me simply do its job?' 'Did the migraine alter my perception somehow?'*

That wasn't exactly impossible. We are, in a lot of ways, slaves to our perception, and it is our perception that makes up our reality. If whatever caused these migraines altered how I perceived my environment, then wasn't it possible that I had simply imagined it? But… wouldn't that make me somehow crazy?

Everything about this just felt… wrong.

I was even beginning to wonder if there was some sort of supernatural component to this. If so, this would be the first time I'd encountered anything even remotely supernatural since Asmodeus possessed me, and when my father and uncle tried to exorcise her. Wouldn't it be more likely that it was just… me? They didn't exactly leave me with a how-to manual either. I wouldn't have any idea what to look for if Lillian was in some way supernatural.

This whole thing was making me feel like I was gaslighting myself. Like I had driven myself crazy. I didn't want either of my companions to know that I was bothered though, so I resolved to keep it quietly to myself. I continued to study Lillian, engaging in the conversation as if nothing had happened.

"I see. I noticed you two have matching rings," Lillian said, sitting up straight in her seat again, flashing her perfect smile while reaching for her wine glass. "Would you mind telling me a little about that?" Her gaze projected a subtle hint of lust as she brought her glass to her lips, the tension of my migraine rising as she did so. I had to take a moment to swallow down the pain.

"It's actually a really beautiful story," Ambers responded excitedly before I could answer. "They were his parents' wedding bands. The meaning changes depending on how you wear them." She held her left hand in front of her while she leaned forward over the table, showing off her claddagh and maybe a little bit more, the ruby embedded in the heart of the ring glistening in the low light.

"Is that so?" came Lillian's curious response, though she continued to stare at us knowingly.

"Yeah," I said, now resting my hands in front of me to show her my ring, trying my best to study her response through the tension of the migraine. "The heart represents love, the crown represents loyalty, and the hands holding the two represents friendship. The way you wear it can have different meanings too." She watched me intently while I explained, like she was studying me. It seemed obvious to both of us that my behavior was in stark contrast to anyone else's in the restaurant, and she seemed to be just as unsure about it as I was.

"When you wear it on the ring finger of the right hand, heart pointing away from you, it means that you are not in a relationship. The ring can sometimes be given as a gift by a loved one or a really good friend and worn in that sense. But if the ring is turned the other way, the heart pointing toward you, it is meant to symbolize that you are in a relationship."

"I see," Lillian purred as her mouth broadened into a gorgeous smile, the migraine subtly worsening as she did. "So, the heart pointing down while worn on the left hand must signify an engagement."

"That's right," came Ambers enthusiastic response. "And when worn the other way, it symbolizes marriage."

"These rings belonged to my parents. They were one of the few things that survived the fire," I stated cautiously, never taking my eyes off Lillian.

Most communication is done nonverbally. In fact, seventy to ninety-three percent of communication between people is done this way. We are usually unaware of our participation in interpersonal, nonverbal communication though, because these actions are so inherent to how we converse as humans and are thoroughly ingrained in our daily lives. Lillian's eyes glistened any time Amber and I described the significance of the claddaghs, especially with how they related to my family history. While Amber dived into a heartfelt explanation of the tradition and history behind the claddagh, Lillian and I regarded each other in silence. The migraine, in turn, slowly lessened in intensity, replacing itself with a growing understanding that there was definitely more to this conversation than what met the eye.

She sat, resting her chin lightly on her thumb, as if trying to puzzle out a question or formulating a strategy, much like a chess player might regard their opponent in the middle of a match. I could see her studying me as I took the moment to note the other patrons and staff in my periphery, and how they still took the occasional interest in our table. At this point, it was easy to note the correlation between the intensity in their regard toward our table and the intensity of the migraine. That in itself was alarming, but it paled in comparison to the completely uncharacteristic behavior displayed by Amber. She had always been friendly and polite, but it was in such a way that she exhibited a sort of professional, humble, cheery confidence. This was something completely new and completely different from anything I had ever seen from her before, and she only seemed to collect herself when the migraine receded.

This train of thought spanned for maybe a moment, a second at most, while Amber continued on with enthusiasm, seemingly unaware of the silent duel taking place between Lillian and I. Lillian seemed to track my own train of thought while I snapped these facts together like puzzle pieces, until a realization finally hit me.

This wasn't a simple job interview.

She seemed to reach a conclusion of her own. Her eyes became more focused, her head, more level. She leaned forward, ever so slightly, and a small smile that creased her lips seemed predatory. The expression was subtle, but easy to read.

Checkmate.

There was a silent buzz that interrupted the conversation and Lillian rolled her eyes, sighing in frustration as she pulled a phone from a red wallet she had apparently kept next to her. "I'm so sorry," she said, glancing at the screen. "I'm afraid I have to take this; this should only take a moment."

"No problem," Amber said with a happy smile while Lillian stepped away from the table, and I regarded her in silence as she walked away. She was clearly annoyed with whoever was on the other end of the line, though I couldn't make out what was being said. Once she was out of earshot, Amber practically turned her whole body toward me, brimming head to toe with excitement while she leaned closer to me. "Holy crap, this is going so well. What do you think?"

"Yeah… I don't know…"

Her head snapped back and she took a moment to regard me, clearly confused. "… Really?" she said back with a jester's grin.

"I'm so sorry I have to cut this short," Lillian came back with an apologetic smile. "But something came up that requires my immediate attention."

"Oh," Amber responded, a little downtrodden. "I hope it isn't anything too serious."

"No, I don't think so," Lillian said as she produced a contact card from her little red wallet. "Thank you both so much for coming to meet with me this evening. I really enjoyed our conversation. Don't worry about the bill either; I'll cover it on my way out."

"Likewise," I said, never taking my eyes off her. "And thank you, I appreciate that."

"Here is my card." She flashed me her gorgeous smile again while she handed it to me. "Please send me an email with your résumé so I can send you an application. Honestly, it's all a formality at this point. I would really like to continue this conversation soon, though, if that is alright with you."

I regarded her plainly and directly, pocketing the card. "I think I would like that" I said barely returning her smile.

"Excellent, I look forward to hearing from you." She turned away and strode off the same way she came in, with the fluidity and confidence of a predator. Every eye in the restaurant seemed to track her as she left.

# Chapter 8

When Lillian left the restaurant, she took my migraine with her, and my head floundered as she went. It took a moment for my brain to reboot, and I clenched my jaw in frustration, sending my thoughts into overdrive.

My train of thought was shattered as soon as it started, though, when Amber grabbed hold of my left hand and pulled me into her. I felt my body turn slightly into her in reflex, and she stroked my cheek with her other hand as she pulled me into a deep kiss. I could feel the anxiety crumble in the heat of her passion, and hard desire flowed in its wake as I felt her trace the warmth of her thigh with my hand. My mind was flooded with the sweet taste of her kiss and my eyes blurred into focus when we finally parted, finding her eyes wide and gleaming.

"I'm proud of you, honey," she breathed. "I'm really excited for you. I think we should go home and talk about it." She never let go of the hand she placed on her thigh, and she slowly guided it up her leg while she spoke. She gave me a cocky little smile as she did, biting her lower lip when she finally stopped my hand just before… um. We'll call it "danger close."

"Yeah, I think we should," I said between heavy breaths.

My little monkey brain completely took over, but somewhere there was a little part of me that also took note of Amber's overt display of affection. Amber was bold when it came to her sexuality, but she typically kept that switch turned off and reserved for 'behind closed doors.'

Noted.

But little monkey brain was freaking amped and ready to break out of its little monkey cage, so I made sure to – *"cough"*—adjust myself accordingly before taking hold of Amber's hand, scooting out of the booth with her in tow. Amber held her head down and fought to contain an embarrassed smile as we proceeded through the restaurant like a couple of excited high schoolers, and only briefly looked up to smile in acknowledgement of the hostess when she gave us her well wishes on our way out.

A cool breeze and the call of ravens met us when we stepped outside, the sidewalks busy with foot traffic as people were going to and from various bars and restaurants in the area. Amber stepped beside me, never having let go of my hand, pulling me into another deep kiss that was far too brief. "Where are you parked?" she asked breathlessly as we parted.

"Down the street." I pointed to my right. "Over by the parking garage."

"Okay, I'm heading the opposite way. I'm going straight home. I'll see you when you get there."

"Okay, I'll be right there," I said, placing a brief kiss on the top of her hand, finally letting it go as I gently pulled away. This elicited a quiet giggle from her while she beamed widely, spun on her heels, and walked away.

The evenings in May weren't particularly cold, but at 64 degrees Fahrenheit, the steady breeze that is typical in North Dakota can often seem to cut right through you if you are not ready for it. My long-sleeve shirt broke the wind some, but it was still just crisp enough to calm my little monkey brain and allow me to put my thoughts in order when I finally made it to my little old Toyota. The radio buzzed on as I turned the truck over, and my mind seemed to shift into gear and flow into thought as I drifted into the evening traffic.

Nothing about this evening seemed to be as it appeared, and I racked my brain as I went over what happened. In doing so, I felt like I needed to break everything down in order to better make sense of it all.

So…

Observation 1: Lillian was gorgeous, and I was far from the only one that seemed to notice that fact. Everyone, including Amber, noticed to some varying degree.

Observation 2: The migraines didn't seem to come by coincidence, evidenced by how they fluctuated with intensity as opposed to the steady throbbing that might have otherwise been typical.

Observation 3: Nearly everyone in the restaurant seemed to shift their attention to my table, and Lillian in particular, as the migraines came and went.

Observation 4: The intensity of everyone's attention seemed to correlate with the intensity of the migraines. Amber included…

I had to mull that last one over for a minute. To say that Amber was unusually friendly this evening would be an understatement, and that was certainly not a side of herself that she showed in public. I have never been afraid of showing overt public displays of affection, but that rarely held true for Amber. At least, not since we became reacquainted. That was a boundary that I was always willing and happy to respect, and I couldn't help but to find myself troubled and confused by this abrupt change.

I knew I had to detach myself from this fact emotionally, at least for now, so that I could concentrate on the other facts at hand. It was hard to do at first. I took a slow, steady breath and shook myself a little while I pushed it from my mind anyway.

Okay…

Observation 5: The most intense migraines seemed to show when Lillian wanted to know something particularly personal. In fact, she seemed to show a particular interest in my parents. The thought cast a shadow of dread through my nerves. From what my uncle told me before his disappearance, that could be bad. Possibly dangerous.

God help me if she was with the Thirteen Pyres Society.

Or the United Magistrate, for that matter.

Was I missing anything?

The early-evening bar-hour traffic wasn't particularly busy; it hardly ever was in small-town North Dakota. So, as I flowed along with the southbound traffic on Third, down the hill from which I came, I tried to piece these observations together, fighting to make sense of what the hell was going on. In doing so, I came to a handful of conclusions. Or, at the very least, a handful of hypotheses worth testing or exploring.

So…

Hypothesis 1: The fluctuating migraines seemed to come from Lillian. This would imply some sort of supernatural ability. That seemed to be the most obvious to me at this point.

Hypothesis 2: This supernatural ability seemed to change the way people acted around, or maybe, more appropriately, toward Lillian. This seemed to include Amber, but for some reason, it didn't seem to affect me in the same way. I must have some kind of resistance to it, and the migraines must be a symptom of that resistance.

Hypothesis 3: This supernatural ability may have been used as a means to coerce information from me. Judging by the way Lillian behaved at the end of the interview, I may have inadvertently given away that information anyway.

Hypothesis 4: Lillian may have set this interview up as a front to conduct a covert form of tactical questioning. If that was the case, when considering her particular interest in my parents, it may be reasonable to assume that she knew about my family history. She may have been trying to determine my family's whereabouts, or maybe to simply confirm who I was in particular.

I eased into my parking space and shifted the truck into park just as that last thought crossed my mind, the radio playing quietly along as I did. I kept the truck running, though, and sat glowering through the windshield while I continued down this little rabbit hole.

My uncle didn't leave me with much information to work with before he disappeared, only some vague warnings that I needed to stay away from certain members of the "supernatural community," including some sort of cult my parents had been involved with called the United Magistrate. Apparently, anyone involved with this cult had been on the run from some enforcers from the Thirteen Pyres Society who were hunting for them, and that they would certainly be put to death if they were found. He had been vehement in his warning that, if I was found, or if I had inadvertently awakened Asmodeus, I might be caught up in this witch hunt as well.

That was basically it. He had given me very little information beyond that, and I was too distraught and overwhelmed by what had happened to my father to dig much deeper into what he said before he left. Hell, the bastard didn't even have the decency to stick around for his own brother's funeral.

I'd spent years since then researching, trying to dig up anything I could on what my uncle had told me. I couldn't find anything. Not a lead, nor a hint, or a clue, that would help me make any sense of what my family had been involved with. The only exceptions came from vague religious texts, some obvious fantasy fiction, and some conspiracy theories that had virtually nothing to do with what I had been looking for. I had essentially given up after a time, and my life had become relatively simple since. It became all too easy to be complacent over the years, and I couldn't help but chastise myself for it now.

I could feel my chest tighten, and my jaw clenched when I realized just how hard I had gripped the steering wheel. I took a moment to take in some slow steady breaths; I knew I couldn't keep a clear mind while revved up like this.

I hated how this evening had taken me so thoroughly off guard. It felt like I was suddenly fighting a defensive battle, and battles are notoriously hard to win while on the defensive. I knew I had to approach this with a healthy degree of caution while maintaining some degree of an aggressive mindset if I were to get ahead of this. The question, though, was how? I had a litany of variables that I couldn't account for and questions that needed to be answered before I could even begin to contend with this. I wasn't exactly a seasoned private investigator either.

I thought about that for a moment though, and it occurred to me that I had at least one lead to work with. Phoenix Energy Solutions. It wasn't much, but it was at least a starting point. If I dug into them a little bit, maybe I could get lucky.

With a huff of breath, I glanced over to the light blue Subaru Outback parked next to me. Amber had evidently made it home before I did. She would be upstairs waiting for me. These last few years would have been exceptionally long, depressing, and difficult without her support, and I knew I had to discuss this with her when I went inside. I hated the idea of it, but there was no way around it.

The little red Toyota made the odd little clicking noises those older vehicles sometimes make when I switched it off, and I climbed the stairs to my apartment in short order, taking them two at a time as I usually do, and eased into my apartment only to be stunned into silence the moment I closed the door behind me.

Amber stood with a hand resting on her hip, facing me in the living room, a cocky smile resting on her face as she waited for me to come through the door. As if on cue, she took slow, languid steps toward me, crossing her arms to her front, gripping the hem of her shirt. I sucked in a breath as the rolling of her hips threatened to drown me, and she slowly pulled her shirt up to reveal her flat stomach and a red-lace bra underneath. Her back arched as she led with her chest accentuating her ample bust, and her curly hair framed her face beautifully as it came free from her shirt when she pulled it off in a smooth motion.

I felt myself letting go of the breath I held, as I reached with my right hand behind my back, searching for the lock on the door. The click was hardly noticed when she placed the palm of her left hand on my sternum and pushed me into the door behind me, grabbing hold of my tucked shirt and pulling it up with a jerk, freeing it from my pants. She pressed herself fully against me then, and she had to practically stand on her toes as our lips met, drawing me into a kiss.

Hard desire flowed through me as I cupped her face in my hands, and I could feel her hips pressing against me while I tasted her, biting her lower lip before gently pulling her head to the side by her hair and nibbling her neck just below her right ear. She reached into and up my shirt then, never having let it go, and the tips of her nails drew up my navel to my chest as she went. I gasped another breath as I felt her nails reach the base of my throat, and she pulled away, gingerly raking her nails back down, grabbing hold of my belt buckle, and finally letting go of my shirt as she did.

My hands dropped and her expression practically screamed of hard desire as she smiled up to me, turned, and started walking toward the bedroom, leading me by my belt buckle. I followed along, hardly resisting her while my hands fumbled deftly with the buttons of my shirt.

# Chapter 9

A couple of things happened at once. First came the loud crack of gunfire, followed by the deafening explosion. My body was slammed by the concussion, jolting from impact under the sheets. I half expected to feel the hard impact of concrete when I fell, but I was greeted instead by the comfort of the mattress when I opened my eyes to the stillness of my bedroom.

Amber and I had fallen asleep spooning during the night, and she was still lying on her side, facing away from me, using my right arm as a pillow. I must have rolled onto my back at some point, and the jolt that I felt hardly seemed to rouse her. My whole nervous system was alight with tension, and my pectoral muscles lightly twitched as I fought to control the pulsing, adrenaline-fueled fear that threatened to control me. I pressed my tongue to the roof of my mouth, hard, and forced a slow, shuddering inhale and held it for a count of four. I released it slowly, focusing on easing the tension in my body as I let it out.

Amber let out a tired little sigh and groaned a little as she rolled into me, resting her head on my chest, clearly unperturbed by the silent battle that was taking place beneath her. Even so, much of the tension seemed to wash away when she opened her eyes and looked up to me. Her eyes sparkled as she absentmindedly traced my sternum with the middle finger and smiled. "Good morning, my love," she said happily, drawing herself into me for a kiss.

"Good morning, lovely," came my tired reply. She pulled away and rolled to her side of the bed, snapping on the lamp next to her.

There were no alarm clocks on the weekends, but she tended to rise early anyway out of habit. I, on the other hand, had never been graced with the gift of being a morning person. The fatigue enveloped me like a weighted blanket, and I struggled to keep my eyes open while she absently stretched, seated beside me in the lamp light. Still, I was none the less captivated by her living portrait, my eyes tracing the hills and valleys of her toned back, until she finally glided into the closet to dress.

I lay there for a moment longer, staring up into the ceiling above me. The stucco cast an eerie, shadowy sort of terrain model in the yellow lamplight, but I hardly took note of it. Instead, I occupied my mind with the memory portrayed in the nightmare that had just disturbed me. It was never an easy thing to do. Revisiting these memories often filled me with a grating anxiety and grief that was often hard to shake off, but I learned a long time ago that shying away from them only increased the intensity of the nightmares, the anxiety, the grief, the misery…

I didn't need a demon to turn me into a monster. All I had to do was shy away from what the past had done to me, and the monster that was inherent in all of us would devour me in due time. There was nothing brave about what I was doing. At least, that's not how I saw it, anyway. This was about preserving myself...

And her.

She deserved better than that.

So, I lay there, under the soft sheets, on top of the comfortable mattress in the stillness of the bedroom, Amber dressing in the closet, and I silently felt through the memory. I sifted through the rage in the violence, the pain in the death, and the grief in the loss. I didn't need to feel it out too much. I didn't need to blow the dam to release the pressure, I just needed to open the spillway enough to prevent any damage to the infrastructure of my mind and my soul.

I didn't have to meditate on this for long either; I'd become accustomed to this practice over time. It only took a few moments for me to calm the raging waters enough to prevent them from spilling over the proverbial dam, cascading down upon my everyday life below. The monster within can sleep another day, It was a sharp contrast to how things had been just a few short years ago.

With a slow breath and a heavy exhale, I willed myself out of bed and dressed myself at the dresser by the bed. Today was a rest day, but gym shorts and a simple blue tank top would do for now anyway. Shambling into the bathroom, I used a flick of my wrist to turn on the light, illuminating the dark. I took little notice of the reflection cast in the mirror above the sink when I turned on the cool water and splashed my face. For a moment I stood over the sink, listening to the water trickling down from the faucet. I let the sound of the water calm my mind and ease me into a trance, gradually slowing my breath. Finally, after a slow and steady inhale, I held it for a brief pause.

"Spirit bound inside of me, asleep forever you shall be." Only then did I take the time to notice the haunted reflection in the mirror, tired eyes staring back at me. I had become all too accustomed to seeing that too, it would seem.

No matter. That would pass as I went through the day.

A small wave of dread washed over me, though, as I stared into my reflection and realized that I had neglected to express my concerns to Amber regarding the interview with Lillian. I knew I shouldn't put it off for too much longer, but I found myself reluctant to bring it up now.

With a contemptuous sigh, I shut off the water and steeled my nerves, pacing away from the mirror. I dried off my face and walked out of the bathroom to see Amber patiently waiting for me to leave just outside the door. I pecked her cheek when I passed, eliciting a happy giggle from her, and strode into the kitchen to make breakfast.

It was the usual, of course: scrambled eggs with sautéed spinach and cheese mixed in. Simple and easy. I put a couple of slices of wheat toast into the toaster and made coffee with the French press on the counter while I waited. Once the toast popped out of the toaster, I served everything on two plates: three eggs' worth for her and four for me. After a pause, I decided at the last minute to grab some red grapes from the fridge, putting them into a bowl for the two of us to share. I had everything out on the table just as she finished getting ready to join me.

She dressed pretty casual today in a simple red sweatshirt and blue jeans. The little diamond on her nose sparkled in the low light as she approached, and she sported her little watch with the blue face along with her claddagh. Her hair was worn down, and it bobbed when she walked with her usual power and quiet confidence.

"Hey, thank you for breakfast, sweety," she said, her green eyes and red lips exploding into a friendly, happy smile that was hard not to fall head over heels in love with.

"Of course," I said, scooping up a forkful of eggs. "Do you have any work planned for today?"

"Not a lot, actually," she said, taking a seat in front of me. "I have another showing first thing Monday morning, so I want to make sure I have all the paperwork ready and my ducks in a row beforehand. It shouldn't take too long. It should be a fairly relaxing weekend otherwise."

"Well, that's good. You certainly deserve a bit of a break."

"Thanks," she said with a smile before taking a bite of her eggs. "What do you have planned for today?"

"Um, not much. Mostly some errands." I could feel a little of tension building in me, watching her bob her head up and down in understanding.

"I see," she said, sipping at her coffee. "Are you going to type up that résumé for Ms. Eldonna today?"

"Well…" I paused. Her eyes tracked up to mine once she took notice and her head cocked to the side, just a little, as an expression of concern crossed over her face. "I feel like I need to talk to you about what happened last night."

"What do you mean?" she said, putting down her cup of coffee.

I froze, trying to sort out how I wanted to proceed. "Did you notice anything strange last night?"

"No, why?" she said with confused skepticism.

"Did you notice anyone acting strangely?"

She simply shook her head no, her eyes locked steadily onto me.

"It's hard to explain… I'm not entirely sure how, but I think Eldonna was using some kind of magic to influence people around her." Her eyebrows shot up at that. "Mostly, I think she was trying to use it against us."

"Kyle…" I waited for her to continue. "Magic? Really?" she said with an exasperated sigh. "Don't you think that sounds a little…"

"What, crazy?" I filled in for her.

She bobbed her head a little.

"How so? It's not like we haven't seen magic before."

"Yeah, but that was a really long time ago. Besides, that was sort of like a fire-and-brimstone sort of thing," she said, bringing her hands up into fists in front of her, opening them quickly, and closing them again at the word "brimstone." "What are you suggesting here? Some kind of mind magic?"

"Yeah, I think so."

"Right." She sighed. "Look, honey, I know you have been really stressed out with school and trying to find a job, and I know you had a really bad migraine last night–"

"That's the thing," I interrupted. "I think the migraine was a symptom. I don't think I was being affected the same way other people were."

"Really?" An eyebrow shot up at that. "Do you think I was affected?" she said with an accusatory tone.

"Yeah, I think so."

"You think so?" she asked, her tone flat.

"Look, there is a lot here that I don't know for sure, but you and I both know how dangerous these people can be," I said, keeping my voice calm. "You remember what my uncle said about The Society, right?"

"And The Magistrate. Yes, I remember." She sighed again. "Are you suggesting that she may be one of them?"

"Look, I don't know for sure. I just think we need to be careful in how we approach things from here."

"You don't know for sure." She rubbed at her forehead, frustration thick in the tone of her voice. "That is a hell of a thing to accuse someone of without being so sure of anything, Kyle. I've worked with her for a while, and I know quite a few people who run in her circles. Don't you think I would have noticed if there was anything off by now?"

"Look, I'm not saying anything definitively," I said, showing my hands, palms up and open pleadingly. "I just think–"

"Kyle," she interrupted. "Don't you think that it's a little more plausible that the migraine made you perceive things a little differently?"

I placed my hands flat on the table, staring at her flatly for her to continue.

"Look, I'm really sticking my neck out for you here. My reputation is on the line. Please, just…" She shook her head before looking back up to me pleadingly. "Please, just fill out the damn résumé."

I felt myself rock back a little as she abruptly stood up to leave.

"I should go. I'll see you later. I love you, Kyle," she said as she put on her shoes and walked out the door.

I rested my chin on the heel of my hand, glowering at the mostly full plate of food on her side of the table, my leg shaking under the table in frustration. My mind raced as I went over my options.

"Awesome," I said aloud in frustration. I cursed a little under my breath, realizing that I would have to sort this out on my own. It didn't take long for the shaking under the table to stop though, when a feeling of gloom washed over me. It made it hard to tell if it was that or the fatigue that made my breath shudder.

Hell, maybe it was both. It was becoming hard to be certain of anything anymore.

# Chapter 10
## Mosul, Iraq

The capital of the Ninawa Province, Mosul, lies within the northern regions of Iraq, and forms the northern tip of the Sunni Triangle. The Sunni Triangle, as a whole, was well-known for being the basis of support for the former president of Iraq, Saddam Hussein, and the Ba'athist party that supported him. When Saddam's government fell after the 2003 invasion, along with the de-Ba'athification that followed, the region fell into chaos when the former Ba'athist members teamed up with insurgents to fight off the Americans and their allied forces.

The city of Mosul itself represented a unique challenge within the Sunni Triangle, as it was considered the sectarian fault line between the Sunni Arabs and the Kurds who occupied much of northern Iraq. When the United States military initially took Mosul, it was only with one thousand Special Forces operators working with thousands of Kurdish Peshmerga, and these operators were unable to stop the armed Kurds from the subsequent looting that would drive large numbers of Arabs out of their homes.

General Petraeus and his 101st Infantry Division would later take control of Mosul and mostly stabilize it, though ethnic tensions grew between the Kurds in the city's east, and the growing insurgency which would slowly take hold in the west. This tension would finally break after the battles of Fallujah to the south drove insurgents north, sparking the subsequent Battle of Mosul in 2004, which storied some of the most brutal and sustained fighting within the region; FOB Marez itself being a frequent target of violent and bloody attacks.

Although no part of the city truly fell under insurgent control, there was a period of prolonged stalemate between the insurgents in the western half of the city and the American forces to the east. That stalemate would slowly break over time, as the newly branded "Islamic State of Iraq" would sustain substantial losses within their greater strongholds to the south and would be forced into their last stronghold to the north. The city of Mosul.

By late 2007, Mosul had become the insurgents' main base of operations, along with their last supply route through which they could move personnel, money, and weapons from abroad into the country. It was here that the insurgents wanted to stage a "decisive final battle," knowing that if they lost their center within Mosul, they could no longer fight effectively in Iraq.

By early 2008, Al-Qaeda and the Islamic State wanted to make it clear they could put up a fight against the United States.

We were in Mosul to put that theory to the test.

The walk back to our compound from the chow hall seemed routine after a couple of months' stay in Morez, and the pock-marks on the concrete barriers lining our compound no longer filled my imagination like they used to, but the continued efforts of the combat engineers never ceased to amaze me as they feverishly replaced or repaired the various battle-damaged structures throughout the FOB. Even so, it was often hard not to notice the blown-out ceiling on one of the hangars near the airfield, or the newly destroyed housing units on my way to the Ranger compound.

It was hard not to think about what that destruction could have meant either.

Some of the smaller entrances into the CHU area could be easy to miss if you didn't know what to look for, but the walk through the lines of CHUs proved to be an adequate short cut to the compound from the chow hall, and I was soon weaving around the T-barriers separating the CHUs from the compound, into an alleyway of single-story, plywood-walled buildings, and around to the awning of one that served as our platoon headquarters.

I was respectably early, but so were a handful of smokers taking refuge under the awning and its scant protection from the blistering Iraqi sun, waiting for the mission brief to start. Locker and Ramirez were leaning lazily on the two-by-fours that made up the shoddily built railing on the opposite end of the awning and broke from their conversation when Locker casually waved at me in greeting. The dark brown contents of the Gatorade-bottle-turned-spit-cup sloshed about in his hand.

"Evening, Sergeant," Ramirez greeted me as I approached.

"What's up, guys, everyone here?"

"The squad is here, Sergeant," Locker said as he spat into his cup. "The Double A brothers are around the corner with Langston, probably up to no good as usual. Everyone else is inside. We are just waiting on the platoon sergeant and PL."

"Dear God," I scoffed. "What are those three up to now?"

"Who knows?" Ramirez took a drag from a cigarette. "Probably trying to feed a mouse to a camel spider or something."

"Jeez, didn't we just counsel Langston for trying to get one to fight a scorpion?"

"Heh, yeah." Locker chuckled, shaking his head. "The spider's gone; you just never know with that guy though."

"I swear, that guy is more of a risk to himself than this war ever could be," I said, the other two huffing in agreement. "Bro!" I exclaimed to Ramirez, slapping his shoulder with the back of my hand. "What's the word? Have you heard anything yet?"

Ramirez's steely-eyed expression softened into a smile, and he relaxed a little into the rail his eyes tracking down to his feet. "Yeah, she's good," he said before bringing his eyes up to meet mine again. "I just spoke with her a little while ago. They took the little one to NICU, but it sounds like it isn't for anything serious." He took another drag of his cigarette before continuing. "Angelina should be able to take him home in a couple of days."

"That's awesome, brother. I'm happy to hear that," I said, extending my hand to him, hardly keeping my excitement contained.

Ramirez broke into a full-faced smile that was a stark contrast to his typically stoic demeanor. It always seemed to underline the wholesome and genuine joy reflected in others around him in those rare instances when it showed. "Thank you, Sergeant," he said as he shook my hand. "I appreciate that."

"So, did you guys finally come up with a name?" said Locker behind his own shit-eating grin.

"Miguel, after her father."

"Ramrod!"

Neither of us noticed the platoon sergeant approach, and all three of us startled when Sergeant First Class Arroyo called out to Ramirez in his booming voice. Our platoon leader, First Lieutenant Wilkins, smiled brightly up to us while he walked next to Arroyo, who was beckoning Ramirez with a crooked finger.

"Moving, Sergeant," Ramirez said as pulled himself off the rail to meet him.

Lieutenant Wilkins, who barely seemed to have a handle on the mountain of paperwork he carried, continued to walk under the awning while Arroyo stopped just outside the railing. "I'll catch up with you in a minute," he said to Ramirez as he passed by. Though he really didn't need to, he reflexively ducked his head a little as he walked under the awning and paused just before turning to hip-check the door open. "Hey, can I get a couple of guys to help me set up?" he said before going inside.

"Yes, sir," came my prompt reply.

"Albers, Arrants, Langston," Locker yelled down to the side of the building as he leaned over the railing, hooking a thumb toward the door behind him. "Get inside and help the LT."

Langston led the other two troublemakers around the awning and into the headquarters, talking enthusiastically about some upgrades he planned on doing to his truck when he got home. It wasn't a subject of particular interest for me, so I had to take their word for it when the other two busted his balls over his poor choice in vehicle upgrades.

The compound itself wasn't particularly large, not much bigger than a high school football field, and it was nearly completely lined with more two-story tall T-barriers that deliberately prevented anyone within the FOB from viewing our activity within the compound. A handful of buildings resembling small, poorly built wooden houses lined one side of the compound and served as the various platoon headquarters, the company headquarters, and storage. These buildings were fairly small, most of them sporting only three rooms, leaving most of the compound open for staging vehicles if they were ever needed.

Locker and I stood in silence while Arroyo and Ramirez took advantage of the semi-private space, aided further by the Spanish neither of us could understand, to speak enthusiastically in confidence. Although I could probably take a guess about what they were saying, I was left to wonder if I could have made better use of those three years of high school Spanish classes when Locker broke the silence between us.

"That must be hard," he said spitting into his cup, never taking his eyes off the other two.

"What's that?"

"Having to miss your child's birth while you're deployed."

I was taken off guard by that and found myself studying him, though he pretended not to notice as he held his thoughtful gaze on Arroyo and Ramirez. Locker rarely, if ever, talked about his family, which always left me wondering whenever he made these sorts of comments.

"Yeah," I said after the moment passed. "I suppose it would be."

The door closed behind me and I glanced over to see Taylor's lumbering form swaying as he exaggerated casually bumping into me, joining Locker and I, nearly knocking me off balance when he did. "Dick," I said in mock protest, shoving him off with an elbow. He exaggerated rocking back and into the railing while eyeing me with a wry grin.

"Bro, this OP looks legit."

"How do you mean?"

"They have pictures of the Emir of Al-Qaeda and some of his commanders in there. This OP is going to be big. They really took their time in planning this one out."

Locker glanced from me to Taylor with a crooked eyebrow. "Really?" he asked disbelieving.

"Yeah, LT is finished setting up. Come check this out."

Arroyo hit Ramirez with an audible slap on the shoulder as the two men broke off and stated walking toward the building. When Arroyo saw that we were still standing outside, he circled a finger next to his head and pointed at the door, but the three of us were already one step ahead of him. We were nearly through the door before Arroyo and Ramirez even made it to the awning, both men smiling broadly.

The plywood-walled main room was empty save for the three desks covered in paperwork and laptops. Our feet falling on the two-by-fours making up the floorboards brought to mind the sounds of cowboy boots walking through the saloons in those old Westerns. It was sort of fitting though, considering how frequently we joked about how these deployments often devolved into something out of the Wild West.

The back room that made up the briefing room, on the other hand, was packed to the brim with nearly forty battle-hardened killers in camo. Most of them were sitting in folding chairs facing the front of the room, while nearly a dozen were leaning against the back wall to the far right of the doorway. As I made my way to the back wall with Taylor, I found myself staring aghast at the display at the front of the room.

You see, Rangers in Iraq typically didn't operate like other units in the Army. Since the early days of counter-insurgency operations in Iraq, Rangers rarely conducted operations greater than a platoon-size element, making us highly mobile and able to hit our targets quickly with extreme prejudice. We particularly specialized in small unit raids, typically hunting down people known as "high-value targets," and we operated at such a high tempo that it wasn't unusual for a platoon to conduct two or more missions a day. In fact, it was far from unusual for a Ranger platoon to conduct well over a hundred missions during a ninety-day deployment. These raids were often time sensitive, and it wasn't uncommon for us to be briefed on the mission details on the way to our targets either.

This, on the other hand, was different. Taylor was right, they had taken their time with this one.

As the LT and helpers finished their work, they revealed a wall nearly completely covered with maps, overlays, a satellite picture of a building with a red $X$, mission details, American units in the area, and nearly ten pictures of men with detailed descriptions for each. Most of these men were older, most of them had beards, a couple of them did not. All of them were highly recognizable, well-known leaders within the upper echelons of Al-Qaeda in Iraq.

Many of the Rangers were talking among themselves, but as I looked around the room, it was evident everyone displayed at least some level of curiosity regarding this up-and-coming mission. It was no wonder why; we had been hunting for these guys, specifically, every single day of the handful of months we had been deployed. Given the level of detail here though, many were starting to openly wonder if we finally caught up to them.

"That's enough, quiet down," said Arroyo with his thick South American accent. "First squad, you up?"

"Up," I said giving him a thumbs-up indicating all my guys were present.

"Second?"

"Up."

"Third?"

"Up."

"Weapons?"

"Up."

"The platoon is all here, sir."

Nearly everyone in the platoon dutifully pulled out and opened notebooks while Lieutenant Wilkins stepped in front of the platoon to give his mission brief. I noticed that Watson, who was sitting directly in front of where I was standing, had something drawn on the outside of his green notebook, which he seemed to be deliberately slow to open. Leaning over his shoulder, I managed to make out what looked like a giant veiny penis drawn on the cover, with the head pointing down toward the bottom. A set of wings sprouted from either side of the head, swooping around and up so that the tip of the wings touched the side of the semi-hairy balls in a picture that was vaguely similar to a set of airborne wings. Above the angelic, throbbing phallus was drawn a "Tab" with the word "Barebone" inscribed within.

Stifling my amusement, I elbowed Locker standing next to me and pointed out Watson's masterpiece. Locker, who was standing cross-armed and rigid, broke down in silent and baffled amusement and elbowed Ramirez next to him. Ramirez, who was Watson's team leader, slowly shook his head, but a slight smirk broke through his stone features.

The lieutenant's umber skin glistened under the fluorescent lights as he wiped sweat from his shaved head. "Well, gentlemen," he said with an exaggerated pause and a wolfish smile. "This is likely to be the highest-profile raid we have done on this deployment thus far."

Everyone in the room fell stone silent with their attention hanging on his every word while the deep baritone flooded the crowded room. It was usually hard not to. At a little over six and a half feet tall, the Virginia native dominated the room with the heavily muscled, athletic build he'd refined as an elite rugby player in Virginia Tech. His sophisticated manner of speaking often left me wondering why someone so wildly intelligent and capable would ever consider turning away practicing surgical medicine to lead a bunch of dirty grunts into combat. Even so, you couldn't build a better platoon leader in a lab if you tried.

"Here is the situation," he continued. "Al-Qaeda in Iraq currently hold a three-story compound in the Ar Rafa'i district of Mosul, through which they plan on coordinating and preparing for continuous and sustained attacks against American and Coalition forces. It is believed that the Emir Abd-al-Rahman, along with several of his key commanders and security detail will be on the premises of the target building later this evening, and are rumored to be preparing some sort of unknown public display in the early morning. Though it isn't yet clear what that public display may entail, for our purposes, it doesn't matter. We will be taking them down tonight in their sleep."

Hungry smiles on eager faces broke out throughout the room. Al-Qaeda fighters came from all over the Middle East, often from thousands of miles away to get their Jihad on; killing Coalition forces and civilians en masse was the name of their game. This emir and his commanders had spearheaded these efforts for months while we worked tirelessly to hunt them down, once missing them by mere moments when they left the objective just before we assaulted it. With the amount of intelligence and planning laid out before us today, however, there wasn't a doubt written on anyone's face that we finally had them.

But there was a sudden jolt down my spine that took me out of my shared silent revelry. This jolt caused my shoulders to momentarily shrug in spasm, taking me off the wall I was leaning on. Taylor was the only one who seemed to notice, giving me a thumbs-up to see if I was okay. I waved him off with a nod, to which he answered with a nod of his own and a look of skepticism before turning his attention back to the lieutenant. I shook it off as nothing at first, but my breath caught when I felt the hairs on my arms and the back of my neck begin to stand on end as if electrically charged.

"For tonight's mission," Wilkins continued, pointing to a picture of the building with the red $X$, "first platoon is to conduct a fast-rope operation to take control of the target building, here, in order to kill or capture enemy insurgents within and retrieve any intelligence found."

It was like a drumbeat thundered in my chest without warning, pulsing into my neck as my heart pumped adrenaline through my body, my breath quickening. I fought to steady my breathing, struggling to understand why my fight-or-flight mechanisms took off so suddenly and with so little warning. It was all I could do to maintain my composure as I searched the room to find the source of my fear.

All around me, all I could see were the same eager and determined faces as before. Many dutifully scribed in their notebooks, but every man in the room had their gaze locked and unperturbed onto the lieutenant as he continued to give his mission brief. I had just begun to wonder why everything had taken on a sharp crystalline shine as stark terror froze me solid when she walked into the briefing room.

She glided in with the grace of a dancer and the curiosity of a child, taking in the lieutenant's mission brief with no concern for anyone else in the room. For a moment, I wanted to shout at her to get out when she walked by Arroyo, who was leaning against the wall by the door, and stood directly in front of three Rangers on the far-left side of the room. Not a soul seemed to even so much as flinch at the fact that she'd entered the room. Indeed, in spite of her bold entrance, no one seemed to notice that she was with us at all.

For a moment, she looked over the display posted on the wall, her hair floating about her as if submerged in water, the same white robes as before clinging to her as if pressed into her by a heavy wind. Her movements became increasingly urgent when she first took in the maps, the pictures, the mission outline. She stepped further into the room to get a better look at the displays the lieutenant concealed from her vision. Still, no one seemed to notice, the Lieutenant not even so much as stuttering or pausing in her presence.

Spinning on her heel to face the crowd, with a look of fear and utter desperation, she slowly and deliberately searched the room until her ancient eyes locked onto mine. I could feel my lungs collapse and my body begin to vibrate as the weight of her gaze slowly pressed into mine, my back pressing into the wall being all I could do to prevent myself from running away screaming.

Her hair drifted around her, framing her head in darkness while her expression seemed to rapidly flow into surprised recognition, then concern, and then sorrow…

With a blinking jolt, she disappeared, leaving me temporarily dazed, fighting to recover my composure in my confusion. The lieutenant's baritone was the only sound in the room.

"Goodwin." Arroyo's voice snapped me back. "What is first squad's role once the over watch and Strykers are in place?"

"We'll be the first one in, clearing the rooftop first, securing the top floor after."

"Good. Second, what are you doing?"

"We will follow in behind first, securing the second floor."

"Good. Waters, how about third?"

"We will fall in behind first and second, clearing the first floor."

"Very good. Does anyone have any questions?"

"Are we going to have any close air support?" said Waters with a raised hand.

"Other than the Black Hawks taking us in, nothing that will be directly attached to this operation," responded Wilkins matter-of-factly. "But there will be Apache attack helicopters in the area we will be able to call on if they are needed. Anyone else?"

No one said a word as Arroyo and Wilkins scanned the room, nodding to their fellow Rangers' silent anticipation with a look of satisfaction.

"Alright, sounds good," Arroyo continued, grimly crossing his arms while he addressed the room. "I think it goes without saying that this is going to be a major raid. The last time anyone hit HVTs this significant, nearby insurgents overran some Iraqi Army outposts in retaliation. We may expect something similar to happen in response to this, so be prepared for a follow-up just in case. That's all I got, sir."

"The raid has been moved to the right, SP at twenty-one hundred," Wilkins continued with a glance at his watch. "That should give you plenty of time to double-check your radios and make sure your gear is squared away. If there are no further questions, you are dismissed."

The room cleared slowly while my head reeled, the Rangers filling the emptying space with excited conversation as everyone herded. My hands shook while I fought to control my breathing, and I waited anxiously for everyone in front of me to move out of the way. Taylor slapped me on the shoulder before giving me a surprised double take and leading me out.

I fell in near the back of the crowd, and the walls seemed to collapse in around me when I squeezed through the doorway into the main room. The herd in front of me was all that kept me from rushing the door, and they were hardly rushing out themselves. It felt like I was walking through a tunnel that was slowly getting smaller, so I leveled my gaze onto Taylor's back, focusing on slowing my breathing, placing one foot in front of the other, until I was finally relieved from my confines by the open spaces of the compound outside. I suddenly had something more tangible to focus on with all my senses under assault by the near oppressive desert sun and blistering Iraqi heat, and finally found all my tension melting away.

The crowd of Rangers nearly all uniformly flowed around the building toward the CHUs and I took the moment of clarity to run through what happened when Taylor fell into place beside me. He regarded me silently at first, keeping pace with me between the buildings. I considered saying something, but it had dawned on me that he'd noticed my moment of panic, and that was the last thing I wanted to bring attention to at the moment.

How crazy would it sound if I started mouthing off about some spirit woman, whom only I could see, who'd followed us into the briefing? Was she following me?

It wasn't until we neared the back of the complex on our way into the CHUs that he finally elbowed me to get my attention. "Roll with me," he said, peeling off from the group, walking into the alley between the platoon headquarters and the T-barriers. I hesitated for a moment, but with a defeated breath, I followed him.

We didn't walk far. Once we were out of earshot from anyone else, he abruptly turned and studied me, hooking his thumbs behind his belt buckle. "What's going on, man? What's on your mind?"

"What do you mean?" Of course, I knew what the hell he meant. What was the point of playing coy?

"This morning, when Arroyo gave us the Warno"–he paused with a shrug–"it seemed like there was something that really freaked you out. Then you went into panic mode during the brief."

He took a moment to give me a chance to respond. The problem was, I didn't really know how he would respond if I told him what I'd seen. I fumbled for what to say, then shrugged in mock confusion.

"Look," he said with a raised hand, bidding me to stop. "You know me. We've been at this for a long damn time. You know I'm not about to go running my mouth off about shit, you can talk to be, bro. What's going on?"

"I don't know, man." I responded with a defeated shake of my head.

"What do you mean?"

"I don't know. I think I'm starting to see things."

"What, like some kind of hallucination?" he said, skeptically.

"I don't know, maybe," I said rubbing the back of my neck.

His voice softened. "Okay?"

He didn't really push after that. I took a moment to think about what I wanted to say, but he simply waited. There wasn't a hint of judgment or anger in his demeanor or the way he spoke; there was only concern in his expression while he waited for me to continue.

Of course, I didn't want to. What I wanted was to "Ranger Up" and soldier on. I wanted to get back to my CHU and speak with my team leaders so we could properly prepare for the fight to come. My men were counting on me to lead them into the fray, and I couldn't let them down.

But I couldn't lie to Taylor either. The guy was practically my brother. He knew me inside and out, better than anyone else I knew; he could usually tell when I was bullshitting anyway. Besides, Taylor was always there when I needed someone I could count on. On nights like tonight, of course, Taylor needed to know I would still be there for him too.

So, I told him about all I'd experienced throughout the day. I told him about the lady in white, how she manifested that morning and during the brief. I told him about her effects on me, and how she disappeared as mysteriously as she appeared. I told him everything while he listened without judgment. Without interruption. He simply listened.

When I finished, he stood in silent contemplation while choosing his next words carefully. "Do you remember what happened with Sergeant Thompson last year in Afghanistan?"

"From Third Platoon? You mean when they pulled him off the line?"

"Yeah, do you remember why?"

"Yeah, I think he started to crack, so they pulled him back to cool off."

"Right, but could you blame him? The guy went through some wild shit over there."

"No, I don't, actually. That was a crazy deployment for everyone."

"That's right. Third Platoon got it particularly bad though. I believe one of his guys actually got hurt. But do you remember what happened after they pulled him?"

"Yeah, he took a week off to cool down at the FOB and went back into the fight."

"I think he spoke to someone while he was at it, but yeah."

We stood for a moment studying each other before I continued. "Do you think I'm starting to crack?"

He huffed out an amused breath. "That's not what I'm saying, but it's been a hell of a deployment, brother. We've had to put up with a lot of shit since we've been out here, and let's face it, the tempo has been pretty insane. I don't think anyone would think less of you if you spoke to someone about it, and I would one hundred percent back you up if you did."

I took that in for a moment. What he was saying wasn't exactly irrational. From everything that I'd heard, Thompson had kicked ass during the remainder of the deployment. Neither of us were going to point out that he later got discharged for PTSD though. Still, I couldn't say that Taylor was in the wrong on this one, and he was still counting on me regardless.

"I'll make a deal with you," I said after a moment's consideration.

"Yeah?" he said with amusement.

"Let's wrap up tonight's OP, and I'll talk to Arroyo about speaking to a chaplain or someone when we get back."

"You promise?" He smirked.

"Yeah."

"Okay," he said with a nod. "You want me there to back you up?"

"I wouldn't turn that down."

"Okay, I'll be there." He extended his hand for a shake, which I took in firmly. "I'm holding you to it, bro."

"I hope the fuck you do," I replied behind a smile before switching grips and bumping his shoulder with mine.

"Alright, I have to talk to the radio guy to get my comms squared away," he said as he walked away. "I'll catch up with you later."

"Cool man, I'll see you at the CHU."

With that, we parted ways. Even though I walked on my own down this dusty, deserted alleyway, I felt far from alone. I took in and reflected on the feelings of gratitude, though I couldn't help but to also acknowledge my worry. But maybe he was right, maybe I'd already pushed myself to my breaking point. Maybe all I needed was a little bit of time to cool off so that I could finish this deployment strong.

*"It's a trap."*

The voice stopped me dead in my tracks. It sounded like a young woman had whispered to me, though it didn't seem to come from any discernable direction. I searched the alley ahead of me, and then behind me. There wasn't anyone there. Even Taylor had left me here alone at some point. I could feel my heart thundering in my chest as the world took on a crystalline shine, until I heard the footsteps shifting on gravel. I turned to face the corner where Taylor and I had taken the detour into the alley, facing her squarely when she finally came into view.

She walked around the corner slowly and deliberately, completely unfazed by the blistering heat from the desert sand beneath her naked feet. Her jet-black hair seemed to defy gravity while it framed her face like a lion's mane. Though she looked barley over the age of twenty, her dark eyes seemed ancient and timeless. She stopped only a few paces in front of me, and when she leveled her gaze on me, it was as if death himself was appraising me, sending more shivers down my spine.

"Be cautious," she stated flatly. "You and your men are falling into a trap."

"Who the hell are you?" My voice came up in a growl through clenched teeth, which would have surprised me if I didn't feel it bubbling up inside me first.

"The execution is merely bait, meant to lure you all inside."

"You didn't answer my question." I could feel my hands tighten into fists while I took a step toward her. "Who the hell are you? What are you doing here?"

"I am a great many things," she said behind a deathly smile. "But for you, I can be a wraith in the shadows, or a beacon in the night." With her hand upturned, she reached out, beckoning me to take it. "I can be a guide in the darkness, your wrath in the fight."

"What are you even saying right now?" I stammered in my fright. "What are you? Who are you?"

She slowly shook her head in a silent no, her steady gaze holding hard onto mine. "You are not listening, Kyle."

That stopped me cold. How the hell did she know my name?

"They mean to bog you down," she continued as she stepped closer. "To overwhelm you. They mean to bring that building down around you, to make it your grave."

"What, the insurgents?" I could feel my voice shake and stepped away from her involuntarily.

She continued to step closer to me slowly, sensually, her hips swaying. "But you can halt the slaughter, Kyle." She raised a hand with a hungry grin when she got within a couple of paces and reached for me as if to caress my forehead. "You have the power to turn the tide against them. Let me in and I can show you how."

"Hold on, stop," I said as I took another step back, bringing my hands up to ward her off or to push her back, "Get the fuck away from me!" With another blinding jolt, she was gone again leaving me breathless.

For a moment, I stood there stunned, trying to catch my breath again. I looked around for her, but the alley remained empty. I could have been the only living soul within the compound for all I could tell. Nearly stumbling toward the opening into the CHUs, I tried to blink away the crystallin shine as it faded out of my vision.

*"It is* there, *look inside yourself."*

Spurred into a run now, I heaved down the length of the CHUs, past the showers and concerned on-lookers, nearly running past my own CHU before I skidded to a stop outside my team leaders' door. I grasped onto their railing, struggling for breath while sweat stung my eyes. It wasn't until I finally caught my breath again and found my composure that I climbed the steps and banged on their door.

Ramirez promptly opened it, and I could see Locker peak around the poncho liner they used to divide the room in two. "I want both of you to make sure everyone has at least two extra magazines for the raid tonight." Ramirez glanced at Locker, who was giving me a curious look, and back again before nodding. "Make sure the SAW gunners have at least one extra two-hundred-round drum on them too."

"Roger, Sergeant. Everything good?" asked Ramirez.

"Yeah man, just make it happen."

# Chapter 11

The warmth of the early afternoon did little to soften my dour mood when the sun blanketed the inside of the little Barnes and Noble coffee shop in its golden light. Sitting in my usual corner table with my back against the wall, I leaned lazily into the chair, fidgeting with the nearly empty coffee cup on the table, silently musing at what seemed like three weeks' worth of wasted research.

Nothing about the hiring process seemed out of place, but I had heard nothing from Lillian since our meeting at The Pirogue just a couple of weeks ago. Since that meeting, any time I had to fill out paperwork for a background check, take the drug test, or anything else that needed to be done before actually working, I first had to work through one of the happy-go-lucky HR representatives assigned to help me through the ordeal. In fact, the whole process seemed to be in line with what you might expect from hiring into any company that works closely with the oil industry.

Even though I learned a great deal about the company in my research, I could find absolutely nothing unusual about Phoenix Energy Solutions itself. The only thing that seemed off was how quickly Eldonna came into her position within the company, though that wasn't entirely odd in and of itself either.

From what I'd gathered, Phoenix was a military-veteran-owned company that established itself in 2012 after their CEO and a handful of others got into a dispute with their parent company and broke off to start a business of their own. Apparently, they thought they could run a generator business better than their parent company, and apparently, they were right. After a couple of years, they managed to develop a truly advanced generator model, along with a powerful business structure that helped them to expand beyond their headquarters in Casper, Wyoming, and into the surrounding states. It wasn't long before they discovered how versatile their generators could be, and their success quickly followed.

Lillian's story was interesting, but there was nothing in it that screamed, "I can play with magic," from what I could find. Originally from Georgia, she apparently had a master's in business along with a master's in water and soil resources through the University of Georgia. She seemed to have bounced around to pad her résumé before landing at Phoenix as the assistant to the COO in 2014, which was also about the time Phoenix really started to take off as a company.

Even her social media was squeaky clean and professional. I found it odd that there was absolutely nothing mentioning her family, personal interests, or anything of that nature in the social media accounts. Odd as that might have seemed, I also had to remind myself with a degree of frustration that I managed my accounts much the same way, even before I discovered the existence of magic.

It was the silent buzz of my cell phone that finally broke me from my musings and pulled me away from the LinkedIn page displayed on my laptop. When I pulled it out, I couldn't help but marvel in surprise at the irony that it was Lillian, of all people, who was calling me.

"Hello?"

"Kyle, it's Lillian Eldonna. How have you been?"

"Well enough, trying to keep busy. How about yourself?"

"Good, thanks. Are you busy now? I don't want to take much of your time."

"Not at all, what can I do for you?"

"Well, I invited the basin lead and the lead mechanic over for dinner at my new home so we can go over how we should move forward with setting up the new shop. Being the lead assistant, I think it would be good of you to join us in this discussion. Assuming you have no prior commitments, of course."

"I do not. When would you like me to be there?"

"Can you be here tonight at six?"

It was becoming increasingly obvious that I was getting absolutely nowhere with my research, and being the not-private detective that I was, I had absolutely no idea how to proceed without obtaining a ghillie suit and performing some kind of Army-inspired reconnaissance mission. As amusing as that idea was, I obviously don't have to explain why that would have been just a bit extreme.

But maybe I wouldn't have to. Being invited to her home could open an opportunity to find some sort of clue into who she really was. Hell, if I played my cards right, I might not have to dance around the issue at all. For all I knew, the opportunity may arise for me to simply ask her about it directly.

"Sure, I can be there by six," I said while glancing at my watch. "Is there anything you would like me to bring?"

"I don't think so," she responded warmly. "We'll have everything we need. It should be pretty casual too, so just bring yourself."

She gave me her address and we ended the call, leaving me to stare pensively at my laptop while fidgeting with my coffee cup.

It was a little short notice, but she at least gave me a few hours to prepare if I needed to. The problem was that I didn't even know where to start. I had so little information to go on that if she was involved with some "magical community," I could easily walk into some kind of trap, assuming that she knew who I was. But then again, the complete lack of information had led me to question whether I had simply imagined this in the first place. I knew that this would make me look particularly foolish if I was wrong, not to mention that Amber's reputation was on the line. That can mean something in a small town like this, especially given her profession. Backing out now might be a hard thing for her to forgive if I was wrong.

I spent a little extra time in the coffee shop trying to game-plan how I was going to approach this situation before finally killing the rest of my coffee in frustration and gathering my things before leaving the store, the flirty barista waving me out as I went.

I was surprised to see Amber's little blue Subaru already parked when I pulled into my parking space outside our apartment. The nice thing about Amber being a real estate agent was that she more or less had the freedom to set her own schedule. Even so, it was unusual for her to come home early, even on a Friday.

After taking the steps up to the second floor two at a time, as usual, I opened the unlocked door to find Amber sound asleep on our brown leather couch, classical music playing softly from the television masking her light snoring. She didn't so much as flinch when I closed and locked the door behind me, and I became consciously aware of the chill in the air as I moved into the apartment.

I carefully removed a fluffy blue blanket from the linen closet, trying not to wake her. She curled herself deep into the comforts of the cushions when I placed the blanket on top of her, wrapping herself in it tightly when I grabbed a book I had been reading lately off the coffee table and sat down on the chair beside her.

A couple of hours passed before she finally stirred. She sat up slowly, stiff with fatigue, rubbing her eyes. She looked around a little while, then yawned and stretched before she finally found me sitting next to her. It seemed a stark contrast from the usual early-bird-conquers-the-day energy that I was so accustomed to seeing from her.

"Hey," she greeted me with a smile. "What time is it?"

"Almost five. How are you feeling?"

"I'm okay, just a little tired. What's up?"

"Just making sure. You haven't seemed like your usual spry self lately. You're not getting old on me now, are you?" I said with a mocking half-smile.

"No." She scowled. Apparently, she wasn't in the mood for my humor either. "I'm fine. I think I'm just getting a little worn down from work."

"I see. You aren't coming down with something, are you?"

"I don't think so," she answered, raking her fingers through her hair. "What about you? How are you doing?"

"I'm doing okay. I'm supposed to meet with Lillian for dinner in about an hour. Apparently, she wants me to meet my boss and the other manager while we go over how we are setting up the shop."

"Hey," she responded with an excited smile. "That's great. Are you excited to finally start working?"

"I don't know." I shrugged. "Maybe."

"What do you mean?" Her expression soured a little. "You don't still think she is some kind of magic user, do you?"

"I just think we should be cautious, that's all."

"Right. Let me guess. Knowing you, you probably tried to research her somehow, right?"

"Some, yeah."

"And did you find anything?"

"If you were part of a super-secret magical cult trying to keep your existence a secret, would you blast about it on the internet?"

"But you didn't find anything, so what if you are wrong? This could be a big opportunity for you."

"Okay, but what if I'm right?"

"And how many opportunities are you going to push aside due to baseless paranoia?"

"I know what I saw, Amber."

"Yeah, you and nobody else in the restaurant while you were battling a severe migraine, I might add."

I raised my hands up questioningly, almost instinctively, but I had nothing to say in response. I dropped my hands back down to my lap with a light slap, and for a moment, the music playing lightly from the television was all that kept the room from descending into deafening silence.

"There are other opportunities that I can look into, many of them local–"

"Like what? The Pen? The Railroad? Because that's worked out well so far," she interrupted as she stood up from the couch. "You are not going to find too many opportunities like this Kyle, and Lillian is practically handing this one to you on a silver platter–not to mention that I really stuck my neck out for you to get this."

"Amber, I–"

"No, I'm tired of being the only one pulling the weight here, Kyle. I'm done having this conversation."

Her words felt like a blow that caught in my throat, leaving me mute from choking when she abruptly turned away from me and stormed into the bedroom.

Pulling the weight? I couldn't believe she would say something so absurd! She may have been making the bulk of the income, but I was hardly slacking off!

I had to stop myself mid-step from following her into the bedroom and saying something particularly stupid, before I realized that I was on my feet at all.

Jeez, talk about a blow to the ego.

Still, I didn't have time to get into a full-blown argument, and I knew that confronting her at the moment would only make things worse. Checking my watch, I decided that freshening up would probably be a better use of my time. Casual or not, getting rid of the two-day-old stubble would probably go over a little better than showing up looking like a homeless Native.

That was an easy enough fix, though. After I ducked into the bathroom and splashed my face with hot water, the razor did its job with ease. I noticed that my hair was a little shaggier than I would have liked, though, but it wasn't too much longer than the high fade I usually favored. The hair might have touched my ears a little now, but I supposed it wasn't too offensive. It'd have to do.

Stepping out of the bathroom, I stopped short of the bedroom door, and I could all but feel the weight pulling down from the center of my chest. After a breath, I tapped the door a couple times with a knuckle before walking in. She stepped a couple of paces outside the closet just as I stepped inside the doorway.

"I have to go," I said, seeing the hurt in her eyes.

"Okay" was her meek reply.

Seeing her pain made me want to go to her, to comfort her, but it was the anger underneath that made me pause and wonder if that was such a good idea. I felt oddly conflicted, standing there in front of her, unsure of what to say or what to do. After spending years refining our relationship, I couldn't think of the last time we'd had this sort of breakdown.

"We'll talk when I get back?"

"Okay, sure," she said with a nod.

"I love you."

She dropped her eyes and shoulders slowly before looking back up to me, I didn't realize how tense she was until then. "I love you too."

We held each other's gaze for a moment, expectant, like we were waiting for the other to speak, before I finally closed the door.

I thought we were better than this.

I thought *I* was better than this.

# Chapter 12

Have you ever been invited to a house that pisses you off at the mere sight of it? Or maybe it doesn't piss you off, exactly. Maybe it just makes you feel a certain kind of way.

I met Cody a few years back, when I was still working on the railroad. He was a fairly successful lawyer, but was also a humble, quiet, down-to-earth kind of guy. Amber and I met him at a local bar one night, I think, and we sort of just hit it off. We met for drinks fairly often for a while, and he even occasionally met with us at our place to drink beer, grill steaks, and generally nerd out over board games and the like.

We knew that Cody was a lawyer, of course, but he never really spoke too much about his work and we never really pried, so we never thought to consider just how successful he was until he invited us to his house one day.

Now, I'm not the kind of person to get upset or jealous about other people's success, especially when it is my friends who come to find that success. On the contrary, I tend to get really excited about that sort of thing. It even motivates me to strive harder.

But seeing Cody's house for the first time didn't just surprise me with how nice it was, although it certainly did. In a way, it felt sort of emasculating. It was one of those places that made me feel both thrilled for Cody while also making me feel like I should definitely reevaluate my life choices. Even though I was making a respectable wage with the railroad, looking at his place still made me feel like I took some kind of wrong turn down the line, and something about that feeling pissed me off, if only for a moment.

Seeing Lillian's house for the first time made me feel much the same way.

My apartment was located just off the Bismarck Expressway on the west side of town, so it only took a couple of minutes to drive across the winding bridges spanning the Missouri River directly into Mandan proper. Once on Main Street, I took a straight shot south under the railroad tracks to Highway 1806. After a handful of miles, the flat highway road turned scenic while it traced the contours of the golden North Dakotan hills, making the drive seem meditative in its seemingly short span.

I nearly missed the turnoff onto the dirt road leading to her property, which was only a couple of miles south of Fort Abraham Lincoln State Park, where George Custer himself was garrisoned just before his famous last stand at the Battle of the Little Bighorn.

Being as this was mostly ranch country, I mistook a couple of the houses along the winding dirt road as ranchers' homes until I noted the lack of anything resembling stables or farm equipment and realized just how close I was to the Missouri River. Although there were only a handful of these houses along the dusty road, most were certainly large enough to be considered mansions, sporting about an acre or two of property between them, and close enough to the river itself to even dock boats if they wanted.

Most of the non-ranching wealthy within Bismarck and Mandan who chose to buy these larger mansions typically did so along the handful of inlets within either of the towns leading into the Missouri River. These inlets served like a sort of roundabout, but with water, during the handful of months of the year when it was warm enough to support their use. There were even several bars and upscale restaurants who built piers along the water's banks on both the Mandan and Bismarck sides of the river, so the river separating the two towns often teemed with boats this time of year.

Living this far south along the river without owning ranch land seemed to indicate to me that not having to deal with the crowds in town, along with the crowds of boats on the river, may have been considered a perk. These were the sort of people that really valued their privacy, though they still managed to remain close enough to town to enjoy its comforts.

To put it simply, these were likely the loners of the Bismarck rich.

The dusty little dirt road finally rounded up a small hill and around a row of trees serving as a windbreak as I neared its end to reveal a house that easily put any of the others along this dirt road to shame.

Sitting on top of the hill sat a two-story work of art perched in the middle of two acres of land, if not a little more. The dirt road turned concrete as it curved into a driveway sporting a four-stall garage with brown doors on the right side of the house. The walls were a patchwork of brown and tan stone with the corner on the left side rounding out into bay windows reminiscent of the towers of an old English castle, although the large glass windows stole away any real illusion of medieval fortification.

It would be hard to sneak up on a place like this if it had the right security setup. But then again, it never hurt to have a little bit of high ground either.

I slowed to a stop next to a metallic-blue Chevrolet Silverado crew cab at the far end of the driveway, as the other two spots in front of the garage were taken by two more behemoths people often refer to around here as trucks.

My little red Toyota pickup ticked quietly next to the lifted Silverado, the way older trucks sometimes do, and I took stock of the trio as I walked around their front. I noted that the white dually in the center seemed pretty new too.

*It must be nice to have that oil money,* I thought, though the early-two-thousands gray Chevy diesel made me smile a little when I walked past.

I nearly missed the security camera on the near-side corner of the garage pointing into the driveway when I took the sidewalk curving toward the front door. It was one of those small ones encased in a black half sphere, easily missed amongst the stone siding if you weren't looking for it. I probably wouldn't want my security system sticking out for all the world to see either, though, if I could afford one.

Noted.

I chuckled a little at myself before taking the sidewalk to the front door, thinking about how it must have looked when I parked my little old rusty red Toyota pickup, which was nearly as old as I was, right next to these younger beasts.

"Small, but fierce," I quipped to no one with a smile.

The curved sidewalk was lined with eight small bushes interspersed evenly within white rocks. The path itself took me to a set of wooden double doors nestled between two pillars supporting an awning above a small porch. These doors were stained a dark brown with intricate frosted-glass windows embedded in the top half of the doors. Metal rods inside the glass were bent into Celtic-looking designs.

I took a moment to study the doorbell, which apparently had another camera embedded inside, before ringing it, trying not to act nervous while waiting for someone to answer. Standing in front of the door, I noticed a simple wooden bench sitting underneath a large window between the door and garage, and I couldn't help but to think how incredibly quaint it was to have it sitting here surrounded by such opulence.

The loud crack from one of the doors opening snapped me from my musings when a portly older man in a gray polo shirt, maybe somewhere in his mid-fifties and mostly balding with some gray hair, stood smiling up to me from inside the threshold.

"Ah," he said, his chocolate-brown eyes smiling from behind his black-rimmed glasses. "You must be Mr. Goodwin," he said with an extension of his hand.

"Yes, sir," I said, firmly taking his hand and giving it a shake. "Feel free to call me Kyle though. And you are?"

"Raymond Evans." He nodded knowingly, letting go of my hand. "Most people call me Ray. Come on in. I'm grilling steaks out back. The other guys are out there by the fire pit," he said, leading me into the house.

Walking in, I was greeted by a living room that took up more floor space than the entirety of my apartment, the windows on the other end stretching up from the floor to its cathedral ceiling.

Immediately to my right, though, there was a rectangular dining room table with eight chairs nestled close to the window I had just mused over a moment ago from outside. There was a wall that partitioned the table partially from the living room, and an empty china cabinet flanked by a handful of moving boxes on the other side.

To my left was a dark-brown-stained wooden staircase leading up to a balcony on the second floor that served something akin to a bridge where you could peer over to the front entrance or the living room from either side.

I hesitated for a moment to consider taking my shoes off to avoid tracking anything onto the sparkling-clean hardwood floors, until I noticed that Ray didn't seem to mind himself, before I gingerly continued following behind.

"You had good timing there." I lost track of him, though for just a moment, when he walked behind the wall that partitioned the dining room from the rest of the house. He stepped back into the carpeted living room with a tray in hand, nearly stumbling into the back of the sectional facing the living room fireplace. "I had just stepped in to grab this tray when you rang the doorbell. I'm not sure if we would have heard you otherwise."

"Well, I'm glad I caught you then."

I couldn't make out where either end of the "bridge" led to–presumably some bedrooms upstairs–but a hallway underneath seemed to lead to a master suite to the left. As we walked underneath the bridge, the dividing wall to my right revealed the little waist-high table with two chairs Ray must have placed the tray on when he'd answered the door.

On the other side of the little table, of course, was a kitchen that was at least the size of my freaking living room. I practically salivated at the dark-stained wooden cabinets, the granite counter-tops, and the island at its center as I briefly imagined the sort of damage I could cause in a kitchen like this.

It was the bald man in a gray suit standing like a fixture next to the island that struck me out of my imagining. He would have practically blended into the kitchen if it weren't for his rhythmic mechanical slicing of the zucchini he was preparing.

"Good evening," I said to him with a friendly wave.

"Oh, don't mind Silent John." Ray paused as he placed his free hand on the doorknob of the door leading from the living room to the backyard. "He doesn't really like to talk," he said as he waited for me.

Silent John barely tilted his shiny bald head up to look at me, his expressionless gaze locking onto mine without him so much as pausing or slowing down his mechanical chopping. His dark eyes seemed lifeless and haunted, making me catch my breath in anticipation, before he dropped his eyes back down to his work.

"Right, nice talking to you, John."

"Don't worry," Ray said, trying to give me a reassuring smile, holding the door open for me as I walked out onto the patio. "He is like that with everyone. He is actually pretty harmless."

"Yeah, Okay." I responded with a nod. "What's his story?"

"Oh, he helps Lillian around the house, that's all." His smile widened as he gently cupped my shoulder with his free hand. "Let me drop this over by the grill really quick, I'll meet you at the fire pit with Chase and Allen."

"Chase! Allen! Come meet your new lead assistant!" Ray called out before I had a chance to respond, sauntering off to a large grill next to the house.

On the other end of the cobblestone patio were two men sitting in white chairs with their backs to me, facing a circular brick fire pit three feet tall with a red cooler between them.

"Hey there!" one of them called out to me with a wave as they both stood up to greet me. He was stocky, though not necessarily out of shape. He was only a couple of inches shorter than me. He had short, neatly trimmed hair that was a faded ginger color, with a beard that was easily six inches in length, also neatly kept.

Soldiers tend to have a certain way they carry themselves that sets them apart if you know what to look for. It's a sort of straight-backed confidence and steely-eyed stoicism that isn't particularly common on the civilian side. It was obvious that he had been out for some time now, but it was easy to see that the old soldier was still in there when he strode over to me in his blue company polo shirt with the welcome smile of a friend.

"Allen. I guess that makes me your bason lead," he said taking off his white-framed Oakley sunglasses, taking my hand firmly into his. "It's good to meet you."

"It's good to finally meet you too, sir," I said, a smile creeping onto my face.

Following his lead came a younger guy, maybe somewhere in his early twenties. He also had a beard, although it was trimmed short, and some of his dirty-blond hair poked out of his blue hat. He was noticeably skinny, though he carried himself like someone who was accustomed to hard work, which was echoed by the dirty blue jeans and flannel shirt he wore. He greeted me with such a vibrant, full-faced, genuine smile that I hardly noticed his dirty work clothes.

"Hi, I'm Chase," he said with genuine excitement and an extended hand. "How are you?"

"I'm doing well, thanks," I said as I shook his hand too, a little surprised at the strength of his grip. "I'm Kyle. It's good to meet you, Chase."

"Likewise," he said, his smile somehow broadening. "Lillian didn't really tell us much about you, only that you might be the new lead assistant."

"I think she mentioned you were in the Army though," Allen said as the two glanced at each other for a moment before appraising me.

"Yeah, I was in for a little while."

"Yeah? What did you do?"

"Infantry, Two Seventy-Fifth. What about you?"

"I was in the Army for a little over a decade," he said with a smile and a crooked eyebrow. "I was a combat engineer though."

"Right on," I said, Allen handing me a beer he had carried over. I could feel a smile creeping back onto my face as I met the old soldier's stare.

It's interesting how so much can pass between two people with so little being said.

"Dang," Chase said, breaking the silence. "At this rate, I'll be the only civilian in the shop."

Allen and I chuckled a little at that when Ray interrupted. "I see you guys are getting along nicely." He didn't really startle us, but we didn't realize he'd joined us from the grill either.

"Sorry Lillian wasn't here too greet you, Kyle," he continued. "She had to take a phone call in her office. She should be here any minute though."

"That's fine," I said while twisting the cap off my beer bottle. "So, what do you do for Phoenix?"

"I guess you could say that I'm a sort of liaison," he said with a shrug and an uncertain smile.

The headache was subtle at first. It started as nothing more than a sort of tension in my forehead just between my eyes and grew gradually. My attention was drawn toward the back door as the pressure grew, but it only took a moment for me to gain my wits and subtly notice that everyone's attention was also drawn toward the door.

Everyone except Ray, who shook himself out of the trance with a sharp sniff and a small jolt, staring between the three of us with an amused smirk.

"I see," I said as a pressure slowly started to build. "What exactly is it that you liaise?"

He seemed to catch his breath when he snapped his attention fully to me, his surprise magnified behind his spectacles.

"Ah"—he coughed nervously—"mostly between Phoenix and a handful of clients."

I had to grit my teeth when a sudden buildup of pressure washed over me unexpectedly, just before Lillian stepped out of the back door. Chase and Allen were immediately star struck by her, slack-jawed and immobilized by her fluid stride and the predator-like confidence in her approach.

Even so, it was hard not to marvel at how easily she seemed to make a simple light-blue button-up shirt and white slacks look like a freaking fashion statement while they clung to her every curve and feature, or how the diamond necklace drew the attention of the eyes to the fact that the top two buttons of her blouse were open revealing her generous bustline.

More than anything though, it was how the ferocity of her gaze, which was somehow enhanced by her lion's-mane hair and hungry grin, had fixated squarely onto me as she approached. It was like her very presence elicited some sort of response from me, in particular.

As she drew near, Ray and I met each other's stare for a moment. The look of surprise he hardly tried to conceal twisted itself into a nervous smile.

"Good evening, Kyle," Lillian purred as she came close. "I'm glad to see that you could join us this evening."

# Chapter 13

"I appreciate the invitation." The tension from the migraine gradually receded as I spoke. The two star-struck men beside me shifted nervously, Allen taking a small pull from his bottle. "This is a beautiful home, too."

"Thank you," she replied with a wry smile. "It's a relatively new build. You missed the grand tour earlier, perhaps I can show you around after dinner. Speaking of—Mr. Evans, how long until dinner is ready?"

"I was just about to fire up the grill, ma'am," came Ray's courtly reply. "Kyle, how do you like your steak?"

"Medium-rare, please."

"Good man," Ray replied with a smile. "I'll get right on it."

"Excellent, thank you, Mr. Evans," Lillian said as Ray excused himself back to the grill.

"That should give us some time to talk things over before dinner, if you want to get started right away," Allen suggested.

"Indeed, I already asked John to retrieve some of the paperwork from the office," Lillian said as she turned away. "Shall we head over to the kitchen table?"

Silent John finished placing a small stack of papers on the table when we rounded the dining room's dividing wall, and he started to walk away with a shamble making no sound or eye contact with anyone.

"John." He stopped and slowly turned at Lillian's call. "Could you pour me a glass of the red please, and anything our guests would like as well."

"I'm okay for now," I said, holding up my still-full beer. "Thank you though."

The others indicated more of the same with theirs, Silent John's reply being only a slight bow of the head before he continued his shamble back into the kitchen.

"I apologize for my home's poor state. I had hoped to have everything unpacked before you all came over." The migraine rose slightly in intensity as she spoke.

Allen waved her off before Chase interrupted with a nearly flirtatious smile. "Oh, it's fine. It's not like you have a small house to fill."

"Right," I said as I pulled out a chair opposite Chase and Allen, who had their backs to the empty china cabinet. "Didn't you just move in a couple of days ago?"

"Yes, that's true." Lillian took the chair at the head of the table near the window. "Of course, I would have preferred this meeting in our office in Killdeer, but our move-in date was delayed. Speaking of, Allen, any word on when that might be?"

"The agent told me yesterday that we can occupy the shop three weeks from today," he said, barely looking up from the paperwork on the table.

Great, more time without a paycheck.

"The good news for you, Kyle," Allen continued, like he was reading my mind, "is that there is some required training we can send you to in our main office in Casper. It's a little over a week from now, so you don't have to wait so long for your first paycheck."

"That is good news, I appreciate that. How long is the training?"

"It's ten-hour days for fourteen straight days, no days off. You'll get a little bit of per diem too, with a refund on travel expenses."

"Dang." I sat up a little straighter, and he showed me a slight smile of his own. "Well, I can't say that I have any issues with that."

"The training isn't all that hard as long as you pay attention and do the homework," Chase interjected. "You'll go over the company's standard operating procedures and they'll teach you the basics on how to fix the generators. It's the same instructor I had a couple of years ago. He is pretty easy to work with."

"Yeah." Allen stepped in while laying out some paperwork on the table. "You should be back up here when the first batch of generators and equipment is delivered, so you will have to hit the ground running as soon as you get back."

The room fell silent when John shambled back with a wine glass and bottle in hand. Every eye tracked him as he took a place next to Lillian. A nervous tension in the room grew palpable when he poured her a glass of the expensive looking wine, and the tension from the migraine rose with Lillian's smile when she took notice of everyone's anxiety.

"Thank you, John." She purred when he finished the pour with a slight bow of the head. "You are too good to me."

Allen and Chase visibly relaxed when the migraine reached a low peak, and I watched in fascination when their attention shifted from Lillian to John as she spoke. The anxiety that gripped them ebbed away while Lillian observed them with a pleased smile behind her now filled glass. Satisfied with their change in attitude, she shifted her attention to me when John took his leave. I could feel my heart pulsing in my neck when her smile turned wry, the tension from the migraine receding with John's departure.

I guess there wasn't any use in her hiding it at this point. It became obvious to both of us that I was immune to her manipulative magic, if not the migraines. The confirmation of her magic left me no less disturbed, though.

"Allen," she said, taking the wineglass from her lips. "How do you plan on organizing these generators when they are delivered?"

"Right." Allen unfolded a page from the stack that took up the width of the table and laid it out for the rest of us to see. It looked a lot like a blueprint of the shop, surrounded by what must have been a fence. "The main entrance to the gate will be here, on the southeast corner, with a secondary entrance here on the north end." He continued as he pointed everything out with a middle finger. "All the generators that are coming from Casper are new, but we will need to service them before we can deliver them to the pads. You will have some hands-on training on how to do that in Casper, Kyle. We will line them up along the north side of the fence until they are serviced, and line them up along the west end once they are ready to go."

"When are the other techs going to be here?" Chase said, nearly rising out of his chair to see while he followed along.

"They should be here the Monday after we occupy the building. The trailer is scheduled to be delivered that morning too, and that will be placed just outside the north entrance to the gate, here," Allen explained, tracing his finger along a road leading out of the gate. "They will help set up the trailer once they get here. That reminds me, Kyle, did you find a place to stay yet?"

"Not yet. The only apartment complex I found in Killdeer has nothing available. I can't find anything in the trailer park nearby either."

"You're probably not going to find anything nearby, unless you want to stay in the trailer with myself and the other techs." Allen said with a frown. "I had to find an apartment in Dickinson in the meantime."

I could feel myself cringing. Dickinson was nearly an hour drive from Killdeer.

"You can thank the oil boom for that," chided Chase. "Killdeer was pretty small to begin with, but people swarmed our little town once the fracking started. They built man camps just north of Dickinson to take some of the pressure off, but they became overcrowded pretty quickly. It was so bad that people were living in their cars because they had nowhere else to go, even in the winter."

"Dang," I said. "That must have been wild."

"It was," Chase continued. "Those apartments are actually fairly new too. They only started building those when the crime got out of hand and the residents started hounding the city council about it. Most of those guys left when the boom ended, but good luck finding a place in Killdeer right now."

"Wow, that's crazy. Were you here for that, Chase?"

"I was. My family owns a ranch north of town, just below Killdeer Mountain."

"In fact, Chase helped us find the location of our new shop in Killdeer," Lillian said behind a friendly smile. "We would probably work out of a shop in Dickinson instead if it weren't for him."

Allen rolled his eyes without a word. Chase nearly blushed behind his wide smile from the praise. "I'm just glad I could help, ma'am."

"Right," Allen continued. "It's a three-hundred-fifty-dollar-a-month pay deduction while you're in the trailer. It might be a little cozy with three other guys there, but it's not a bad setup until you find other arrangements."

"I'll have to run that by the fiancée. I can't imagine she will be thrilled about sharing the space, but I might be able to sweet talk her into it."

"I didn't know you were getting married, congratulations," Allen said with a friendly smile.

"Thank you, I appreciate that," I replied with a smile of my own.

"Unfortunately, the trailer is for workers only," Allen said, dropping his smile. "Sorry."

"Okay. Worst-case scenario, Amber will hold on to the apartment while I rack out in the trailer. I'll figure something out," I said with a nod before taking a pull of my beer.

The rest of the meeting went fairly smooth after that, with Allen leading most of the discussion. He continued to go into detail regarding the phases leading up to "operational status:" how and when the initial deliveries were going to be made, how we were going to organize the shop, and the general op tempo leading up to operations. His brief was military-like in its organization, though it was oddly refreshing, which left me smirking at the irony of it.

I guess it's true what they say about old habits.

Lillian, on the other hand, kept mostly to herself, content in letting Allen lead the discussion while taking the occasional sip of her wine.

"Sorry to interrupt," Ray said, poking his head around the partition. "The steaks are ready if you want them."

"That would be wonderful, Mr. Evans," Lillian eagerly replied. "Shall we continue after dinner?"

"We can probably do that," Allen replied. "I'm pretty much finished though."

"Great," Ray said. "I'll ask John to help clean up the table while I bring everything out."

"Anything I can do to help?" Chase offered.

"No, John and I can handle it," Ray said with an appreciative nod. "Just let us know if you need anything."

Allen waited for Ray to duck back behind the partition before continuing. "Most of what I'll need from you, Kyle, will have to wait until the equipment and supplies get there. I have a folder here with some points of contact, though," he said, pulling one out of the pile of paperwork. "I'll need your help hiring on a supply guy, so you'll have to cover down for him in the meantime. You won't have to worry about that until after your training though."

"Okay, sounds good," I replied with a nod.

The ghost of a migraine returned when Silent John shambled around the partition, his expressionless features remaining completely neutral, his empty eyes refusing to meet any of ours. None of the others seemed remotely bothered by him this time; they even seemed grateful for his help when he quietly gathered the papers on the table.

"Thanks, buddy," Allen said with a friendly pat on John's shoulder.

"Yeah, I appreciate the help." Chase added with a smile, handing over a couple of papers of his own.

Silent John provided little acknowledgement of the two men, his movements measured and deliberate as he swept his haunted gaze over the table with a thousand-yard stare. Chase and Allen seemed completely satisfied with his demeanor, casually taking their seats, and chatting themselves when John took his leave with his stack.

The migraine practically vanished by the time Ray joined us to set plates and silverware on the table. "I hope you don't mind if I sit next to you," Ray said, placing a plate to my left.

"Not at all. Is John joining us though?" I said, indicating the empty space at the far end of the table he had apparently left open.

"Well–uh…" Ray said, stopping short, wide-eyed with uncertainty. Chase and Allen seemed to take notice, though Chase continued to speak with Ray, glancing from me to Lillian almost pleadingly.

"John has work to do in the office," Lillian supplied for him. The migraine returned subtly as she spoke. "He's elected to eat in there until he's finished."

"That's right," Ray chirped nervously. "I—ah, I'll be right back with the steaks." He nearly ran into John on his way out, nearly causing him to drop the bowl of salad and tray full of sliced potatoes, though John moved, nonplussed with his unchanging, haunted expression. Lillian seemed to barely suppress an amused laugh behind her wine glass, though she wasn't hiding her smile when she paused to side-eye me before taking another sip.

I could only hope that I hid my frustration better than she did her amusement.

Granted, my migraines weren't exactly helping with that frustration, but I could at least breathe a sigh of relief when John left, taking my migraine, again, with him.

Before coming here there was a part of me that hoped I was wrong about the migraines, or Lillian's odd ability to influence people around her. I quickly lost count of how many times I had second-guessed myself over the previous weeks, or how I chastised myself for not listening to Amber, especially after coming up completely dry from my research.

Now it seemed like I had woefully walked into the lion's den, only I wasn't the only one who had to worry about getting mauled.

But what did it say about Chase and Allen that they showed little to no resistance toward Lillian's psychic manipulation, or that she used it against them so readily? How much could they possibly know about what was going on behind the scenes when she had such a firm hold on them?

Or Amber…

And what the hell was the deal with John?

Question after question swirled around my head as I stared into the contents of my mostly full bottle of beer, each one adding to my mounting frustration. It became apparent to me that I had to separate Chase and Allen from Lillian if I were to confront her. I had no way of understanding the depths of her manipulation, or if she could use them against me, if I didn't catch her alone.

"I hope you boys are hungry," Ray said as he entered with a tray full of steaks and started divvying them out.

"Starving, thank you," Chase said eagerly when Ray slapped a mound of meat on his plate.

"Thank you," I said when mine crashed down on my plate like a meteor before Ray finally took his seat. I took a minute to marvel at it. It took up nearly my whole plate and was by no means a thin slice. It was beautifully marbled and cooked perfectly medium-rare, the cooked smell of meat and spices making me salivate like Pavlov's freaking dog. "Where did you get these things? This is massive."

"Chase was kind enough to supply us from his family's ranch," Lillian said, taking up the potato tray and loading up what little space was left on her plate.

Chase seemed to blush a little at the attention. "Yes, well," he said, pushing his glasses up with a smile. "This cow was freshly butchered, and we didn't have much room left in our freezer for it. It wasn't any trouble."

"Of course, he is being modes," Lillian said teasingly, passing the potatoes to me. "Speaking of, how is everything going on the ranch lately?"

I could feel the echo of the migraine returning as the meager pile of potatoes battled with the steak for supremacy over my plate. The pressure was barely noticeable, just enough for me to register and take notice of it while casually paying attention to the conversation at hand.

"Things have picked up since our ranch hand left," Chase said, now cutting into his steak. "My parents own the ranch, and the county is paying them to re-fence along a road that runs along the property. My fiancée and I are doing what we can to help, but between that and keeping up with our two hundred head of cattle, it's been tough to keep up with the deadline since he left."

"Do you guys have a lot of ground to cover?" I asked, swallowing a mouthful of meat.

"We still have a few miles to cover. We have a tractor we Frankensteined together, and that helps speed things along, but its definitely not OSHA approved and it's still a slow process," Chase joked.

The pressure in my head spiked slightly, drawing a sharp inhale from me in its abruptness. As if on cue, Ray, who listened quietly to the conversation, exchanged a questioning look with Lillian, though hers seemed mocking behind her wine glass.

"Have you been able to make any progress renovating that beautiful old house of yours?" she asked, keenly placing her glass on the table and taking up her silverware. "I seem to recall something about your old hand helping you before he left."

Chase had to take a moment to finish chewing before he could answer. "No, not since he left. Pretty much all our focus has been on the fence"

"That's such a shame," she said matter-of-factly. "It's sad to see such a beautiful home fall into such disrepair, especially with your rich family history behind it."

I felt myself cringing against another spike in pressure and had to stop myself from reflexively rubbing a hand against the throbbing migraine, opting to occupy my hand with the beer bottle instead. A light bulb expression seemed to show itself in Ray when he took notice of my subtle breakdown in composure, and a brief moment of understanding seemed to pass between him and Lillian. Even Allen seemed to take more interest in the conversation while he quietly ate his meal.

Chase, on the other hand, seemed to pause before continuing. "Kyle, didn't you say that you need a place to stay?"

I could see a smile creep at the corners of Lillian's lips as she feigned interest in her meal.

"My fiancée and I both do," I responded simply.

"Well, we have room in the old house," he said sheepishly. "The whole house is vacant, actually. The old hand had it to himself before he left."

The kid didn't slouch much, but he seemed to sit a little straighter all of a sudden. He was leaning a little forward with a smile in his excitement and shifted the occasional glance at Lillian, seeking her approval. Lillian, for her part, was content with the reassuring, flirtatious smile she gave him as she cut into her steak.

"I'm living with my family a little over a mile away from the old house, so you and your fiancée would have it all to yourselves. Aside from the cows outside, of course," Chase continued. "I'll have to run it by my dad, he owns the house, but I don't think he'll take issue with it if you offered to take a day or so out of the week to help out around the ranch."

"That's really generous," I responded politely, the migraine receding as I spoke. I tried to make it look like I was considering his offer when the tension ebbed away, and I looked up from my plate to see that Lillian was patiently watching me with an unreadable expression.

Another one of Lillian's little puzzle pieces had just fallen into place, even if I still couldn't see the whole picture. Whatever it was that she wanted, it was growing increasingly obvious that she wanted me close.

"That's actually not a bad idea, now that I think about it," Allen chimed in. "You are only working Monday through Thursday, Kyle. If you put in some work on the ranch on Fridays, you would still have the whole weekend."

*Seems like I'll just have to play along then, for now,* I thought.

"I would have to run that by Amber," I said to Chase, "but I think we can make that work. I appreciate that, Chase."

His whole face lit up with another one of his warm smiles. "That's great. I'll let my dad know. Have you ever worked on a ranch before?"

"No, but I worked a little bit of construction in college and my father taught me a lot of carpentry growing up, so I can definitely help with the fencing at least. I can probably help with that old house of yours too, but I don't know much about ranching."

"Well, we can definitely teach you that part," he said reassuringly.

Most of the rest of the meal revolved around Chase telling us about his family's ranch and his family history, beginning with some of the chores they typically did every day. He spoke with a great deal of enthusiasm when he described the little home his parents lived in at the base of a small mountain, and the picturesque views it provided overlooking the Badlands set off into the distance, or how the frigid cold of the north made for unique challenges when herding cattle along the rolling hillsides.

It would have made for a pleasant dinner for me if it wasn't for the awkward company, even if it seemed like I was the only one at the table who thought so. There were moments when the notion nearly slipped my mind, if only we weren't occasionally interrupted by Silent John when he came to clear the table of empty plates or to refill our drinks. Even so, the sun had gone down behind Lillian long before anyone took notice, shadowing the fields behind her in darkness before our conversation even slowed.

"Well, I'm afraid it is getting awfully late, gentlemen, and I have a great deal to do in the morning," Lillian interjected suddenly. "I have extra rooms available, so of course you are all welcome to spend the night if you are not up to leaving right away. I know at least a couple of you have a long drive to look forward to."

"I should probably get going then," Allen said before rising out of his chair. "Dickinson isn't that far."

"Are you sure you are okay to drive?" Lillian asked, rising herself.

"Oh, yeah," Allen said, waving her off. "I only had a couple, I'll be okay."

"Do you mind if I stay the night, ma'am?" Chase asked somewhat sheepishly.

"Of course. I'll have Mr. Evans show you to the guest room," Lillian said with a motherly smile.

"Right," Ray said with a stretch and a groan while standing from his seat. "It's upstairs, I'll show you where it's at."

"Thank you, I appreciate that," Chase said, standing up to follow.

"Kyle, would you mind accompanying me to my office before you leave? There is some additional business I would like to discuss with you. It shouldn't take very much of your time." There was no sign of the migraine when she asked. In fact, it completely diminished, and the fact that she didn't use it at all when she asked was almost startling in and of itself.

She looked at me expectantly, almost pleadingly, in the silence between us. It took a second for me to realize that Ray had also paused with Chase at the partition to await my answer.

"Sure," I said uneasily. "I can spare a little bit of time."

Her teeth shone as she blossomed into a smile, though there was a hint of excited restraint in her eyes. "Excellent." She said, "I'll have John show you to the office. I have to grab something first, then I'll be right there."

"Wait here, Kyle. I'll grab him for you." Ray said with a knowing smile and nod to Lillian before turning to leave, Chase following close behind.

She gave me a light squeeze on my elbow when she passed and tilted her head with a flirty smile that would have left my heart pounding, if only it wasn't already.

I again wondered what kind of game she was playing. If she knew she couldn't use her magic against me, then how did she intend to proceed? That was kind of a hard question to answer when I literally knew nothing about her or what she was capable of, unless she intended to go about this using the old-fashioned psychological method. I knew how to guard against that, at least.

I grabbed my nearly empty beer and slammed what was left of it in my frustration, half wishing it was something a little bit stronger. It was only my second one of the evening, so I wasn't exactly going to drown myself into intoxication; it was really more of a placebo for easing my frustration, waiting for John.

It wasn't long before he shambled around the partition to stare wordlessly at me with his haunted thousand-yard stare.

"Lead the way," I said with an outstretched hand. I wasn't exactly expecting him to say anything when he turned to lead me down the hallway beneath the bridge and to the door at its far end. He didn't exactly disappoint me either.

I probably shouldn't have been so impressed with the size of the room, though naturally I was. It was nearly as large as my entire freaking apartment. The door opened into the center of the room, with a massive dark-stained wood desk and large bay windows behind it. Towering bookshelves lined the wall to my front and an unlit fireplace sat in the wall to my right. There were unpacked boxes placed throughout the room, though the bookshelves and the desk, complete with a dual-screen monitor, seemed to already be in order. There were two expensive-looking brown chairs on either side of a matching couch facing the fireplace with a small table between them and the fireplace, and the room was dimly lit by a handful of lamps set around the room.

The room was nice, but that wasn't really the first thing that caught my attention. It's hard to explain, but you could say that I felt it before I saw it. It was a sort of a light pull at first, right at the edge of my senses. As I drew near the door, I could feel it beckoning to me like it wanted me to find it, and the closer I got, the harder it was for me to ignore.

As soon as Silent John opened the door, I fixated on it immediately. The closed book sitting on top of a wooden bookstand behind the couch pulled at my senses, beckoning me inside.

Cautiously, I stepped closer. My paranoia took over, and I started to wonder if this was going to be some sort of trap. I tried to place more of my attention on John as he silently walked next to the desk to stand like a statue, facing me with his creepy-as-hell stare.

"Okay," I said to him after a beat. "Just, ah, let me know if you need anything, bud."

Nothing.

Solid granite.

"Cool," I said, giving him a thumbs up.

He blinked.

The book was beautiful. It was as large as any college textbook I might have owned and bound in brown leather, but the spine was reinforced with bronze. The front was decorated with a silver-and-gold inlay depicting the tree of life, with silver roots and gold branches, and the whole tree was encircled with what looked like rope twined in a silver-and-gold strand. There was a bronze clasp that held it closed with what looked like Nordic runes etched around a Celtic knot.

Still wary, I drew closer to it, cautious of its steady call. Nothing about it seemed threatening to me though. It welcomed me like a friend, but it was just a book. A big, beautiful book that wanted me to pick it up. To hold it. To read it. To share whatever secrets it held captive within, if only I could figure out how to open it.

I traced my fingers over the branches and roots of the tree, and then over the rope encircling it. It took a moment for any skepticism I might have had about the gold or silver being real to fade before I wondered how it could have been embedded into the leather so perfectly. But when I traced my thumb over the knot on the clasp, the runes exploded into a crimson light, and I jerked my hand back in surprise when static electricity struck at the pad of my thumb.

"Damn it," I said as I shook out my hand, more out of surprise than pain. I looked over my shoulder to see that John didn't seem to even move so much as a muscle. He just continued to stare at me, unchanged.

That was when I heard the book click, and I looked back to see that the clasp had unlocked itself. I stared at it for a moment, hard. I still wasn't sure if I wanted to touch it again, less so after it shocked the hell out of me. But I could still feel it, I could still feel its call. I knew that I could resist it if I wanted to, but I wasn't sure if I did.

Looking at the clasp, I saw that it was stained a shade of crimson that wasn't there before. It took a moment for me to realize what it was before I looked to see a small dab of blood on my thumb.

"What the hell? It actually took blood to open it?" But that didn't seem to matter anymore. The book still called to me, but with the promise that it wouldn't hurt me again. So, I opened it, just to the front page.

### Book of the Body

### Miriam Ann McAllister

*What a strange coincidence,* I thought, *that the author had the same first and middle name as my mother.*

"Do you believe in fate, Kyle?"

I didn't hear her come in. I jumped a step away from her on pure reflex, sucking in a breath in fright. She leaned back against the door behind her with an amused smile and silent chuckle.

"Jesus, Lillian. Am I going to have to put a bell on you?"

"Maybe we can discuss that later." Her gaze fixated on the book while she took slow, languid steps toward the bookstand, and I noticed that she casually held a picture frame to her side. "Well, do you?"

"I can't say that I ever have." I eyed her suspiciously, backing away from the book stand.

"Me neither, but sometimes I have to wonder." She slowly traced the edge of the first page before turning them one by one, her expression transfixed with a look of awe.

"I've been in this business for a long time, Kyle," she continued, handing me the picture frame without taking her eyes from the book. "There were times when it seemed like everything we worked so hard to achieve would fall apart around us, and that everything simply seemed… hopeless."

"I can imagine, you came into the company pretty early on. It's always hard for a new company to get off the ground," I said before taking the picture, and my heart nearly stopped the first moment I studied it.

It was an old, faded black-and-white photograph of a wedding party of six people. The three men on the right were dressed smartly in their suits and ties, all of them wearing the sort of caps that were popular among the Irish in the nineteen forties. It was hard to tell for sure, but it seemed like all the bridal party wore white, not just the bride. It seemed like it was a fairly typical wedding photo for the day, but that wasn't what struck me.

I knew some of the people in the photograph. I didn't recognize the gentleman on the far right, but the man next to him was my uncle Donald, the one who disappeared after my failed exorcism. The groom was clearly my father, though maybe in his early twenties. My mother, who was the same age as my father, wore her dark hair back, barely showing underneath her white veil. I had rarely seen her so happily depicted in photographs before, with her dark Native complexion contrasting beautifully in her white wedding gown. I didn't recognize the woman on the far left, but the woman between her and my mother was Lillian.

"But now that we finally rebuilt our old alliances, and now that we finally acquired the tools and funding to win," she continued, looking up to me with a kindhearted expression, "now that we've again found ourselves on the precipice of war, can you imagine my surprise when I stumbled upon the one person alive who could guarantee our success? And to do so completely by chance."

The picture shook slightly in my grip despite myself. My voice caught in my throat, my mind racing to formulate a response, only to come back empty. I could only stand frozen in stark silence for her to continue.

"Kyle Goodwin, the son of Miriam, The Blood Witch."

# Chapter 14

There was no bomb cleverly disguised, there was no elaborate plan to unravel, no ambush emplaced waiting patiently, waiting to destroy me. There was only this book, this picture, and this incredible woman accosting me.

The picture of the reality I'd built in my mind shattered in light of her revelation, my mind racing into overdrive to put the pieces back together. My thoughts were slow to crystalize when this new picture came into focus, but now I had new pieces to work with.

"You were part of the Magistrate," I rasped, finally, clearing my throat.

"The *United* Magistrate, but yes." She folded her arms in front of her, leaning a hip against the book stand as she spoke. There was nothing impatient or authoritative in the way she addressed me. Only patient concern.

"And you knew my parents," I said, still trying to gather myself.

"Your mother more so than your father, but yes. We were acquainted before the war, when she was still a member of the Society, though I wasn't aware of them at the time." She turned her attention back to the book as she continued, slowly turning the pages again as she scanned them. "I hadn't yet come into my magic when I first met her, so naturally I had no idea of its existence outside of fairytales, nor of your mother's associations."

"Society? What are you talking about?" I asked.

She seemed taken aback, staring at me questioningly for a moment. "The Thirteen Pyres Society, they are the dominant governing body within the wizarding realm. Did your parents not tell you?"

"No, that's not what I meant," I said with a slow shake of my head. "Not exactly, anyway. They stifled my powers before my magic could manifest as a child without ever telling me. I guess they thought it would be a permanent fix. My uncle warned me about the Society when my magic briefly broke through my mother's spell binding, saying that they worked for the Magistrate and that the Society was hunting them."

"What did he say about them?"

"Only that the Magistrate was some sort of rebel alliance fighting against the Society. He told me that my mother stifled my powers after they went into hiding to keep their true identity secret, and that if we were discovered, they would execute us."

"Well, your parents, most definitely," she countered. "Probably not you though, unless they believed that you've violated one of their laws of magic. They might have placed you into a forced apprenticeship, though I'm not sure that would have been much better."

*No, they would definitely execute me, I chided her silently.* Willfully accepting the possession of a demon was all it took to break one of their laws, but I would not tell her that. I still had little idea of who she was; there was no way in hell that I was going to trust her with that information.

"That's how the war began, in fact," she continued. "They called it the Blood Witch's War, in honor of your mother's efforts to bring down the Society. They called her the Blood Witch, believing that it would denigrate her, that it would drive a wedge between us and anyone who would otherwise wish to join us. But your mother wore that name like a banner, and in the end, it was the Society's abuse of power that brought us all together."

"Hold on," I interrupted. "You said that she worked with the Society, but you make is sound like she started the whole mess."

"She did. In fact, she was a member of their high council." She turned her attention back to the book, turning the pages one by one, scanning them with interest as she spoke. "She sat upon the ninth seat, known as the Pyre of Science. Her contributions to the magical community were world-renowned. Some were even so bold as to compare her to the likes of Einstein. As loved and respected as she was before the war, she became equally feared once it started. She was arguably the most powerful and destructive shadow walker of all time.

"Do you know what that is?" she asked, briefly looking up at me. "A shadow walker?"

"Yes, I do," I responded. "I made that discovery when my powers manifested."

"Oh," she said with genuine surprise, quickly laughing it off. "That's incredibly rare, even through blood-lines. I shouldn't be surprised, though, considering who your mother was. Tell me, were you ever able to control your powers?"

"No, they are still held under my mother's spell binding. I've only been able to manifest them under extreme duress."

"I see." She nodded thoughtfully.

"But if she had so much influence within the council, why did she turn against them?"

She smiled sadly before returning her attention to the book. "It was because of me, actually," She said, finally. "I was a young girl when I first befriended Miriam, years before I came into my powers. I looked up to her like a big sister. I visited her often on my way home from school, and later, from work."

She stopped turning those pages suddenly and a broad smile shone on her face. I was too far away to make out what she was reading, but she grew visibly excited as she read the text, tracing her fingers down the page as she did. I waited patiently for her to continue until she finally looked up into the empty fireplace, her smile faltering before she continued.

"Late at night, on my way home from one such visit, I was attacked. I knew my attacker, in fact. He was a stubborn brute of a man whose affections I had previously denied, and who absolutely refused to take no for an answer."

She paused for a moment more, pulling a bookmark from underneath the book. It was fairly simple: a rectangular piece of baby-blue paper with a length of string tied off one of the narrow ends. It occurred to me the direction this story was about to take, and I grew increasingly uncomfortable as she slowly fidgeted with the string, twining it around her fingers.

"I screamed at first, while he dragged me into the alleyway," she continued. "And I cried, and I begged, and I pleaded for him to stop. That is, until he drew the knife, and I had no choice but to let him…"

She still didn't look at me. I could hear the pain in her voice as she placed the bookmark in the crease of the open page, and I could feel a part of me breaking when hearing it. I didn't want her to continue. I didn't want to share in that pain, but I knew I had to.

"I silently wished someone would hear the struggle or see what was happening to me. When he ripped the clothes from my body, I practically willed someone to come to my aid, to stop that bastard from hurting me, from violating me… but nobody came. I felt utterly helpless. Alone."

She straightened her posture to compose herself, breathing in deep through her nose, setting her gaze back onto the fireplace. "I tried to push him off me, and when I did, I felt my power flow into me. I could feel it energizing me, so I tried to push a little more, just a little harder, and that's when he plunged the knife into my side."

She slid her left hand up her side, stopping just below the ribs. "That's the funny thing about adrenaline, you don't always feel that sort of injury at first. But when he stabbed me, it seemed to trip something in me, because my power pooled into him from my hands and he instantly burst into flames.

"I was more surprised than anything at first, when he stumbled away from me screaming," she continued, balling her fist, taking it from her side and holding it just out in front of her, gazing at it as if inspecting it. "But I wasn't finished with him either. I let loose with everything I had. I turned that entire alleyway into an inferno with him inside it."

With a snap of her fingers, the scant wood inside the fireplace burst into flames.

It would have been grand theater, but I wasn't exactly going to shy away from the fire gently crackling underneath the mantel. It wasn't like I hadn't seen this sort of thing before. Still, I couldn't help but feel some empathy for her. It's a story I've heard far too often, something I would never wish on anyone.

"So, you defended yourself," I stated flatly.

"Yes," she said, not taking her eyes off the flames.

"Against a rapist that probably would have killed you."

"Yes," she said sadly. "Unfortunately, the Society didn't quite see it that way. I lost consciousness in the alleyway. Expending so much power at once was simply too much for me to handle. Anyway," she said, drawing her attention back to the book. "I awoke in the hospital sometime later and the Society took me into custody soon after."

"They kept me prisoner for some time, holding me in some sort of abandoned warehouse to interrogate me before the trial. They accused me of murder through the use of magic, eventually holding their little kangaroo court with all thirteen council members present, including Miriam."

"And they found you guilty… for that?" I said, trying to keep the skepticism from my voice.

"Indeed," she said, now addressing me directly. "You see, Kyle, the Society is very strict in the way they enforce their laws, and there is very little gray area in the way they interpret them. So yes, they found me guilty and sentenced me to a summary execution, but Miriam stopped them before they could follow through.

"Miriam was a long-time advocate for change in the way the Society enforced their laws and the Society as a whole was largely split on the issue. She witnessed countless executions committed under similar pretenses, and when it finally came to witnessing me, a long-time friend, subjected to the executioner's ax, she decided that she had seen enough. She rallied her supporters and stole me away before the executioner could follow through.

"As a matter of fact," she said with a smile. "Your father was one of them."

"My father was a member of the council?" I said with some surprise.

"Well, no." She waved her hand. "He was a captain of the Pyre Guard. You could think of them as sort of enforcers or foot soldiers for the Society. That wasn't long before that picture was taken —"

The book launched the little blue bookmark across the room like an arrow before slamming shut. Lillian and I both jumped a step away from the book when the bookmark itself slammed into the door with an audible thwack. There was a metallic click as the clasp closed, leaving us in stunned silence, the only noise coming from the still-lit fireplace.

Lillian and I exchanged a surprised look before she turned away from me with an amused laugh to retrieve the bookmark while I studied the picture I'd nearly forgotten, still cradled in my hand.

"When was this picture taken?" I asked.

"Nineteen forty-eight, I believe," she said, returning the bookmark to the book stand. "Not long before the war started."

"Your timeline seems a little off," I countered. "My father was nearly sixty when he died, that wasn't until after my last deployment to Iraq."

"I'm sure he seemed awfully spry for his age, too," she said with another one of her seductive smiles. "Tell me Kyle, did you ever wonder why you always looked so young for your age?"

"I always assumed that it had something to do with all dem squats," I said with a mocking smile of my own.

"I'm sure that helped." She said, shaking her head, not so amused.

Apparently, I needed to work on my jokes. I never claimed to be a comedian.

"You are by no means immortal, but access to magic grants the practitioner an extended life span."

"Do you have any idea how crazy all this sounds?" I asked her flatly.

She nodded once before stepping up to the book, pressing her thumb on its clasp without taking her eyes off me. "Miriam's grimoires cannot be opened without her blood or the blood of her offspring. But don't take my word for it," she said, backing away from the book, beckoning me to it with an open hand. "Look again for yourself."

I hesitated for a moment as she briefly straightened her blazer and clasped her hands behind her, standing straight-backed and positively regal, waiting for me to inspect the book again. I didn't hide the heavy sigh when I stepped back to the bookstand, though I realized when I did, that I could still feel the book calling to me. I realized it was never overpowering or overtly distracting. It was more like the steady beckoning of an old friend.

When I placed my thumb on the clasp, like I did before, the shock didn't come nearly so much of a surprise, and the runes glowed crimson as the clasp came undone. I turned the pages, slowly at first, deliberately taking my time inspecting their contents. Most of them showed formulas and diagrams that I had no hope of understanding, but it only took a handful of pages for me to come across what looked like a journal entry dating back to the early nineteen fifties.

My breath caught high in my chest as I tried to read what my mother wrote, but my vision seemed to blur and my mind raced, barely comprehending what I was looking at.

Lillian placed a gentle hand on my shoulder, stepping next to me without a sound. "Your mother wrote her grimoires during the war, compiling all her decades of research and development into them."

"Grimoires? You mean, there are more of these?" I asked, failing to hold back my surprise.

"Yes," she said, smiling up to me again. "This and two more, one for each of the pathways of magic: the way of the mind, the way of the body, and the way of the spirit. Within these books lie some of the most powerful magic anyone's ever recorded, and we have all three."

"So, let me guess," I said, closing the grimoire and clasping it shut. "You want me to open my mother's grimoires for you and help fight in your little war. Is that right?"

"You have done a great deal of fighting already, Kyle, and I know you are already well acquainted with its dark underbelly." She glided away from the bookstand to casually lean against the back of the couch. "I won't ask you to do so again if you don't want to. But think of it – you can finally learn your family's true history, we can help you understand why and how your mother stifled your powers, and we can even help you undo the binding and teach you how to control your magic.

"The Society plays an important role in maintaining stability and balance within the magical realm. Humanity itself depends on the maintaining of that balance, so we don't want to completely destroy the council. That would only serve to undo its critical infrastructure and create an unprecedented chaos in both the mortal and ethereal realms.

"What we want, Kyle, is justice. Not just for me, but for the countless victims of their so called 'legal system.' But to achieve that, we need to be both efficient and destructive, such that they'll have no choice but to either comply with our demands and step down completely or face annihilation.

"Yet, to do so, we require the knowledge held within this grimoire," she continued, placing a hand on the book. "This, along with the others, and you are the only one who can open them.

"You are also a former special operations soldier, an elite. Your tactical knowledge and training would be invaluable, and you can even conduct your training within the safety and seclusion of Chase's family ranch. In time, if you are anything like your parents, you may even decide to take up the fight yourself, when you have seen the crimes the Society has committed against our people."

"Our people," I breathed.

"Yes," she replied with a nod.

The light of the fire cast shadows that danced on the smooth brown leather and gleaming metal surfaces of the book, and the weight of it all seemed to press down onto me all at once.

I thought of a choice I once made that sent a once promising career crashing into flames, almost literally, leaving me to wonder if I would ever find anything so fulfilling again. It was a decision made in a hopeless time that utterly destroyed what remained of my family, killing my father in the process, leaving me to question every aspect of my reality with little hope of ever finding answers.

For years, I longed for the day when I no longer had to worry about keeping my emotions in check, for fear of losing control and awakening the demon Asmodeus and the destruction that would bring.

Even so, the grimoire called to me…

And I remembered…

If it weren't for the choices that I'd made, I doubt that I would have been able rekindle my relationship with Amber. She was my rock and my strength; I never would have come so far without her. There was a point in my life when I thought that I had lost everything that I cared about; my friends, my family, my future. But I was also given a second chance, and she had been there to help me every step of the way. I was given an opportunity to start again, to rebuild, to find myself, and if necessary, to fight.

I'd lost so many people in my life who would never know such an opportunity again…

And the grimoire still called to me.

"The ranch," I said, finally. "Is Chase on board with the idea?"

"Oh," she said with a devious smile. "I think he can be persuaded."

"Oh?" I mocked, my voice coming out stern while my arms crossed. "By manipulating him with your magic?"

Her head snapped back, and she stood a little straighter. "It's not so much manipulation. I merely highlight people's desires and bring them to the surface.

"As for Chase, he worked for Phoenix long before I met him. He joined the company so he could legitimately earn enough money to buy his father's ranch. It wasn't exactly a hard sell for us to bring him up here, and his future ranch needs a capable hand. I'm sure he can be persuaded to help us if we offer to pay his father for the ranch on his behalf. I doubt I would even need to use my talents for that much."

"Right," I said. "And Amber?"

"She is a realtor, of course she would want to sell me this home. She made a lot of money out of the deal. I only helped motivate her to do so. Not to mention that you are engaged. Why wouldn't she want to help you find honest work?"

"Oh, stop," I said in rebuke. "Your so-called talent runs deeper than that and you know it. You used your magic to pry information from Amber, and you tried to do the same with me. You only stopped when you realized I was immune."

"Not at all." She folded her hands in front of her as she spoke, gaining back some of her composure, though her tone began to harden. "She never once told me of your magical origins. All the information she gave was freely given and would have likely been provided without the use of my talents. You are free to ask her about it, of course."

She paused a moment and leaned back into the couch again when I didn't move to object, her tone softening. "Every magic user has a particular set of talents that they lean on, Kyle. Your mother was adept at weaving illusions, for example, where your father was skilled at bending the elements to his will. As I said before, mine is simply to raise an individual's desires to the surface." She raised her palm up in front of her as if to show me. "And in time, we can help you discover your talents as well, if you haven't discovered them already."

"Right, and what's his story then?" I indicated, turning our attention to Silent John, who stood like a statue right where I'd left him.

Lillian pursed her lips slightly. "He was a member of the Pyre Guard." She paused for a slow breath to consider him before she continued. "Sometimes, you can bring someone back to life like this after they die, provided you can get to the body soon enough. That's one of Raymond's main talents."

"That's... dark."

"And for us, sometimes it's necessary," she said with a sideways glance. "So, what do you say about my offer?"

I studied Silent John for a moment more, who only continued to provide us with his haunted stare.

"It's an interesting offer, Lillian," I said flatly. "Maybe even one I might consider. I can't help but to wonder, though – if the Magistrate was the good guy here, why would my uncle Don warn me to stay away from you?"

"That's a good question, and I don't blame him for doing so," she said matter-of-factly. "Associating with us after the war could have been dangerous. The Society may have executed you for doing so. But we've since rebuilt our alliances and expanded beyond them, becoming arguably more capable than we were at the start of the last war. But you don't need to take my word for it." Her smile became wry. "You can ask your uncle about it when he returns, now that he's rejoined the Magistrate."

"Who—what?" I stammered. "What are you talking about?

"How do you think we discovered who you where?"

"We lost track of you when you left Wyoming," she continued before I could answer. "But I had a strong sense that I might have found you when I met Amber, I just needed to bring you here to be certain."

"If that's true, why am I speaking to you instead of him?"

"He was sent on a diplomatic mission," she said with a huff. "It's taken him longer than expected, but time can move in odd ways in the Otherworld."

"The Otherworld. What—like the land of the Fae? The Tuatha De Danann?"

Her eyebrows shot up. "Well," she said with a smile. "I'm impressed. You've done your research."

"Yeah, a bit," I said through my disbelief. "Do you have any idea when he will be back?"

"It's hard to say," she shrugged. "He's been gone for several years, which was expected, but we have reason to believe that he's nearly finished with his mission and will be rejoining us soon."

The Fae? The Otherworld? It seemed like it was way too fantastical. How could any of this even be real? But then again, it wasn't all that long ago when I discovered that there were more to demons and magic than mere fantasy, and I had often wondered if there might be something else creeping in the shadows. Still, could the Tuatha De Danann really be out there?

Could my uncle?

For years, I'd longed for the day when I didn't have to look over my shoulder for fear that The Society or the Magistrate would find me. I slogged through countless hours and mounds of research material for a way to finally rid myself of this demon, for a chance at a normal life, or maybe even to regain access to my magic.

All of this still seemed to be a little far-fetched though, like it was a little too good to be true. With Lillian's use of magic and this apparent literal zombie standing next to me, there were far too many red flags going off for me to be certain of anything. Not to mention that the last thing I wanted was to be drawn into some mystical war and possibly put Amber in danger.

And the grimoire still called to me…

"There is a lot going on here, Lillian," I said finally. "I may need some time to consider your offer, and I would like to speak with my uncle first."

"Of course," she said with a nod. "That is completely understandable. Please understand also that we may not have much time. We've been waiting for your uncle's return to make our move, but we have reason to believe that the Society caught wind of our intentions. We may have to move preemptively before he gets here if they force our hand."

"Fair enough," I said, making sure to address her squarely. "I'll talk to Chase about moving into the ranch and I'll put in honest work with Phoenix in the meantime. But let me make myself perfectly clear." I took a step closer to her and she drew herself straighter at the seriousness in my tone. "If you use your so-called talents on Amber again, if I so much as suspect it's happening, there is no deal. She stays out of this. Understood?"

"Yes," she said flatly. "I understand completely."

"Good. Have a good evening, Ms. Eldonna," I said, making my way to the door.

"Oh, and Kyle." I stopped short, my hand barely on the doorknob as I turned to face her. "Nobody can know of our little conversation here this evening. We have gone to great lengths to maintain our secrets and will continue to do so. I hope you understand."

I unconsciously squared myself up to her, fixing her with a hard stare. "Did you just threaten me?"

Her gaze floated over to John with a lazy shrug. "More of a promise."

I followed her gaze to John, who stood haunted, completely unmoving in the spot we'd left him. "Understood," I said firmly, stifling a cold shudder running down my spine.

I found Chase lounging alone in one of the chairs by the fire pit, seemingly content with a beer in his hand while he stared hypnotically into the fire. The wind was howling through the trees, but howling wind wasn't exactly outside the norm in North Dakota.

"Hey, man, how's it going?" I said, breaking him from his trance.

"Hey, Kyle." He turned in his chair to look at me. "How was your meeting?"

"It was good. Hey, is your offer to let Amber and I stay at your ranch still on the table?"

"Yeah," he said with an excited grin. "I would have to run it by my dad first, but I don't think he would mind. He would actually be really grateful for the help."

"Awesome, I appreciate that," I said, pulling my phone from my pocket. "Let me get your number."

I casually scanned the tree line while Chase typed away on my phone, bracing myself against the chill of the wind when I saw something at the edge of the riverbank. I had to focus on it for a moment. I couldn't quite tell what it was at first, until I realized that someone was kneeling ankle deep in the water.

She wore a red gown that was tattered and worn. Long dark hair flowed with the wind behind as she her pulled a burgundy shirt out of the calm waters, fervently scrubbing it in her hands like she was trying to remove a stain. She shone far too bright in the absence of the evening light, and I realized that the howl I was hearing wasn't coming from the wind.

It was coming from her.

It was more of a song than any howl of the wind, long and somber. Standing to her full height, she looked to me sorrowfully with the shirt still clutched in her hand. With a flash, she transformed into a raven, shirt and all, and flew with the current of the river. I struggled to keep my breath under control as I searched for her when she disappeared along the riverbank.

"Here you go," Chase said, startling me slightly. "You okay, man?"

"Yeah, I'm good," I said, taken aback, but unable to explain what I saw. "Thanks again man, have a good night."

# Chapter 15

The glare from the streetlights danced along the windshield as I drove along the expressway into Bismarck, though I hardly noticed them through the quagmire of thoughts that turned my brain into sludge. I practically drove on autopilot all the way home, hardly realizing when I pulled in next to Amber's blue Outback until I threw my truck into park.

I took the stairs to the apartment slowly, weighed down by a dread that made every step seem like climbing a steep mountain slope. It was a rare form for me. Although we spent little time occupying this little space, it always felt the way a home should, like a sanctuary, or a safe space of sorts. Looking back, every home we occupied always felt this way, but every step I took weighed just a little heavier than the last until I concluded my ascent.

I paused for a moment, staring at our apartment door, bracing myself for the bombardment of questions that would come the moment I walked through its threshold. I wasn't sure if I was ready to face her yet or if I wanted to share what I had learned. I took a breath in a vain attempt to calm my nerves before entering, though I doubted that it really helped.

I was instead greeted by the quiet darkness of the living room lit by the scant light above the kitchen stove, though there was a tiny sliver of light creeping from underneath the office door.

With a sigh of relief, I closed the door, kicked off my shoes, and stealthily made my way into the bathroom. I closed the door quietly, hoping that I hadn't disturbed Amber from whatever it was she was doing in the office, only to blind myself with the bathroom lights when I flicked them on. Blinking away the pain, I let the sound of the water from the faucet calm my mind and ease me into a trance, gradually slowing my breathing. Finally, after a slow and steady inhale, I held it for a brief pause.

"Spirit bound inside of me, asleep forever you shall be."

Though it was the only spell that I still knew, I wondered, and not for the first time, if it had any effect whatsoever. I thought back to the magic of the grimoire and how its power coursed both within and then through me in a way that was familiar, yet nearly forgotten. The magic that pulsed from that book reverberated in me like an echo, a silent reminder of what it was like to wield true power, a tidal wave compared to anything I had managed to summon since that failed exorcism so long ago.

*Was this spell just another lie?* I wondered. *Was it just a placebo my uncle gave me, meant to placate me for the time being? After everything I learned tonight, after all that was uncovered, how can I trust even this simple little spell when everything I knew about my own family turned out to be a lie? Hell, how can I trust it when I couldn't sense even the slightest trickle of magic on my own to begin with?*

*And what about the* apparition? I caught myself grinding my teeth in frustration when I mulled over that particular puzzle. I remembered thinking, for the briefest of moments, when I first saw her along the edge of the riverbank, that it might have been Asmodeus. She was the only genuine spirit I had ever encountered before today, but the spirit by the river seemed nothing like her.

Asmodeus could alter her appearance, but her changes were always something subtle, like the length of her hair or the outfit she wore. She always presented herself as someone who was young and beautiful, someone who could have been of Arab descent. This new apparition was exactly the opposite. She seemed very old, Caucasian, and practically decrepit. If she were alive at all, any real sign of youth would have faded a long time ago, along with the condition of her ragged clothes.

I also recalled how utterly terrified I was of Asmodeus when I first encountered her. That faded fairly quickly after the possession. But I wasn't afraid of this new spirit, mostly just confused and creeped out. I started to wonder if it was just an ordinary ghost wandering the riverbank, but given the circumstances, I doubted it was something so coincidental or mundane.

"Right," I huffed in silent amusement. "Because ghosts are somehow 'mundane' now."

With a reluctant sigh, I clicked off the bathroom light and walked around the kitchen table toward the kitchen when I heard the office door click open.

"Hey," Amber said quietly, peeking into the living room from around the door. She gave me a welcome smile before sliding around the door and clicking it closed behind her, careful not to spill the large white coffee mug in her hand.

"Hey, hon," I said, self-consciously placing my hand on a seat next to me. "It's a little late for tea," I teased, noticing the strings from the teabags spilling over the side of her mug.

"It's chamomile," she responded happily. "Decaf. How did it go?" She gave me a quick kiss before taking a seat on the other side of the table, her red curls flowing freely over the light pink robe she wore as she cupped the still-steaming mug.

"It…" I felt my chest tighten as I took a seat and I tried to swallow through it. "I don't know."

"What do you mean?" she asked, tilting her head slightly in concern.

I took a slow breath to steady myself before answering. "It… could have been better, I think."

"Oh." She seemed to droop a little in disappointment with her pause. "I see. So, what happened?"

I laid it all on her.

I told her about the grimoire and the photograph. I told her what I learned about my parents' relation to the Magistrate, the Society, and their involvement in the war. I watched her run her hands through her hair, horrified when I described Lillian's "talents," and her silent expression of empathetic sorrow at Lillian's story of self-defense. I even told her about Silent John and the apparition by the river. While only offering Cliff Notes for the meeting with Allen and Chase, I spared few details about my meeting with Lillian, Amber sitting in contemplative silence when I finally finished.

"I just…" She sighed in frustration. "I don't understand, all she wanted was a house. Do you have any idea how crazy this sounds?"

"About as crazy as an Army Ranger who finds out that he is a *wizard* after being possessed by a demon?" I tried to sound humorous, wiggling my fingers like I was casting a spell. "I wouldn't have believed it if she hadn't shown me my mother's grimoire, or her wedding picture for that matter."

She scoffed. "I wouldn't have believed it either if you hadn't literally burned a house down."

"Wow," I said, taken aback. "That wasn't exactly… me."

"Right." She slouched in her chair uncomfortably, sipping her tea. "That was out of line. I'm sorry. What do you want to do about it then?"

"I don't want to go anywhere near this," I told her firmly. I tried to conceal an impatient breath before I continued, frustrated by the feeling that this conversation was about to take a turn for the worst. "Whether it's Phoenix or the Magistrate, they are both one and the same to me at this point. Besides, there are literally more jobs available than there are people right now, I think we will be alright."

"To what end? Are we going to just keep running until the Society shows up at our door too?"

"We've done pretty well so far. If we are a little more careful, we can —"

"Have we though? Really?" she asked sarcastically. "The Magistrate found us by chance. How long do you think it will take before the Society finds us once they actually start looking, especially now that this war is about to kick off?"

"This isn't our fight, Amber."

"How is it not? What do you think they are going to do when they find us? They are going to execute you, Kyle." She jabbed at the table, punctuating her point. "The moment they find out about that demon, you are dead."

"Well, what would you have me do then? Do you want me to just throw myself into some war that I don't know how to fight, with weapons that I don't even know how to use? That's a real easy thing to suggest when you've never had to wash your friend's blood from your hands."

She sank back into her chair, and I only then realized I had been close to shouting. My hand ached with how hard I grasped the chair next to me. It squeaked in mild protest when I forced myself to relax.

"If we ally ourselves with the Magistrate, there is no way to know how this could end," I continued, softening my tone. "They lost against the Society in the last war and were massacred because of it. If we involve ourselves in this, we'll likely put ourselves directly in their line of fire. If they lose again… If something happens to you…" My chest grew tight and my throat felt like it was about to close. I had to swallow hard against it to continue. "I can't lose you too."

She sat for a moment studying me, sadness and worry widening her eyes while they sparkled in the lamplight. "What about the demon?" she continued, softly. "Even if the Society never finds us, it's only a matter of time until she wakes up again."

"I still have the spell Uncle Don gave me," I said with a shrug.

"The way you spoke about this book, this…" She spun a hand in the air, searching for the right word.

"Grimoire?" I supplied for her.

"Right. This grimoire. You made it sound like it was the first time you handled magic since the fire." She paused for a breath, shrugging. "Kyle, I've seen the nightmares. They're getting worse. How can you be sure that this spell is even working anymore?"

I had no way to answer her question, all I could do was shake my head with a shrug of my own. Of course, she was right. The spell was the only thing left in my arsenal I felt I could use to control this demon. But feeling the power of the grimoire, the way it called to me, the familiar magic that flowed into and through me seemed to only cast doubt to the effectiveness of the spell. The grimoire's call was the first time I felt anything resembling magic since the fire. The so spell might actually be useless after all.

"What if the Magistrate can help?" she asked. "If your uncle Don is with them, it might be worth working with them."

"We don't even know if he is actually with the Magistrate. Besides, how do we know we can trust them when Lillian all but admitted that she has been manipulating you with magic?"

"Did she though?" she asked, folding her arms. "Do you really think I've been magically manipulated?"

"I don't know," I said with a sigh. "That's the thing about manipulation, you might not know it's happening until the damage is already done."

"Right," she said, taking a sip of her tea. "Well, I never told her about your magic, the demon, or anything regarding your family's history. She found all that out on her own. Besides, she didn't say that you had to fight, nor do we have any other leads on what happened to your uncle."

"So, what would you suggest I do then?"

"Just do what you already promised Lillian: work with Phoenix until Uncle Don comes back. When he does—"She held up a hand before correcting herself. "If he does, we'll see if they can help us get rid of Asmodeus."

I gave her a weak smile. "You make it sound so simple."

"It never really is with us though, is it?" she said sweetly, standing up from her seat to join me on my side of the table. "Just think, we might actually have a chance to finally rid ourselves of this demon. Once this is all over, we can finally be free."

"Do you really think it's worth the risk?" I asked, taking one of her hands into mine.

"I do, because it's not just the two of us we have to worry about now," she said, producing a little white piece of plastic from a pocket in her robes.

"How do you mean?" I asked suspiciously.

"We have a legacy to protect, and we can't let some demon be a part of it anymore." My breath caught high in my chest when she placed a hand on my shoulder and kissed my cheek, placing the plastic stick on the table in front of me. The instructions on the damn thing were clear as day, but I couldn't wrap my mind around what they were trying to say.

Two clear lines for pregnant, one for not pregnant.

Looking into the window, I could see, just as clearly as what was posted on the label, two solid red lines. I wrapped an arm around Amber's waist, drawing her close to me, refusing to take my eyes off of the pregnancy test like I was trying to solve an unsolvable problem, until it finally hit me.

We weren't exactly trying for a pregnancy, but after I finished with my studies, we weren't exactly trying to prevent it anymore either.

But damn… that happened so… fast.

"Amber," I said, finally meeting her eyes again. "We're going to be parents."

"Yeah," she said with a vigorous nod and smile. "We are."

I wrapped her into my arms fully then, drawing her into my lap and myself into her.

"I'm going to be a dad…"

# Chapter 16
## Mosul, Iraq

The stars were countless, as they often were on nights like this. The airfield lay on the outskirts of the city, just far enough away for the light pollution to not diminish their magnificence. On some of the slower nights, I might have stolen a glance up into the night sky to be drawn away from the heat of the desert and into the calm of memory.

There were many memories to draw from, nearly an entire childhood full of them. They were the memories of a young boy full of wonder in a faraway place, on a ranch draped under a night sky not so different from this one. The insurmountable worries of that little boy seemed so inconsequential to the grown man now, but I tried not to dwell on any of them. Not in moments like this.

My mind drifted instead to the quiet and the stillness of the nights on the ranch, to when the boy wondered what kind of man he would become, before war could teach him. Before war could forge him.

Or maybe, I sometimes wonder, if the heat and the trauma of war had warped him?

It was deceptively cool this particular evening in Mosul, a stark contrast to the blistering heat of the previous afternoon. Once the sun went down, the desert seemed to suck away all of the heat, leaving me to shiver against the cold, though it rarely dropped below 70 degrees Fahrenheit this time of year.

A chill ran through me. I shivered against it, telling myself that it had nothing to do with the spirit I'd hallucinated earlier in the day, or the unknown danger I was about to lead my fellow Rangers into later in the evening. Trying to convince myself it had nothing to do with the fact that I might lose myself or another one of my men to this godforsaken place, in this godforsaken war.

"No," I told myself. "It has to be the cold."

I let my mind wander back to the memory of the boy and allowed myself to relax a little, breathing in the cool mountain air while the dry desert wind kissed my face. The moment seemed fleeting though when Taylor strode out of the hangar door and socked my shoulder.

"What's up, old man?" he said, stumbling past me.

"Old man?" I said with a scoff. "What, did they run out of mirrors for you to break?"

"Nah, that got boring," he said with a wry grin. "I came out here to look at an ugly ass troll instead."

"Well, you'll probably see plenty of those on the OP," I said with a smile of my own before taking in more of the sky.

"Truth," he agreed. "You good, bro?" he asked after a moment.

"Yeah." I said after a breath. "Just taking in some fresh air."

"Thinking about the mish?"

"More about what we talked about earlier, about talking to someone when we get back."

He studied me for a moment before responding. "You're going to, right?"

"Yeah, I intend too. I just worry that it won't turn out the way I would like."

"You worry too much, man." He squeezed my shoulder. "Trust me, I'll be right there with you. It'll be okay."

"Yeah, I appreciate that, man."

"Yeah," he said after a moment, taking in the night sky himself. "Sounds like they are ready to load up. You ready to go?"

"Yeah, bro," I said, turning toward the door, fist-bumping his shoulder on my way in. "Let's get after it."

Taylor was right on my heel when I walked into the hangar, though it was chock full of anxious Rangers and air crew busily tying up loose ends for the launch. Our gear was lined up in the order we would enter the aircraft, right where the helicopters would normally be if they weren't outside waiting for us.

It was a pretty relaxed affair. Nobody had their kits on while we waited, being as we were ahead of schedule. Most of the guys were milling around their gear, chatting casually while they waited for the call to come. Langston and the Double A brothers were among a couple of exceptions huddled around the far end of the hangar.

"How's it going, guys?" I said to Locker and Ramirez, sitting next to my gear beside them.

"Just another day at the office, Sergeant." Locker said, spitting tobacco into a cup.

"I hear that, brother," I said behind a silent chuckle. "Everyone ready to go?"

"Good to go, Sergeant," drawled Ramirez, lying with his back on his gear and hands laced behind his head. "We just finished checking our guys a little while ago."

"Awesome. I know we are nearing the tail end of our deployment, but let's not get complacent out there. I know that we have a few distractions right now, but let's make sure our head is still in the fight tonight. I don't have to express how big of a deal this OP will be."

"Do you actually think the emir will be there tonight?" Ramirez asked skeptically.

"I sure as shit hope so," I replied flatly. "They put a lot of planning into this for it to be another dry hole."

"Yeah," Locker said before spitting into his cup again. "With our luck though, that little shit will probably scamper off as soon as he hears our helicopters outside." That elicited a chuckle from Ramirez and me.

Things changed quickly when the soft whine of the helicopters filled the hangar from the outside and Arroyo strode into our little holding area with a pointer finger extended up to the ceiling, spinning in the air beside him, bellowing at the top of his lungs. "Let's go chock 1, get your shit on and get ready!"

"Speaking of…" I said, standing up and offering a hand to help Ramirez. He took it with a grin and the two of them immediately started yelling for their respective teams to don their gear, though they were already spurred into action by Arroyo's announcement.

There was a moment of what could only be described as controlled chaos when everyone put on their body armor, checked their gear, and were double-checked again by their leadership. We didn't have to wait long for the large hangar doors to open to reveal the hulking aircraft under the night sky, the helicopter's crew chief motioning to us from outside to follow him into a Blackhawk.

The huge rotors weren't spinning when we went out to meet them, but the engines shrieked with a ghostly howl that seemed to spur my very soul into motion as we approached. The crew chief entered first while I stayed outside and counted men onto the aircraft. Once I was satisfied that all my guys were accounted for, I jumped in with them, clipping into my seat.

It was cramped in this particular helicopter with all our equipment, but that was fairly typical. Military vehicles, including the UH-60 Blackhawk helicopter, weren't built for comfort. Things might have been different if we weren't so heavily laden, but with all our body armor, assault packs, weapons, and other equipment, we were knee to knee and shoulder to shoulder in our seats. Nobody was going to be comfortable on this flight, but we didn't have to be. It was going to be a short flight anyway.

We sat like this for several minutes, unable to speak to each other through the incredible noise of the aircraft while the air crew went through their final checks before takeoff. Soon, the main rotor began to spin gently, shaking everyone inside. The crew chief who had led us inside strapped himself into a seat that allowed him to lean half out of a window, along with a mini gun that swung outside by a long swiveling arm attached to the airframe. Just as the main rotor really started to pick up speed, though, he pulled himself back into the cabin and gave me a thumbs-up and a barely discernible grin from behind his flight helmet. I gave him one in kind, and we exchanged a fist bump before he spoke into a microphone in his helmet and stuck his head back out of the window.

I could feel a familiar pull at the pit of my stomach when I watched the earth retreat from beneath us. The vibration that shook us in our seats all but vanished as we gracefully took to the sky.

Awareness of a strange dichotomy overtook me anytime I flew in one of these hawks. Adrenaline pulsed through me like an electrical current, but I sat calmly in my seat. My breathing was deep and full, but slow and steady, in through my nose and out through my mouth. My mind flowed through the scenario laid out in the mission briefing, all while taking on a Zen-like clarity among the roar of the engines.

I looked into the faces of the men around me, all of whom were about to fast-rope into a night of uncertainty. Eyes that ever so recently shone with compassion and love now expressed neither remorse, nor fear, nor emotion at all behind the evil green glow of their night vision goggles. Their collective gaze seemed to beckon me to join them in the nights hunt, and a hungry, predatory sort of pride overcame me when I flipped my night vision goggles mounted atop my head over my eyes. The darkness broke into clarity and the night became an alien world of green and black.

It was a world that we knew well. We were in our element—indomitable and unstoppable. We owned the night, and the darkness could no longer hide our prey.

The crew chief leaned back into the aircraft and held out his hand to me, fingers spread, and yelled inaudibly over the noise of the helicopter. That was fine, we did this often enough for me to know what he was trying to say.

"Five minutes!" I screamed at the top of my lungs, repeating the gesture to my men without any hope of them hearing me, satisfied when they repeated the same back to me.

Those minutes seemed like seconds when the crew chief leaned back in from his mini gun to hold up his pointer finger, yelling noiselessly into the aircraft.

"One minute!" I screamed again, repeating the gesture. This time, the cargo doors on either side of the helicopter flew open and Rangers prepped the ropes while I prepared to count them off. The open doors provided a clear view of a city bathed in green, and I could see the target building's hulking form off the right side of the hawk as we banked onto the approach.

It's one thing to see an objective through aerial photography; that'll only give you a basic idea of what you will deal with when you get there. It's another thing altogether to see it in real time. It wasn't exactly a skyscraper, but the three-story building that was to be our objective clearly stood out among the two-story buildings surrounding it. Buildings such as homes were often walled off, creating a sort of courtyard for the residence, so I wasn't surprised to see that here. What I was surprised by was how much standoff it created around the target building as it fenced in a large parking lot in the back as well.

These insurgents chose well, I realized. If we had come in from the street like we normally would, this could have been a real slugfest, assuming they had the numbers to hold it.

Without warning, noise like a giant buzz saw ripped through the roar of the engines on the right side of the aircraft, and I looked on in horror as the mini gun came to life and poured a stream of light onto the roof of what was clearly the target building.

Son of a bitch, so much for the element of surprise!

I glared at the crew chief when he pulled himself away from his mini-gun and leaned into the cabin with his hand balled into his fist, his pointer finger and thumb extended out like he was trying to pinch something in the air. I repeated the gesture to him, reminding myself that he probably had a good reason to blow our cover the way he did.

"Thirty seconds!" I screamed to my men, passing the gesture to them as well. The helicopter positioned itself over the building and the ropes dropped. The moment the end of the ropes hit the ground, the crew chief gave the signal to go, and I immediately shouted at my Rangers to exit the bird, coordinating their decent from either side of the helicopter.

The entire squad emptied the aircraft within seconds, just like we had practiced countless times before. I barely had to coordinate anything, really, and my turn seemed to come as soon as we started. Instinct and training took over without even so much as a thought, and near-blistering air from the rotors and empty Iraqi desert screamed over me the moment I took the rope and pummeled me through my descent.

My feet hit the concrete roof with a thud, and I sprang out of the way of the ropes to find that my squad had already secured the rooftop.

Awesome. So far, so good.

I took stock for a moment as the ropes thudded to the ground behind me, now released from the Blackhawk, its hulking form floating away to leave us in the oppressive silence of its absence. All my guys were easily accounted for, but it took me a moment to realize that the dark patches on the far end of the building were bodies. When I approached them, I noticed right away that they were already cleared, not that there was really much of them left *to* clear.

When I was a young private, a squad leader once told me something interesting about bullets and the effects they can have on the human body. To paraphrase, he said that the 5.56 from our M4 carbines poked holes into people, while the 7.62 took limbs off people, and the 50 cal blew people apart. The mini gun that the crew chief hit these guys with fired a 7.62 round, but when firing at a rate of around six thousand rounds per minute, it was a lot of 7.62 to take in all at once. Needless to say, it did more than just take their limbs off.

I also noticed what looked like an AK-47 rifle, RPK machine gun, and a rocket propelled grenade launcher ready to fire by the small pile of bodies, and I felt a small shiver crawl up my spine when I did. Any one of these weapons could have taken down our helicopter or killed any one of my men before the ropes even hit the ground, stopping the mission dead in its tracks before it even started.

I popped a chem light with a sigh of relief to mark the bodies, mouthing a silent thanks to the crew chief that killed them before leaving the dead to join my men.

"Viper 1-4, this is Viper 1-1," I said, walking to my Alpha team, who had already stacked up by the stairway door at the far corner of the building. "Rooftop secure, moving to the third floor."

"Viper 1-1, roger," came the Overwatch over the radio. "Nothing observed on the third, shifting fire to the second."

That sounded odd, I figured *someone* would have stirred with all that noise. I didn't dwell on it though; it was time to move. My Bravo team fell in behind me as I signaled my Alpha to breach the door, and we were immediately flowing down the stairs to the third floor.

The stairway was nearly pitch-black, but our descent was fluid and practiced, my Alpha team silently fanning out into an empty room as soon as they reached the bottom. I came in behind them, noticing right away that the room was large, like some sort of conference room with a small table set up in its center. To our left was a string of doorways that lined the wall until they reached another stairway at the opposite end of the room.

I wordlessly signaled my Bravo team to take the first room closest to us. My Alpha would take the second while I positioned myself behind the table, careful not to silhouette myself in the window on my right.

The table wouldn't exactly stop a bullet, but I probably wouldn't need it too. The enemy wouldn't be using night vision inside a dark building, or at all for that matter. The table would conceal me in the darkness while I provided security for the two teams moving in and out of this room, searching and securing the others as they went.

Silently, they breached the first one, and then the second, my Bravo team leap frogging the second and stacked on the third when the roar of engines steadily drew near. Soon the whole building seemed to shake as the Blackhawk pummeled the rooftop above with its main rotor. The floor vibrated beneath me as I crouched. The clutter that could have been office supplies on the table seemed to rattle a cue to the team to open and flow into the door.

At first there was shouting, though I couldn't make out what was said through the noise of the helicopter above. The shouting grew more urgent, then the noise of gunfire erupted from inside the room, momentarily drowning out the noise from above.

*Shit, are they okay?* I could feel my heart pulse in my neck for a moment that felt like an eternity. *Come on, Locker. Give me an up!*

A soft light shone through the open doorway, shadows dancing in its light as Locker peeked through and signaled that the room was clear. Ramirez flowed past with his team and stacked onto the next doorway while I let out a slow, controlled breath to steady my nerves.

*Thank* fucking *God!*

It was so subtle at first, I almost didn't catch it right away when the sixth door cracked open just a little. My attention fully snapped to the door as it opened a little more and I could see the silhouette of a figure peeking his head into the room. Ramirez and his team pushed into their next room at that moment, seemingly unaware of what was happening just two doors down from them, leaving me alone with this shadow of a man.

He said something intangible in Arabic, almost questioningly as he opened the door, fully exposing himself and the AK-47 he held diagonally along his torso. My laser snapped on, flooding the room with light. The green dot danced up his chest with each successive pull of the trigger.

Things always seemed to slow down in moments like this. His body stiffened when the first round entered just below his sternum. His shoulders rolled inward, and he leaned back when the second and third punched in just above that. The room echoed with thunder and light when the last two rounds punched into his face and his lifeless body thudded with his back to the floor.

The room dimmed again when the laser went out, punctuating the stunned silence. That silence was brief. A man yelled from inside the room in a language I didn't understand before unleashing a burst of fully automatic fire from inside the doorway, bullets slamming into the wall in front of me before the door slammed shut from the inside.

I didn't notice that Locker and his team had already entered the main room among the commotion with their weapons up, moving cautiously to the fifth room, ready to engage anything that came out to greet them. I signaled them the okay to clear it and they were in the room in a flash, silence once again punctuating the conference room as they cleared theirs without incident.

Ramirez entered with his team into the main room as they did, and his team moved onto the still-closed sixth door. He looked to me for assurances, and I used a hand signal indicating that there was still an enemy in the room he was about to enter.

With him now being the first man in the stack, he took it on like it was a non-issue. With a quick signal of Ramirez's hand, his second man pulled security on the door while Ramirez opened it and tossed in a grenade in one fluid motion. The man inside yelled in panic and fired a burst through the now open door until the grenade exploded. That wasn't an issue though; we were all well clear of the door. The whole building seemed to rock with the explosion and the team flowed immediately inside once it did.

I have no idea if that man was still alive when they went inside, all I know is that he died violently.

The sound of engines grew close again as Locker and his team moved on to the seventh door. The Blackhawk above seemed to shake the building to its foundations while my two teams cleared the last two rooms without incident. I breathed a heavy sigh of relief and stood from my spot behind the table when Locker finally placed a rifleman and his SAW gunner by the stairway for security.

"Viper 1-6, this is Viper 1-1," I said over the radio. "Third floor secure, LOA."

"Viper 1-1, roger, pushing to you." the lieutenant responded. "Viper 1-4, shift fire first floor."

Locker and Ramirez met with me near the table to report on what they'd found, and a line of Rangers flooded the open room when I gave them instructions. Wilkins and Arroyo joined me as second squad flowed by to meet the security team by the staircase. Taylor, who was among them, racked knuckles with me as he passed by.

"Alright, Goodwin, what do you got?" the lieutenant asked.

"I'm sure you saw the three dead on the roof. We have four EKIA up here too. We are green, green, green, and green, sir," I said indicating the status of my squad and 'Enemy Killed In Action.' "I already have guys searching the EKIA right now."

"Awesome, good work," Wilkins responded. "Finish your search and get your guys into a security posture when you're done. White light the area if you have too."

Taylor's squad had already moved down the staircase, and the three of us jumped as the sound of gunfire punched up the stairs and interrupted our conversation. Waters and his third squad were positioning themselves near the staircase, getting ready to descend.

"You got it, sir. We'll be ready if you need us," I said into the sudden silence. He moved over to third squad without a sound.

"Good job, Goodwin," Arroyo said with his thick accent. "The fight isn't over yet though, stay frosty."

"Roger that, Sergeant."

With a pat on my shoulder, he left to join third squad as well.

A battle waged on the second floor. There were periods of silence punctuated by gunfire. Sometimes there was yelling, sometimes in English, sometimes in Arabic. The worst part was the waiting. My skin practically crawled from the anxiety as I waited impatiently for an update, hoping to God that none of my brothers would get hurt, or God forbid, killed. When it finally came over the radio, I exhaled a heavy breath in relief, but my jaw ached when I watched third squad flow down the stairs and into the fight.

I would have driven myself insane if I just sat there alone, silently anticipating the outcome of the battle at hand. Besides, I still had a job to do. My two teams had already taken to searching the other rooms, so I decided to switch on the flashlight attached to my rifle and search the room I was already in.

I wasn't ready for what I saw.

I hadn't noticed before that there were no chairs, and the table wasn't cluttered with office supplies. The short end of the table was facing the window I had recently been so worried about. I had apparently been taking cover along one of its long ends. There was a folded tripod lying on its side with a digital camera next to it at its center. There were eight knives lying neatly along the length of the table, each of them with a blade nearly as long as my forearm. I dreaded turning around, but when I did, I found a black flag adorned with Arabic writing, some within a white circle in its center.

I wasn't standing in the middle of a conference room. I had been taking cover in a film studio set up for a damn execution.

*The spirit earlier… or whatever* she *was, didn't she say something about an execution?*

"Hey, Sarg," Locker said, striding out from one of the other rooms, Ramirez right at his heels. "The EPW search is done. We set up security in the other rooms."

"Good, I'll check it out in a minute. I want someone on this window though," I said, shining my light below the windowsill.

"On it," Ramirez said, about to turn away—but he stopped short. I could vaguely see his eyes grow wide in the dim glow of my flashlight. "Damn."

"Holy shit." Came Locker. "No blood on the floor, maybe we got here in time?"

"I'm sure we'll find out later. I'll finish up here. Get our security set in but make sure your guys are ready to move."

"Roger," came their collective reply before leaving me to complete their tasks.

"Goodwin," the Lieutenant said voice from the staircase as he came to join me, clearly out of breath.

"Over here, sir."

"Hey, we're finishing up downstairs." He took a moment to lean a hip on the table, wiping his brow before continuing. "We may have taken on a little more than we can handle though… oh." He pushed away from the table, hesitantly stepping back to take in the scene.

"Yeah?" I said, hoping to gain his attention. "How did we do, sir?"

"Um, yeah." His eyes snapped back to mine momentarily before drifting back to his slow scan of the studio. "We were lucky, no casualties," he continued. "White from third took a round to the chest though."

"Holy shit."

"Yeah, he's okay," He said, walking to the other side of the table, eyes locked onto the camera. "The plate caught the round."

"Damn," I said with relief. "Lucky."

"Yeah, someone in third took a graze to the shoulder. Doc already patched him up though. It wasn't more than a scratch."

"Wow."

He picked up the camera, turning it over to examine it in the sparse light of the flashlight. "We took some prisoners, a handful of them are on our list. We also found that they were keeping several hostages." He swallowed as his voice shook. "Mosul's governor… his family was with them. His children… I didn't even know they were missing." He looked up from the camera, scanning the room with a look of horror and disgust. "I guess they were planning an execution."

"Are we surprised by that, sir?" Not meaning to sound so cold.

He shot me a look like he wanted to hit me. Not that I could blame him. The insurgents that came to fight from outside of Iraq were absolutely brutal. They had no regard for the lives of the Iraqi citizens, even going as far as to murder and torture anyone they so much as suspected of helping us Americans. They often had no qualms with forcing their target to watch as they did their worst with the victim's family, leaving us to pick up the pieces in their aftermath, sometimes even filming their actions to spread on the internet for propaganda.

Scenes like this weren't exactly common, but the insurgents weren't exactly trying to win the hearts and minds like we were either. If you spent enough time in Iraq, you would at least hear of these killings, and it seemed like everyone who had been on previous deployments with me had seen at least one.

Sometimes I forgot that this was the lieutenant's first deployment. Sometimes I forgot how numb I'd gotten to all of this.

"So," I said, after a sigh. "We took zero casualties, killed a bunch of bad guys, snagged some of who we were looking for, and we saved some hostages. It doesn't get much better than that, sir."

"Heh, yeah," he said, dropping the camera to the table. "Now we just need to get everyone back."

"I don't seem to recall us expecting a hostage rescue. Do we have enough room in our trucks for everyone, sir?"

"Barely, but I think so," he said as he was making his way to leave. "Once we're finished downstairs, we'll bring the Strykers around and load up. They'll pick up Overwatch on the way, third will load up with the hostages and POWs when they get here. Everyone else will follow."

"Sounds good, sir," I said, watching him go.

"How is your security up here?" he said, pausing before he left.

"I have the front fully covered. The rear might be an issue," I said, pointing to the window by the table.

"I wouldn't worry about that too much," he said after considering it for a moment. "Taylor has a good handle on it, just keep a shooter there for now."

"Will do, sir."

"It might be a few minutes before we are finished downstairs, so hang tight for now," he said as he left for the stairs. "I'll let you know when it's time to leave."

"Take this window over here." Ramirez said to Albers as they came into the room.

"Hold on," I said, taking hold of Albers by the arm and turning him around, making easy access of his assault pack. I practically threw the camera inside before closing it up and directing him back to the window.

It didn't take long to check my squad's security positions. It helped that my team leaders actually knew what they were doing. Even so, while checking every individual's position, I felt myself again relieved that the powers that be made this an air assault mission, taking the roof first instead of taking it from the ground like we usually did.

This place was a veritable fortress. The green-filtered lights from the city gave away little to the surrounding buildings or their shadowy alleyways. This was easily the tallest building on the block by at least one story, giving us plenty of fields of fire throughout the area. The walled off courtyard only sported two main entrances, the main gate in the front and the parking lot entrance in the back. The wall surrounding the building pushed out to nearly one hundred meters in some places. Even if we stormed in with our heavily armored Strykers, the rocket-propelled grenade launcher on the roof could have really made things hell for us.

Popping back into the main room, I looked over to Albers, dutifully pulling security through his window and into the still night. I could almost hear the spirit's warnings as I watched him stand deathly still in the shadows.

*They* mean *to bog you down,* I remembered her saying. *They mean to bring that building down around you and make it into your grave.*

*Well, that doesn't seem likely now,* I thought. *We practically won this fight.* A sense of relief and guilt washed over me then. *I thought I was going crazy, I guess this just confirms it…*

"1-4 Victor, this is 1-6, move to pick up Overwatch." Came the lieutenant's voice over the radio. "All other Victor elements, bring your vehicles to the target building for extract."

"Nice," I said, popping my head into the room Ramirez was in. "Did you catch that?" I asked him with a thumbs-up.

"Roger," he responded with a thumb of his own.

"Locker," I said, barging into his. "Did you catch that?"

"Sounds like the Strykers are coming to pick us up?" he responded from his window, his SAW gunner, Arrants, standing with him.

"Yeah," I said, peering out the window. "We'll cover third while they load the extra bodies into the vehicles. Once they're loaded up with second, we'll follow in behind."

"Sounds good," Locker responded just as machine gun fire sounded down the street. "What the hell?" We both tried to peer out the window to make out what was going on down the road without exposing ourselves, but we couldn't make out anything significant. We could only see the flash from the gunfire.

"Viper 1-6, this is Viper 1-1 Victor," a calm voice said over the radio as the sound of one of our .50 caliber machine guns silenced the enemy guns in the distance. "Be advised, we are taking small arms and RPG fire on our way to you."

"Roger," was the Lieutenants only response.

"Heh," Locker chuckled next to me. "I guess they didn't want us to leave without saying goodbye."

"I guess not," I said with a chuckle of my own.

In the courtyard below, I could see a team of Rangers lead a group of people handcuffed to the gate, followed by another team, just as the ghostly whine of the Stryker drew near. It's lumbering hull slowed to a near stop as it approached the gate when the world went white in a flash. The deafening boom shook the entirety of the building, shattering windows and sending the three of us scrambling on our feet. I managed to brace myself with a hand against the wall next to the window before nearly taking a knee on the newly formed pile of glass at my feet.

"You guys okay?" I shouted to Locker and Arrants.

Locker: "Yeah."

Arrants "I'm good."

Smoke and dust poured into the window for a moment, just as the three of us stood together, the smell of cordite filling the air. It took a moment for the scene outside to clear, but every single individual who had once stood in the courtyard below now lay in the dirt, and I couldn't tell who was injured or if any one of them were okay.

It took a moment more for enough of the dust to clear to see that a section of the wall had collapsed in. I could see six roundish figures on top of the vehicle. *No, that's not right,* I thought, trying to adjust my night vision. I didn't need to, my night vision worked just fine. I just couldn't comprehend that the improvised explosive device was powerful enough to lift the sixteen-ton, eight-wheeled tactical vehicle off of the ground and flip it onto its roof, driving it partially through the wall and blowing off two of its wheels in the process.

The three of us stood stunned for a moment, shocked into silence. "Holy shit," Arrants cursed next to me.

That's when someone fired a rocket into the courtyard.

# Chapter 17

"What about Rowen?" Amber kept scrolling away on her phone, waiting for me to respond with her knees propped up on the dashboard.

I had to mull that one over while I monitored the car in front of me.

"Rowen isn't bad," I said finally. "It sort of gives off Lord of the Rings vibes though."

"I thought you liked Lord of the Rings." she said, peeking up from her phone.

"I do, but it's not what I want to think about when I'm calling for our son," I responded, not looking away from the road. She sucked on her lip with a quizzical look before turning her attention back to her phone. "The beacons are lit!" I chided her with a smile. "Gondor calls for aid!"

She flopped her head back into her seat, dropping her phone into her lap with a defeated laugh. "And Rohan will answer!"

I stifled a laugh trying to act stoic. "Muster the Rohirrim!"

"Yeah, yeah." She picked up her phone again with a shake of her head. "Okay."

"How about Logan?" I said, changing lanes.

"Okay, Wolverine," she said with a mocking grin. "Besides, that's a pretty common name right now."

Normally, I hate moving. I always have, though I wouldn't blame anyone for accusing me of having an addiction to it, considering how frequently I have over the years. My one saving grace this time was that I moved most of my things before my training event in Casper. All that was left were some bare essentials Amber would hold onto while she tied up loose ends in Bismarck.

It never hurt to have my best friend with me on a long trip though.

"What do you think about Malakai?" She continued scrolling on her phone.

"Is he trying to become a wizard?" I wiggled my fingers for emphasis. "Maybe we can teach him magic."

"I mean, I suppose you could," she said with an eye roll. "We can even call you Dumbledore."

"I prefer Snape, thank you very much," I said in mock indignation, placing a hand on my chest.

"You would." she said, exasperated. "Snape, Snape, Severus Snape."

"Dumbledore!"

Her bubbling laughter drowned out the music playing over the little old Toyota's speakers, and I found myself easily carried away in the stream of her mirth. Huffing a laugh of my own, I habitually placed my hand on her thigh, and she cast me a loving smile before lacing her fingers into mine. "I don't think we're going to get anywhere with the boys right now. Why don't we go over some girl names?" she said, returning her attention to her phone. "What do you think about Sage?"

"Didn't you have a bully in high school named Sage?"

"Oh, yeah." She looked up from her phone, tilting her head to the unpleasantness of the memory. "I kind of hated her."

"I think we all kind of hated her."

That wasn't true at all; she was a blond-haired, blue-eyed, super popular preppy girl. It felt good to say though.

"How about Amanda?" I suggested.

"Could you think of anything more generic?"

"Didn't you just suggest Sage?"

"Bite me," she said with a side eye.

"I might want to do more than simply bite you, love."

"Down, boy." She squeezed my hand with a smile. "What do you think of Juniper?"

"Oh," I said, taken aback. "That's not bad. I might have to mull that one over." She smiled up at me, rubbing my thumb with hers in our entwined hands.

The hour-and-a-half drive west from Bismarck to Dickinson was a straight shot with little to see aside from endless miles of farmland and the barest changes in elevation. It wasn't until you took Highway 22 north to Killdeer that the scenery really became interesting. Farmlands gave way almost completely to ranch land on the northward journey from Dickenson, weaving around progressively larger and steeper hills on the climb towards the Badlands.

The winding valleys and lush meadows were a portrait of green and golden hues, though the canvas was scarred with hulking oil rigs that occasionally littered the landscape. Semi-trucks traversed the highways screaming by with apparent reckless abandon, taking turns way too fast and barreling at speeds that often went far above any posted speed limit. They didn't exactly travel in convoys, but it put things into perspective when I thought about how bad it had been in the days of the big oil boom; before the downturn that was so great the railroad was forced to lay me off even though I was working on the other side of the state.

Killdeer itself appears when you least expect it. The road eventually crests one of the endless number of hills in the area and practically runs into a roundabout that sits at the southernmost part of town. Past that, an industrial park sprawls out to the base of a foothill, the foothill itself blanketed by the few homes that make up the town itself. A winding road took us to the top of the hill, crested by the county's high school and wellness center.

"Wow." Amber perked up in her seat as she took in the sight of the Badlands and Killdeer Mountain Range miles away. "Is that where we are going?"

"Yeah," I told her. "We'll turn off at a bend in the road a couple of miles from here. That'll take us past Killdeer Mountain and right into a driveway at a fork in the road."

"I didn't realize that North Dakota had views like this. It almost reminds me of home," she said, taking in the rolling sea of green and gold as we came over the crest of the hill.

"Just wait until I take you up to the top of the mountain," I said with a squeeze and a smile, which she returned in kind.

"Home," I quietly mused to myself. "How funny is it that I spent nearly a decade without ever thinking about it, but now I can't shake it from my mind."

As promised, the dirt driveway at the fork in the road led down into a depression along the side of a hill. From there the dirt road split, the left bend going back up into the side of the hill toward an old two-story house, the right looping around an old workshop. Several other buildings sat along the spur of the hill, though I wasn't sure what most were used for exactly.

Hey, I might be from Wyoming, but I'm still a city kid.

Or an "Urban Indian," depending on who you ask.

For a farmhouse, it was fairly well-maintained considering how old it was. It had been in the same family for four generations, and no one except a couple of farmhands had lived in it for the last couple of decades. The peeling paint needed some attention, maybe some trim, and the porch probably needed to be redone, but I watched as Amber's face lit up in wonder as she marveled at the sight of the little white house set between two oak trees.

"Oh my God," she said breathlessly, with a wide grin. "It's cute." Her grin dropped as soon as we stopped, her face scrunching into a grimace. "You know, I almost forgot what that smelled like."

"What's that?" I gave her a grin of my own.

"Cows." She spared me a full seconds glance before taking in the house again. "It might be a while before I get used to that again."

"What, it doesn't bring back any memories of cow tipping or mudding on my uncle's ranch, does it?" I teased.

"Well, first of all," she said with a smirk. "The cow tipping never happened. Second, that wasn't even your uncle's ranch. He was a hand and Mr. Hubbard wasn't even remotely happy about it."

"Yeah, we should probably keep our noses clean this time."

"That would probably be wise," she said, knowingly.

"They have horses, though."

"Really?" She exaggerated with a gasp. "Do you think we can take them mudding?"

"If we ask nicely, they might even let us ride them." I laughed, stepping out of the truck.

Dropping the tailgate, Amber and I started grabbing boxes from the bed. Not that there were many to grab, about a dozen or so medium and large boxes held down by a couple of ratchet straps. It was a small truck after all.

Small, but fierce.

She didn't make any remarks about the crumbling concrete patio steps leading up to the front door or the rusted metal handrail that wobbled when you grabbed it, but the disappointed look and realization of the work that needed to be done became evident before we even walked through the door. Walking inside, I thought she was going to drop the box she carried.

The front door opened right into the unfurnished living room, with a small open kitchen directly to the right. Walking in behind me, she only took a couple of steps onto the hardwood floor before pausing to look around and dropped her head with a defeated sigh. "Jesus, Kyle." She chuckled a little before looking back up to me. "When was this place last updated? The seventies?"

"Maybe the eighties," I said with a laugh.

"Didn't you say that a couple of people lived here recently?"

"Yeah, they were just a couple of part time hands that worked for the oil field." I explained. "They managed to update a few things while they were here, internet, satellite, that sort of thing. Apparently they were laid off when the oil prices dropped, so they skipped town before they could do much more than that."

"Right," she said with another exasperated sigh. "We really have our work cut out for us here."

"Well, that was part of the deal. As long as I help out around the ranch, including the house, we can live here for free."

"Well, it has potential, I'll give it that." She cast another uncertain look around. "It's been a while since I've worked with power tools though."

"I'm sure you'll do fine. Besides, no one expects you to do anything like that, though I doubt they would complain if you did." She shot me a glare like she was going to protest, but I interrupted her before she could, "Unless you would rather help with the goats, that is," I teased.

Her big green eyes shot open. "Goats?" she said in disbelief. "Are you serious, they have goats?"

Goats happened to be one of her favorite animals, so I had a feeling that might win her over. "Yeah, they are just up the road. We passed them on our way over here."

"Do you think I could do both?" she said with a smirk.

"I doubt they would mind, but let's put these boxes away first."

A short hallway at the far end of the living room led to the master bedroom, a bathroom, and a stairway leading upstairs. The old stairs creaked as we labored up them, but the second floor was fairly small with two modest bedrooms and a linen closet between them. One bedroom opened right into the stairway, so that was the one I went into first.

"What is this room for?" Amber asked, dropping her box next to mine.

"Well, I thought I would leave that up to you," I responded, bending over a little to avoid the low-sloped ceiling. "I figured one of these bedrooms could be your office and the other could be for the little one, once they are old enough."

"Oh, okay." She strode to the only window in the room, overlooking the front yard. "This is a beautiful view," she said, breathlessly.

"Unless you would rather work out of the basement, of course," I jabbed playfully. "We can make it into a makeshift dungeon for you."

"Won't you need the space to practice your witchcraft?" she chided with a smirk.

Walking backward out of the room, I waved my hands mockingly before leaving for the stairs.

I could hear the rumble of the gray lifted behemoth of a truck before I could see it when I stepped outside. I knew what it was and who it belonged to before I saw it. The distinct roar of the early two thousands four-door Chevy diesel echoed down into the dirt road, churning a hurricane of orange dust in its wake, Chase's grin practically gleamed from the rolled-down driver's window. He slowed to an easy stop by my little red Toyota, leaving me thankful that the wind was blowing the other way when he strode out of his truck with a tan cowboy hat in his hand.

"Hey, guys." His eyes were practically squinted in enthusiasm behind his glasses when he reached for my hand to shake, which I gladly accepted. "So, this must be Amber." Amber was only a step or two behind me, and he took her hand with equal enthusiasm. "I'm Chase Landreth. It's great to finally meet you."

"Good morning. It's nice to meet you too, Chase," she replied with a modest grace.

"I saw you guys driving past the mountain, so I thought I would say hi and lend a hand if you need it."

"Mountain?" Amber asked skeptically.

"Yeah, that one right there." Chase said, pointing. "My folks live in a house near the base."

Amber looked to me with a disbelieving smile and crooked eyebrow. I merely responded with a shrug. It wasn't hard to know what she was thinking. Amber and I grew up with the Bighorn and Teton Mountain Ranges practically in our backyards, with their soaring peaks and indescribable landscapes permanently coloring our childhoods. Killdeer Mountain looked more like a respectfully large hill to the two of us in comparison, even if it was the second highest point in the state of North Dakota.

"It probably doesn't look like much now," he continued. "But the view of the Badlands from up there is amazing."

"That's what Kyle keeps telling me," she said with a polite smile. "I'm excited to see it."

"Well, maybe I can take you up there?" he said, returning a smile of his own. "I was going to check the fence line anyway, you guys are more than welcome to tag along. It would be a good opportunity for you guys to check out the property too."

Amber and I looked toward each other for assurance and found each other nodding in silent agreement.

"My dad wants to cook us a steak dinner tonight," he said like he was trying to sweeten the deal. "He would love to meet you guys. You are more than welcome to join us if you're interested."

"Yeah, that would be great," Amber said with her refined modesty. "I would love to meet him too."

# Chapter 18

With Chase's help, it didn't take long for us to unload the rest of the cargo into the house. Not that it would have taken long anyway; my little Toyota only carried so much at a time. One particular black plastic tuff box, which was nearly as heavy as I was, had the three of us cursing out loud when we struggled to shimmy it up the stairs, in near constant danger of dropping it or falling down the stairway ourselves. Thankfully, we managed with Chase humbly accepting my profuse gratitude.

We then loaded ourselves into Chase's diesel and drove the short distance to the workshop, where we loaded the material we needed to fix fences. There wasn't much to grab, mostly just a line of rolled barbed wire, wire cutters, fence posts, and a few other odds and ends. All things considered, I could have fit everything we needed inside the bed of my truck, though I doubted my little fierce Toyota could have handled the terrain.

I made a mental note to trash-talk him about it later.

We loaded back into his truck with me in the back seat, country music playing softly on the radio as we drove slowly along the nearby fence line. "I almost forgot—this came for you the other day," Chase said, handing me an envelope he kept on his dash. "I think it's an invitation to the grand opening this weekend."

"Oh, okay," I said, taking it from him, stuffing it in my back pocket. "Thank you."

"Yeah, we got everything ready at the shop while you were gone. Some of the bigwigs are going to be there. It sounds like Lillian wants to make a spectacle about it."

"Huh," I said, a little more gruff than I intended. "Sounds like fun."

"How do you like real estate?" Chase asked Amber, sitting next to him.

"I like it a lot, actually," she replied with a smile.

"Yeah?" he prompted.

"Yeah. Honestly, I wasn't sure if I would at first though." Chase passed her a questioning look without responding. "It's a lot of hard work, especially when you are just getting started, but there is something really rewarding about finding someone's dream home. It didn't take long for me to really fall in love with it."

"That's really cool," he said, carefully maneuvering over a small hill. "What are you going to do when you move down here?"

"Same thing." She braced herself while Chase drove over a ditch. "My license allows me to work all over the state of North Dakota, so I'm going to work out of Killdeer and Dickinson when I move here."

"Wow, that's a lot of traveling."

"Right," she said, with a nod. "We still have our apartment for a few months. I'm going to tie up some loose ends before coming here, then I'm going to work part time after the little one comes."

"I'm so excited for you guys." Chase beamed. "I think you guys are going to make great parents."

"Thanks," she said with a shy little laugh. "That's kind of you to say."

"Good luck selling anything out of Killdeer though," he said without looking at her.

"Why do you say that?" she asked, incredulously.

"Since the oil boom, Killdeer has been overpopulated, and the city council refuses to issue building permits. Families can spend generations in an area like this, especially with the sort of wages the oil fields offer."

"So, people are reluctant to move or otherwise sell, and there is nothing new to buy," she added.

"Exactly. The opposite is true for Dickinson though. You'll probably have better luck down there if you can put up with the travel."

She seemed to consider that for a moment. "Do you think that'll change when the oil picks up again?"

"Who knows, maybe." He shrugged. "Man camps were a big deal north of Dickinson when workers couldn't find housing up here last time. Even then, the city only allowed a single apartment complex to be built. Crime spiked hard when that filled up too. The city might have learned their lesson from the last boom, but I doubt it."

She bit her lip in consideration for a minute before something caught her eye. "What is that?" She pointed at a brown mass along the fence line between two metal posts bent in toward each other.

Chase squinted over the steering wheel, peering through his glasses, struggling to get a better look while the massive truck lurched forward. "I'm not –" Wide-eyed realization struck him. "Oh, no."

He punched the accelerator, the whole cab bucking in response to the rugged terrain as we ascended near the crest of a hill. Almost by instinct, I lurched to the driver's side door, nearly striking my head on the ceiling from the truck going practically airborne before coming down hard on my seat.

In a flash, Chase flew out of the truck almost before coming to a complete stop, sprinting to the mass near the tailgate with me hot on his heels. He slid hard on his knees, his arms spread out in front of him, carefully examining the mass in evident horror. I still had no comprehension as to what was going on, merely following him by sheer instinct until I was right on top of it.

It was a young calf, its eyes wide in terror, foam building on its mouth through wheezing breaths after what must have been hours of struggle, pain, and exposure. Barbed wire wrapped itself tight around its throat, torso, and legs, drawing dark brown tendrils of dirt-caked blood where barbs ripped through its soft flesh.

Chase placed a calming palm on the calf's head, hushing it softly. The calf lurched at the touch, its hind legs half kicking as it wheezed a low, exhausted bellow; it was a sound that left my chest tight in breathlessness. Wordless understanding passed between Chase and I as we exchanged looks; this calf wasn't going to make it. Not unless we did something soon.

"I need wire cutters." He passed a hurried glance between Amber and I when she stumbled to a stop next to him.

"On it," I said, already on the move.

"And clean rags. I keep some under the back seat."

Amber shook herself from her stunned silence. "Okay, I'll get them."

I rushed up to the side of the truck and tried to vault into the bed mid-sprint, attempting to channel my inner parkour athlete.

It didn't work.

I swung my legs over to my right side, bracing myself over the ledge with my arms locked tight, but my hands slipped on the side rail, and I tumbled into the bed at a roll. Pain half blinded me when I cracked my head hard on the floor, but I scrambled with a groan to the two sets of wire cutters in a tool belt near the cab. Amber was looking up with concern from the back seat but continued to dig for the rags when I peered up to look at her. Wire cutters now in hand, I scrambled to the guardrail to make another daring leap but paused mid step.

The once panic-stricken animal fuming in its pain and exhaustion was now relaxed, docile, eyes blinking softly in its calm. Chase kneeled beside it with his eyes closed, one hand placed softly but firmly on its head, the other on its side. Both sat nearly motionless, save for Chase's noiseless chanting calming the calf. I sat frozen for merely a moment until Amber slammed the door, sending me over the rail like a runner to a gunshot, breaking Chase from his trance.

We reached the calf nearly at a sprint, Chase and I locking eyes as I handed him a pair of wire cutters. If he understood what I saw him do, I couldn't tell by his expression. "We need to cut away the wire," he explained, breathlessly. "Amber, can you cover these wounds when we do?"

"Yeah," she said, surprisingly calm. "I can do that."

We set to work without another word, cutting and twisting the wire away while Amber bandaged the wounds, careful not to catch ourselves on the barbs in the process. The calf, for its part, remained docile and mostly still during what should have been some of the more painful moments, barely wincing when we pulled the barbs from deep within its muscle and sinew.

Only once did the animal whine in pain when I pulled a strand away from its groin. Chase placed a hand on its head with a quiet whisper, calming the calf in an instant. Our eyes met when I released the calf from the strand, and a shade of guilt shadowed his expression. "We need to get her in the bed," he explained. "Amber, can you grab the blanket in the back seat and take it there?"

"Yeah" was all she said before she darted off.

Chase turned to me, doubt and quiet weariness weighing heavily on his expression. "We got this," I reassured him. "This isn't over yet; we can do this." His doubtful expression seemed to deepen, but he steeled himself just a little before giving me a nod. "Okay."

I'm not a world-class powerlifter or anything, but I'm not exactly frail or weak either. Since I'd been out of the military, I'd taken the time to lift weights and generally take care of myself, so lifting the one-hundred-and-fifty-or-so-pound calf and carrying it to the bed of the truck wasn't exactly an issue. Still, it unnerved me to an extent when I lifted the now quieted animal to the bed of the truck where Amber patiently waited with the blanket laid bare, a move that should have left it protesting in pain.

"I'll drive," Chase said, closing the tailgate. "There is a calving station nearby that should have what we need. Can you two tend the calf until we get there?"

Amber and I exchanged a glance. As concerned as she was, she definitely seemed calmer than Chase and I. "Yeah, we got this. Let's go."

Chase left without another word, racing to the cab of the truck while Amber and I fumbled for rags to cover the worst of the still exposed wounds.

The rags that we used to staunch the wounds were questionably clean at best, but that was the least of my concerns. I had to rapidly reach into the dark recesses of my mind on the fly to remember how to apply improvised pressure bandages, and then use them to apply pressure to a gunshot wound on the soldier's arm—

No, the calf…

I blinked and shook the image out of my vision, disturbed and revolted by the momentary flashback. A glance at Amber told me she didn't seem to notice anything amiss as she continued to cover a wound on the calf's neck. It was a subtle moment, I thought, so I took a breath to regain my composure, clearing my head before returning to my work.

Stress can be a useful tool if applied correctly, but it can also be invasive if you are not paying attention to it. It can attach itself to you like a tick, unfelt as it grows steadily, feeding on your calm, poisoning your mind with its disease. Imaginative minds such as mine can be particularly affected, strange things can happen to it if you are not careful.

This flashback wasn't too bad. Some are more invasive than others.

Some can make you feel like you are losing your mind.

We only had so many rags to work with, but some wounds were more superficial than others, so we focused on the more serious ones, a couple of which could have been life threatening if left alone. It was easy to see right away that not all the wounds could be covered, so Amber and I worked deliberately, communicating what we needed and what we were doing every step of the way.

Carefully evaluating as we worked, I pointed out that the humerus in its front right leg may have been broken, evidenced by a bulge showing near the top of the leg. Like I said before, I wasn't exactly a big ranch guy, but I learned early in my childhood from my ranch hand uncle that some breaks might mean the inevitable death of an animal. Amber knew this too; I could see the heartbreak in her expression.

"We need to splint this," I told her.

"Kyle…"

"I know, I know." I held up a hand defensively. "That isn't our call to make though, we should at least do what we can first."

Her expression was grim, but she nodded. "What can we use then?"

"All I see are a couple of rags and some fence posts."

She looked around for a moment, bracing herself against the rocking of the truck as we continued gingerly across the terrain before throwing aside the tool belt and grabbing hold of a long-handled wrench. "Will this work?"

"Well, it doesn't get much more improvised than that," I said, a little bemused. "Screw it, let's give it a shot."

I took the wrench from her and tightened it down with a rag above the break, nearly toppling over when the truck suddenly jolted. The calf raised its head, eyes open wide as it bellowed in pain. I carefully tied another rag on the bottom of the break, trying not to jostle the animal any more than I had to.

When I finished, Amber had leaned over the calf's head, gently stroking its muzzle to soothe it, and I found myself taken aback. "It's okay," she cooed, trying to meet its eyes with hers. It blinked as it let out a low whine of pain. "It's okay, little one, we'll take care of you. It's okay."

There was little more we could do for the calf, so I sat leaning against the rail, watching in amazement at the spectacle. It occurred to me then how incredibly calm and rational she was throughout this chaos. She never really froze, complained, or panicked like most people would, working thoughtfully and diligently in concert with Chase and I.

In moments of stress and chaos, you often see people as they truly are while the environment strips away their masks and pretenses, laying them bare for the world to see. I sat amazed at her strength of character, her grace and compassion as she gently tried to comfort and calm the poor calf like a mother would a child, knowing full well that it may have to be euthanized when this was over.

It can be easy to fall into a routine with someone you have been with for a while, but it can be immensely gratifying to see the reasons you fell in love with that person on full display.

I made no attempt to hide my admiration when our eyes met. "Hey." She smiled softly through tired eyes.

"Hey," I replied with a smile of my own.

"How are you?"

"I'm hanging in there. You?"

"I'm doing okay." Her kind expression floated back to the calf before reaching back up to me with a shade of worry. "Are you okay?"

"Yeah, I kind of banged my head a little on the bed chasing after those wire cutters," I said, rubbing my head. "It probably sounded worse than it was though." I gave her a nervous smile, hoping that was all she was referring to.

"That's not what I meant." Her eyes softened a little. "Are you still with me? Are you okay?"

I could feel my heart sink a little in my shame. "Yeah, I'm still me. I'm okay." I nodded reassuringly. "I didn't think you noticed."

I felt embarrassed, I hated talking about this sort of thing. It was always hard to open up about these flashbacks, even to her. Sometimes, especially to her.

"You sort of— "she bit her lower lip in consideration before continuing – o "disassociated a little. It didn't last long."

"I'm sorry, I–"

"No, don't," she interrupted. "Don't ever apologize for something like that. "You're safe now and I love you. I just want to make sure you understood that, and that you are still with me."

In truth, I felt weary. With time, you can almost figure out what triggers you. The operative word being "almost." It doesn't help that triggers can change too, sometimes into something completely random, making it difficult to see a flashback coming, making it particularly worrisome knowing that a bad episode could bring me closer to inadvertently waking up Asmodeus. Still, the more you learn to recognize your potential triggers, the easier it can sometimes be to avoid, or at least lessen the severity of the flashbacks. This one wasn't particularly bad; in fact, these flashbacks were becoming increasingly rare and less severe over time. But the flip side was that it made me feel even more like a hopeless failure anytime they came.

"Yes, love." I gave her an encouraging smile. "I'm still here, it's still me. I love you too."

"Good, I'd have to kick your ass otherwise," she said with a playful smile.

"You're welcome to try any time, love," I teased with a smile of my own.

"Yeah, yeah, okay." She laughed with an eye roll before craning her head over the rail behind her, looking toward the front. "Looks like we are getting close."

# Chapter 19

Chase slowed the truck to a stop in front of a large shack connecting several outdoor pens to a series of gates, flying to the tailgate as soon as we parked. "We need to get her inside," he said, the tailgate coming down with a crash. "How is she?"

"Not good, I think she broke a leg." I indicated the splint. "I think we stopped the worst of the bleeding though."

He grimaced, looking her over. "Okay, that's not good."

"No, not really," I said, looking over the calf too. "Do you have any poles or maybe a couple of broom handles lying around? I might be able to make this blanket into an improvised litter."

"I might have a couple of two-by-fours in the back." was his hurried response.

"Yes, grab those. I might be able to make that work."

"Okay, hang tight," he said before running off. He was back within a few seconds with a length of wood in each hand. The blanket was already folded in half under the calf, so the first board was easy to manage. We just had to place it between the folds. The other one took a little longer only because tying knots with blanket corners can be kind of awkward. The knots didn't need to be perfect though; they just needed to hold long enough to get the calf inside.

The knots nearly came undone when Chase and I took either end of the blanket litter and strained to take her to what looked like some kind of washing station in the back of the main room. Chase pulled a phone out of his pocket once we put down the litter by a drain set in the floor. "Amber, there is a fridge in the next room with a cooler full of antibiotics and some formula. I have a bottle in there too, it looks like a giant baby bottle. Could you grab those for me, please?"

"Sure," she said before hurrying to the only other door in the room.

"Can you call my dad and let him know what happened?" He handed me the phone with the screen already unlocked. I just had to hit the call button on the screen.

"Yeah, I'll be right back."

I stepped outside to make the call, but it rang for what seemed like an eternity before finally going to voicemail. Frustrated, I called again. Again, it rang without end while I tried to regain my calm. It wasn't his fault that we stumbled into this little emergency. Still, the call went to voicemail anyway, so I left a message before jabbing my finger onto the screen, hanging up in frustration before storming back into the calving station.

I wasn't able to practice magic for long after Asmodeus possessed me, so I wasn't going to claim to be some kind of expert on the matter; the exorcism saw to that. Still, the demon taught me enough to recognize it if I saw it. If I hadn't seen Chase channeling into the calf earlier, what I walked into might have taken me by more surprise than it did, though it was still enough to halt me at the door.

Chase had drawn a wide circle of water from the garden hose near the center of the room. The calf lay on its side, the focal point near the drain with Chase looming over it. Tendrils of water wound themselves in toward the calf from the outside circle, crawling up its hindquarters, its legs, and its head. Chase kneeled near its head with his eyes closed, chanting while he firmly held one hand over the calf's eyes, the other pouring a small stream from the garden hose over the broken leg.

The splint had already been removed, though the bulge from the break still showed clearly on its upper leg. Water trickled directly over the bulge making its steady splashing onto the ground the only noise I could hear, though I doubt I could have understood what Chase was saying if he'd been speaking loud enough to do so.

Suddenly, and with no warning, Chase grabbed the leg below the break with one hand and jerked the leg out while pushing in the bulge with the other. The leg snapped back into place with an audible crack, and Chase froze for a moment before coming back onto his heels.

All the calf did was blink.

I don't know if you've ever broken a bone, but it isn't exactly pleasant. Well, the breaking itself can be kind of hit or miss, but moving it after breaking it can bring forth a level of pain that can bring you to your knees. This calf should have been thrashing around screaming after Chase reset the break, but all it did was blink while I sat in the doorway, dumbstruck, watching the scene unfold before my eyes.

Chase kept pouring water onto the wounded leg, silently chanting, quickly losing his breath, and he soon dropped the hose on the floor next to him, catching himself from slumping forward onto the calf. Breathing heavily, he wiped his sweaty brow with a shaky hand before finally catching my eye.

Fatigued as he was, he sucked in a shaking breath in his surprise when he noticed me studying him, eyes wide in fear behind his glasses. A moment passed between us, my surprise transforming into understanding.

I realized he never intended for anyone to catch him using his magic. He must have sent Amber and I on our little errands intending to give himself space to perform without an audience, thinking he would've had enough time to save the calf's life with no one the wiser. Hell, if his father answered the call, there was a good chance that I would've been on the phone with him still.

"Is this what you wanted?" Amber burst into the room cradling a baby bottle as big as my thigh and a box of formula close to her chest. A little red cloth cooler swung from a strap at the crook of her elbow.

Chase passed a worried look from Amber, to me, and back again. "Y-yeah, could you mix up the formula for me, please? You can use the water from the hose."

"I couldn't get a hold of your father," I said as I joined them. "I left him a message letting him know what's going on though."

He gave me a quizzical look but continued, "That's okay. I don't think it's as bad as we thought."

"No?" I prompted.

"No," he said, pulling antibiotics and a syringe from the cooler. "She is a little dehydrated and malnourished, but with some food and a little bit of rest, I think she'll be okay."

Amber and I exchanged looks before she asked, "What about the leg?"

He shrugged as he prepped the syringe. "It was just a dislocation, albeit a bad one. I'll have to keep her in one of these pens until the leg is stable enough for her to roam again." He paused a moment while he plunged the antibiotics into the animal. "We'll just have to clean some of these scrapes first."

Blood-caked mud splashed onto the floor when Chase and I rinsed off the wounds. The calf suckled hungrily from the bottle with its head propped on Amber's leg while she gently stroked its nose, preemptively hushing the calf before we started peeling away the improvised bandages.

"Oh good," Chase chirped with relief. "These don't look so bad either."

Amber gave me a quiet smile that quickly changed when she saw my skepticism. "Really?" He gave me a concerned glance, he seemed to have sensed my skepticism as well. "She lost a hell of a lot of blood in the bed of that truck."

"True," he said with a nod, bringing his attention back to the calf. "These bandages really seemed to help. It's amazing how resilient these animals can be sometimes. I think we just need to rinse her off for now," he said, handing me the hose. "Mind taking over? I need to call my dad."

"Sure," I said, taking the hose.

I watched Chase carefully as he hurried out of the room, my mind racing through the possibilities until he walked outside, closing the door behind him.

"What's on your mind?" Amber asked, breaking me from my concentration.

"Does any of this seem weird to you?" I asked her.

"I mean, kind of. I've never saved a calf's life before." She pursed her lips thoughtfully. "How do you mean?"

"Look." I pointed out into a wide arc, drawing her attention to the water on the floor.

"A circle." She nodded, concluding with a frown.

"Right, you can use circles to draw in and focus magical energy. Do you remember how bad some of these cuts were bleeding?"

"Yeah." Her eyes got suddenly wide in realization. "You think he used magic to heal the calf?"

"I do, but I think he did more than that. Do you remember when you dislocated your arm playing volleyball in high school?"

"Yeah, it sucked." She winced. "It wasn't as bad as when I broke my foot in college though."

"Right, but do you remember how hard it was to load you into the car to take you to the hospital?"

She grew stiff in alarm, nodding for me to continue.

"I'm pretty sure I caught him using some sort of mind control magic to subdue the calf before we loaded her into the truck. I walked in on him using it again as he was setting the leg too."

"Oh my God," she said, putting the hose down by the drain. "I thought that violates one of the laws of magic?"

"It does if you use it on a human. I don't know how that works with animals though. Either way, it was probably the only way we were going to save the calf. With a small ranch like this, that might've been a big financial loss for them to lose a cow like that, even if it was just a calf."

"Why would he try to hide it from us then?"

I shrugged. "He probably doesn't know anything about our background. If he didn't think we were *normal*," I said, using air quotes, "he might not have bothered to try."

"Is he working with the Magistrate?" she said, glancing at the door.

"I don't know if he is yet," I said, following her gaze with mine. "It might be worth asking him, though."

The hollow croak of a raven sounded nearby when I stalked outside, closing the door behind me. Chase was gazing out into the pasture like he was looking for something but turned to give me a tired smile when he heard the door click closed, putting his phone in his pocket.

"Hey, how is she?" he asked wearily.

"Good, I think we are finished in there."

"Okay, good." He flashed me a tired grin. "Heck of a first day. It's pretty rare that we have to rescue a calf like that."

"Right." I chuckled. "I'm not even fully moved in and I'm already playing Superman."

"Well, I appreciate it." he said, snorting a laugh.

"Not a problem, Chase. That's why I'm here. I'm happy to help."

He gave me an appreciative nod. "We'll probably have to kennel the calf with her mother in one of these stalls for a few days." He looked out into the prairie again, searching. "I thought I saw her on the drive up here I sort of hoped she would've followed us, looking for her calf."

"I'm sure she'll be easy to find. By the way, that was a pretty interesting trick you used earlier to subdue the calf."

He looked at me suspiciously but shrugged. "I've helped raise every one of our cows since they were born. It's easy to make them compliant when they grow to trust you." He flashed me another one of his smiles. "You'll learn to do that too if you stay long enough."

"Right on." I nodded. "The way you healed her was pretty cool too. I've never seen anyone use magic like that before."

He dropped his smile. "What do you mean?"

"The way that you used water to draw a magic circle, and how you used that water to mend the break after you set it. Or how you used it to clot some of her wounds." His eyes grew wide in fear, but he didn't try to deny what I was saying. "It's just that I've never seen anything like that before. But then again, I've never seen mind-control magic performed either."

"Wow." He held up his hands defensively. "I've never used that on a person before. I didn't break any of the laws of magic."

"Relax." I held up a hand, trying to calm him. "I'm not exactly with the Society. I can't imagine that I would be so friendly about it if I was."

"I guess not," he said, lowering his hand suspiciously. "Who are you then? What do you know about magic?" I noticed he was still tense, like a rabbit ready to bolt.

I hooked my thumbs through my belt, tying to come off as unthreatening as possible, for all the good it did. I'm not exactly a small guy. "To be honest, I'm not really much of a practitioner. I'm actually kind of a nobody, really." He nodded a little bit, though he still looked fairly unsure. "I'm told that my parents were fairly well known though, albeit probably not for the best of reasons."

"Okay?" He nodded again for me to continue.

"My mother was Miriam McAllister." His eyes shot open in near-instant recognition, leaving him at a loss of words. "Some people knew her as Miriam, the Blood Witch."

He took a sharp breath in fear, taking a stuttering step away from me. I held up a hand bidding him to stop. "My parents cut ties with the Magistrate after the war and went into hiding, long before I was even born. I don't even recall them ever practicing magic before they passed away either." He didn't exactly bolt, but his expression deepened with suspicion.

"I'm not a member of the Magistrate, nor have I ever worked with them," I said, finally putting my hand down. "I was recently approached by a recruiter though."

His suspicion melded with curiosity. "Really?" he asked.

"Yeah, they are setting up a base of operations here. Have you heard anything about it?"

"No." He shook his head slowly.

"You sure?" I asked him flatly. "Not even from Lillian or that assistant of hers?" I paused for a moment, trying to remember his name. "Raymond?"

"What? N-no," he said, defensively putting a hand up again. "Why would she… No way… Are you saying she is Magistrate?"

"Yeah. Do you remember that meeting we had at her place with Allen and Raymond?"

"Yeah, and Silent John."

"Right," I scoffed, hardly believing that I almost forgot about *that* creepy bastard. "Do you remember when she took me into her office after the meeting?"

"Sure," he said, skepticism thick in his voice.

I told him about the meeting without excluding too many details. I told him what I learned about Lillian's relationship with my mother and the Magistrate. His eyes grew wide in horror when I told him about Lillian's and Raymond's special "talents," but remained silent when I told him about the grimoire. It wasn't until I concluded with the offer she made to me and what she planned to do with his family's ranch that he finally broke his silence.

"Oh my God." He gasped. He took his hat off to run a hand through his hair, gazing at the ground while he sorted through everything that I told him. "She offered to help me pay for the ranch." He shot me a glance before he started pacing angrily. "She can't do it though. My family stayed neutral in the war. We didn't have a choice. We had to, and they knew that."

I wasn't going to interrupt his storming around, but I made a mental note to ask him about that last little tidbit later.

But that's when he stopped short, suddenly wide-eyed. "And they have the entire Blood Witch's Codex?"

It was my turn to be surprised. "The what?"

"Your mother's grimoires," he elaborated. "The Blood Witch's Codex."

"Ah, yeah," I said with a nod. "That's what she said."

"And Donald McAllister too… Jesus," he swore, putting on his hat. "We need to tell my dad."

# Chapter 20

"It was pretty bold of you"—she rolled her hand as she spoke— "to just walk up and ask him like that."

"Ask him what?"

"About his magic," she clarified. "How did you know he wasn't Magistrate or something?"

"I guess I didn't." I shrugged. "But, I mean, they're trying to recruit us. I didn't see any harm in being up front about it."

"I guess not." She shrugged from the passenger seat, monitoring the road ahead. I spared her a glance, a little confused about the sudden show of aggression. I decided not to push it though, there wasn't any sense in spilling blood into the water right before meeting Chase's father.

The Landreth family farmhouse wasn't far from the old white home we would stay in. The mile or so drive left little time for us to chat as we followed Chase up the road. Not that we needed to follow him; it was easy to find. A newly built barn off to the south side of the road with a pen full of goats served as a landmark for a winding gravel driveway mostly concealed by a row of trees. The driveway split at the end, the mountain looming like a sentinel over a hay barn connected to a pen with horses on the left bend, the right leading to a single-story home nestled into the side of a hill.

"This is cute," Amber said, admiring the scenery. "It sort of reminds me of the mountains back home."

"Sort of," I said, a little amused. "I remember those mountains being a little bigger though."

"I mean, yeah. It's like a little mini-Bighorn." She flashed a wolfish smile, nearly pinching a pointer finger and thumb together.

"Or a teeny tiny Teton." I laughed.

We crunched our way up to the middle door of the three-stall garage connected to the left side of the home, parking between Chase's lifted Chevy and a skid steer at the far end. The hill the house sat on sloped sharply down below a white-painted deck that wrapped itself around the right side of the house, exposing a sliding glass door below the deck leading into the basement.

Chase waited for us to park before getting out of his truck, greeting us with an exhausted grin. "Looks like the old man already has the grill going," he said, pointing to the silver beast blowing smoke on the deck next to a couple of metal chairs. "He must be inside getting everything ready. Don't mind the dogs in the mudroom. They are more likely to lick you to death than they are to bite you."

"What kind of dogs are they?" Amber asked, following closely behind Chase, who led us to the main door of the house.

"Just a couple of old blue heelers," he said, pausing at the door. "They're mainly working dogs, but they're very friendly."

Nothing could have prepared us for what came next.

Poor Amber took the brunt of the assault. A tidal wave of fur skittered across the concrete floor from the other end of the mudroom, colliding into our shins in a cacophony of excited barking and whimpers, halting us at the door before we could close it. Paws pinned us to the walls, tongues lashed out at our hands, and we bent down to reflexively rub their attached heads.

But damn them, they were too good.

Poor Amber went down first as one of the fur assassins rolled over to its back at the touch, pleading with her to join him. Amber sank down into the rolling mass like a ship sinking beneath the waves, laughing and cooing her complete lack of distress along the way. Absent my friend, it wasn't long before I sank down to join her into the deep, chasing after the dog's exposed underbelly myself.

I found the dog's chest with my hands, rubbing with immense satisfaction and vigor to the glee of the animal, who writhed and whimpered in my grip. The trap was sprung; the very dog that overtook Amber whipped its head around to meet my ear with its wet nose, only to lick the lobe it had so cleverly sought after.

We never stood a chance.

It was Chase who saved us from the fury, clapping as he called for the attention of the pack of three to bring them into a set of kennels in the back. Dutifully, they heeded his call and scurried to their individual cages, leaving Amber and I to follow Chase through the main door leading into the home's interior with elated smiles on all our faces.

Chase quickly led us past a laundry closet and down a short hallway made mostly of a couple of doors for bedrooms and a bathroom before the hallway opened into a large kitchen with an island set in its center. Beyond the island stood a large wooden dining table directly to the left of the sliding glass door leading to the deck. There wasn't anything separating the living room from the dining room to the left of the table except a couple of old leather chairs that faced the television set, though a large wooden door on the far wall presumably leading to the master suite served as a midpoint between the two.

Everything in the kitchen, from the granite countertops, to the appliances and the painted walls seemed to be fairly new; or at the very least, no more than a decade old. Even so, everything seemed well worn and used. There were heavy scrapes and flecks of mud on the tiled floor, marred by the sort of heavy cowboy boots Chase seemed to be fond of. Though I wouldn't exactly call it a chaotic mess, most of the counter space was covered by dishes, tools, and a pile of paperwork.

Pictures adorned the walls throughout the house, some in color, some in black and white, nearly all of them showing the ranch and its various inhabitants in various stages of their lives. As new, or at least as renovated as everything was, it gave off a cozy and warm feeling that even made a stranger like me feel sort of at home.

Chase went to open one cabinet near the kitchen sink but paused before looking at us. "You guys want a beer, a glass of water, or anything?"

"I would love a glass of water," I said after Amber declined.

Chase pulled a couple of glasses out of the cabinet as an older man, somewhere in his mid-fifties, stepped out of the master bedroom with an expectant grin.

"Oh, hello there. I thought I heard someone coming in." his cowboy boots thudded across the tile floor as he stepped into the kitchen with an outstretched hand. "So, you must be Kyle and Amber."

"That's us," I said, taking his firm grip fully into my own. "It's good to finally meet you, Mr. Landreth."

He stood nearly six feet tall in his blue jeans and button-up flannel shirt, and moved like someone in their mid-thirties in spite of his age. Piercing blue eyes shone through rimmed glasses, though he brimmed with cheer. A thick, but neatly trimmed white mustache danced on top of his upper lip as he spoke.

"It's good to meet you too, Kyle. No need to be so formal though, I'm just a simple rancher," he said, with an energetic and wholehearted smile. I was already beginning to see where Chase got his cheery demeanor from. The concept of "North Dakota nice" was definitely a tangible thing, but some people seemed to be bred with it. "My name is Walter, but most people call me Walt."

"It's good to meet you, Walt," Amber said, mirroring his excitement as she shook his hand. "Thanks for the invitation, you have such a beautiful home."

"Thank you." He replied warmly. "I've been meaning to meet with Kyle for a while now, but we kept missing each other."

"Perks of being on the school board, I suppose," I supplied.

"Yeah, well, it's been a mess over there lately," he said with a shrug and a nod. "But I'm glad you made it over and I hope you brought your appetites. How do you like your steaks?"

"Medium-rare, please. Is there anything I can do to help?" I asked.

"No, we got it. All that we ask is that you enjoy yourself," he said before giving Amber a nod.

"Medium-rare too, please," she said with a smile.

Walt nodded his approval. "Well, I better go check on them then. Chase, mind getting the table set?"

"Yeah, I got it," Chase said, setting our water glasses on the counter as Walt hurried onto the deck.

"Hey, Chase," I said after a moment. "Are these anything like the steaks you brought to Lillian's party?"

He was just about to pull some plates from another cabinet before pausing to consider. "I think these ones are a little bigger, actually."

"Dang," I said, earning a quizzical glance from Amber. I felt myself grinning at her, "You are in for a treat."

# Chapter 21

"I heard you guys had an exciting day today," Walter said as we finished setting the table.

It was a great spread for the four of us. Steaks nearly the size of our dinner plates were stacked like a mountain in the center of the table. Dishes full of mashed potatoes, asparagus, brussels sprouts, biscuits, and gravy adorned the rest of the space between us. It was hard to be patient with the smell of it all assaulting the senses, distracting us from the chaos of the day that left us practically starving.

"You could say that," I said, sitting down in one of the seats against the wall. "We found a calf tangled in barbed wire while we were fencing. It was hurt pretty bad; I wasn't sure if it was going to make it. Chase took charge though, and we managed to save it."

Chase gave me an uncertain look from the chair opposite mine, like he wasn't prepared to address the elephant in the room. Walter, on the other hand, brimmed with pride as he took a seat next to his son.

"Well, I'm glad everything worked out then," Walter said, folding his hands on the table. "Shall we pray?" I exchanged a look with Amber, who was sitting to my right, though we didn't say anything. We simply bowed our heads respectfully.

It's not as though we didn't believe in God or the afterlife. My father was Irish Catholic, and he strongly encouraged the faith, though it was never forcefully imposed. He was practically my hero growing up, so it was natural for me to take the practice to heart. My devotion didn't last long when I left home, but I never fully abandoned my faith either.

It is sometimes said that there are no atheists in a foxhole, but in my experience, that wasn't always true. Sometimes people find their faith in war, or their faith may further solidify as a way for them to cope with the stress of combat. I would never want to take that from anyone. The world can be cruel enough without having to take someone's spiritual security blanket away from them by force.

But for some people, war can leave them questioning.

Amber's story wasn't quite so dramatic, though I would hesitate to say that it was any less traumatic. Her drunken, abusive father often tried to force his faith on her.

Religion can be less of a comfort when it serves as a reminder of your abuser.

Still, we bowed our heads respectfully, my heart growing heavy over Walter's reciting of the Lord's Prayer.

"Help yourself, folks." Walter exclaimed, beaming when he finished. "We only have one rule when it comes to supper time. If you leave hungry, it's your fault."

"Thank you, we appreciate it." Amber half giggled. "I've never actually visited this side of the state. It's beautiful here. How long have you all lived in the area?"

He looked at her over his glasses with a smile, somehow managing to fit a serving of potatoes beside his massive steak. "Well, I would be the fourth generation of Landreth to own the ranch. If memory serves, we settled this area in 1907 after my family came to America from Scandinavia."

"Wow," I exclaimed. "How old is the other ranch house then?"

"Oh, that was built in the early seventies. I was still a kid when they finished that one. We were barely living in anything more than a shack before that." Turning in his seat, he looked over a handful of photos in the kitchen, searching through them until he finally pointed at one near the end. "Matter of fact, it's that one over there."

We all turned our attention to the old black-and-white photo on the wall. To call it a shed would be a compliment, though. It was small, maybe holding a couple of rooms at most, and it looked like it was only just tall enough for someone like Walter to stand in, if only just barely. Even in the old black-and-white photo, the little home looked old with the siding practically falling off in some places, and visible cracks in the one window showing in the picture.

"That right there is the original home my family built when we moved here to homestead," Walter explained.

I could almost feel my eyebrows shoot up into the ceiling. "Your whole family lived in that?"

"Yes, sir. My folks along with my two brothers and I grew up in that tiny, little space, right up until my father built that one right next to it." He gestured to a picture of the old white house Amber and I would soon move into. "We tore that old shed down as soon as that house was built, which was all well and good. It was practically condemned by then anyway."

Genuinely impressed as I was, I had little time to respond as Walter continued to regale us with the long version of his family history.

He spoke in depth about the long voyage his family took by boat to Boston and the long, harrowing journey through the frigid American wilderness into humble North Dakota. He went on about how his family was able to build up the ranch through the Homestead Act and how they could do so successfully in spite of the hellish blizzards and frigid cold.

Through photographs he had displayed on the wall, he introduced family members who fought in World War One, World War Two, and Korea. He even went as far as to fetch an old flintlock dueling pistol he proudly kept as a family heirloom, which I was more than excited to examine myself.

We finished our steaks long before his story trailed into the modern day, where he described how difficult it had been to run such a small ranch and raise a family in a modern economy. Though it must have been a struggle, the old retired teacher somehow managed to get by in spite of the difficulty, if just barely.

"What did you teach?" Amber asked over a glass of water.

"I was the shop teacher," Walt responded with an air of humble pride. "In a small town like this, you only really need one… or maybe two. I taught a range of subjects from wood working to welding, and even some minor automotive. I did that for a little over thirty years before I finally retired."

"So, you were teaching full-time while running a ranch? That's pretty impressive," Amber said with a slight nod of her head. "I can't imagine how you found the time to do all that."

"Well, I'll just say that I got really good at time management." Walter's smile widened, "I had a lot of help from Mrs. Landreth in the meantime, but the oil they found on our land made it easy to walk away from teaching once they started pumping."

"I'm sure that has been a bit of a relief," I added.

"It has. It's allowed me to spend a lot more time with my family." Chase looked up to meet his father's glance with a smile when Walter squeezed his shoulder. "It's allowed us to invest heavily in the ranch too, maybe even expand a little."

"Expand?" I asked, hoping he would elaborate.

"Well, sort of," Chase interjected. "A family who lives in Denver owns the southern lot; we just sort of rent it. We have been trying to negotiate a fair price to buy the lot, but we have always had issues with the negotiations."

"Right," Walt continued. "They recently had a couple of deaths in the family, so they are trying to sort out the land rights. The issue is that they could always kick us off of the lot and use it for themselves or sell it to someone else. If they did either, it would be the beginning of the end of the ranch."

"I see," I said, addressing Chase. "Is that why you wanted to work with Phoenix?"

"Yeah, for the most part." Chase's eyes seasoned with shame before he averted his gaze into the table and spoke. "I wanted to work with Phoenix so that I could pay for the ranch, just like Dad did with my granddad."

"Does Lillian know about all this?" I asked flatly.

"Yeah, she does."

"And she never told you about the training grounds?"

"No," he said quietly, shaking his head.

"But she did offer to help you buy the ranch, including the south lot, right?"

He nodded down at the table before finally looking up at me. "Yeah."

I took a moment to absorb this new information as it became all too obvious why Lillian chose this ranch for her training grounds and why she would want to go through Chase in particular. Why go through the effort of pushing herself, magically or otherwise, to do what she wanted when all she had to do was to make the right promises to save a family legacy? Ulterior motives or otherwise, it was hard to deny the effectiveness of that kind of sales pitch.

Not to mention that the physical location would have been nearly perfect. The wooded valley at the base of the mountain could practically hide an army, let alone a rebel training camp.

"Ah, training grounds?" Walter asked, shifting a confused look between his son and me. "What are you talking about?"

"Dad, there is something that I need to tell you," Chase said, giving me an uncertain look.

"Okay, what is it?" Walter asked, looking uncertain.

Chase's uncertain expression deepened as though unable to break the bad news to his father, practically beckoning me to do so for him. Not that I could blame him; it's never easy to confess one of your mistakes to your old man, regardless of how patient he is or how old you get. Being the son of an old cop, I think I know that about as well as anyone.

"Sir," I continued on Chase's behalf, "are you familiar with the United Magistrate?"

"Ah, what?" Walter asked, though I could see a hint of the apprehension he tried to conceal in his confused expression.

"We didn't know this before we were hired on, but the Magistrate seems to be using Phoenix as a means to siphon money into their organization." Any mirth in his expression, whether fake or otherwise, had disappeared almost completely. It was startling when contrasted with the warm demeanor from before. Still, I continued, "I believe they are trying to help Chase buy the ranch from you so they can use it to reignite the war with the Thirteen Pyres Society."

"Th-they can't do that." He balked, stuttering in his surprise. "First of all, who are you? How would you know something like that?"

"Well, I'm not exactly a practitioner, but the Magistrate did try to recruit me recently. Apparently, they want me to help them fight in their war."

"That doesn't make any sense," he said, skeptically. "If you aren't a practitioner, why would they want you to help them fight?"

"That's fair. In all honestly, I'm kind of a nobody, but it might make more sense if you were aware of who my parents were."

Amber sat quietly next to me, though she sat stiff as a board with tension, fighting to maintain her composure. I only really noticed when she took a slow, long gulp of water, giving me a sideways glance.

I made sure to fold my hands on the table in front of me, in plain view of Walter to see before I continued. "My mother was Miriam McAllister, commonly known as the Blood Witch."

His eyes grew wide in fear at the mention of my mother's name. He sat straighter, pressing his palms on the edge of the table like he was about to push off and bolt, his own words catching in his throat.

"Sir, please," I pleaded. "Like I said, I'm with neither the Magistrate, nor the Society."

"So… who are you with, then?" he asked, almost accusingly.

"I'm unaffiliated," I said, trying to soften my tone. "My mother stifled my powers when I was an infant to hide her identity and largely kept her past a secret. She died when I was a child and my father died nearly a decade ago. I only recently learned about their relationship with the Magistrate."

He seemed to relax a little, but he shifted a skeptical glance between Amber and I, nonetheless. "Stifling someone's powers isn't an easy thing to do, and it can be quite dangerous for the person you are trying to do that to. And to do that to your own child…" he said in disbelief, practically to himself. "What about you?" he asked finally, addressing Amber. "What is your connection to all this?"

Amber blinked in surprise and shrugged. "I guess that makes me the supportive fiancée."

"Oh, okay," Walter scoffed, removing his glasses and putting them on the table. He was clearly tense, and it seemed wise to give him a moment to sort things out while he rubbed his face in his hands. Amber, Chase, and I quietly shared a nervous look among ourselves, uncertain of what else to say until he gave me a bleary look over his hands, replacing his glasses.

"I just... I don't understand," Walter finally stated. "The Blood Witch's War practically annihilated the Magistrate. And who is this... Lillian? What does she want with the ranch?"

"Her name is Lillian Eldonna. She is working as some kind of liaison between Phoenix Energy and the Magistrate," I supplied.

Walter's eyebrows scrunched in concentration for a moment, but his expression quickly shifted into eye-opening fear. "My God, Lillian Eldonna..." he said, sinking into his chair. "The succubus... You really don't know what you got yourself into, do you?" he asked Chase, who practically wilted into his seat.

"Succubus, sir?" I asked, a little surprised. "Like, the sex demon?"

"Sort of, but not quite," he said, with the patience of an old professor. "There are different kinds of succubi, but a demon of lust possessed her and turned into one after the fourth stage."

"Fourth stage? How does that work, exactly?" Amber asked this time, though I was no less interested to find out.

Walter took a drink of water, taking a moment to consider what he was going to say before continuing. "Right, so there are four stages to a possession. The first stage is the only one that is involuntary. It's when the demon makes itself known to the potential victim."

"How does it do that?" Amber asked, giving me a sideways glance.

"It interferes with the auditory and visual systems of the brain, somehow," Walter explained. "It makes it so that it can communicate with you in such a way that nobody can see or hear it but you. After that, it needs your consent for the other three."

"What happens then?" Amber asked in a professional tone she sometimes used to hide apprehension. It was subtle; you might not have even recognized it if you didn't know her well enough to know better.

Walter regarded her though, with a hint of sadness. "The demon first welds its spirit with the victim's, so that they essentially become one. Then they do the same with the victim's body, and then finally, the mind. The victim becomes increasingly more magically powerful with each consecutive stage, but by the end of the final stage, the two become completely welded together and indistinguishable from one another in every way."

I never went into detail with Amber about how I became possessed. I only told her it happened when I was deployed to Iraq. It was hard to look her in the eyes in the middle of Walter's explanation. I couldn't bring myself to witness the pain inflicted by the betrayal.

"When you say 'weld,' do you mean, like, joining two pieces of metal together?" I asked, joining the sides of my two pinkies together.

"It's more like…" He paused, pursing his lips. "Damascus steel. If you join two different kinds of steel together in a forge and fold them a few hundred times, you might come up with some cool patterns in the steel, but it essentially becomes a single piece of hardened steel."

"And that's how Lillian became a succubus?" Amber asked. "By welding her mind, body, and spirit with this… lust demon?"

"That's right." he responded grimly. "She became fully possessed during the Blood Witch's War. As a matter of fact, it was rumored that even the Blood Witch herself had become partially possessed by the end of the war."

It was my turn to be taken by surprise. "But they were just rumors, right?"

He regarded me again with a degree of sadness, choosing his next words carefully. "Rumors, yes, but they were not entirely unfounded. Once the Society started to gain the upper hand, she drafted her Blood Witch's Codex for her disciples to follow in the event of her death in the war. When she lost the bulk of her disciples in the war, she became dispirited. She came upon a wealth of power that she never previously displayed before, becoming particularly found of her blood magic. Shortly after she finished drafting her grimoires, she disappeared with her books, along with your father and uncle."

I could feel myself going cold in spite of the summertime heat. The memories I had of my mother were few since she'd died when I was young, but neither she nor my father ever gave me any reason to believe they were influenced by a demon. It was hard enough to imagine that they could withhold their magical abilities from me, let alone a demonic possession.

"Is it possible to exorcise a demon when you are possessed?" Amber asked calmly, though not without worry.

"In the first stage, yes. Depending on the strength of the demon, you can sometimes even do it yourself," Walter said. "After that, it sort of depends."

"Could my mother have done it?" I asked.

"It depends on the strength of the demon, and the magical strength and willpower of the possessed," Walter answered with his teacher-like professionalism. "It never hurts to have some help by another practitioner either." Walter took a sip of water before continuing. "Once the demon becomes attached to your spirit though, or God forbid your body, getting rid of it usually means losing a part of yourself with it.

"If it's a lesser demon, though, it might not be that big of a deal. You can think of a lesser demon like a smaller demon that can only attach itself to a smaller portion of your soul. It might only take a small portion of you with it after the exorcism. In fact, you might be able to fully recover from it. But the stronger the demon…"

"The more of yourself you lose," Amber supplemented, no less distraught.

"Exactly," Walter said. "It's not unheard of for people to die in the process either. Once the possession reaches the fourth stage though, the welding of the minds, the practitioner is generally considered a lost cause."

I could feel a sinking feeling in my chest, my mind racing.

Was that how my mother died?

No, she died from a stroke.

Or was that just a cover up?

Was I a lost cause?

I'm not exactly a skilled practitioner and Asmodeus isn't exactly a lesser demon. Hell, she is mentioned in biblical texts, for Christ's sake. How could a non-magical jackass like myself possibly stand up to something like that?

Amber seemed to lose much of her composure, slouching in her chair, staring blankly into the half-filled glass she cradled in her hands. When she looked at me with a hopeless expression, I could only imagine what she was thinking.

"You mentioned something about training grounds?" Walter asked, breaking the silence. "What exactly did you mean by that?"

Amber, Chase, and I exchanged another look, though Chase seemed to intentionally avoid his father's heavy gaze. "I don't really know much, sir," I said after a slow exhale. "All I really know is what Lillian told me."

So, I told Walter about the night of the meeting at Lillian's estate. He managed to hold himself together now that I wasn't completely blindsiding him, though without saying anything, he seemed to take a keen interest when I mentioned Raymond Evans and Silent John. Much in the same way that I told Chase and Amber, I told him what I learned about Lillian's relationship with my parents and how my mother started the war by saving Lillian from the Magistrate. He sat in contemplative silence when I told him about my mother's grimoire, and his mostly stoic demeanor didn't really falter until I told him about Lillian's plan for the ranch and my role in those plans.

"They have to know that they can't do that though, not without serious consequences," Walter finally said.

"What makes you say that?" Amber asked.

"Because I am a member of The Thaumaturgic Order of the Freemasons," Walter said matter-of-factly, as if that should have explained everything.

"Freemason, sir?" I asked skeptically. "Like the cult?"

"No," he scoffed. "It's hardly a cult. My lodge acts as neutral arbitrators for disputes within the magical community, and liaisons between the magical and non-magical world."

"I see," I said, recalling my railroad days when the union I belonged to settled disputes with the railroad company through a third-party arbitrator. "So, if the Magistrate used your ranch as training grounds for the war, it would create a conflict of interest if your lodge wanted to arbitrate the dispute."

"Exactly," Walter said. "It would be like erasing The Geneva Convention in its entirety, and there would be no one to stop the Magistrate from committing their war crimes in their next war. The Freemasons would probably excommunicate my family before that happens, but that would still put the Magistrate in conflict with my lodge.

The Magistrate would essentially fight a two-front war at that point, since the Society would presumably fight against the Magistrate too."

"Not unless I bought the ranch first, Dad," Chase said, quietly. "I'm still not affiliated; my application hasn't been accepted yet."

"That would be the loophole, wouldn't it?" Walter said, regarding his son, who continued to avoid his gaze.

"What did you say to her offer?" Walter asked me finally.

"Well, I told her I would think about it," I told him bluntly.

Walter blinked in surprise. Even Chase regarded me with no absence of concern. "What is there to think about?" Walter asked.

"My family started a war to protect the sanctity of a young woman's life after she was found guilty of murder for killing a man in self-defense. And not just her life, but countless others who were presumably put to death in a kangaroo court for breaking laws they didn't even know existed, over what could have sometimes been considered accidents. Even after losing the war and going into hiding, my father still became a cop who was considered to be one of the most highly respected members in his department and loved within his community.

"My war-fighting days may be behind me, but I have to admit, that sort of thing speaks to me on a level that I can't even begin to describe. Sure, the Magistrate may seem shady as hell, but why would I not want to at least hear what my uncle has to say when he gets here?"

Walter regarded me with a strong, stoic expression, slowly nodding before he asked, "Are you going to be able to reconcile what The Magistrate and your family did in the last war while you are supporting them in this one?"

"I don't even know what they supposedly did," I said, defensively. "Every time I bring up my mother's name, people act like I am the spawn of the devil himself, but all I've heard is how my parents rose up against a tyrannical government entity to save innocent lives and lost in the process. So please, tell me, what am I supposed to reconcile with exactly?"

"Oof," Chase exclaimed, like he was taking a punch in the gut.

Walter, for his part, placed a steady hand on his son's shoulder, as if to indicate that Chase should stop himself from continuing. "You really don't know, do you?" he asked, genuinely, like the answer should have been obvious all along.

Which only pissed me off more.

"Know what?" I said behind clenched teeth.

Walter let out a shaky breath with closed eyes before looking back up at me. "Please wait here, there is something I need to show you." He stood up from the table and walked into the living room like a man carrying a great weight on his shoulders, taking his time down a flight of stairs that was concealed behind a half wall on the far side of the living room.

"I'm sorry, Kyle," Chase said, slumped into his chair. "This is so well known within the magical community; I forget sometimes that there are people who still don't know about it."

"About what?" I asked, exasperated.

He looked up at me with a sad expression behind his glasses. "I think it would be better for my father to tell you," he said delicately, finally, before looking down at his folded hands resting in his lap.

The warmth of Amber's touch grounded me, her fingers entwining with mine underneath the table. Her emerald eyes were filled with hope, and she gave me a gentle smile with a squeeze of her hand as if to say, *It'll be okay, I'm right here.* I squeezed gently in thanks, drawing myself closer to her while we waited for Walter to return.

We didn't have to wait long for Walter to come up the stairs with a large manila folder in hand. We waited in quiet anticipation when he laid the folder on the table without taking a seat, gripping the back of his chair as he stood.

"What I'm about to tell you isn't… going to be easy to hear," he said, without looking at me.

I hesitated to take the folder when I saw the inscription on the top right corner, where my uncle's name, Donald McAllister, was clearly written.

"There was a string of disappearances a few years ago during the last oil boom," he continued. "I developed this dossier when some of the bodies turned up."

Amber's hand squeezed in apprehension from under the table when I finally reached for the folder, drawing herself close to me when I placed it between us. I opened it to find the cover page which included a brief physical description and a clear photo of a man who looked not so dissimilar to my father. He was tall, six-foot-two according to the description. He looked much younger in the photo than I remembered, with an athletic build that was a little leaner than I remembered, at roughly two hundred pounds. His stern look was all too familiar though, with his piercing blue eyes, short-cropped brown hair, and neatly trimmed beard.

There was a brief description of his magical abilities as well.

Primary: Way of the body-favoring the elemental.

Secondary: Way of the mind-minor illusion evocation observed.

Weakness: Way of the spirit-little observed.

"It later turned out that those recent murders had nothing to do with your uncle," Walter said, as I looked through the dossier. "But the state of the bodies that were found bore some resemblance to others that were found in the war, and it made a lot of people within the Freemasonry worry that there might be some sort of resurgence within the Bakken."

A brief description of my uncle's history was outlined in the next couple of pages. Apparently, he was discovered, along with my father, by the Society after their powers manifested with puberty. After a forced apprenticeship, they were later indoctrinated into the Pyre Guard and quickly gained in both rank and influence. That was, of course, until they broke off from the Society to take part in what the dossier referred to as the Blood Witch's War.

"You're not entirely wrong about the Society and the questionable ways in which they administer justice. The Magistrate even tried to capitalize on it, billing themselves as liberators." Walter took his seat again before he continued, mournfully. "They might have even intended to be, at least initially… but all of that changed when they really started taking casualties."

I stopped reading when he took his seat, hanging on his every word. "That's when they started getting desperate. They recruited more than your conventional wizard and… well…" It was all he said before gesturing to the folder with a nod, beckoning me to continue with a worried sigh.

Amber's eyes were wide with worry, but the slight squeeze from under the table gave a clear signal too.

So, I turned the page.

The descriptions paired with the pictures in the following pages depicted the scenes in detail, although I didn't need to read them to understand what they were. The pictures themselves left little to the imagination in their graphic detail.

Several featured improvised torture chambers held in what could have been a basement within any family home. Some still held the broken and butchered bodies of the victims within Others only showed the bloody aftermath of the various misdeeds.

There were a few depictions of the classic Viking "blood eagle," the victim kneeling with their arms stretched out to their side, rope suspending them upright with their back torn open, their lungs resting on their shoulders. There were others, though, who were depicted in similar fashion, only they were suspended by their hands off the ground between trees.

There were more near the back of the folder depicting crucifixions, where the victims were then disemboweled and burned on the cross they were nailed too.

Some of the written descriptions were more detailed than others; a few included only the dates, locations, and the names of the victims depicted. It was obvious that some were taken after the bodies were found, while many were taken by the perpetrators themselves, who were sometimes depicted in all-black hooded cloaks with their faces covered in black balaclavas. These pictures annotated the names of the suspected assailants, my uncle's name being highlighted in every description.

In every photo, as gruesome as they were, it seemed obvious that each scene was meant to be discovered. To send a message. It didn't seem like there would be any other reason why the victims would be so obviously maimed or broken only to so easily be found, aside from general masochism.

It took a moment for me to recognize, in horrified realization, that some of the torture victims, and even some of the crucified, were much younger than many of the others around them. Some of the victims weren't even teenagers.

The message these people were trying to convey became completely clear. It was the same message the insurgents in Iraq would send to anyone who worked with us, though the methods they used were vastly different.

If you work with the enemy, we will kill you and destroy everything you know and love.

"This is ridiculous!" Amber exclaimed. "There is nothing here proving his family did any of this. "How can you sit here and tell me that this is his uncle when you can't even see their faces?"

"Keep looking, you are almost finished," Walter said, dourly.

With few pages left, I kept turning. I didn't have to look much farther to see what he was referring to.

It was another crucifixion, a black-and-white photo with a family of five hanging dead on the cross. Flames engulfed their bodies, and several black-clad individuals stood in the foreground. This time, however, their faces were revealed.

Amber's breath hitched, her voice catching in her throat. I could feel her shaky hand gripping mine hard under the table. She obviously recognized these shadowy individuals too.

The camera showed practically my whole family, along with others I couldn't recognize but whose names were clear. My mother carried a small rod, or it may have been a wand pointed down at her side. Her long dark hair spilled around her dark features and onto her chest, giving her a menacing look within her black hood. My uncle had a long, decorative staff planted firmly at his side next to her, and I even found Lillian in the picture, her arms crossed with a smug smile on her face.

It was seeing my father in the picture that hit me the hardest, though. He stood proudly next to my mother in the same type of black-hooded cloak, his old 1911 held loosely, but clearly by his side. It was impossible not to recognize. It was the same 1911 my father claimed was given to him by my mother in his early days in law enforcement. It was the same pistol he taught me how to shoot with, the same one he used to obsessively clean and care for any time it was so much as thought about.

It was the same pistol that I still sometimes trained with and obsessively cared for to this day. It was even occasionally used as my every day carry pistol when the days were cold and my clothes were baggy. It was the same one that was sitting in my little red truck on this very day.

My shaky hand turned, finally, to the last page, which briefly described a battle that had taken place on a beach near Charleston, South Carolina, shortly after the last picture was taken. According to the report, the United Magistrate had won the battle, but not without taking severe casualties, so much so that it was considered a turning point in the war. My family had soon disappeared, never to be seen or heard from again. It even theorized that my family had either been too seriously wounded to continue fighting or were killed outright in the battle.

"A Pyrrhic victory," I said, unable to hide the latent sorrow in my voice.

"Precisely," Walter said dourly.

I could all but feel a black hole sinking in the center of my chest. It was becoming harder and harder to maintain my composure with each shuddering breath as I concluded my reading, sinking into my chair.

"The Magistrate would often use these methods to draw away supporters from the Society and draw the Society itself into a fight," Walter began to explain.

"This is nonsense," Amber interrupted. "How can—"

I gripped her thigh to steady her, her surprised look landing on me hard. "Do you mind if I step outside for a moment?" I asked the group at large. "I think I need some fresh air to clear my mind."

"Of course," Walter said simply, without another word.

# Chapter 22

My body shivered with each shuddering breath in spite of the warm summer evening, my hands going numb, gripping hard onto the deck's wooden railing.

How could this have happened?

How could this even be possible?

How could this be my father, the man who coached my Little League and ran fund raisers?

My lips started to tingle, my head bowed with my face going numb, my eyes closed tight.

This was the man who taught me how to hunt, how to fish, how to swim.

I clenched my teeth, fighting hard against a throat that tried to suffocate me, swelling shut.

He taught me the value of selfless service, honor, integrity.

He was kind, never so much as raising his voice to anyone, while always fighting to be the first through the door to take down burglars or violent criminals.

My chest was constricting, doubling me over while I fought to breathe against a thousand-pound weight.

How was I supposed to believe that a man who'd dedicated his life to service, a man who'd sacrificed so much to literally save lives, would be the same man who could torch bodies nailed to a cross?

I was beginning to lose control of myself. I needed to take it back before I lost myself completely.

I pushed myself up from the railing, standing straight, forcing myself to take in shuddering breaths, pressing my tongue hard against the roof of my mouth, concentrating on slow and steady exhales.

One right after another… and then another… and then another.

Slowly, the tension eased from my shoulders, and eventually my arms. My breathing finally under my control, I drew my attention to the three small circles I'd lightly traced into the wooden railing. "Spirit bound inside of me, asleep forever you shall be," I mouthed quietly to myself with eyes closed.

Placebo or not, it was still something I could put my mind to, to put it at ease. I didn't feel like I had much else to hold on to anymore.

A cool breeze gently kissed my cheek, contrasting the warmth of the early summertime evening. I took it in, filling my lungs to completion while I beheld the majesty of the mountain looming over the woods, the valley, the ranchland before me. The moonlight casting itself across its rocky features in a break in the tree line left me marveling at its beauty, and for the briefest of moments, I thought, *It wouldn't be so bad, living in a place like this.*

I heard the sliding glass door close gently behind me, "Hey, are you okay?" Amber asked, walking up next to me.

"Yeah, I think so," I said with what I thought was a reassuring smile.

"Are you sure?" Her fingertips lightly traced the back of my arm. "You know you can talk to me."

"Yeah, I'm just trying to reclaim what little is left of my dignity." I tried for another smile. "I have that 'strong, stoic Indian' persona to maintain after all."

"Just as long as you are not like that with me," she added with an amused chuckle. "You don't believe any of this, do you?"

"Did you see the last picture in the folder?" I asked softly.

"Yeah, but it's just one picture. Pictures can be altered; it doesn't prove anything."

"Maybe, but they didn't exactly have Photoshop in the nineteen forties either." She pulled her hand away, hurt evident in her eyes. "Besides, it's a dossier. That's not supposed to provide proof of anything."

"So… what? Are you saying that you believe this crap?"

"I'm starting to think that it is not beyond the realm of possibility," I said softly, but sternly.

She startled in surprise. "How can you say that?" she said, taking a step back. "This is your family we are talking about."

"Yes, the same family who stifled my powers, this vital part of my identity, just so they could hide from the Society and their literal war crimes. I had to find out what I was on my own, as a full-grown adult, after a literal demon from the freaking Bible possessed me." I was far from shouting, but I knew that my voice had grown cold, my nerves beginning to fray again. "And then, what? They just–"

"You fucking killed him, Kyle," she nearly shouted, stopping me cold like a punch in the chest. "I was there, remember? Your father died trying to protect you, trying to save you from that demon. I watched you practically blow him apart, and you almost killed Don and I before he could stop you."

Her words were like ice water, stopping me cold, constricting my chest, leaving me nearly unable to speak. "That wasn't me," was all I could say, nearly at a whisper.

Not a day had gone by that I didn't remember the night of the exorcism. The heat of the fire, the smell of the smoke, the burning flesh, the sounds of voices pleading… all haunt my waking memories.

"Do you think I wanted this?" I asked, watching the hot anger melt into dreadful realization in her expression.

"Kyle, I –"

"Do you think I wanted to be an orphan?" I didn't raise my voice, but I couldn't keep the venom from the words that I spoke.

"Kyle, please."

"Everything I loved, everything that I knew and that gave me purpose burned away and died that day."

"Kyle, I know. Please, I'm sorry," she pleaded with hands raised between us defensively, as if to push me back. I've never yelled at her; I've certainly never struck her, nor would I. But every fiber of her being seemed to plead for me to seize control.

To stop myself. To see reason. "Please, I didn't mean that." Her voice shook with genuine concern… and fear. "I'm sorry."

A long silence stretched between us, filled only by a raven's *kraa* and wind sweeping through trees, until I finally turned away from her, gripping the railing tight. "Then you need to choose your next words carefully."

For a moment, she stood there, taking a steadying breath, before finally joining me at the railing. "I just think…" She bit her lip, regarding the mountain thoughtfully. "I don't know if it was the right thing to do, but I think they did what they did to protect you. I still think it is worth talking to your uncle about it when he gets here."

"I think we've waited long enough, Amber." There was no malice in my voice, but the hurt shone in her eyes anyway. "He has been gone for so long, and he left us with nothing more than vague warnings about these groups of people whom we couldn't possibly know of or learn anything about. It was only a matter of time before any of them found us, and they did."

"It's only a matter of time before the demon wakes up again too," she said, softly, finally meeting my eyes with her own. "What then? What if the Magistrate can help us?"

"What if what Walter says about them is true? I don't know if I could trust them." She let out a heavy, slow breath, but she didn't say anything. "She is a succubus," I continued. "Fully possessed by a demon, and she is with someone who turns people into literal zombies. Who is to say someone like that wouldn't try to convince me into taking sides with Asmodeus?"

"What do you suggest we do then? Keep running?" she asked, softly.

I just shook my head and looked toward the dining room table, where Walter and Chase seemed to be holding a heated discussion of their own.

"The Freemasons? Really?" She seemed exasperated. "We don't even know who these people are."

"What do we know about the United Magistrate? I've never exactly heard of the Freemasons burning entire families on the cross or dishing out blood eagles, have you?"

She lightly shook her head with a sigh. "We know your uncle, though," she said, folding her hands, leaning heavily on the railing. "It was your uncle Don who taught me how to ride a bike. He was the one who taught me how to ride a horse too. He helped me with my homework when my own father was too drunk to see straight. He took me in and protected me when my father would…" She closed her eyes from the pain of the memory and didn't continue. She didn't need too; I remembered the bruises all too well.

She hugged herself tight, collapsing into herself with a tear streaming down her cheek. I reached out to her, placing a hand softly on her shoulder in comfort. She stiffened but didn't pull away. "He was more of a father to me than my own father ever was. I don't know how I could turn away from him like that."

"I can only imagine how hard that must have been. I'm glad that he could've been there for you." She looked at me bleary-eyed as I gently took her hand into my own. "Really, I'm grateful for every single day that my family took you in, I can't imagine where we would be right now if they hadn't. These people that Uncle Don is working for though… I've seen this sort of thing before."

I had to take a steadying breath of my own, but she waited patiently for me to continue. "The torture chambers that we found in Iraq… filled with broken, mutilated bodies… some of them children…" She blinked in surprise, but I continued. "We don't know for sure if Uncle Don is actually working with the Magistrate right now, but these people… they sound like the sort of people I used to hunt down in Iraq. They sound like ISIS to me, but with magic.

"If the Magistrate is anything like what Walter says they are, then there is no way that I can work with them, let alone fight in their little war. Besides, like you said before…" I lightly rubbed my thumb over her claddagh for subtle emphasis, and she finally took my hand into hers. "We have a legacy to think of now."

"You never told me about your time in Iraq," she said, wiping a tear away.

"You're right, I don't think I ever did. I can sometime if you want me to."

"I would like that, but only if you want to," she said, squeezing my hand a little.

"I don't think we ever really talked about the fire either. Maybe we should when this is over."

"Yeah, I would like that." She glanced into the dining room. "Do you really think we can trust them?"

"I don't know, but I'm willing to explore that over the alternative."

"Yeah, okay," she said with a nod, biting her lip. "About the possession…"

"Yeah?"

"What stage are you in?"

"Stage II, cancer."

"Psh, screw you," she said, stepping into me, nuzzling my chest.

"Maybe later. I wouldn't exactly turn you down though," I teased as I enveloped her into my arms, though I earned a playful hit in the ribs for my efforts.

"I'm scared, Kyle."

"I know, I am too," I said, nuzzling my face into her mass of curly hair. "We'll get through it though, I promise."

The dining room table had already been cleared, save for our respective drinks, when we quietly returned to our seats. Chase sat in his seat, clearly vexed, but spared a quiet smile and a nod when we joined him while Walter placed the last of the dishes in the dishwasher.

"Are you okay?" Walter asked, looking up from his work.

"Yeah, sorry. That was a lot to take in," I said, before taking a long drink of water.

He nodded in understanding. "I'm sorry it had to come out like this. I'm sure that it was hard for you to hear."

"I only have one sticking point though," Amber interrupted. "Where is the evidence? How can you be certain that Kyle's family was involved in these so-called war crimes?"

Walter started the dishwasher and washed his hands before answering patiently. "Your skepticism is valid, all things considered." He dried his hands on a kitchen towel, walking back to join us. "My order works hard to insulate the general public from magical affairs, but I can assure you that there are whole archives and graveyards filled with all the evidence that you require."

"Is there any way the Freemasons can help us?" I chimed in.

That earned a suppressed look of surprise from both Chase and Walter. "How do you mean?" Walter asked.

"If these people are who you say they are, then I want nothing to do with them, let alone to involve myself in their little war. But I don't want to involve myself with the Thirteen Pyres Society either."

"So, you are asking for what? Some kind of sanctuary?"

Amber and I shared an uncertain look before I responded. "If something like that is possible, maybe."

"It's possible," Walter said, taking a moment to consider. "What you have to understand, though, is that I have to report on this. I don't really have a choice in the matter, and in the eyes of the Masons, you will already be directly involved with the Magistrate. All three of you." He glared at his son for a moment before continuing. "You would have to completely cut yourself off from them, almost publicly, before the Freemasons would even consider helping you." He tapped a finger on the table a couple of times while he considered further. "You might even be able to make an argument about coercion too. You have to at this point, actually, if my order is going to accept your claim."

"Okay." I said, and an idea all but came to me. "How soon will you have to report on this?"

"Soon," Walter responded pointedly. "I can't really put something like this off."

"Would the Society have access to the report?" I asked.

"Not directly, but they could request it if they wanted to."

"Okay," Chase chimed in this time, following my lead. "But wouldn't their names be stricken from the report if they managed to claim sanctuary beforehand?"

"Absolutely," Walter stated. "But how do you think you will be able pull that off?"

"Here is what I suggest," I said, pulling the invitation Chase gave me out of my back pocket and placing it on the table, drawing surprised looks from Chase and Walter in kind. "Start your report but hold off on submitting it until after the party on Friday. It's a grand opening celebration, so representatives from Phoenix Energy, who are non-magic-using civilians, should be there. We can cut ties with them simultaneously and you can submit your report and the claim for sanctuary as soon as we get back."

"That's risky, Kyle," Walter said, after a steadying breath. "Having civilians there might not be enough to protect you while you are there."

My thoughts drifted toward Silent John, and Lillian's silent "promise" to keep things under wraps. "M-hm." I nodded in otherwise silent understanding.

"It's about as good of an opportunity as any, Dad," Chase said. "I think it'll be risky regardless of how we do it, but having civilians there might at least serve as some kind of deterrent."

The three of us looked quietly to Amber for input, but she sat slumped in her chair, defeated, without sparing more than a glance between us. "Okay," she said finally, with a shrug. "Sure." I took her hand into mine under the table to comfort her, but it was a gesture she barely acknowledged.

"Okay." Walter nodded and said, finally, tiredly. "I'll get the paperwork started."

# Chapter 23
## Mosul, Iraq

The IED blast already knocked all the occupants within the courtyard prone, probably saving them from the rocket as it slammed into the ground among them. The Rangers on the ground immediately sprang to their feet, ushering prisoners and rescued hostages alike back into the compound just as a hail of gunfire erupted from the building kitty-corner left of ours.

But that simply wouldn't do.

Death blossomed from nearly all the open windows on our third floor, and some from the second, as a torrent of gunfire and tracers flashed into the structure across the street, guided by infrared lasers from individual weapon systems, providing badly needed cover fire for the shadowy figures below to reoccupy the building.

Rounds slammed into the brickwork like sledgehammers as Arrants thundered rounds from inside our room in response, light flashing like lightning from his machine gun within the nearly cramped space, with Locker firing right next to him.

"Control your team, I need to check on Ramirez!" I shouted at Locker through the gunfire, who gave me a thumbs-up to acknowledge.

Stepping out of the second room closest to the descending stairs, I made a beeline to the other end of the conference-room-turned-execution-chamber where I knew the other team was set up, nearly running into Ramirez's hulking form as he stepped out of a room near the stairs we'd descended from earlier.

"You guys good?" I shouted, offering him a thumb-up.

"Yeah, we're good." He shouted back. "We're taking heavy fire from the building kitty-corner left. There's an open area between that and the building to our front they keep trying to cross. Langston is knocking them down so far, but a couple almost made it."

"Locker has good eyes on that occupied building." I shouted above the noise. "That open area is Langston's primary, keep it locked down. We cannot let them cross into that other building."

"Roger that, we won't let them," he shouted before returning to the room he came from.

I turned to the shadowy form kneeling by the table near the window overlooking the rear parking lot, using the table as cover as he vigilantly kept a watchful eye for potential targets. "Albers." I shouted, and he turned to face me. "You good?"

"I'm good, Sergeant."

"What do you got?" I moved to join him.

"There were a handful of guys who tried to come in through the parking lot," he said, pointing toward the entryway. "Second squad took them down pretty fast though."

Looking to where Albers was pointing, I saw what looked like five bodies with weapons strewn about, no more than a couple of paces from the now open gate.

"Well, that's why they call it a fatal funnel," I said, with a pat on his shoulder. "Make sure you keep an eye on those buildings on the other side of the parking lot too."

"Rah, Sergeant," he said, returning his attention to the window.

"Goodwin," Lieutenant Wilkins huffed, out of breath from running up the stairs. "What is your situation?"

"This way, sir." I led him into an unmanned room between my two teams, noting a desk pushed against a wall as I kicked aside debris and a sleeping bag approaching the shattered window.

We were still being decisively engaged by the enemy, though we seemed to have gained some semblance of fire superiority as we continued to play tennis with bullets over the courtyard and across the street. Enemy rounds slammed into the walls around the outside of the window, but the lieutenant, to his credit, calmly and patiently listened with calculated intent while I briefly explained the situation.

"Has anyone occupied that building directly ahead of us?" he shouted above the noise.

"Not that I can tell, sir, but they keep trying to send guys over from the building to the left."

"Overwatch is kitty-corner right," he continued with a nod. "The other Strykers are getting pounded right now, but they will be here soon. I need you to cover Overwatch and their movement to that center building so we can secure that downed Stryker."

That made sense. If the enemy managed to gain a foothold in the center building, Overwatch would be all but cut off from us and left out to dry while the ruined Stryker on the other side of the courtyard would be left at the mercy of the enemy. But if Overwatch made it to the center building, they would have enough firepower to fend off the attackers while also being better positioned to secure the wreckage. We might even be able to send over a team to plus up their numbers if we needed to.

"You got it, sir, what about close air support–"

The whomp of a sudden explosion shook the floor beneath our feet following a flash that briefly lit up the night sky. The lieutenant and I both reflexively braced a hand on the walls beside us.

"Jesus," I cursed, just as a torrent of gunfire cracked through the open window, slamming into the wall on the other side of the room.

"Viper 1-6, this is 1-4 Victor."

I could see the look of shock beneath the green glow of the lieutenant's night vision when the sergeant in charge of the Stryker came over the radio. "This is Viper 1-6, send it," he calmly responded, despite his obvious stress.

"Viper 1-6, we were hit by a VBIED. We are alive and okay, but immobile, over."

VBIED is short form for "Vehicle Born Improvised Explosive Device." They are vehicles laden with explosives, such as mortar rounds or artillery shells, sometimes driven by suicide bombers, often creating devastating explosions causing incredible damage to whatever is nearby. They are not always driven though. In cities, they can sometimes be found unoccupied along the side of the road, waiting for an unsuspecting victim to walk or drive by.

The lieutenant and I exchanged an astonished look. IEDs and VBIEDs were common. You did everything you could to avoid them, of course, but they were seen frequently enough that we'd practiced drills that we repeatedly rehearsed in the event that we were hit by one. But to see one used in a complex counterattack like this was practically unheard of, especially at this later stage in the war.

A cold chill ran down my spine as I recalled the words of the specter from the day before. *They mean to bog you down, to overwhelm you.*

"Roger that, 1-4 Victor," the lieutenant said into the radio. "I'm sending another vehicle to support you. Hang tight, we'll be there soon." He took a breath before addressing me directly. "Our first priority is to secure this downed Stryker in the courtyard. I need you to cover Overwatch as they move into that center building. Once they are set, we may have to send either you or second squad to support 1-4 Victor."

"Yes, sir, what about close air support?"

"CAS was pulled away last minute. They'll be here in about twenty minutes. We have a quick reaction force on their way too, but they might not get here until after CAS," he said grimly.

"You got it, sir, we'll handle it," I said with more confidence than I felt.

"Overwatch, this is Viper 1-6," the lieutenant called over the radio as he left the room and rushed down the stairs. I didn't care enough to listen to a response. I instead called my team leaders to join me in the conference room.

It was hard to see their expressions, even with the enhancement of the night vision goggles, but I didn't need it to gauge their moods. I could see the stoic and physically imposing form of Ramirez's body slowly stiffen in apprehension as I explained away the situation. Locker, who was a little more animated, shifted from one foot to the other.

"I don't know if we have twenty minutes, Sergeant," Locker said, shaking his head.

"We're going to have to find it," I told him sternly. "If Overwatch can take that center building, we can hold out until our support arrives. Just control your teams. Suppress the hell out of that occupied building and kill anything that moves in that open area. Move Arrants and his SAW into that center room for better coverage if you have too —"

The window next to the table exploded into the conference room, throwing glass shards across the room as rounds punched into the walls around us. "Jesus!" Locker cursed as we ducked under the incoming gunfire for cover. Albers, who had ducked out of the way of the initial volley, took a knee by the table and returned fire with his green laser guiding his aim over the parking lot.

"That's for second squad to worry about." I shouted over Albers's concussive furry. "Cover for Overwatch and kill these fucking bastards."

"Roger that!" Locker shouted as they broke off to control their teams.

Keeping clear of the window, I moved over to Albers to take in his situation. "What do you got?" I shouted over his shoulder, watching lasers from the second floor dance across the face of the buildings on the other side of the parking lot, chasing after muzzle flashes as they erupted from its various windows.

"That whole building just lit us up, Sergeant." Albers shouted as he loaded a fresh magazine into his M4. "I think they might try to push into the parking lot again."

"Alright, keep an eye on it for now," I said, placing a steadying hand on his shoulder. "Watch your ammo, we might be here a while."

"Roger, Sergeant," he responded and started taking slower, more precise shots.

Moving back toward the line of office rooms, I saw Locker had already moved himself and Arrants into the room the lieutenant and I had previously occupied, his two riflemen occupying their own separate rooms to their right. Ramirez was with Langston, who was laying absolute hate with his SAW, occupying the farthest left room. So I moved into the room Watson occupied, careful not to trip over the legs of the dead insurgent who lay next to a table that bisected the room.

I found myself grateful for the building's sturdy brick walls when more rounds punched into them from outside near the windows, further contributing to the melody of battle. Watson, to his credit, took controlled, methodical shots from inside the room, his laser punching out to chase muzzle flashes across the street with each shot.

"How are you doing, Watson?" I asked, peering out the window next to him.

"Good so far, Sergeant," he said without looking at me, keeping his weapon at the high ready in spite of the added weight the M-203 grenade launcher mounted to the bottom of the barrel of his M4. "They are still taking plenty of shots, but the shooting has slowed down a little."

"Did Ramirez tell you what's going on?" I asked, taking in the scene. This room held a better vantage point from the rooms I had occupied before, and I could see that the open area between the middle building and the occupied one wasn't a large space either. It could have acted as a simple courtyard if it were fenced in, and the sight of it left me nearly astonished. These Rangers had to have been quick on the trigger to knock insurgents down before they could reach the middle building, but that didn't seem to stop them from planting nearly a dozen bodies into that open ground.

"Roger, we're covering Overwatch so they can take that center building."

"Yeah, any sign of them yet?"

"I just watched them leave the rooftop on the building to the right," he said, pointing through the window. "That's about it though, but we should see them soon."

From our vantage point, we could mostly see into the smaller courtyards walled off between the center building and the building Overwatch occupied, though there was a small walkway between the two courtyards leading from the street into the alley behind the buildings.

Shadowy figures assembled on the rooftop of the center building from the stairway near the back, creeping to the walls on the outer ledges.

"Holy shit, is that Overwatch?" Watson cursed beside me.

That didn't make sense. Taking the alley would have left them exposed to the enemy with no actual way for us to cover them, let alone see them. I would have expected them to come out of the front of the building, through the courtyard, and possibly into the street where we could better cover their movements.

"No way," I said, and as if on cue, men poured out the front door of the building Overwatch occupied. The rooftop on the center building erupted into gunfire as a rocket-propelled grenade launched into the side of the building Overwatch flowed out of, sending Rangers scrambling for cover behind the walls of the courtyard.

"Watson, lob a grenade onto that rooftop!" I shouted, lighting up targets with the laser from my rifle, punching rounds into the enemy across the street. Lasers from nearly every window on my third floor wiped to the rooftop of the middle building, following my own, just as nearly every window of the middle building sparkled with muzzle flashes, sending a hailstorm of rifle fire back at us.

"Viper 1-6, this is 1-1." I shouted into the radio, pulling back from the window. "The enemy has occupied the center building to our twelve. Overwatch is pinned down and cut off, over."

The radio crackled to life as numerous transmissions tried to push through at once. I had no way of knowing if the lieutenant heard what I said. I didn't think he needed to.

Watson's M-203 thumped as he sent a grenade into the chaos of the rooftop, but it seemed to make little difference. We were engaged by two buildings at once on this side of our compound alone. Nearly an entire squad of Rangers were caught out in the open in front of us, helplessly clinging to what little cover they could find behind a fragile concrete wall while we desperately fought to provide what little covering fire we could.

My heart sank in my chest, and I could all but hear that specter's voice ring in my memory once more: *They mean to bring that building down around you, to make it into your grave.*

Watson wasn't exactly a big guy, but he was quick, agile, and fairly strong for his size. I didn't see it coming when he shoulder-checked me, my hips slamming into the desk as I toppled over it.

Something hit me.

I didn't know what it was, but it hit me like a truck; everywhere, all at once.

I hit the ground. Hard.

Everything went quiet.

Dark.

# Chapter 24

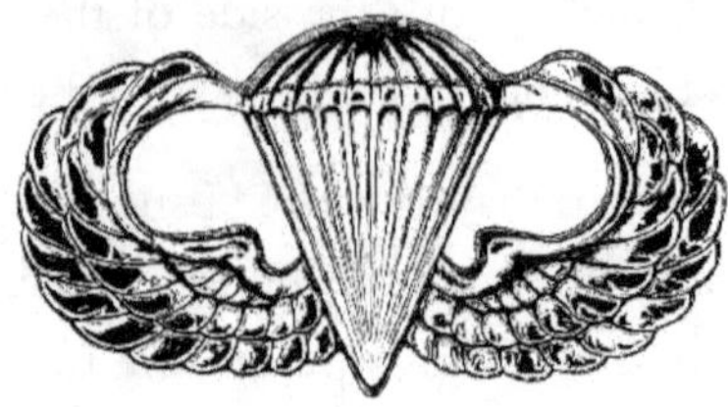

It's hard to overcome fear, though I doubt you would be shocked to learn that.

I once had a fear of falling, not at all to be confused with a fear of heights. In fact, there were moments growing up near the mountains in Wyoming, where I stood at the edge of a cliff reaching hundreds of feet into the air, feeding on the thrill of the danger as my toes reached out toward its precipice—a flightless ending should a strong enough wind have taken me just right.

God help me though if I stood on a wobbly stool, where the sensation of falling constricted my innards, sending me toppling into a panic.

It was in Airborne School where I learned how to overcome that particular fear.

The three-week school is broken up into phases, and you are required to jump off progressively higher platforms with each phase. Granted, you are strapped to a harness that slows your fall if you jump off anything higher than knee height, so you are never truly falling.

That is, until the final week, when you are required to jump out of a perfectly good airplane in flight.

Five times.

The lead-up to it was fine. The only thing that ever really intimidated me was the rappel tower, but that quickly evaporated when I had instructors practically yelling in my face to get into my harness and jump off the platform. It wasn't until the day that I finally had to jump out of a C-130 in flight that it really started to hit me, and I was barely strapped into my parachute and reserve when it did.

Rows of wooden benches filled the hangar. The roar of airplane engines from outside could be heard above the noise of the hundreds of paratroopers seated within. It seemed busy at first, the jump-masters feverishly shouting instructions as I quickly donned my parachute for the first time, only for the chaos to subside once they checked to make sure I had put everything on correctly.

The hours sitting on those hard wood benches didn't help to calm my mind either. The weeks leading up to it were chock-full of stories from the instructors lamenting the perils of an airborne operation, how it was not uncommon for someone to land concussed with a head injury, broken legs, a broken back, or God forbid died. There is even a popular cadence about one unfortunate soul who died on a jump, lovingly referred to as "Blood on the Risers." They also made it a point to tell you, nearly every single day, that the school was an all-volunteer course, and you could quit at any time.

I could always recall how the noise of the C-130's powerful engines seemed to howl like specters from outside the hangar, triggering adrenaline cascades through me as time ticked endlessly by on those benches. The slow, steady breaths I took only seemed to add to the anxiety, while thoughts of the inevitable leap of faith loomed ominously in my mind, threatening to steal my courage away from me.

Finally, the instructors told us to stand and load, single file, onto the bird.

I knew I could quit at any time, even then, at that moment. It would be as simple as taking off my harness and refusing to jump. They would send me to a leg unit where I wouldn't have to worry about jumping again; I would be okay. But that's not what I wanted. I knew that if I wanted to be at my best, I needed to be among the best. I needed to be airborne. I needed to be a Ranger. I needed to accept my fate.

*But how?* I thought as the wash of the aircraft's enormous engines rushed into me, the file of paratroopers lining up behind the open ramp to get counted on. *When?*

I also knew that, once I stepped onto the ramp, there wasn't really a way for me to turn back. Not really, not without enduring some serious consequences. "It has to be now," I told myself. "It'll be my own little *point of no return*, I just have to make it onto the ramp."

The hundred or so yards it took to walk to the ramp felt like a mile, the warm rush of the wash threatening to blow me away, the cacophony of noise threatening to deafen me, step by step, until I finally took that fateful step.

The fear didn't subside so much as I was able to accept whatever would happen from that step forward. Whether I would be okay, broke a bone, or landed in a heap of my own gore, I was going to take this leap of faith and accept my fate.

It was a practice that I took with me wherever I went, both while serving in the Army and outside of it. Anytime I found myself in a particularly fearful situation, where I wasn't sure if I would make it out unhurt or alive, I would set my "point of no return" and accept whatever this world would hold for me on the other side.

To this day, that is still one of the best jumps that I ever had.

# Chapter 25

I sat at the kitchen table and waited, fidgeting with an old folding knife I found in one of the few boxes remaining in the apartment, failing to keep my frayed nerves at bay while Amber dressed in the other room for the party.

The plan seemed simple enough. I had all week to dwell on it, even if I had to keep the idea of it largely to myself while I worked in the shop, playing nice, dutifully embracing my various tasks, being friendly and engaging toward genuinely good men whom I would likely never see again. The days slowly ticked by on the calendar as I kept those cards held close to my chest, not unlike how the minutes slowly ticked by in those moments I spent waiting for Amber, seated at the kitchen table as I was.

It all seemed like a lie, like I was living some kind of odd double life.

Which, in a sense, I guess I kind of was.

Except, of course, there was Chase, who seemed to keep up the charade far better than I seemed to.

Many of the generators had already arrived at the shop, as planned, by the time I finished my training in Wyoming, along with the trailer they used as living quarters for the handful of techs who arrived with it. This meant there were plenty of spark plugs to install inside generators that also needed fresh oil to fill when I finally arrived from my training in Wyoming, with Chase ever present if a more complicated issue presented on any one of the units.

Not too infrequently did I crawl into the confines of these machines beside him, trying to share a knowing glance or smirk that was never reciprocated, only to be met with the same cheery regard he shared with any of the other techs in the shop instead. This was all well and good, I supposed, though it left me with a feeling of wanting and loneliness. It was the only time I would ever see the young man, and I often wondered if he was so well practiced due to keeping his magical abilities and knowledge of it a secret for so long.

"Did you really dig that out of a box?" I didn't notice Amber coming out of the bathroom to join me in the kitchen before she spoke, breaking me away from my musings. It took me a moment to realize that she was referring to the knife that I still fidgeted with before I pocketed it with a shrug.

"You are not planning on using that on someone, are you?" she teased with a smirk.

My mind drifted to the eight-inch blade I kept with my father's old 1911 and three fresh magazines in the back seat of my truck, "I certainly hope not."

"Right," she said, seemingly unconvinced, grabbing her purse from a chair. "Well, I'm ready when you are. Shall we…" She looked me up and down, breaking into a fit of giggles. "Oh no. We aren't going to be *that* couple, are we?"

That puzzled me, but the moment left me when I noticed that my burgundy polo shirt and dark blue slacks matched the burgundy shirt she wore under her blue blazer and dress.

"Hey now, I came here like this," I said with an amused chuckle.

"Yeah, I guess," she said, also amused and shaking her head.

"But, I suppose, no one will doubt that we came together," I said with bobbing eyebrows.

"Oh my God," she said, shouldering her purse, playfully slapping my arm in mock reprimand when she walked by me toward the door. The mirth was a welcome change after spending nearly a week apart, and with the tension that remained after she left for Bismarck the morning following our dinner with the Landreth's.

The Bismarck Expressway took on a life of its own in the twilight hours of evening. The orange hues and shimmering gold light glistened from the green valleys and distant hills below the winding heights of the road, Mandan proper leaving me underwhelmed when we dipped into the main street. I found it odd how this seemed to match the mood within the little red Toyota when the mirth from the apartment seemed to evaporate, only to coalesce into a quiet tension between Amber and I on the highway south of town.

"Don't you think this is a little... I don't know... extreme?" Amber finally asked, breaking the silence between us.

"How do you mean?" I spared her a glance, but she continued to stare thoughtfully out of the window from the passenger seat.

"This just seems like a giant knee-jerk reaction to everything that is happening." I waited patiently for her to continue through the pause, though I could feel my grip tighten on the steering wheel. "I mean, what do we know about these Freemasons? How do we know we can trust them? Are we really going to throw away everything we've worked for over the word of random people we know nothing about?"

"I've never heard of the Freemasons ever committing atrocities or war crimes either," I retorted.

"What about your father? What about your uncle?" she asked, finally looking at me directly. "Have you ever heard of them hurting anyone that wasn't a criminal? I've only worked with Lillian for a few months, but I would still trust her over some random cult."

"Sure, but were they not also a part of some random cult? And how would you explain Silent John?" She went silent at that. "Lillian basically told me they killed a guy and turned him into some kind of thrall. How is that in any way moral or good?"

"Yeah but... that was during a war."

"And there are rules to warfare, Amber. They are there for a reason."

She went silent for a moment, the barely audible noise from the radio filling the silence between us. "What are you going to do for work after you quit your job tonight?"

"There is plenty of work in the area and we have plenty saved to hold us over in the meantime."

"So, what? Are we just going to rely on my income until you finally find some kind of work to do?"

"Did you not hear what I just said?" I was starting to feel my patience slipping, though I kept my voice calm and level trying to hold on to it. "But yes, between that and the work on the ranch, I think we will be alright. Besides, if all goes well, neither the Society nor the Magistrate can touch us after tonight anyway."

She withdrew completely now, staring silently off into the landscape as we drove by.

"Amber, I need to know if you are still on board with this."

"Yeah," she said, nearly at a whisper. "I am."

Silence stretched between us. The rolling hills drifted lazily by the winding road, the occasional herd of cattle greeting us along the fence line. It only reminded me further of how much I hated fighting with her.

"Do you remember when we were young?" I asked softly. Some of the tension seemed to ebb from her shoulders, a smile slightly creasing her face, though she held her gaze out of the window, anyway. "We often dreamed of owning a ranch of our own, out in the countryside."

"I doubt the Landreths' would sell us the ranch." She kept the smile, but it couldn't mask the sadness in her eyes.

"Maybe." I shrugged. "But we'll have a beautiful house all to ourselves. We can fill it with everything we said we ever wanted—a room with a library, oak bookshelves lining the walls…"

"… The patter of little feet greeting me in the office." She placed a hand on her stomach, some semblance of hope filling her expression.

"A white picket fence in the yard, with dogs and littles to chase them."

"Tools in a shed to build a deck with." Her hand met mine, lacing our fingers together as she pulled it into lap.

"Teaching the littles how to ride."

"Or gently pushing them on a tire swing."

"We want the same thing here, at the end of the day." I gave her a slight squeeze as I spoke. "Something quiet, honest, without some ominous threat looming over us… A home, where we can live away from all this… And after today, we can have it."

"That is one hell of a promise."

"Yeah, well, you know that I'm good for it," I said with a shrug.

She sighed heavily, nodding down to her hand still resting on her stomach. "The room upstairs has a nice view of the front yard," she said, after a quiet moment. "It would make a cozy library."

Gravel crunched under the tires on the approach to Lillian's estate, her driveway packed full of vehicles that revealed themselves when we rounded past the row of trees marking the edge of her property. I parked behind a white Ford F-150 with Phoenix Energy Solutions logos plastered along its sides, which I took to be Allen's work truck, leaving me barely enough room to park on the concrete pad without hanging out on the dirt road leading in.

"Ha! I blocked the bastard in," I said devilishly, eliciting an exasperated laugh from Amber. "Hey." I gave her hand a squeeze so she would look at me. "We got this."

"I know," she said with a squeeze in return.

"I love you."

"I love you too."

A raven's call punctuated the muted noise emanating from inside the house. Shadows danced across the lit blinds on the windows, and figures could be seen walking around through the frosted glass on the door as we approached.

Amber rang the doorbell when we stepped onto the patio, holding herself with a stance of utmost confidence and professionalism that completely eclipsed the apprehension that I felt standing next to her. I wondered to myself how she could so readily muster her composure, trying to draw my own strength from her example while I stared into the unblinking eye of the camera on the doorbell, until the loud crack of the opening door revealed Raymond's portly figure beyond the threshold.

"Ah," he said with a full-faced smile, pushing his glasses up the bridge of his nose with a finger. "Kyle, Amber, welcome. Come on in."

"Raymond, it's good to see you again," Amber said with polite enthusiasm, stepping inside as Raymond moved aside to let us in.

"Likewise," he acknowledged with a nod. "Kyle, it's good to see that you made it." He took my hand into a sturdy handshake. "There are a few people here I would like to introduce you to."

And there it was, the point of no return.

# Chapter 26

"Lillian's done a lot with the place," I mused, walking inside.

A classical symphony orchestra was playing from the speaker system, setting the mood. Beethoven maybe? I've never been a music expert or anything. That was always Amber's passion, not mine. In any case, the music filled what would have been a quiet space, save for the handful of people chatting inside. The china cabinet was fully stocked now, with a beautiful array of decorative plates, bowls, and cutlery on the other side of the dinner table, which was itself adorned with silver placemats and a bouquet in its center.

"Yeah, it almost feels like a home now," Raymond quipped with a chuckle, leading us into the living room, where two gentlemen sat talking on the sectional in front of the lit fireplace. "Mr. Johnson, Mr. Cabida," Raymond interrupted. "Have you met the new basin lead assistant?"

Both men placed their glasses of red wine on the dark wood living room table before standing to greet us on our approach. "I don't believe I have," said the older of the two, a bit bewildered by the interruption.

"Mr. Johnson, It's good to meet you, sir." I shook the older man's hand respectfully, recognizing him as the CEO. "And you too, Mr. Cabida," I offered, recognizing the COO in kind. "We never met, though I recognize you from company photos during my training. My name is Kyle Goodwin, and this is my fiancée, Amber."

"It's a pleasure to meet you both, but please, call me Greg," Mr. Johnson said as he enthusiastically introduced himself to Amber, who greeted him with polite enthusiasm.

"And I'm Jason," the younger COO, somewhere in his late forties, introduced himself, offering a stiff handshake.

Both men were dressed entirely business casual, with Greg's full head of entirely white hair and mustache neatly kempt. He wore his gray polo with a Phoenix emblem embroidered on his left chest pocket. Jason, on the other hand, stood nearly as tall as me, with neatly cropped hair, dressed in a form-fitting blue button-up shirt.

"I'd hate to interrupt your conversation," I said, addressing them both. "I wasn't expecting either of you to be here."

"Well, I would hate to miss out, with us opening a whole new branch in the Bakken," Jason said matter-of-factly. "I've only met a handful of the crew up here; It would be a shame to miss an opportunity to meet the hard-working men and women that helped make this happen."

"Patrolling the line, sir?" I said with a knowing smile.

"Indeed," he said with a curious smile of his own. "Did you serve?"

"Yes, sir, the Two Seventy-fifth."

The former Green Beret's smile broadened. "Well, it's a little different from regiment. How are you liking it here so far?"

"It is, sir, but we have a good crew up here. I appreciate the opportunity."

Greg's confused glances snapped into realization. "Oh, you were a Ranger."

"Yes, sir, out of Fort Lewis, Washington."

"I deployed with a lot of good guys from Lewis. I think you will like it here," Jason said knowingly. "Why don't you grab a drink and well catch up later?"

"I would like that, sir; I look forward to it," I said with a polite nod.

"I can get it for you," Raymond offered. "What would you like? We have a merlot that has been a hit lately, or I can get you a beer instead?"

"I would love a water," Amber said with a polite smile.

"Could I get one too?"

"Of course, I'll be right back," he said, turning into the kitchen, where Silent John had apparently been standing like a creepy statue near the kitchen sink next to another man I hadn't seen before. He seemed tall, with an athletic build in his tailored suit. His dark eyes barreled into me from beneath his flat cap and wolfish grin.

"Kyle, Amber," Chase greeted us at the back door, closing it behind him before walking over with his cheery smile. "Hey, I'm glad you made it." He herded us nearer to the dining room table before continuing. "I wasn't sure if you guys were going to make it."

"Yeah, sorry. That's my fault," I answered him. "Where is Lillian?"

"She is in her office talking to someone from the Magistrate, I think. Most of the party is outside."

"The Magistrate?" I asked, trying not to sound alarmed. "Are you sure?"

"I think so, yeah. At least the guy Lillian is talking to is. There are a couple of them here." He rubbed his hands nervously, his eyes shifting around. I guess I couldn't blame him, I could feel a shiver creep up my spine.

"Did you talk to her yet?" Amber asked, nerves evident in her voice too.

"Not yet, I didn't want to until you got here." He took a steady breath. "We need to be careful here."

"How do you mean?" Amber asked.

"I don't know about the guy in the kitchen, but I think I recognized the name of the guy Lillian is talking to. Owen Carter," Chase said, looking over his shoulder.

"What is his story?" I asked, looking past him to see if anyone was listening in.

"If he is who I think he is, he is near the top," Chase said, looking back to me with worried eyes. "He was one of your mother's disciples. A shadow walker."

Amber and I exchanged surprised looks, my voice catching in my throat. "I thought all her disciples were dead," she started in alarm, nearly at a whisper.

"Not all of them. There were a couple that we lost track of after the war." Chase matched her tone.

"But a shadow walker? How?" I said, trying to be more mindful of our environment, thankful that we were in a fairly well-lit area of the house. "How many of them are out there?"

"I know there aren't many out there," he said, pushing his glasses up his nose. "He is the only one I'm aware of right now, but shadow walkers rarely like to advertise themselves either."

"What does that mean for us?" Amber asked.

"It means that we need to be really careful about what we say." I answered her, Chase nodding in agreement. I continued to survey the room around me as I spoke, growing increasingly paranoid about every little corner or absence of light, finally leveling my gaze on the floor at my feet. "And stay away from the shadows where you can."

Amber spared me a concerned look; Chase's was more questioning.

"Ah, here you go." Raymond rounded the corner with drinks in hand. "What are you guys doing all alone over here? Most of the party is outside."

"Thanks, Ray," I said, Amber and I taking our glasses. "We're just chatting, we'll be out there soon."

"Okay." gave me a quizzical look. "I'll see you out there." I tipped my glass to him as he walked away.

"I think I need to use the restroom." Amber spoke into her glass of water before looking up to me sheepishly.

"Okay," I said, taking her glass from her. "I'll keep a look out for you."

"Thank you, I'll be right back," she gave my arm a light squeeze before passing down the hall beneath the bridge and past the stairs.

"Is she going to be okay?" Chase asked, looking after her.

"Yeah, I think so. Probably just the nerves getting to her."

He let out a heavy breath. "Yeah, I get that. It doesn't seem like your typical *grand opening* party."

"No, I think they have something bigger in mind tonight," I said, considering my glass, wondering if it was even safe to drink.

"Any idea what that might be?"

"It's hard to say." Lightly scanning the room, I added, "It sort of has the feel that this is some sort of diplomatic mission for the Magistrate."

"How do you mean?"

I pursed my lips, trying to solidify my thoughts before I answered. "It's sort of like how diplomats from different countries come together to solidify an alliance. It might be something military related, economic, so on."

"That would make sense though, if the Magistrate was using Phoenix as some sort of cash cow," he reasoned.

"Yeah, but I feel like Lillian could handle something like that on her own. Why would she invite someone like a disciple of the Blood Witch? That almost feels military. And then you have the matter of inviting us."

Chase wiped at his slight beard, his eyes opening wide as silent realization dawned on him, but I nudged him gently into silence before he could voice his concern. The man in the flat cap walked casually out of the kitchen and stopped, sparing me a knowing grin when he spotted me.

"How ya doing, hey?" he said with a slight Irish accent as he walked over with a hand casually in his pocket. "Parden the intrusion, but who might you lads be, if you don't mind my asking?"

He seemed younger than I originally thought, somewhere in his late twenties. He carried himself well too, like someone who could have been an athlete, but I've always had a hard time discerning that from someone wearing a suit. He was neatly shaved with a near perfect smile, but these smaller details were overshadowed by the intensity in his dark eyes. They were like staring into a tiger's eyes if its eyes were brown.

"Mayo Declan," he introduced himself with an extended hand.

"Kyle Goodwin," I said, taking his vise-like grip into mine. "This is Chase."

"Is it?" Mayo said, Chase giving an uncertain smile as he shook his hand. "It's good to meet ya. So, you must be Miriam's boy, the Blood Witch's son himself." He fixed his gaze hard onto mine, and I could feel a tension building in my forehead, just between my eyes. It was subtle at first, hardly noticeable until it hit me like a flood, his grin widening as he spoke. "Lillian said you might make a show of it tonight."

The sudden onset of the migraine nearly sent me into a panic. Blinking through the pain, I set my eyes searching for Amber, who hadn't yet returned from the bathroom. I noticed, though, that the two executives on the sectional carried on their conversation unaffected, and Chase, for his part, seemed to search around nervously too. It quickly became obvious that he was only keyed up due to my own concern.

Mayo's sneer dissolved into confusion when I put the pieces back together. Anger boiled up inside me, chasing away the migraine that quickly receded entirely. It was hard for me to resist getting into his face. To wrap my hands around his neck. To throw him to the ground and beat him.

"So it would seem," I responded, finally. "And you must be with the Magistrate."

"Yes I am." Some of the mirth in his expression returned. "It broke me heart to hear what happened to your parents though. I knew your da more than your mom, but the three of us went way back."

"Really?" I said, hardly concealing my disbelief.

"Eh, I'm a bit older than I look, son." His smile returned. "Your uncle Donald will be glad to hear yer back under the fold, though."

"My uncle Don… is he here?" I said, reeling in disbelief. Whatever energy I had directed into my animosity toward Mayo suddenly shifted itself, pulling me toward the back doors, toward the party outside. I could see them through the enormous windows, a crowd illuminated as dark silhouettes around the fire pit, as my mind raced to wonder which one he could be.

"No, lad," Mayo said through an amused chuckle. "He is out east at the moment, getting ready for the show to start."

*Oh, but of* course *he wouldn't be here,* I thought, drawing myself back into the conversation with present company, swallowing my disappointment and my anger with slow, steady breaths.

Mayo smirked up to me with his highly punchable mouth, "Don't worry lad, he will want to get in touch with you soon. Believe me. Did Lillian tell you what we had planned?"

"No, she didn't." I hoped to sound more stoic than I felt.

"Well, I won't spoil it for her then. I'm sure she will want to fill you in herself."

I could sense Chase slowly stiffening next to me when someone strolled in from the hallway, slowing as he passed us a curious look on his way to speak to the executives on the sectional. He seemed to be in his mid-fifties, but he was lean, like a runner, and he walked like a man in his thirties. He looked somewhat out of place with his dark, slicked-back hair and his blue button-up shirt, though the executives were quick to pay attention to him when he bent down to speak to them.

"Right," Jason said, placing his drink on the living room table before standing, Greg standing with him, walking hurriedly out of the back door. "Looks like Lillian would like everyone to gather around here for a moment."

"Well, I need a word with Mr. Carter there," Mayo said, surveying the room before addressing Chase and I with a knowing grin. "We'll catch up later though, eh?"

"Sure," I said pointedly.

He gave me an all-too-friendly pat on the shoulder with an arm that I couldn't help imagine breaking before he walked away.

"You good, man?" I asked Chase, trying to sound reassuring.

"Yeah, I think so." He wiped his beard and shook his head. "It's just a little much right now."

"I know, man. We'll get through it though." He nodded without saying a word but breathed a heavy sigh of relief when Amber walked sheepishly, with her head down, out of the hallway to join us.

"You okay?" I asked, handing back her glass of water. She took it and nodded without answering, taking small gulps before wiping her mouth. I placed a reassuring hand on the small of her back with her standing next to me.

"I'm feeling a little nauseous, but I think I'm okay." She placed her head on my shoulder for a moment, gently pulling away when the crowd filed into the living room from outside.

"All rise," I whispered, stealing myself against a migraine gently growing from within my forehead, threatening to blind me as it dug itself further into my skull. "And gather for the queen of the United Magistrate."

# Chapter 27

I could feel her coming, my migraine pulsing lightly as she came closer step by lazy step, biding her time as the crowd slowly filed into the living room. It was unnerving, really, how I'd nearly become accustomed to it now that I anticipated it coming. I felt like I could understand it, in a way. Like I understood her intention when she lightly exerted her will upon the growing number of inhabitants within the living room.

There were a little over a dozen in all, most of whom worked directly with Phoenix in some capacity. They brought in a jovial mood, some laughing and joking as they conversed with one another, eagerly including even the executives and the Magistrate's representatives in their boisterous conversations.

"I'll give her one thing," I said, quietly. "She really knows how to set the mood." I noticed that even Chase's mood seemed to perk up a bit.

"I'm not sure if I want to do this anymore," Amber said, nervously.

I nodded in understanding. "She is magically manipulating the mood in the environment to lighten the mood so everyone will be more friendly and accommodating."

"That's… hardly the most sinister way to manipulate people," she responded.

"No," I said, amused. "I imagine it is useful when you are trying to mediate a diplomatic mission."

"Wait, you can sense that?" Chase asked, surprised.

"Yeah," I said, meeting his confused gaze.

"How? I thought you didn't have access to your magic."

"I don't." I shrugged. "It's… hard to explain."

"Oh… I can feel it now too." Chase surveyed the room with a concerned look. "I never noticed that before."

Lillian entered from the hallway, standing tall with her hair flowing freely like a lion's mane in her modest black dress. A sweet smile blossomed, a star in her own show as she stood underneath the walkway with a wineglass raised in a toast.

"Good evening, everyone." The crowd grew quiet in tandem with the intensity of the migraine, the pressure of it receding once she had everyone's full attention. "Thank you all for coming in celebration of our grand opening here in the basin. And to our special guests from the Magistrate, thank you all for allowing me to host you in my humble home this evening."

My spine stiffened when Owen Carter and Mayo Declan raised their glasses to toast her; I guess their involvement wasn't as secretive as I originally thought.

"For all of you who don't know him," Lillian continued, "Greg Johnson is the founder and CEO of Phoenix Energy Solutions, and I believe he would like to share a few words with you."

"Thank you, Ms. Eldonna." Johnson confidently took her place on the floor, speaking with his wineglass in hand. The migraine ebbed to a low hum, giving me room to think while he droned on about the company history, which I frankly didn't care to hear about.

"What sort of diplomatic mission?" Chase asked in a hushed voice.

"I think they are getting ready to hit the Society," I said, surveying the crowd, who were hanging on Greg's every word.

"How do you figure?" Amber asked, glancing up at me.

"If it was just about money, Lillian could handle it on her own. Why introduce the military arm of the Magistrate to Phoenix if it wasn't military related? And there was something Mayo said about my uncle being out east, getting ready for a show."

"Why invite us, then?" Chase asked, keeping his eyes on the speaker.

"Because, sometimes, it's nice to have a place to fall back to after a strike." Chase looked almost sick when I spoke.

"Oh," was all he said, looking up to me, uncertain.

"We still have the civilians here, we'll be okay," I tried to reassure him, but I was starting to wonder how we were going to make our move, or if we were going to be able to at all, when I spotted Mayo himself staring at me from the other side of the room next to Owen. He wore a knowing smirk and gave me a slight nod that left me with a sickening feeling that he might have overheard our little conversation.

Lillian quietly sauntered over to us from behind the CEO as he finished his speech, her black dress hugging her elegant curves in her stride. "Kyle, might I have a word?" she all but purred when she got close, her lips curling in hungry anticipation.

Amber shot a concerned look between us, eyes wide when the migraine suddenly spiked again, though her apprehension seemed to wash away when Lillian spoke. "It'll only be a moment, dear."

I ground my teeth against the pain, and the anger for her pushing herself into Amber again. "Um… yeah." I tried to play it off as more or less surprise, though I suspected that I probably wasn't playing it off well at all.

I was never really much of an actor anyway.

With a nod, she beckoned for Silent John, who still hovered near the kitchen, to follow while I took her lead underneath the bridge and down the hallway. The migraine dissipated completely as we walked with Silent John falling in behind me, replaced by something that felt oddly more familiar. Even welcoming. I felt a smile creep as it beckoned me closer, pulling lightly at the edge of my senses at first, but growing steadily as we drew closer to the door.

It was the first thing I noticed when I walked into the enormous office space, nearly untouched since I'd last seen it. The book's backing glistened in the lamplight, the silver-and-gold inlay refracting the light while it sat like a centerpiece on the bookstand behind the couch in front of the fireplace.

I wondered in that moment if there was a way I could barter or steal it from her, though I still didn't have the faintest idea how. With its decisively impenetrable locks and considering how I was the only one who could open it, I knew it would be just as safe now as it had always been. Getting Chase and Amber out of here alive and unharmed had to remain my main priority—I would have to address this concern at a later time.

"I was beginning to think you wouldn't make it tonight," she said, tracing a finger along the top of the book's cover, walking lazily to the bookshelves on the other side of the room, Silent John clicking the door shut behind us.

"A wizard is never late, nor is he early. He arrives *precisely* when he means to." I retorted, in mock authority.

She turned to me with an unamused glare, eyebrows crooked. "Can't say I've ever been a fan of Tolkien."

"You see, that's how I know we can't be friends." I took a couple of steps toward the book, noticing Silent John taking a position near the desk with a realization that I was getting flanked, and I started to wonder if the click I'd heard was actually the lock on the door.

"Is *that* the reason?" she mocked, folding her arms as she casually leaned against the bookshelf. "I was given the most distressing news, something I really felt the need to discuss with you."

"And what would that be, Lillian?" I absent mindedly traced the gold and silver inlay on the book, half mesmerized by it, though still keeping Lillian and John within my periphery.

Lillian sucked on her lower lip to consider, "It's come to my attention that you might break away from our agreement."

I stiffened, gritting my teeth, a cold realization dawning on me. "The thought had occurred to me."

"But why?" She pushed away from the bookshelf, walking slowly around the couch toward the fireplace as she spoke. "Now that we are here, standing at the precipice of revolution, where people like you and I can finally come out of the shadows and live in the light." She waved a hand and a light fire sprang from the fireplace. I lightly scoffed at the dramatic effect, but she continued. "Free from being hunted by these tyrants who would sooner see us die, not necessarily for what we have done, but for simply being who we are."

"What did she tell you?" I eyed her coldly without turning my back to Silent John.

"Who, Amber?"

"Who else?" I took a couple of steps back, toward the end of the couch, where I could still see Silent John in my periphery while I addressed her. As casual as I tried to make it, it probably wasn't the most subtle move, but I wasn't particularly fond of the idea of standing directly between them, with my back turned toward either one of them.

"She was concerned about you." She nodded in understanding. "She believes, and rightfully so I might add, that you might be throwing away a profound opportunity in favor of the Freemasons. What can they offer you that I cannot?"

"I've known enough of war to know that I don't want any part of it," I said, surprised by the calm in my voice.

"After tonight, there won't be much of a war to fight," She said, standing straight backed and proud with a wolfish grin. "Mr. Declan came a long way to secure the financial backing and support from Phoenix, and Mr. Carter has been instrumental in providing part of the spell we need for our little attack."

She paced slowly toward the other end of the couch, speaking softly. "We have everything we need to drop a little surprise for the Society's little gathering tonight, and afterwards, they will be left virtually leaderless, fractured, and in shambles. It's a shame Carter and Declan won't be here for the festivities." She chuckled, amused.

She stopped short of the book stand, placing a hand lovingly on top of the grimoire, her eyes glistening in the firelight as she studied the inlays. "The other half of the spell is in here, written in your mother's own hand. All we need is for you to open it for us."

"And who else will be attending this little gathering?" I said, holding my ground. "I know about the families that you massacred during your last war. I have enough on my conscience—I don't need the loss of innocent lives weighing it down further."

Her shoulders slumped slightly as she blew out a heavy sigh, glaring up at me. "Every war has its collateral; you should know that as well as anyone. The government you fought for wasn't innocent of its crimes either. Remember Abu Ghraib?"

"Yeah, and the people responsible were put to justice by our government too." I seethed, "That was a far cry from your Magistrate's massacring families, putting them to the cross or mutilating their bodies for your amusement. We are not the same."

"Those were desperate times for us." She waved it off. "Besides, what do you think your uncle would say on the matter?"

"Maybe I'll ask him if I see him. That is, *if* I want to hear him out in the first place," I said, giving her a hard stare. "I won't stand in your way, but I'm not going to help you fight in your little war either."

"Shame." She nodded in understanding. I heard a drawer close as she gave Silent John a stiff nod, taking a couple of steps from me. "Just don't kill him, we still need him."

John flicked a wrist, an extendable baton snapping open as he stalked toward me, handcuffs dangling in his left hand. He held the handcuffs out to me as he drew near, his right hand up and ready to strike, the intention clear. I could let him cuff me willingly, or else I would be in for a fight.

If you were going to fight someone who had a weapon while you were empty-handed, my first piece of advice would be not to. You would probably end up getting your ass kicked for your efforts if you tried. But if you were backed into a corner with no other choice, my second piece of advice would be to go after their weapon hand if you can. You will probably end up taking some shots from your opponent's other hand in the process, but you might stand a chance if you disarmed them first.

I feigned compliance at first, holding my hands out to him, palms up, like I was willing to allow him to place the cuffs on me. Once he got close though, I lunged, grabbing his right wrist with both hands, rolling with the punch when he struck me with his left. He shoved me hard into the wall behind me, but I hung on, pulling him in close, twisting his wrist so that he would let go of the baton.

I caught the baton before it fell, slamming an elbow up into his face, following it up with another, making him stumble, creating just enough space for me to plant a foot hard into his chest. He all but fell into the desk behind him, catching himself on it before it could topple over, knocking the dual-screen monitor and other contents over for his trouble, shaking the daze out of his head before looking blankly back up at me.

"Stop this!" I snarled, raising the baton into a fighting stance, ready to strike. Blood dribbled out of his mouth as he stood, unfazed.

The nice thing about a suit is that it can be relatively easy to conceal some smaller weapons. That's only really a perk, though, if you are the one wearing the suit.

His left hand darted to his shirt, lifting it up, his right hand digging into the appendix holster he wore, pulling out a pistol with a freaking silencer on it. I threw the baton hard at his face, immediately closing the distance, grabbing his wrist and pointing it away as I slammed into him. He lost his balance as I pushed, leaning hard onto the desk.

The slide clacked between us, slamming a round hard into the ceiling above. With a twist and a pull, I wrestled the gun out of his hand and pistol-whipped him in the head, sending him sprawling onto the floor. I moved a couple of steps back, creating distance between us, working the slide as he stared blankly back up at me.

"I said fucking stop!" I shouted, but he found the baton and grabbed it, standing slowly as he fixed me with his blank stare. "I *will* fucking shoot you."

"Stop messing around and finish this, John." Lillian sounded bored from the other side of the room. "We still have guests to attend to."

He took a step, baton raised to strike. The slide clacked twice in my hand, a round punching through a windowpane behind him. He stumbled once, looking dumbly at the red stain forming on his white shirt at the center of his chest, and looked back up to me, taking another step forward.

I stood, dumbfounded. The round the pistol fired was no smaller than a 9mm round; the weapon was some kind of a Glock. The 9mm round didn't pack much of a punch, but the round I planted into his heart should have been more than enough to drop him within a second or two.

I planted a round into his brow without thinking before he got too close, snapping his head back, the back of it spewing gore as he dropped lifeless to the floor.

I leveled the gun hard onto Lillian, my mind racing while she casually rubbed the bridge of her nose. "Ray is going to be so disappointed when he finds out that you broke his toy." She chided, "Do you have any idea how hard it is to make one of those?"

My mind was racing, how was I going to explain this? How was I going to walk away from this when I practically shot a guy in his own home, with a party going on in the next room?

"Hey, would you like to hear a terrible cliché?" she asked jokingly.

"Do you want to get shot in the face?" I growled, holding the pistol steady.

She pouted and snapped her fingers. "Good help can be *so* hard to find."

She didn't so much as move – she simply blurred and slammed my head into the wall behind me. Shooting stars clouded my vision as she held me by the throat in an iron grip, one-handed. I still held on to the pistol, so I pressed the silencer into her ribs and pulled the trigger twice.

Nothing.

Jammed.

She erupted into a full-throated laugh, pressing herself against me. "I guess I'll just have to take care of it myself." She drew me into a deep kiss, my skull all but split from the surge of pressure that blinded me with pain. With a growl, she slammed my head into the wall again.

Pain.

Dark.

# Chapter 28

The darkness enveloped me like a cloak, long in its stillness. I drifted silently into its endless night, painless, dreamless, thoughtless. My breath found me first, coming light and steady, drawing me weightlessly back into myself.

I slowly became more aware of my body, each breath becoming heavier than the last, my arms and legs becoming heavier still. My head lolled on my chest, heavier than the rest of me, seated as I was. My wrists ached, so did my ankles.

But damn it, my head ached worst of all.

I shuddered a breath, opening my eyes to a blurry, blinding white light, closing them again to brace against the nausea that twisted my insides, constricting my throat.

"Ah, there he is." His voice came from off in the distance; I could only just make it out.

"Why hello there." Her voice was soothing, closer than the last.

"Are you with us, sport?"

I shuddered another defiant breath, lifting my far-too-heavy head, fighting another flood of nausea as the world spun around me. "Take it easy, buddy. You're okay." A hand shook my wrist as he spoke.

A harsh groan erupted from deep within my chest, my eyes straining to open, blinking away the blurry light until Raymond's broad grin finally came into focus. "I was beginning to wonder if you would wake up before we started our little ritual," he mused, wiping saliva from my bare chest with a cloth.

My hand jerked to his, straining against the handcuffs that restrained me and held me to the armrest. I tried the other, violently, a cutting pain searing at the edge of my mind from my wrists held firmly in place. I tried to kick the bastard. The legs of the chair squeaked against the floor as it budged, but my foot barely moved at all. Pain scraped against my shin from the shackles that secured them.

Lillian's vise grip clamped hard onto my wrist and right biceps, restraining my arm against the chair's armrest, squeezing me like a tourniquet. I strained against her too, but I might as well have tried to pull my arm out of hardened concrete for all the good it did me.

"Hang on, Kyle," she soothed, sitting in a chair next to me. "I'm almost finished." A needle was stuck inside the crook of my arm with an IV tube, crimson with blood, trailing to a bag filling on the floor.

Ray sat back into his office chair slowly, regarding me like a disappointed father would a petulant child. "He has some fight in him, I'll give him that." He dropped the cloth onto a table next to him. There were a few other things on there too: a bowl full of water, a scalpel, a bottle of black ink, a fine-tipped paintbrush, a notepad, and a black bag.

Lillian grinned at him, keeping me firm in her vice grip. "Indeed, are we surprised?"

He looked from me to her, sadly, before wordlessly consulting his notebook.

My head still swam—from a concussion, I concluded. It must have been a mild one since I could still string some semblance of a coherent thought together. Struggling was apparently useless, so I tried to take stock of my situation instead.

The room was empty and ordinary, like any other empty bedroom, void of decoration on its plain white walls and hardwood floors. I sat near the back of the room facing the door, an empty closet next to it.

So, I must still be in Lillian's house then.

"Where is Amber and Chase?" I asked, a sinking feeling growing in my stomach.

"They are in the other room, waiting patiently for the ritual to start." Lillian smiled, sweetly.

Two knocks came from the door, Owen Carter himself stepping inside without a prompt. "The guests have all cleared out, and Declan and I will be leaving too." His voice came out smooth and calm, at a low base as he addressed Lillian, his eyes meeting mine.

Lillian released my arm, exaggerating a pout to Carter, lounging in her chair. "Must you leave so soon? I would hate for you to miss the ritual."

"I'm afraid so," he said, his eyes darting between Lillian and I, though otherwise expressionless. "There is a troop of Pyre Guard chasing our decoy in Jamestown. We have a chance of ambushing them down there. Otherwise, they might catch wind of what is going on over here when the fireworks start."

"Indeed, they certainly would," Lillian said, worriedly.

Ray spun lazily around in his chair to face him. "You want to take any of my thralls with you?"

"That shouldn't be necessary. You might want to keep them with you anyway in case the authorities show up."

"Alright," Ray said with a nod, spinning back around to his notepad. "Best of luck then, drive safe."

Carter turned to leave but hesitated at the door. "Are you sure this is going to work, turning him like this?" he said, nodding to me.

"All we need is his living blood to open the book," Ray said, with a heavy sigh.

"And we have his pregnant girlfriend in the other room for the ritual; we have everything else we need," Lillian added.

"And the ranch kid, you are sure you'll be able to work him over?" Carter addressed Lillian directly.

"Of course." She smiled sweetly, tilting her head to him as she lounged in her chair. "I've been playing around in his head for months now. It'll be no trouble at all once I have my way with him."

Carter nodded slowly, clearly reading into the context, then fixing his sad gaze onto me. "It's too bad," he said finally. "I had hoped to train the kid."

"Mentoring your mentor's son," Lillian mused. "That would have been poetic."

"Don is going to be pissed when he finds out about this."

"He will be hurt when he finds out what the Society did to him," Lillian shrugged, "But he'll be okay."

"Yeah," he said, sadly, closing the door on his way out.

A sudden sense of dread enveloped me then, washing over me like a cold shower when I finally put some of the pieces together. They needed me to remain alive if they were going to open and transcribe the grimoires, but they would also need me to remain compliant. It suddenly became obvious why they had me strapped to a chair, alone, with Ray and his toolkit full of magical items. Why else would he have me here if he would not turn me into one of his thralls?

"Wow, hold on," I said, trying to hide some of the panic from my voice. "What about Amber? What are you going to do with her?"

"She is the conduit." She casually pulled the tube from the now full IV bag, placing them into a bag next to her.

"What, for the spell?" I asked, watching blood ooze out of my arm.

She giggled playfully. "Of course. We had other plans for the recipe, but I'm afraid we are out of time for that now. With your noncompliance, I'm afraid she will have to do."

"Look, this is woefully unnecessary," I said, raising my hands, the handcuffs clanking against the hard wood armrests. "You are clearly holding all the cards here. She is innocent and it is me you want. She doesn't have to be involved in any of this. If you let her go, I will help you."

She sat back in her chair, regarding me. "How long do you think I can trust you to work for me while holding that knife to your throat, especially now that you are consorting with the Freemasons? I'm sorry, Kyle, but you should have thought about that before you betrayed me in the first place."

"What about Donald? Do you really think he is going to be okay with you parading his nephew around as one of your thralls?" I tried to reason, doing all I could to conceal the fear in my voice as she stood up to leave, taking her bag with her.

"I believe he will be devastated to learn how the Society killed his nephew." She spoke calmly, matter-of-factly, as someone might if they were lamenting a story to a child. "He will mourn your loss for a time, and he will come to understand when we tell him we needed to do this to gain access to the grimoires. He will then take his righteous fury and vengeance upon the shattered remains of the Society, leading us to victory, just as he was always meant to. In time, we may even hold a proper funeral for you and all the others we lost along the way."

"Hold on…" I pleaded.

She paused only briefly before opening the door.

"Farewell, Kyle." She barely spared me a glance, the door clicking shut behind her.

"Lillian, wait!" I all but shouted, panic-stricken, the cuffs rattling from the strain.

"She is gone, Kyle." Raymond stood from his chair, producing a stick of white chalk from his black bag, hunching low, then drawing a circle around my chair. "This will be easier for you if you relax."

Every aspect of my body was electric with tension, though I stopped straining against the cuffs. I drew heavy breaths, trying to calm my mind, trying to think of some way out of this. All I could do was to keep him talking, maybe stall him a little.

"How does this work exactly?" I asked, grasping at straws. "What are you planning on doing here?"

"Well," he said, completing the circle and sitting in his chair. He spared me a glance before consulting his notebook again. "I was able to discern how your mother's spell worked. It blocks magic from entering you through your spirit, which might explain why Lillian wasn't able to influence you. Succubae draw energy from a person's spirit, after all." He casually flipped a page in his notebook. "I'll have to remove it before we start."

"Sounds kind of risky," I said, glaring at him.

"Maybe, but you won't be given a chance to use magic anyway," he said, glaring at me over his glasses. "You'll be unconscious."

"And then what? You lobotomize me?"

He gave an impatient sigh. "Not really, your brain will remain intact. Your spirit though, I'll need to access it to enthrall you. You'll get to keep a part of it, but I'll have to destroy the rest."

"So, you get to rip apart my soul, but I get to keep just a little part of it." I huffed. "How generous."

"Sure, and you get to keep all your memories, so none of your military training has to go to waste. You will even be able to strategize, solve puzzles, that sort of thing. You'll be hard as hell to kill too."

"Hell, you can drive me off the lot today and you won't have to worry about my personal agency nor my ability to speak. Sounds like one hell of a deal."

He gave an amused chuckle. "Something like that. Your mother was the one who figured out how to do this, believe it or not. Keeping this piece of your soul will grant you a great deal of autonomy. Traditional thralls were no better than zombies. It's what separates them from, well, you."

"Or Silent John."

"Mhm." He nodded into his notebook.

I thought about that for a minute. "So, you knew my mother then."

"That's right." He grabbed the scalpel from the table, swiveling lazily in his chair, studying me intently. "We were friends, once upon a time. I wasn't one of her apprentices, but she coached me in the way of the spirit. I wouldn't be the necromancer I am today without her," he said, idly testing the blade in his hand with a thumb.

"You are about to mutilate her only son," I said, calmly. "Lillian is about to murder her only grandchild. What do you think she would say about that?"

He drew in a heavy breath, sighing slowly. "I've done a lot of things I'm not proud of, Kyle, this only being one of them. If this works out, people like me will be able to practice our art without constantly peering over our shoulder, in constant worry that the Society and the like will be there, hunting us." He stood over me, the scalpel gripped firmly in his hand. "Once I get my hands on the book of the spirit, none of this will matter anymore anyway."

He gripped my right wrist, pinning it down, cutting into the webbing between my thumb and pointer finger with the scalpel before tossing it onto the table. I ground my teeth against the sudden pain as he took my hand in his in a bloody handshake. I squeezed, hard, blood covering his hand like a glove, dripping onto the armrest that restrained me. He winced at the strength of it and pulled against me, but the blood made it hard to hold onto him and his hand soon slipped away.

He sneered as he stumbled away, nearly falling into the open closet behind him before catching himself.

"You're making a mistake, Raymond," I said, sadly. "Did anyone tell you how my father died?"

He studied me skeptically for a moment, carefully adjusting his glasses with his clean left hand. "They said it was a fire."

I closed my eyes and nodded, trying my best to resign myself to what was to come. "Yeah, a fire." I sighed, sadly, my body relaxing into my acceptance.

I threw myself at my restraints, shackles snapping, the cuffs grinding bloody against my wrists. The chair creaked but didn't break. There was no way for me to fight this; there was no way for me to talk myself out of this chair either. No way that I could clearly see, anyway.

My lifeblood still oozed from the crook of my arm, dripping lazily to the floor. The cuffs restrained me, coated by a thin sheen of red where they ground against my wrists. My heart sank at the hopelessness of it, my eyes drawing down to the circle drawn around me. Even if I could wield magic, it would be easily contained within this chalk outline. I realized then that there was no way out of this, no one was coming. I was completely on my own.

But that didn't matter nearly as much as knowing that Amber still needed me. Our unborn child still needed me, and I was powerless to save either of them on my own.

For a warrior, death is a constant. Death is everywhere. You live to slake death's lust and hunger for departed souls. You thrive in the knowledge of being his instrument as you drive your force and will into the enemy while you plunge his very being into death's open and eager maw. Death can come easy for a warrior, in a way. A warrior may sacrifice their own life for the ones they love.

But what of your soul, the very thing that tethers you to this world and the next? Would you risk your soul to wither and decay, damning yourself for eternity for the chance that your loved ones may have a life worth living?

*Could she* help, *this demon* inside *me?*

*Insanity!* I thought, tears blinding my vision. I thrashed harder, more violently against my restraints, pain lancing up my shins and along my arms until the chair tipped over, toppling me to the ground with a crash.

"I think we've had enough of that," Raymond said with a huff, righting my chair with a groan.

My breath hitched. "Come and take me then, if you think you can." I growled in challenge, glaring hard at him with a grin.

*Could I* even *reach her?*

God help me.

He hesitated for a moment before righting himself. He closed his eyes, drawing a bloody line down the center of his forehead to the bridge of his nose, muttering silently to himself as he stepped closer to me. "I'm sorry, Kyle, really," he said, stopping just at the edge of the circle he'd drawn around my chair. "I wish it didn't have to be this way."

He struck out, grabbing my forehead with his bloody hand. My head felt like it was going to split open, my body arching uselessly back against the chair. I wanted to scream, and maybe I did, against the blinding pain.

Everything hurt.

Until it didn't.

# Chapter 29
## Mosul, Iraq

I awoke to groaning in the darkness, the sounds of a dying man's final moments. That was the first thing I remembered. Then came the pain. It was all-encompassing, every part of me alight with it.

I could hear someone on the radio sending up a report with tension thick in his voice. Two of our own were wounded on the third floor.

My floor.

The thought barely registered, though I had a nagging feeling that I needed to do something about it. My eyes fluttered open into more darkness; shuddering breaths shook pain into my tight chest. Flashing light and booming gunfire snapped my mind back into focus.

I was hit.

I pawed at my legs. They were still there, thank God. My right leg was wet, though. My clothes clung to me below my right knee. There was a burning pain there too, and in my left arm. But everything still moved, everything still worked. That was a good sign.

Someone dragged me into the conference room. I could dimly see a figure kneeling over me in the dim light. They must have taken my vest apart to check me for wounds. I was still lying on the backpiece. They had taken my helmet off too.

"Sarge." So, it was Locker then. He was holding my radio in his hand. "You good?"

"Don't get blown up, bro," I rasped, my chest still tight. "It fucking sucks." I sat up, batting away his steadying hand. Locker was my senior team leader; it would have been his job to take over the squad if I went down. I couldn't blame him for stepping up, but it still pissed me off he wasn't with his team. "I'm good. Where's the rest of my kit?"

"I called it in," he said, sliding over the front half of my vest. "Watson is hit too."

I unclipped my utility belt, snatching a red lens flashlight from a pouch, and ripped open my IFAC, a sort of standard issue first aid kit every soldier is required to carry. "How bad?" I asked him, but I realized right away that I didn't need to. The groans told me everything.

Combat wounds are nothing like they are portrayed in the movies. Hollywood often shows soldiers taking a bullet or having their limbs blown off, and then they scream on the ground. But that is not how it really happens.

It is worse. In reality, truly bad injuries sap your energy, preventing you from screaming. It is a moan, a deep cry of utter desperation. It is visceral, a soul-wrenching groan of true pain manifested into sound. This was the sound that Watson made. It is a sound that never leaves you. It's a sound that haunts your sleepless nights until you are old, and you join your dying friend in the afterlife.

"Bad," Locker said. "An RPG hit your wall; he took a lot of the blast. It took a chunk out of our wall too."

I froze, a shiver of panic shooting up my spine. "Are you and Arrants okay?"

"Yeah, we're good. He's in there now putting in work. Overwatch is pinned down in their courtyard. We're trying to provide cover fire, but they're getting worked over down there. It isn't looking good."

I found my helmet next to me, my night vision still attached and somehow still working. Behind Locker, Albers was kneeling over Watson, working feverishly to patch his wounds. I tried not to think too hard about it when I ripped open my pant leg, exposing my bleeding shin. I flashed my red lens onto my leg, just long enough to get a sense of the damage. It didn't look as bad as it felt. Tiny holes peppered the skin, slowly leaking blood. Shrapnel wounds had a funny way of being like that sometimes.

"How long was I out for?" I asked, tearing open a packet of gauze.

"Not long, Albers pulled you out right away. You started to wake up as soon as I pulled your kit apart." There was a pull tab on our vests that made it easy to do. They came apart as soon as you pulled it. They were much easier to put back together than the standard-issue vests the regular Army were issued. Perks of the job, I guess. This basically meant that I really wasn't out for long, maybe a minute, if not a little more. That was a positive, but we had to get moving. Minutes can mean an eternity in a gunfight.

"Get back to your team and get them onto the roof. See if you can get a better vantage point from up there," I told Locker, nearly dropping the pack of gauze.

"Roger." But he hesitated. "You sure you're okay?"

"Yes, go." He left without another word, pulling his team out of their respective rooms, and leading them up the stairs.

My hands were stiff when I worked the gauze over my wounded leg, all dexterity nearly gone from them. The booming gunfire around me tempted my nausea with every burst, but I managed to keep it down, finishing my wrapping just as our platoon medic stumbled up the stairs with exhaustion. Evidently, he had been putting in work too.

"Albers!" I shouted next to me, clipping my vest back together. "Link back in with Ramirez and get back into the fight." My arm didn't seem as bad as my leg; it would have to wait.

The medic stumbled onto his knees next to Albers, giving him a reassuring nod. It was well understood that if you were hit, you were expected to perform self-aid if you could. If you couldn't, it was understood that everyone was expected to leave you where you were until the fight was over. Every weapon system that wasn't in the fight meant a greater opportunity for the enemy to gain fire superiority and kill all your friends. The medic was really the only exception, but even he carried a rifle in case things got really bad. That didn't make the job any easier to deal with, though.

Albers stood but paused, looking down mournfully at Watson. He bent down one more time to say something to him that I couldn't quite hear before running into a room, joining Ramirez.

"The radio called for two," the medic shouted above the gunfire, looking around confused. "Where is the other one?"

"There is only one!" I shouted back, putting my vest back on.

"You sure?"

"Yes I'm sure, get the fuck out of here."

The medic nodded, lifting Watson into a fireman's carry, taking him down the stairs as I snapped on my helmet, found my rifle, and braced myself against the table next to me. I tried to stand, my head swimming with the effort, pain shooting into my shin, my leg giving out from under me, nausea leaving me retching on the floor.

"Fuck," I cursed out loud, clearly worse off than I had thought. But I had to get back up. I had to get back into the fight. I braced myself on the table, with both hands this time, my weapon clattering onto the tabletop, and pulled myself up. My equilibrium was warped, my head lilted, threatening to topple me over again. I barely kept myself from falling over a second time while I stood there, fighting to regain my senses.

The world spun around me, under the green glow of my night vision, the symphony of war playing all around me. I had to keep moving. My men needed me. I couldn't lose anyone else. I pushed myself off the table, half stumbling to the back window of the conference room to check the progress outside. Brief flashes of light sparkled from the building on the other side of the parking lot, lasers danced around the outside of the building to meet them. The fight didn't seem too intense on this side, but it was just enough to keep second squad occupied. Bodies littered the gate opening to the parking lot; they'd evidently tried to make a push outside. I doubted they would make that mistake again. Most of the chaos came from the other side of the building anyway.

Half limping, half stumbling, I crossed the conference room into the ruined office Watson and I occupied. The dust hadn't fully settled yet, giving off a smell of pulverized concrete, the sharp sent of cordite, blood, and death. The dead insurgent inside lay askew on the floor next to the tipped-over desk. Everything was covered by a thin blanket of dust and rubble. A hole had been blown out of the outside wall where it met with the inside wall to the right and I could see into the room Locker and Arrants had just occupied.

I marveled at the destruction, how the rocket must have struck the wall just right, so the two joined walls could absorb just enough of the blast that I could survive. Wonder and relief both washed over me with the realization. I almost laughed. Some of the energy from the blast spilled into the other room, though it looked like most of it funneled into this one… into Watson.

That's right, it wasn't just luck. It was Watson who saved me. He pushed me over the desk, placing himself between me and the rocket, absorbing the blast with his body.

The wonder and relief morphed into shame and dread. *I should have seen it coming. I was the leader here; I swore to bring him home. That should be my blood on the wall. It should have been me, wheezing and dying on the floor. Not him. Not Watson.*

Enemy rounds slapped into the outside wall, drawing my attention. *I can't dwell on that now. The others are still here, still fighting.* I drew myself toward the window, careful not to expose myself to the gunfire and observed absolute mayhem outside.

Lasers streaked out of windows, searching for victims who fired back with a chaotic torrent from across the street. My Rangers were disciplined though. It's easy not to be in the face of such overwhelming gunfire. Our machine guns were "talking," one gun shooting a burst, then another directly after. It was a method used to provide continuous fire support while still conserving some ammunition. It meant that the gunners were aware of how little ammo they still had too.

Tracers streaked from both sides over the smoldering wreckage of the overturned Stryker half in the courtyard, flashing into windows like angry hornets, or over the roof of the building across the street. You would almost think that we would have a clear vantage of the roof the enemy insurgents occupied. Only its high walls provided them with good cover as they returned our fires with theirs or quickly peeked over the ledge to strike at the Rangers in the courtyard next to them.

Those Rangers were in a bad spot. They managed to duck behind the concrete wall surrounding the courtyard they occupied, but there was no way for them to maneuver out of it without getting mowed down by the withering fire from the rooftop or the floor below—a floor that we could neither see nor engage.

Lasers finally lanced out from our rooftop, searching for targets on the roof across the street. Locker and his team must have been in position then, though their added vantage seemed to help matters only a little. Still, something was better than nothing.

"Ramirez," I called over my radio. "Take your team onto the roof with Bravo team, see what you can do about that enemy rooftop."

"Roger, Oscar Mike," chirped the radio, and Ramirez's guns were quickly silenced. Locker picked up his team's rate of fire, but my stomach dropped when a figure with a shouldered RPG launcher crested the rooftop and fired into the gathered Rangers in the courtyard below. They were well dispersed, but the blast knocked a man down, limp onto the ground.

A laser from our rooftop latched onto the insurgent and he dropped with a jerk of his body, but there were several more on the roof with him, practically untouchable behind their cover. My heart sank at the hopelessness of it all. It wouldn't be long before Overwatch, pinned down and helpless, would succumb to the onslaught, and all I could do was stand there, alone in this empty room, and watch them die.

Shivers ran down my spine with a jolt, making me catch my breath. I looked around the room, searching through the green glow of my night vision for something that could have spiked my attention, and the world around me took a crystalline shine. I became acutely aware that I had not become afraid this time, no adrenalin dump accompanying the gripping sense of terror that preceded her like before; just a heightened awareness of my surroundings, and a sense that I was being watched.

Everything went quiet.

It was as if someone hit the pause button on a TV remote, the melody of war suddenly silent. I drew myself back into the window, baffled by the stillness outside. Several lasers stretching out from above and below remained fixed on targets across the street, unmoving and solid like bars in a broken cage. The deadly streaking glow of tracers slowed to a near stop, creeping through the darkness like stars descending from the night sky to join us humble humans down below.

*"They will not last."* The voice didn't come from any discernable direction, though it was hard for me not to recognize it. Still, I found it odd that I was so at peace compared to the terror that was nearly all-encompassing before.

She glided next to me like an apparition, her hair drifting about her as if submerged in water, her white robes clinging to her body as though pressed by a strong wind. Her dark, ancient eyes avoided mine, taking in the scene outside as she approached the window.

"Who… what are you?" I asked, nearly breathless.

"I've had many names, many titles, but none of that matters now," she said grimly. Sensing my hesitation, she gave me a sidelong glance. "Asmodeus."

"I don't understand, how are you doing this? What are–"

"I am not long able to hold this state, such as I am," she interrupted, calmly. "Perhaps soon you will understand, if you only listen. I need not tell you of the scourge they have become"—she gestured broadly to the insurgent-occupied building across the street—"nor of the massacre your friends are about to endure right in front of you. They will dance upon your bodies and parade your corpses down the streets before they are done with you. A celebration of victory for their false caliphate."

She turned to face me squarely, searching my face. "You are badly injured. You won't last long like this, but you have the power to stop this slaughter, Kyle." She gestured to the trapped Rangers across the street. "You can still save them. No more of your friends… no more of your men need die today."

"I don't understand," I said, taking a hesitant step back from her. "How?"

Her ancient eyes dug into mine, a note of longing etched into her young Persian features. "I can show you." She held out her hand, beckoning me to take it. "If you accept me, I will unshackle your will, sharing my spirit with your own. You will become untamed, unburdened by the mundane and mortal, willing fire and fury the likes of which extend beyond your imagining." She nodded slowly to her outstretched hand. "All you have to do is accept me."

It was an odd thing, studying this apparition. It was as though she existed somewhere between standing on solid ground and floating just above it, partially real and partially imagined. I felt like I was losing my mind, standing in the quiet stillness of what should have been a chaotic battle.

My eyes tracked the dark streaks on the floor leading toward the conference room. Watson's blood trail. He was one of mine, his well-being was my responsibility. I swore to lead him. To keep him safe. To do everything in my power to bring him home. His life ebbed from him in his final moments, leaving him gasping on the floor where my body should have been; not his. He was still young, still full of life and possibilities. He shouldn't have given his life for mine in my moment of confusion. Of weakness.

The young Ranger still lay prone from the blast in the courtyard outside. There was no telling if he survived. Maybe he didn't. It was only a matter of time before the Apache gunships would show to provide their desperately needed support, but we didn't have time to spare. Sooner or later, the insurgents would find a way to maneuver around those stranded Rangers and massacre them like an executioner's firing squad, and we would fight for our lives soon after.

A quiet rage built up somewhere between the cracks of my helplessness, bubbling up like molten lava, burning away everything it touched. Asmodeus still looked at me with her pleading eyes, still quietly beckoning me to take her hand into my own. Hallucination, apparition, it didn't matter. I had to do something. Anything. I couldn't let any more of my brothers die.

"Okay." I took her hand into mine, as warm and as real as any I held before. I took a deep breath, forcing myself to make peace with this new point of no return. "Whatever it takes, help me bring my men home."

"As you wish." She smiled sweetly, a loving gaze etched behind her deathly eyes.

My vision flashed, blinding me for an instant. I flinched from the booming gunfire, the cacophony of war resuming outside my window, punctuating her sudden absence.

The light from the night vision burned my eyes as I watched someone finally pull the fallen Ranger back toward the safety of the wall. I blinked the pain away when I flipped them up, and opened my eyes again, stunned.

I could see everything. I could make out every detail, every shadow became clear, as if someone had turned a light switch on within the world in its entirety.

*Be not afraid.* Her voice seemed to come from within me. I looked down at my gloved hands, opening and closing them slowly. It took a moment for me to realize that they were moving on their own.

"Pay close attention," it was my voice this time, mouthed smoothly through lips I could not control. I was merely a tacit observer in my own body, seeing only what she wanted me to see, my body moving under her complete control.

"The spirit draws in the energy," my voice said, and I began breathing the energy in, drawing it in through my chest. I could feel it pooling into me. My bones seemed to vibrate with its power as it spilled into my limbs. I spotted a shadowed area cast by the courtyard next to the building. "The mind forms the energy in accordance with your will." Another shadow, tucked away in the corner of the room. "The body is the conduit, releasing it into the world."

My hand reached out, releasing a near-imperceptible amount of energy into it. I flowed like a rush of water released through a dam into the shadow, and I was suddenly standing in the shadow of the courtyard wall outside.

A vicious laugh vibrated deep in my chest. "You are the wrath that never sleeps." The wall stood between me and the building my platoon occupied, and I took little notice of the violence around me. Nobody seemed to take much stock of me either, though I could see shadowy figures in the windows across the street.

"They think they can hide in the shadows." I seemed to take special note of an unoccupied room in the insurgent's stronghold. "But you are the shadows." With a small push, I flowed back into the shadow.

*"With eyes wide open, you see the unseen."* It was her again, words voiced only inside my head. The room was empty, though the whole building seemed to shake with the noise of automatic rifles firing at random. That didn't seem to matter now; nobody knew that I was here. Gripping my rifle, I crept through the open door into a short hallway leading into a main room in the back.

*"With your essence cloaked in the shadows, the dead lie in your wake…"* Bodies littered the floor, most of them dead, others barely living. None were a threat, so none of them mattered. I took little stock of them while I crept through the darkness.

A flight of stairs led to the second floor, a man half carried another with an arm over his shoulder, carefully making his way down when I made it to the foot to meet them. *"While the living stumble blindly before you, searching for a light to save them, only to be reaped in the dying of the night."* The whole building was dark. He probably thought I was on his side of the fight if he saw me at all, though I could see him clear as day. I shot him and his friend twice in rapid succession, their bodies tumbling down the stairs together in a mass of limbs and death.

I didn't take the stairs; the shadows were easier and numerous. Doors lined the hallway; some were closed, most were open. *"No door can bar you."* Another shadow led into a closed room where two men stood inside, shooting from a window. I shot them both in the back without hesitation.

Another shadow. Another room. More of the enemy. I shot them too. *"No wall can keep you."* The door to this room was open, so I crept into the empty hallway and through another open door. More of them were inside. There was no way for them to know I was among them until they died. *"There is no stronghold you cannot enter."*

I kept a mental tally of my round count as I went, so I knew this magazine was almost empty. I tried to plead with her to reload the weapon, to say something. Anything. There was no use; she was in complete control while I silently panicked within the prison of my mind.

Another shadow, another room. Two men were inside, one firing through the window. The other in the back froze while reloading his rifle, watching me practically walk out of the wall in front of him.

*"There is no man you cannot break."* The man in the window died first, the second man watched in horror as his friend crumpled lifeless to the floor. He raised his rifle as I raised my hand, willing energy into my splayed fingers just as he pulled the trigger. Automatic fire thundered inside the enclosed room, rounds jackhammering into an electric-blue dome just outside my reach. I poured more energy into the dome, each round pulsating into my brain, threatening to break my will.

His weapon clicked, lifeless, out of ammunition. Stars danced in my vision, fatigue washing over me as I was nearly drained. But not quite. The insurgent dropped his empty magazine, desperate to reload. My hand closed in front of me. With a murmur in a language I did not know, energy poured into my fist, and I punched. The air rippled; kinetic energy broke into the man's chest, crashing him into the wall behind him where he slid to the ground, unmoving.

Gasping for breath, I took a moment to steady myself as I became weighted down by fatigue. More so, I could feel some of my lost energy ebbing back with each breath, though a little slower than before. I chanced a glance through the window as my breath steadied, and I was shocked to find the pinned-down Rangers taking cover behind the courtyard wall in front of me, desperately returning fire from the rooftop above me.

I'd single-handedly cleared the second floor!

I searched the room for another shadow while reloading my weapon; it was easy to find. *"In the cold of the night, a deathly walker holds dominion."* I walked into it and onto the rooftop, veiled by the shadow cast by the exterior wall. There were nearly a dozen men up here with me, all armed to the teeth. Most were taking cover behind the wall, trying to avoid the incoming rounds cracking over their heads, though they would frequently chance a peek over the top, firing briefly before taking to their cover again. Some were facing the target building my platoon occupied. The rest were facing the pinned-down Rangers in the courtyard. None of them saw me.

An insurgent with an RPG launcher finished loading a round and stood, about to launch a rocket into the pinned Rangers below. With only a fraction of energy, a brief whisper, and a snap of my fingers, his rocket jammed. Every weapon on the rooftop went silent.

Every weapon but mine.

It was like shooting fish in a barrel. I punched round after round into their confusion, one man dying after another. Some tried desperately to clear their malfunctioning weapons before they died, a couple tried to make a run for the doorway next to me. That only made them die faster. Others cowered against the wall, pleading with hands stretched out, screaming. There was no mercy in what I did, they all died in the onslaught.

Only a handful remained when my magazine went empty. None of them charged me, they were too terror-stricken after watching all their buddies die around them. They went for the door instead, though they had to cross the span of the roof to get there. With a closed fist and a whisper, I punched out my hand, fingers spread, and a gout of fire erupted from my palm to meet them.

A wall of flame hit them mid-stride. Their bodies curled and dropped to the ground without a scream. The heat was blistering, leaving me gasping for breath while the inferno stole the oxygen from my lungs and everything around me. I quickly darted into the doorway before the noxious smell of the burning dead could overwhelm me, back into the shadows within. *For too long you've dwelt in slumber."*

I darted from one shadow to the next, from the stairway to the first floor, then to the wall outside the target building, then back to my blown-out room on the second floor. *"But tonight you rise, a shadow walker."* I nearly fainted, barely catching myself on the overturned desk before I could fully collapse onto the floor. My limbs filled with lead, weighing me down with exhaustion that I had to fight through for each shuddering breath.

*"Breathe, slow, deep into your belly."* I did as she instructed, gripping the edge of the table with both hands. Much of the gunfire died down on this side of the building, though sporadic shooting could still be heard in the rear. This floor of the building, though, remained quiet.

"I have to go," I told myself out loud. "I have to get back to my men." I stumbled out of the room, my slung M4 clacking against the door frame when I nearly tripped into the conference room. My head pounded. I didn't feel any of the effects of the concussion when Asmodeus took over, but now it seemed like every little jolt threatened my nausea.

*"Use the shadow,"* she said as I searched for the stairs. They weren't hard to find. As dark as everything was, the whole place seemed to be covered by shadow. *"Find your energy."* I didn't feel like I had much left in the tank, but I still had some. I could feel it all around me; I could almost draw more if I wanted to. If I could figure out how. I focused on a nearby shadow instead.

*"Search within the shadow, consider your destination. Search for a shadow within."* I hesitated. There was still a part of me that doubted that this was real, that believed I was going crazy. How could I simply go along with this new voice in my head? But I couldn't shake the violence that was still fresh in my mind. So, I reached out, into the shadow, energy pooling down into my fingertips.

I remembered the rooftop. There wasn't much up there, only the doorway leading to the stairway and the short wall encompassing the top. Still, I could imagine the shadow cast by the doorway and tried to focus on it. *"Link the two in your mind, and push."*

That part was as easy as breathing. I flowed into the shadow, stumbling in surprise when my feet found the rooftop outside. My men were all in a line along the edge of the building, facing the building across the street. None of them seemed to know that I was there.

"Viper 1-1, this is Overwatch. We're moving to take the building to your front. Shift fire, over."

The radio call shot electricity down my spine. I couldn't believe it; the pinned-down Rangers were actually going to take the building I had just cleared. "Shift fire, second floor!" I shouted to my squad, all but sprinting to join them. "Shift fire, second floor!"

My team leaders echoed my command, their Joy's echoing them. "Overwatch, this is 1-1, shift fire confirmed." The Rangers in the courtyard moved into the building, one team after the other. They must have made quick work of that first floor. There were only a handful of gunshots before they came back over the radio.

"Viper 1-1, first floor clear. Moving to the second, shift fire."

"Shift fire, rooftop!" I shouted to my squad. "Shift fire confirmed," I said into the radio after my squads echoed chorus.

It wasn't long before I could hear helicopters in the distance. All the fighting seemed to stop all at once as the Apache gunships finally approached. Air support had that effect on people sometimes. The insurgents knew they would only die if they kept fighting with even one of those flying around. They always seemed to prefer to drop their weapons and melt into the cities, to live and to fight another day.

"Viper 1-1, second floor clear. Moving to the roof, lift fire."

"Lift fire!" I shouted the command, though they'd already stopped firing a long time ago. "Locker, Ramirez, set your men around a perimeter. I want 360-degree security." I realized that I still wasn't using my night vision as soon as I said it and flipped it back over my eye, adjusting the brightness as low as it would allow while the teams adjusted themselves around the outside edge of the rooftop. Its light no longer blinded me, though it somewhat hindered my vision. I could see better without it. I could even see the Apaches off in the distance.

And her.

She stood silently next to me, the warm Iraqi wind catching her hair as she smiled, taking no heed to the warriors surrounding us while she surveyed the battlefield. Nor of me for that matter. It would take close to half an hour before the quick reaction force got here to pick up the rescued, the dead, and the wounded. I wouldn't dare to say anything to her until they did.

There was something about that hungry smile that terrified me.

# Chapter 30

The room was shrouded in darkness, a circle of light illuminating the floor around me from an unknown source above. It was disorienting. There were no walls that I could see, no ceiling above me. All I could see was the smooth, hard floor on which I stood near the outside of the circle. Everything else was draped in an inky black.

"Hmm." Her voice hummed sleepily behind me, iron chains rattling as I turned to find the source. She laid directly in the center of the circle with her back to me, writhed in chains shackling her wrists, ankles, waist, and even her neck directly to the floor.

I froze like a scared rabbit when she pushed herself off the floor into a seated position, her legs crossed beneath her. Asmodeus smoothly pulled her hair out of her face, freezing my breath in my lungs when her eyes locked onto mine, her mouth splitting into a predatory grin. "Here to finish me off, my love? Tell me, how is your dear ol' dad?" Her grin faded into confusion. "No, this isn't you," she said before I could respond. "This is somebody else."

My blood thawed at the mention of my father. Even now, I wanted to lash out at the memory of what she had done. "No," I said through a clenched jaw. "It's the Magistrate. They've taken us prisoner."

"I see, though they are trying to do more than that, it seems." She nodded her understanding. "No doubt one of their necromancers attempting to rend your soul to transform you into one of their abominations, judging by the way they invaded us. Tell me, who precisely is responsible for this?"

"Lillian Eldonna." I huffed a breath, trying to calm myself. "Raymond Evans is the one trying to turn me. He has us shackled to a chair as we speak. I don't think we have a lot of time."

Her face went slack with surprise. "Trying to turn *us*, you mean. Raymond is someone I'm only loosely familiar with, though Lillian… now that is something." She laughed. "He will be in for quite the surprise when he realizes he cannot tamper with your spirit. Now, how did she take you if she couldn't seduce you with her magic?" She flashed a wry smile. "Did you *let* her?"

"No," I stammered. "How did you know that?"

Her smile broadened. "Succubae consume from the spirit itself, slowly draining their victims of their humanity. But with us bound, neither Lillian nor her half-rate necromancer could hope to damage your spirit. Your soul is already spoken for."

Her words sent a cold shiver down my spine. "I thought it was my mother's spellbinding that stopped her from influencing me."

She pursed her lips. "A reasonable assumption, but no. The spellbinding would have done little to stop either of them. It merely acts as a plug, preventing energy from flowing into you. But you failed to answer my question. The last thing I remember, I was in the midst of burning your father's house to the ground."

"That was a long time ago." I only just realized that my hands had balled into fists. It took everything I had not to lunge at her, to beat her within an inch of her miserable existence.

I silently lambasted myself for my anger and what I was about to do. Sure, she probably saved the lives of many of my friends and fellow Rangers that day in Iraq, but she nearly took everything I knew and loved after, before she could be subdued. I could only imagine what it would mean if I asked for her help a second time, or what I might lose. Even so, Amber was still in danger, and without my magic, I had no idea how I could help her on my own. Not to mention that I did not know what happened to Chase either.

It seemed like I had little choice. Besides, I had already crossed my point of no return.

"Lillian got to me through Amber," I finally said, swallowing a lump that had formed in my throat. "She used her seduction on Amber… I guess. Now they have her and they're going to use her for some sort of ritual."

"And now here you are." She spread her arms wide, chains rattling noisily. "Trapped with me within the confines of your own mind. Let me guess, you've come to ask for my help?"

"You weren't exactly my first choice," I seethed.

"I would imagine not." Her eyes narrowed. "What sort of ritual?"

"I'm not sure. I get the impression that it is supposed to target the leadership of the Thirteen Pyres Society somehow. They pulled it from one of my mother's grimoires, the Book of the Body."

Her expression hardened, her eyes growing fierce in their intensity. "And now that they have your blood, they can access it," she scoffed. "Generally speaking, it takes a body to directly target a body with magic. There are a variety of ways that can manifest, depending on the intent, but it usually takes more than one to kill at a distance."

"Amber is pregnant." I felt hollow when I said it. The words seemed to slip from somebody else's lips, not my own. I had to fight to detach myself from the emotional torrent that was welling up inside me, though it seemed like a losing battle when it feverishly clashed against the confines of my mind.

She pulled in a slow, heavy breath. "Your mother was notably efficient in employing her magic. That would certainly be enough for what they need."

"How do we stop them?"

"Even with your magic, you wouldn't stand a chance in a one-on-one fight with either the necromancer or with Lillian. You simply don't have the knowledge or experience to contend with their decades of practice. If you were to surprise them somehow, maybe ambush them unaware, then maybe… *maybe* you would stand a chance."

"Well, nobody knows about you, for starters," I explained. "And everyone is under the impression that I don't have access to my powers. Are you able to fix that?"

"What, your powers?" she said smirked. "My reawakening all but guarantees that, Shadow Walker. That's all that I am limited to, though, such as I am." She raised her hands, gesturing to her manacles.

"That should be all I need for now, thank you," I said, trying to keep my voice stern.

"Always so polite." She slowly took to her feet, a cacophony of chains rattling until she stood at her full height. She steadied her gaze on me like a hungry tiger, and just as lethal. I could practically feel myself shrinking from the weight of it. "But consider this, you will be chasing a woman possessed by an entity who bore witness to time's conception, and a man who has practiced his art for decades before you were even born."

She lifted her chin in her self-confidence. "Without me, you would surely die in this chair. But I am timeless. Theology has spoken my name in its various forms for centuries across the globe. Imagine the power you would yield if you would but release me. If you would accept me, your victory would be all but assured. You can run home with your beautiful Amber and soon-to-be child to live a life of your choosing. Assuming they are still alive, of course."

"A life of my choosing?" I scoffed. "That is a fine thing to promise, coming from a demon of chaos. I seem to remember trying to live some semblance of a life before you took it all away from me, nearly killing my entire family in the process."

"I also illuminated aspects of your identity that you never would have uncovered on your own, not to mention the lies your own family fed you to keep it a secret. If anything, I helped free you from this farce of a life you were living so you might find one of your own making." She crossed her arms. "Tell me, Kyle, have you yet uncovered anything of your family's past?"

"I have a little, yes," I said.

"And yet you still wish to defend them?"

A part of me wanted to spit in her face, to deny everything that she was saying. My life all but fell apart that day on the ranch, and everything I recently learned about my family's history ran completely contrary to the type of people I had always known them to be. Still, I couldn't completely discredit what Asmodeus was saying either.

Regardless, none of it mattered if I was to be turned into a thrall, or worse. It didn't matter if I was handcuffed to this chair, powerless to defend myself or to help Amber. Without Asmodeus or my magic, I wouldn't have a family to raise by the end of the night.

But I couldn't risk my family to the influence of a demon either.

Not again.

"My answer is no, Asmodeus," I said, choosing my words carefully. "You may hold claim to my spirit, but I will not subject my body to your influence, nor my mind to your will. We are running out of time. Will you help me or not?"

Her gaze cut into me like daggers. "It seems I have no choice," she relented with a sigh, gesturing to her manacles. "We'll need a plan. How do you suggest we find Amber?"

I rubbed my claddagh with my thumb, taking a small measure of comfort that, even within the confines of my subconscious, it was still there. "I may have a way to do that, but we need to get out of this chair first."

"Alright," she said. "Then pay attention. We may only have one shot at this."

# Chapter 31

I stirred from unconsciousness with a searing pain and pressure in the center of my chest, and a warm, wet sensation down my stomach and into my seat. It was all I could do to open my eyes or otherwise brace against the pain. I quickly realized that it was Raymond's hand on my chest causing the pressure, though that didn't necessarily account for the pain. I could hear him chanting, fully focused on his attempts to force his will into me and failing. With his attention fully on me, I couldn't let him onto the fact that I was awake.

I had only one shot at this.

Something changed in me, though. It was as if my awareness of my environment shifted as energy slowly drifted into me. I had to pull it in to use it. With my eyes closed and my head lolling, I drew in slow, shallow breaths, forcing myself to wall off the pain into a separate segment of my mind so it wouldn't leave me distracted.

I imagined a furnace in the center of my chest, right where Raymond placed his palm over my heart, imagining each small inhalation as fuel for its fire, each exhalation as the fire's smoky waste. The warmth of the furnace pooled into me as the energy I needed slowly started to build. The whole process was slow, with Raymond's chanting buzzing in my ear and the pain in my chest begging for my distraction. The tone of his voice shifted too. He was getting impatient.

*"Easy,* Shadow *Walker, you are doing well."* She must have sensed my growing unease. *"Be patient, your time will come."*

"What?" Raymond pulled his hand back. "What is this?"

Time was up.

I pooled a small sum of my energy into my fingers, focusing on the cuffs, and snapped. They immediately loosened.

"Wha–" Raymond gasped, pulling away, but he wasn't fast enough. I lanced power down my arms, into my fist, and punched out, taking him off his feet, sending him smacking into the closet behind him, where he crumpled to the floor.

"Damn, that was easier than I thought it would be," I said, shaking off the cuffs still dangling on my feet.

*"You didn't need* that *much energy for the restraints. You should have used more for your attack."* Asmodeus's voice came to me clear, like a whisper in my ear.

"Right," I said aloud, looking from inside the circle still on the floor, then to Raymond. "I'll have to remember that next time. How about this circle?"

*"It's a simple containment* circle, *meant to keep energy from escaping or interfering from the outside. A physical body can cross it, as you can see from Raymond."* His groans sounded from within the closet. Apparently he wasn't dead yet.

Coughing with a wince, he looked up to me, bleary-eyed as I stepped over the circle. "I didn't break a rib, did I?" I asked as I approached.

"Wha–" A punch to the mouth shut him up, rendering him unconscious.

With all the excitement, I didn't notice the blood draining from my chest onto my stomach from a pentagram carved into me over my heart. "Son of a bitch." I swore, searching for a cloth or something to cover it with. I spotted the white t-shirt I'd worn earlier and used it to wipe away the blood. I noticed my red shirt too, though I left it alone.

The wound was no bigger than the size of my palm, and it was fairly superficial. It wouldn't take long for it to clot either. I might have even appreciated the scar it would inevitably leave behind if the pentagram were more my style. Sadly, it wasn't. I would have to deal with that at another time.

Pressing the reddened t-shirt over the wound, I gingerly opened the door and peered into the hallway outside. The house seemed empty, or at least this floor was. Nothing stirred as I peeked out, so I assumed, if it was Lillian's house, that I was alone in the basement. The room I was in was at the end of a short hallway that opened into a larger open room at the other end to my right.

Stepping into the hallway without closing the door behind me, trying my best to stay as quiet as possible, I realized I was prowling in the depths of what was essentially an enemy stronghold without a weapon, and that I still needed to clear the area to find some trace of Chase or Amber. There was only one place I knew for certain where I would find one.

"I need a shadow," I whispered.

*"So, make one."* She sounded like she was growing impatient.

"Right," I said, and looked at the light in the hallway. I concentrated on it, and with a snap of a finger, the light went out with a pop. I was taken aback by the clarity of what I saw in the midst of the darkness. It had been years since I had seen the world through night vision or the shadow walker's sight. The hallway revealed itself to me in the darkness, and I could see that I was enveloped in its shadow.

*"You need to hurry,* Shadow *Walker."*

"Thanks for the reminder, demon," I snipped. Walking to the end of the hall, I searched within the shadow for another one outside. I could feel one above me, just on the outside edge of the house, confirming that I actually was in the basement. I focused on it, pushing a trickle of energy into it, and walked outside.

I could immediately tell that I was at the side of the house opposite the garage, clouds covering the nearly full moon, shrouding the world in darkness. This suited me just fine.

*"That was a* little *slow."*

"Yeah, I'm a little out of practice," I said, stalking to the corner toward the front of the house.

*"You* will *need to be faster than that. There is a reason they call it shadow-walking, not shadow-staring-at-a-wall."*

"Thanks, you're being *super* helpful right now." I peeked around the corner. The driveway was mostly empty, save for a couple of trucks and my Toyota. It was sort of out in the open since I'd parked in the rear of the other vehicles that had already left. Otherwise, the area looked clear. Remembering the security camera, I snapped my fingers, and ran for the truck, hoping the hex worked.

Skidding to a stop, I crouched, taking one last look around to ensure the area was still clear before opening the door and ducking inside. I dug for my go-bag, relieved that everything was still there. I undid my belt and strapped on my concealed-carry holster, pausing when I spotted my emergency roadside bag.

This was a fairly common item in the upper Midwest, especially in the uppermost regions like North Dakota, where it wasn't entirely uncommon for the temperatures to dip 40 degrees below 0 Fahrenheit, or for snow drifts to build as tall as some houses. Emergency roadside bags had a variety of items, such as blankets, flares, reflectors, or water. Getting yourself stranded in the middle of nowhere in the dead of winter can be deadly under extreme conditions, so these simple bags can literally save your life.

Mine had the addition of a basic first aid kit, and I considered applying a basic bandage to my wound before going back inside. I knew I could apply one pretty fast, but I also spotted Chase's truck still in the parking lot and decided against it. The bleeding wasn't bad and might even stop soon on its own. Not to mention that time was of the essence. If Chase was still inside I would need to extract him before I would otherwise lose the chance to do so. There was no telling what would happen to him if I wasn't able to, and there was no telling when the ritual might begin either.

After clipping on my knife holster and checking my father's old 1911, I threw my now bloody white t-shirt on and ran back to the shadow I had previously walked out of.

*"Better,"* she said after I made my way back into the basement hallway. *"But you need to be faster."*

Ignoring her, I glided into the first room where they'd held me earlier, mostly seeing if Raymond was still there. I half considered putting a bullet in the unconscious man, who still lay crumpled within the closet I had left him in. He wasn't much of a threat at the moment and murder wasn't really my style, so I flowed back into the hallway, opening the door into the next room.

This one was set up much like a typical bedroom, but it was completely void of any decoration or character. It had a simple twin bed, a chest of drawers, a simple wooden chair, and a basket half full of clothes. Otherwise, it was about as empty as Silent John's personality. Creeped out, I moved on without closing the door behind me.

It was remarkable how at ease I felt, tactically moving through the hallway like so. There was a small part of me that was a little unnerved by the idea of doing it alone, but it was amazing how something I hadn't practiced in years came back to me so fast. I felt like I was in my element, invading homes, and tactically clearing rooms like I did so long ago.

The rooms seemed large, as far as bedrooms go, so there were only four in this section of the hallway. I leveled my pistol to the third door as I approached, pausing as I gently tested the doorknob, found it unlocked, and flowed inside.

This one was set up identical to the one before, only this one had an occupant. He stood silently from his chair, a middle-aged man in a button up shirt and slacks, and stared at me with the same dead expression as Silent John when I cleared myself out of the doorway.

Another thrall.

"Stop right there. Don't move," I said sternly, leveling my pistol at him. "Where are they keeping Chase?"

Ignoring my commands, he casually opened the chest of drawers next to him, pulling out a pistol. I shot him in the temple, the sound deafening within the enclosed space as he dropped to the floor.

So much for the element of surprise.

*"We need to hurry, that might draw more of them here."*

"Moving," I whispered, moving toward the next room. Again, I lined myself up to the doorway, but this time I was far more deliberate with my entry.

Chase flinched away from me in the chair he was tied to within the darkness of the room. "Chase," I said, throwing on the light. "Are you okay?"

"What?" He blinked away the light. "Kyle?"

"Yeah." I knelt next to him, testing the knots binding his wrists to the chair. "Are you good, man? Are you hurt?"

"No, I'm okay," he said, opening his eyes. "What's going – Jesus, are you okay?" He gasped, staring at me wide-eyed behind his glasses.

"Yeah," I said, glancing down at my blood-soaked shirt. I must have looked like a damn trauma victim. "It's not as bad as it looks." Frustrated with the knot, I pulled out my knife and started to cut. "They tried to turn me into a thrall. I got away."

"Wow, Kyle," he said in disbelief. "Are you sure you're okay?"

"Yeah, but we need to get you out of here, buddy," I said, nearly clear of the first knot. "What happened? Where is Amber?"

"I'm not sure. Lillian brought me into her office after you. I thought you were still in there, but she jumped me as soon as I walked in. That was the last thing I remember before waking up in here."

"You left Amber alone?" I glared up at him, furious.

"I'm sorry." He shrank back into his chair. "I didn't see any other choice."

I wanted to scold him, but I put it aside. That wouldn't help anything right now. "They took her as some sort of sacrifice for a ritual. They're trying to kill off some of the leadership in the Society," I said, finally cutting through the rope and moving onto the next one.

"What?" he asked in disbelief. "How?"

"They pulled a spell from my mother's grimoire, the Book of the Body."

"Their headquarters is on the East Coast, can they even cast something that far?"

"I don't know," I said, glaring up at him. "Can they?"

He paused for a moment to consider. "Maybe. They would need one hell of a power source to hit someone that far. They'll also need a body to direct the spell, but they would need a lot of energy to power it. Something like a ley line or a nexus."

"What the hell is that?" I asked, nearly through the rope.

"You can almost think of a ley line as a stream of energy that runs through the earth, a nexus is where two or more ley lines meet." I cut free his other wrist and moved onto his feet. "We have a smaller ley line that runs under our property," he said, rubbing his wrist. "We tap into it sometimes when we need to. Remember that shed where we healed that calf?"

"Yeah."

"That sits over a ley line." A door slammed in the hallway. "Oh no," he said, staring into the doorway.

"To hell with this." I stood up and shut the door, flipping the lock in the doorknob. It wouldn't buy much time, but hopefully enough. I put the knife in its scabbard and walked back to Chase. "Stand up," I instructed, helping him to his feet.

I immediately pushed him onto the mattress. "Hey," he said, the simple wooden chair flopping around clumsily behind him. The ropes securing his ankles were tied near the bottom of the legs, so I simply yanked the chair up, toward his buttocks, pulling it free.

Someone tried the doorknob as I pulled Chase to his feet. "Shit," he cursed. "What do we do now?"

"Follow me." I took him by the wrist and pulled him toward the open closet. It was empty, and there was just enough shadow for me to use inside. I didn't focus on anything in particular, only reaching for anything available that I could use upstairs. I pushed a little energy into the shadow and walked with Chase in tow.

I became immediately entangled in clothing hanging from some sort of rack, coat hangers rattling noisily as Chase and I searched for a door within the confined space. There was no use being quiet when Chase and I found it. Anyone on the other side would have known we were there. With my gun up, I burst through the door into the room on the other side, relieved that Chase and I were its only occupants.

"Graceful."

I scoffed, ignoring her. I wasn't about to get into the habit of responding to the demon out loud, not with someone else in the room.

It was Lillian's office. We emerged from a closet set in the far side of the room. It seemed to be just as I had left it, save for the blood stain where Silent John had died and the pull of my mother's grimoire calling to me. Stepping silently around the couch, I noticed that both the book and the pedestal were gone.

Chase stood frozen, staring at me wide-eyed and in shock. "You…"

"Found my powers, yeah," I supplied for him.

"… Are a shadow walker… like your mother…"

"Yeah, but I'm not her," I said, gently. "And we need to get you out of here."

He shook his head slowly, gathering himself before walking warily over to me by the door. I would have taken us through another shadow, but Chase was shaken enough as it was. I didn't need to traumatize him further if I could help it. Thankfully, the main floor was empty, making it easy for me to clear our way out the front door and into the driveway with Chase at my heel.

"You need to get out of here," I told him, keeping a wary eye out for anyone who might have followed us, approaching his truck.

He opened the door, but didn't get in. "What about you?"

I shook my head. "I need to find Amber. I'll meet up with you at the ranch when I do."

"No," he said sternly, closing the door behind him. "I'm coming with you."

Wincing at the noise, I was a little taken aback by his sudden show of bravery. It didn't escape me that finding Amber was a borderline suicide mission. I had no idea what Chase was capable of either, magically speaking or otherwise, but Lord knew I could use the help.

"He'll only get in the way." She walked into view near the edge of my vision to my right. I tried not to make a show of my surprise, knowing that Chase could not see her slowly walking toward the tailgate, leveling her eyes on him like a predator on the prowl. "He is a healer, unskilled in the arts of war. He will only get himself killed, and you along with him."

I hated to admit that she was right. Someone who could heal magically might be useful, but it wasn't like we were rolling in with heavy armor or artillery, and we didn't have anyone pulling any form of security for us either. Once I found Amber, speed had to be our security, and I had to take advantage of any element of surprise I could manage. Lifelong ranchers weren't exactly trained in the fine arts of stealth craft.

"If we fail and you are captured, or God forbid killed,"—I shook my head—"nobody will know what happened here."

"I don't care, I–"

"Look," I told him sternly, placing a hand on his shoulder. "I appreciate what you are trying to do, but someone needs to tell the Freemasons what the Magistrate is doing." He shot me a hard look. "Someone needs to tell them that the Magistrate is operational and targeting family members of the Freemasons. Your family in particular. Besides, this is dangerous enough. I can't look after you and go after Amber at the same time."

He looked like he was about to protest but seemed to decide against it. Reluctantly, he climbed into his truck and paused before closing the door. "Hey Kyle," he said, clearly worried. "Thank you."

"Don't mention it brother," I said, fist-bumping the hood. "Drive safe."

He shut the door without another word, his gray Chevy roaring to life just as the front door of the house slammed shut. Four more thralls rushed into the front lawn and got on line, pistols up and ready to shoot.

But I shot first.

I emptied the remainder of the magazine into the crowd, running to the only other truck besides mine in the driveway. I knew I hit a couple of them, their bodies jerking with the 45 ACP rounds punching into them. They didn't go down but hobbled to the side of the garage near the front door with their buddies, who were taking cover as soon as they realized that someone was shooting back.

If they were anything like Silent John, I realized, they would probably need to take a hit to their central nervous system to go down. I didn't necessarily need to kill them right away, I just needed to keep their heads down so that Chase could make his getaway. I would have to find a way to maneuver around them and take them out once he was in the clear.

Their volume of fire wasn't high, though. After a quick reload, I placed shots where I could into the corner they hid behind while Chase took advantage of the shift in chaos to speed out of the driveway. Rounds slammed into his truck as he pulled away, punching into its bed and shattering glass until the tree line obscured him from view.

*"You're thinking too much like a soldier, use your magic!"* Her voice shook me from my tunnel vision.

"Right," I said, all but kicking myself for my stupidity. With Chase gone, two of them started laying down a base of fire while the other two maneuvered around to my truck. Four-to-one odds were far from ideal and these guys were acting like they knew what they were doing. In the Army, we tried not to attack the enemy unless we had three-to-one odds in our favor. If I stayed put, they would flank me and take me out.

"Damn it!" I heard Raymond shout, slamming the front door.

Great, now it was five to one.

"Get out there and kill that son of a bitch!" He sounded rough, his shouting more of a wheeze than a yell. I wondered if I'd broken a rib after all.

Rounds punched into the truck from two different sides, and vehicles were not very good at stopping bullets. Taking cover behind the engine block, I focused on the shadow underneath the truck, connected it to a shadow next to the house, and rolled into it.

I half expected to find myself resembling a moist human pincushion when I rolled out of the connected shadow, sighing in relief when I found myself to the contrary. "*Lucky,*" she all but whispered in my ear.

"No shit," I whispered back, sprawling to my feet and moving to the corner of the building.

I was behind them now. Normally a competent team might have tried to pull some sense of rear security, but with Raymond's chastising, every eye and every gun focused on the truck I just rolled away from. He should have let the professionals put in their work.

I snickered a little while reloading a magazine when I realized it must have been Raymond's truck they were shooting at.

Grasping his chest and barely breathing, Raymond had apparently already hobbled to join the two by my truck while the two by the garage picked up to maneuver around Raymond's truck at his insistence. With a snap of my fingers, the guns by my truck went silent.

I stepped out, inhaling deeply through my nose, drawing in my power, and reached out my hand. "Burn!" I snarled.

A gout of flame erupted from my open palm, completely enveloping the two thralls and Raymond's truck in a cone of flame. The two thralls went down without even so much as a murmur.

Fire worked well too, apparently.

I nearly overdid it, almost taking out the grill of my truck and engulfing the side of the garage in a wall of flame in the process. Stars danced in my vision, exhaustion nearly taking me down to my knees while I smiled up at Raymond, whose expression was of open-mouthed shock and surprise, seated firmly on the ground next to my truck.

"That wasn't your truck, was it Ray-Ray?" I chided.

He looked furious, painfully holding his ribs while bracing himself against the driver's side door. He probably would have shouted something back if he could breathe.

The two remaining thralls charged me, which I thought was funny. I shot them both in the head as they approached, crumpling them to the ground at my feet.

I leveled my gun onto Raymond, who started to stand. "It's over, Ray," I said, stepping closer. "You're too wounded to fight. Let's give this up."

He shook some sort of bracelet clear of the sleeve of his left arm, hunched over as he held his ribs with his right. "Not hardly."

He raised a hand and I fired, twice, rounds sparking off a clear red shield out in front of him, his white smile glistening behind it. He snapped his fingers with his right hand and punched with his left. If he knew how to throw a punch, instead of telegraphing it, I might have died where I stood.

I rolled as a red streak of energy detonated the ground where my feet had been, knocking me off-balance onto my back, stealing my breath away. He hobbled up to me, drawing energy for another strike when he stopped, wide-eyed. Panicking in my vulnerable state, I brought my gun up, willing it to work after the snap.

I hardly noticed how the orange–red runes lit up the length of the slide like burning embers.

Raymond punched with a snarl. I yelled, pushing my will into the firearm, and fired.

A red streak of energy detonated in front of me and around me, shaking the ground beneath me. My ears rang, eyes shut against the flash of blinding light. When

I opened them, I was shocked that I was okay, as an electric-blue dome originating from the gun barrel enveloped me.

Raymond stood, hunched over and fatigued in bewildering confusion. I lined up my sights, pushing in more of my will. Blue runes lit like burning embers along the slide, and I fired. His upper body exploded into a slurry of blood and gore, sending his legs tumbling near the truck behind him.

"What the hell was that?" I stood, shocked by what I'd done.

"You got lucky, that's what," she scolded, walking out of the corner of my vision to my left – I nearly shot her out of fright. "If it wasn't your father's pistol, you would have died."

I glared at her, holding my tongue. The runes faded from the slide as I examined it until they disappeared completely from the naked eye. "I've handled this thing all my life. I shot and cleaned it more times than I can remember, but I've never seen these before."

"Nor would you," she explained simply. "Your mother made it for him on the onset of the war. She had a talent for creating magical artifacts others could not. The runes are magically imbued; you could never tell without proper discernment. Most magical items present that way, often making them hard to find."

"How does it work?" I asked her, awestruck.

"Well, you've seen the shield," she said with a smile. "It also stores kinetic energy each time it is fired, to be used later for a powerful blast, or numerous smaller ones depending on how it is used. As far as activating it? I'm not sure, though it seems you are well on your way to finding out."

"Could I… replicate this?"

"Perhaps." She nodded her head. "With the proper grimoire."

"Which one?" I asked, ejecting the magazine. Only one round remained, though I still had one more in the chamber.

She tilted her head, considering. "The Book of the Mind, most likely."

"That'll have to be a problem for another time then," I said, reinserting the near empty magazine from earlier, leaving four rounds remaining. I walked back to my truck with a sigh, checking the ruined pistols dropped by the thralls hoping to find more ammo. No luck; they carried Glocks chambered in 9-millimeter. Their ammo was useless in my 1911.

"So, what's next?" she asked, watching as I hurled a Glock through Lillian's office window in frustration. "How are you going to find Amber?"

Embers danced in the air above the garage, the fire spreading onto the roof. I rubbed my engagement band with my thumb as I watched, weighing my options. Finally, a thought occurred to me.

"It was my father who found my mother, the night that she died," I said, examining the claddagh. "My uncle used to say they were inseparable, and they always seemed to know what the other was thinking. My mother was Native, so she never took much interest in Irish lor or history outside of this ring. What do you think the chances are…" I looked to the demon to see if she would fill in the blanks. She stared back with only a silent shrug.

I focused on my father's old claddagh, worn on the ring finger of my clenched hand, drawing in energy with deep breaths. Closing my eyes, I pictured Amber's claddagh, my mother's old ring, connecting the two in my mind with a small push of energy. There was a gentle pull, like a small magnet drawing my hand toward the tree line.

Excitement welled up inside of me when I opened my eyes to a gentle red glow illuminating the heart in the ring, a Celtic knot smoldering with amber as it connected the wrists together around the band.

"Clever," Asmodeus said, flashing a hungry smile.

Inhaling deep through my nose, I drew in my power, reaching out with my right hand. "Burn!" I snarled, a fountain of flames erupting from my open palm, blowing in the front door of the house with the force of a cannon ball. The fire flowed into Lillian's million-dollar home, consuming it in an inferno within moments.

# Chapter 32

As the sky continued to darken, the rolling hills transformed into a blue-gray world of shadows beneath the condensing clouds blocking the waning moonlight. I couldn't tell if the chill running through my spine was from the cool evening air or the palpable smell of death that followed me into the cab of the vehicle. For a moment I meditated on the gentle pull of the ring, easing my mind into stillness with the hum of the engine and noise of the radio filling the silence.

In war, an unfocused mind can get you killed. The excitement of finding Amber, the fear of losing her, and the rage I felt toward her abductors all solidified, swirling in my mind like a hurricane, threatening to throw me off-balance. I even unconsciously reverted to old wartime driving habits in my anxiety, looking out for obstacles or roadside bombs as I sped along the highway, which was completely nonsensical and irrational given the situation. I needed to detach myself from the situation if I was going to come out of this on top.

"These are not normal clouds," Asmodeus calmly pointed out. She mostly sat quietly next to me, examining the cloud cover outside the window. The very idea of sharing the cab with a demon that nobody else could see did nothing to calm my nerves.

"How do you mean?" I asked, trying to sound more stoic than I felt. "Is it the spell?"

"It has to be; you can see the clouds condensing up ahead." She sounded calm but focused, nearly the opposite of how I felt, but exactly how I needed to be.

"How powerful does a spell have to be to change the weather?" I asked, completely aghast.

"Powerful. I'm beginning to think your friend was right—they must be using a nexus nearby." Her words were sullen, bringing with them their own sort of weight.

"Are we too late?" The sinking feeling in my chest made it hard to speak.

"It's hard to say. There is no way to know until we get there, unless they activate the spell first."

"Okay," I said softly, steeling my resolve, my forearms growing tense from gripping the steering wheel too tight. Nothing more needed to be said. I punched the accelerator, focusing hard on my ring. Thankfully, we didn't have far to go.

We drove north along Highway 1806 until it curved west, passing by the veterans cemetery. The pull of the ring signaled northeast, then east when the road curved north again.

Asmodeus stared at me curiously. "What is it?"

"I think they're in Fort Abraham Lincoln," I explained, turning the truck around. "The entrance is near the cemetery."

"You've been there?"

"I have, a couple of times," I said, completing the turn and punching the accelerator. I had to raise my voice over the roar of the old pickup's four-cylinder engine.

Small, but fierce.

"It's where Lieutenant Colonel George Custer and his Seventh Cavalry Regiment were stationed before the Battle of the Little Bighorn during the Great Sioux War."

"Ah, the Battle of Greasy Grass. Custer's last stand," she offered contemplatively.

I felt myself smiling in appreciation. "If that's where they are, I can see three places where they might conduct the ritual."

"Go on," she prompted, her attention fully on me.

"The easiest way to infiltrate would be the reconstructed Indian village on the far northeast side of the state park. It would take a while to get there, but there is a thick tree line and a dike along the river that we can use to cover our movement. They built a handful of earth lodges, sort of like what the Mandan tribe used to live out of back in the day. Trees surround the entire village, so it will be easy to get in close and ambush them if they are there."

"That makes sense," she seemed to confirm for me. "People tend to congregate around strong ley lines and nexus."

That sort of brought my hopes up. "The second would be a reconstructed parade ground the cavalry used. It's out in the open, but there are several old stables and barracks along the perimeter, and Custer's old house is on the west end near the base of a hill. It's on the way to the village though, and it's close enough to the river that we can recon it along the way."

"Assaulting through open terrain would prove challenging, though," she pointed out matter-of-factly.

"Right, not without taking the high ground first. But that isn't even the worst option."

"Which one is that?"

"The third option I can see is the old infantry post on the far northeast side of the park. It sits atop a large plateau that overlooks everything. They wouldn't have much up there in terms of cover or concealment, aside from a couple of blockhouses, but their vantage point would be rock solid. I might be able to find a draw with shrubbery that I could crawl through toward the top of the hill, but there is a good chance they will see us coming and fire down on us before we could do anything about it."

She looked at me with a worried expression. Neither of us needed to explain why assaulting uphill, alone, and virtually weaponless, would be the next best thing to a suicide mission. "Let's hope they are at the village then."

Driving just past the cemetery, I turned into the only entrance on the south side of the park, driving slowly down the winding road with my lights off. There was a house tucked into the wood line before reaching the parade ground that I wanted to avoid, so I pulled in behind a bush along the side of the road, hoping it would conceal the vehicle from road traffic, before finally turning off the engine, plunging us into silence.

"Are you sure you are up for this?" Asmodeus asked from the passenger seat, concern thick in her voice.

"Are you really so concerned for my safety, fair spirit?" I asked her, my level voice threaded with mockery.

"Do you have any idea how difficult it is to find someone willing to be possessed?" She scowled. "Most mortals are useless to me. The vast majority of magic users resort to exorcism before a conversation can even begin."

"I can't imagine why," I jeered.

She sighed heavily in frustration, which was an oddly funny thing to hear from an incorporeal spirit. "You do not know how much potential you have," she said, turning her gaze back to the window. "Especially as a shadow walker with your parentage. Whole battles have been determined by the simple presence of a shadow walker on the field, your mother's actions being a profound example."

She turned to face me again. "The fact remains that you have neither the knowledge nor the skill to engage in mystical combat. Not yet. You of all people should know by now that mere potential isn't enough to win a fight."

"What would you have me do then?" I growled, gripping the steering wheel tight. "Should I just leave Amber here to die? And then what?"

"As opposed to charging into combat with only four rounds in your pistol, wounded, fatigued, and concussed?" Her voice softened, her expression almost pleading, "Let me train you. What happened with Raymond was lucky at best. He would have killed you easily if you hadn't injured him first. I can show you real magic. I can make you into a veritable force to be reckoned with, such that when you are ready to strike out against them, you can ensure that something like this can never happen to another innocent again. You do not know what you are up against here, Kyle. If you go out there like this, you will certainly die."

Truth be told, she wasn't entirely wrong. My previous magical display left me drained, and the resulting fatigue left me feeling like someone tripled the force of gravity. Even if I could draw in more energy, it wouldn't be nearly to the extent it was before. It was late, nearly three in the morning. Sleep was beginning to call my name. That was something I could handle easily enough, but the migraine from the resulting concussion was setting in now that the adrenaline was wearing off, and it was getting difficult to keep my eyes open. I'm pretty sure the wound on my chest had already clotted, though my blood-soaked shirt stuck to it, painfully pulling at the forming scab.

All of that goes without mentioning the lack of ammo or the fact that I had no idea what I was getting myself into. For all I knew, Lillian had a pack of thralls with her along with another magic user. I wouldn't last in any magical duel and a firefight would be virtually out of the question. This fight would end before it would even truly begin.

"So why me?" I asked her warily. "What do you get out of all this?"

She considered me for a moment. "Without a corporeal body, I can be nothing more than a passive observer to all this. I'm completely unable to influence anything in this world without you, especially with what is to come."

"What would that be?" I asked in all seriousness.

"I'm afraid you will see the beginnings of it here," she said ominously, her flat tone sending shivers up my spine.

I lay my head back into the seat and weariness swept over me, threatening to draw me out of consciousness. "The problem," I said, forcing my eyes open, "is that I can see no future for me without Amber. I cannot begin to tell you how often we dreamed about the house with the white picket fence and children playing in the yard."

I picked my head up and looked the demon dead in the eyes. "It's the only thing we ever really fought for since we locked you down, and I'll be damned if I'm going to let them take her away without a fight. I will burn this whole damn park to the ground if I have too."

Her glare was pure venom, piercing me like a viper ready to strike. I would not back down from her again, not this time. "Besides," I said with a smirk. "I thought you would appreciate a little chaos."

# Chapter 33

A light rain fell, pattering on the leaves of the bush next to me, tapping on the hood of the truck as it brought with it a chill in the windy evening. In combat, you are either too hot or too cold, too dry or too wet. There never seems to be a comfortable time to fight and you really just have to learn to accept it.

Oddly, it was feeling like another day at the office. I would have cited the weight of body armor being a notable exception, but the weight of fatigue and weariness were more than making up for it.

For a moment, I knelt in place between the bush and the truck, taking in the environment, drawing in the surrounding energy. It was easier than expected, almost surprisingly so. "Can you feel that?" I asked the demon standing over me.

"I can." She nodded to me. "We're near the nexus. We must be on top of a ley line."

Good news, and lucky. I was going to need whatever advantage I could steal.

I sat a moment longer, looking and listening for any sign we were spotted, growing increasingly frustrated by the rain hampering both senses. The bush I parked behind sat near a tree line running parallel to a dike used for flood protection along the bank of the river, the thick foliage haunting the landscape in the frigid rain.

"This is a natural choke point," I informed the demon. "We are stuck between a ridgeline to our left and the Missouri River to our right. This is the only real entryway into the park too, so I will need your help keeping an eye out for spotters."

She glared down at me. "I only see what you see, Shadow Walker."

"Right." I sighed. "You tend to notice things that I don't, though. Just help me out here, okay?"

She rolled her eyes. "I'll do what I can."

Fighting in the wood line meant fighting on a more even playing field than you would urban combat, assuming that the enemy wasn't particularly dug in. Everything is far more straightforward, more two-dimensional. It made it easier to spot the enemy before they could spot you, but it also meant having to move slower, as the simple act of walking could produce enough noise to give you away.

Time wasn't a luxury I had though. I darted into the woods, stalking parallel to the dike like a cat on the prowl, moving only as fast as I dared to minimize sound. Moving from tree to tree, up a small hill and down onto relatively flat ground, I was constantly on the lookout for some sort of sentry, until I finally made my way to the edge of a clearing.

My knee sank into the cool earth at the base of a tree, one hand steady against its rough bark, the other tight on the metallic grip of my pistol as I took in the open parade field with ragged breaths.

Little light shone into the valley, the hills on the other side looming over Custer's house like giants threatening to devour the empty field below. Long wooden barracks and stables lined the parade field like the open rib cage of an animal long dead and mostly buried by time's passing. The river babbled behind the break in the dike behind me, competing with the rain slapping the leaves above me, drowning out the deafening silence beyond the tree line that sheltered me.

"I don't see anyone out here," I said, pulling the front of my shirt stuck uncomfortably to my shivering chest. "I thought I would have seen someone pulling watch by now."

*"We can rule out the parade field, then."* I didn't bother searching for her. With her whispering in my ear, I knew she wouldn't present herself to me if I tried.

The gap in the tree line made for easy access through the gap in the dike into the river, but it was too wide for me to shadow walk into the woods on the other side. Though I didn't see anyone in the dark, the gap still made for a good place to post a spotter to monitor the road leading into the park or the tree line unseen.

The Army referred to this as an "open danger area," or ODA, for a reason. It left you exposed, easily spotted, and vulnerable to anyone waiting for you to cross if you were not careful. You generally wanted to avoid areas like this if you could, but in this case, it seemed that I didn't have much choice.

With a silent groan, I pushed myself to my feet, my knees protesting with the effort. "Ah," I grimaced, drawing a heavy breath. "I'm not eighteen anymore. I'm getting too old for this shit."

*"Stay focused."*

"Thanks, you're super helpful as always." Wiping rain out of my face, I focused energy into the shadow of the tree, connecting it to the nearby stable, and pushed, immediately creeping along the side of the stable to the corner on the other side. Finding the next tree, I pushed more energy into the shadow, and myself with it, until I could take another knee next to the tree deep into the wood line.

The ODA was lava.

Checking my surroundings, I looked back into the parade field and found him almost immediately. Now on the other end of the park, a small house converted into the welcome center stood at the entrance of the parade field with a thrall standing just on the outside with a rifle slung on his chest.

"There's our guy," I whispered through a smile. "I must have missed him running through the trees."

"Not very subtle," she said standing next to me, dry in spite of the rain.

"No," I said, watching him carefully. He didn't seem to think anything was amiss. "Oh, what I wouldn't give for a suppressed rifle right about now."

"He might not be alone. We might have to find an alternate route to escape when we are finished."

"Maybe, but there is a reason we took this route to get here. That may have to be a bridge we burn later." Keeping low, I pushed energy into the ring, concealing its glow behind the tree. "Shit."

She followed my gaze toward the rings pull, her eyes wide upon meeting mine. "This is suicide, Kyle."

"We'll see," I said, getting to my feet.

The original infantry fort wasn't built to defend from the east. The "Mighty" Missouri River provided a natural fortification in that direction, and the Natives of that era, fierce warriors as they were, weren't exactly known for their proficiency with cannons. You could see the eastern bank just fine, along with the Indian village on the lower slant of the hill, but most of its attention was focused on the north, west, and south from its vantage point at the peak.

The river, however, provided more than enough water and sediment from flooding to feed the lush tree line at its base, with deep draws extending up from the woods like fingers clawing their way toward the peak. The vegetation wasn't enough to hide a large force of numbers, but it was more than enough to conceal a force of one on a nearly moonless night.

Several vehicles were parked in the village that I could see near the tree line. I paused on my way toward one of the draws to have a look, not daring to step foot into the village itself.

"I count four," she said, standing next to me again. I nearly drew my gun on her again.

"Jeez," I seethed in a whisper. "Do you have any idea how unsettling that is?"

She put a finger up to her mouth without talking, then pointed to the trucks in the village. Blank stares abounded among the thralls I could see spread out along a perimeter surrounding the trucks, each with an AR-15 slung.

A whole fire team.

"How many of these things do they have?" I whispered breathlessly.

"It's hard to say. There may be more, we need to be careful."

Nodding to the demon, I slunk back into the forest, careful not to make a sound above the pouring rain.

The clouds above swirled in a churning vortex above the hill. The rain pelted me at an angle like icy needles thrown by the wind. My hands and knees sank into the wet earth as I moved, my body straining with the effort of pulling myself up the hill.

I had to low-crawl to stay below the top of the brush inside the draw near the top of the hill. The higher I ascended, the lower I had to crawl to remain unseen. The brush all but disappeared near the crest, though there was just enough of a divot in the ground for me to pull myself up by my stomach, my skull all but dragging against the ground. Climbing as high as I dared, I peered over the ledge of the high plateau, gripping my pistol tight as I steeled myself against the thought of getting shot in the face by some random thrall standing guard above me.

I saw the nearest blockhouse first, looming in the open like a sleeping giant. I watched it for a moment to see if I could spot any movement, which turned out to be useless. The miniature fortress resembled a box sitting on top of another box, only the top box was canted at a forty-five-degree angle. Even with my shadow walker sight, the scant slots along the walls were too dark and narrow to see through, and any approach on foot would have left me an easy target for anyone inside to pick off.

Short grass bent with the wind in front of my face, each gust threatening to reveal more of my face to the blockhouse. I could see another figure standing stone still in the rainfall, just inside the blockhouse's guarded perimeter. Probably another thrall, I surmised, but I couldn't see more than that from my viewpoint.

I was already exposed to view from the blockhouse. Raising my head any more would've made me an easy target for anyone inside to take the crown off my head with an easy rifle shot. I would need to gain a better vantage point of the field somehow.

*"Please don't charge the building."* Annoyed with her agitation, I shook my head at the thought of it.

My shirt furled up to my collarbone, my chest and stomach scraping painfully against the ground as I pushed myself back down the draw toward the thick shrubbery below. Even with the rain, the ground felt like sandpaper against my exposed skin, scraping against the wound in my chest. I wondered if it would open up again, but it was hard to tell with the moisture from the rain.

I pushed myself down to where the vegetation grew thicker. I wouldn't be able to walk through any given shadow. It had to be big enough to at least crawl through like a tunnel. Finding one under a small bush, I focused my mind toward the block house on the hill, trying to connect the two. Doing so from where I spotted it near the top would have been hard enough, but the farther the distance, the greater the focus and the more energy it took to connect shadows. I was already running on fumes.

Still, a vague form of the blockhouse came to mind as I pushed energy into the shadow. The shadow finally gave way, and with stars flashing in my vision, I crawled into it, nearly at the feet of another thrall.

He took a step back just as I lunged into him, my shoulder taking him by the hip, drilling him into the ground with a thud. A rifle stock thumped weakly against my shoulder as I swam up his guard, striking his head with my pistol, once, twice, ripping the rifle out of his hands with the third strike to his temple.

With the thrall blinded by blood and concussed, I stood, and my heel struck like a piston down onto his head with repeated strokes. His head cracked, then caved, then burst open spilling blood, bone, and brain matter onto the hardwood floor.

Footfalls thundered above me with someone rounding the stairway. Grabbing the discarded rifle, I holstered my pistol and walked into the shadow behind the thrall, descending the stairs with his AR-15 up and at the ready. I struck him at the base of the neck with the buttstock, hard, chasing him down the stairs as he fell, stomping his neck until it cracked for good measure.

I brought the rifle up to my shoulder, ready to shoot anyone who might barge into the door as I stumbled to a nearby port in exhaustion. The thrall outside seemed oblivious to the chaos inside, staring expressionlessly past the blockhouse with his AR-15 slung across this chest. I nearly collapsed in relief and exhaustion.

But he wasn't the only one out there. Far from it. There was a large circle drawn within the perimeter of the three blockhouses, four thralls evenly dispersed outside with rifles slung. Behind each stood a chalice on top of a wooden block. A small, covered flame burned in the chalice nearest me, and it took a moment for me to realize that someone had placed each chalice in accordance with one of the cardinal directions: north, east, south, and west.

Lillian stood near the eastern edge dressed in a white gown, flipping through my mother's grimoire sitting on a podium. My hand gripping the AR-15's pistol grip hard, it took everything I had not to shoot her right then and there. In front of her, two more circles were drawn into the ground with tables inside draped in white cloth. A fifth thrall prepared a table with plates and other various items I couldn't quite make out.

Amber lay on top of the other table with another chalice at her feet. Her red hair sprawled in stark contrast to her white robes and white table cover, unconscious. I watched her intently for some sign of life, bracing myself against the wall one-handed, breathing heavy with fatigue and fear that I might be too late.

"What am I looking at?" I whispered.

As I was speaking, Lillian stood tall at the podium, giving the thrall at the table a stiff nod. The thrall left the table to stand just outside the main circle. Once he was outside, Lillian snapped a finger and a small blaze spread along the circle, connecting the outside chalice's in a fiery ring.

"A very powerful spell." The image of Asmodeus appeared next to me, sharing the porthole to gaze outside.

"Thanks," I scoffed. "So helpful, as always. I think we established that already, so what else do you got?"

A slight smile crept into her eyes, my annoyance clearly amusing to her. "Your mother used this spell once. It destroyed the Society's headquarters at the time. That's how the war officially started."

"Oh, wow," I said, taken aback. "How did that work out?"

"Apparently they were trying to target the Merlin." She smirked, "It went for his dog instead."

"Oh no," I gushed. "Not Fido." She beamed a wolfish grin. "So, how does it work?"

She pursed her lips, drawing her attention back to the circle. "It's fairly complex. It combines a couple of spells, in a way. It needs a tracking spell to guide it. I assume that's what the thrall was preparing at that table."

"So, it's more of a magical cruise missile than it is a magical bomb."

She shrugged. "With it's trajectory and power, it's more of a magical nuclear missile, but yes."

"Hold on, they nuked the Merlin's dog?"

She nodded with a smile, not taking her eyes off the ritual. "Him and a handful of his staff, yes. They needed a physical piece of the Merlin to guide the spell, a hair follicle, a nail clipping, that sort of thing. They confused the dog's hair for his."

"Damn, no wonder they went to war." I shook my head in baffled amusement. "Where is the Society's headquarters now, exactly?"

"Savannah, Georgia" she said coldly.

I felt like I took a punch in the gut. I was loosely familiar with Savannah. One of the Ranger regiments was stationed there. "They are not just going after the Society; they are going to destroy Savannah too."

"Depending on how much energy she puts into the spell, yes."

I honestly couldn't give a rip about the Society. They weren't even a factor in my consciousness. They could have their little war and burn in it for all I cared. I came here for my family, but there was so much more at stake now. Savannah wasn't a small town. The weight of it nearly crushed me.

"The other circle inside contains the main component of the spell. The warhead, if you will," she continued. "The sacrifices needed lie within, the spirit of the innocent, the mind of the unwilling, and the body of the lover. To activate the spell, everything within the circle must die." She gave me a hard look. "She only needs a physical representation of your mind. Your blood is the only part of you in the circle. The rest of you should be fine."

"Right," I said, shouldering the rifle. "I'll just shoot her then and be done with it."

"Wait!" Her hand flashed in front of my rifle, stalling me. "You wouldn't be able to shoot her right now if you tried."

I lowered my rifle, glaring at her to continue.

"The more complex the spell, the greater the need to protect it from outside contamination." I listened intently, watching Lillian pace the inside of the circle with a burning bundle of sage held in front of her. "This is the purpose of the outside ring. Once the fire ring is lit, the grounds need to be purified. The ring itself is there to protect the spell from both energy interference and physical contamination."

I sighed in frustration. "How do I defeat it then?"

She studied the circle intently before answering, "Each chalice is a weak point, representing one of the four primary elements."

"Earth, wind, fire, water," I said, following along.

"Exactly, and this is where she is most vulnerable. Now that she has initiated the process, she has no choice but to continue even if the protective circle should fail. To do so, you will need to counter one element with its opposite. But you must be careful." She gave me a hard look. "If you take it down, and you disrupt the spell itself before it is finished, any amount of energy gathered could detonate on top of this hilltop."

I examined the burning chalice near me. It was covered by what almost looked like a handmade rooftop, protecting it from the rain. That made sense considering that water was the opposing element to fire. I considered shooting the rooftop for a moment, but the rain might not put out the fire fast enough. The protective circle might shield the chalice from rifle fire anyway. Searching farther along its perimeter, I found a chalice filled with dirt on the west side of the circle. It would be a tough shot, but there was a chance I could hit it.

"Right," I said, examining the rifle in my hands. It was a simple AR-15 with an AGOC, a four-power scope with a reticle that was illuminated with ambient light. There wasn't enough light in the area to light up the reticle, but I wouldn't need it to.

"What are you doing?" she asked, watching me turn over a corpse at my feet.

"Assuming the other two towers have two thralls each, that'll make nine thralls with us on the hilltop." This one had two spare magazines inside pouches attached to his belt. I started yanking them off. "Once that circle goes down, we will be in for one hell of a firefight. If the other four at the village try to join the party, that'll make thirteen, nearly half a platoon. I'll need all the ammo I can get."

"You cannot be serious." She stared at me, awestruck and wide-eyed.

"Does it look like I'm joking?" I glared at her, attaching pouches to my belt.

"Kyle, what you've done up to now is impressive, but you can't hope to take all of them on your own." Ignoring her, I moved to the other corpse, nearly tripping over the one at my feet as I went. "Look at you, you can barely stand! What hope do you have of using magic like this? Do you plan to shoot your way out?"

"If I have too, I'm sort of good at it," I said, attaching more pouches to my belt. That made five magazines with thirty rounds each. Not great, but not bad either.

She scoffed. "If you plan on going on a suicide mission, at least let me help you."

"This again?" I stood, drawing myself back to the porthole. "I thought we went over this already."

She stood defiantly in front of me, her eyes burning holes into my own with their intensity. "Listen, I know I cannot stop you from doing this, but you are concussed, wounded, and outnumbered. How long has it been since you were this fatigued?"

I refused to back down from her. Not this time. Not with so much on the line.

Her expression softened, her voice pleading. "My claim to your spirit already gives you many advantages you wouldn't have had." Let me into your body, Kyle. You could endure far greater pain and fatigue. You could sustain more grievous injuries and heal faster from it. More importantly, you could fight this battle refreshed, unburdened by the pain and fatigue you already carry. You could win this battle with mere snaps of your fingers. All you have to do is let me in."

With the two of us standing mere inches apart, there was a part of me that wanted to rage at her, to throw her aside for daring to stand in my way. But she wasn't wrong either. Exhaustion weighed me down, slowing my every move. Everything within me all but begged me to crawl into a hole and hide from the world. To sleep. To rest.

Though I was a little out of practice, fatigue was something I could manage. But the pulsing migraine from the concussion made it nearly impossible to concentrate, making drawing in energy or using magic almost more effort than it was worth. Even something as simple as shadow walking felt like a monumental task. That went without mentioning the fourteen-to-one odds against me outside. Even with this little fortification, it would only be a matter of time before they overwhelmed me if I stayed here.

I could feel my will starting to slip.

"Okay, but what happens when we win? What then?" Confusion flashed in her eyes. "How much of me will remain if I let you take me?" She tried to speak, but I cut her off, keeping my voice level. "I was ignorant of what you were before I accepted you into me in Mosul, but now I know. I don't have to look far to find out what happens to me if I accept you either – I just have to look out this window."

"Kyle, I -" I walked through her, waving her off. She was only a projection of my mind, after all. And she was right, she couldn't stop me if she tried.

"Kyle, you'll die."

Looking out the window, a memory flashed in my mind of Watson shielding me from the blast. I turned to her standing next to me, pulling my pistol from it's holster. "I should have died a long time ago."

Stepping to the window, I drew my pistol sights onto the chalice full of dirt. "So, essentially, an explosion is just condensed wind moving rapidly, right?"

"In a manner of speaking, yes."

I pushed energy into the pistol, stars sparkling in my vision. "I've got a jar of dirt," I sang aloud, pulling the trigger.

The explosion blew apart the legs of the thrall standing next to the chalice, launching him into the air, the fire ring behind him blowing out completely. Holstering my pistol, I grabbed the rifle, sighting in the thrall in front of me. He shouldered his rifle just as a bullet punched through the back of his skull.

# Chapter 34

The moment the second thrall fell, the volley of fire came. I went for a third, shooting a few rounds of my own, but it was no use. I don't know if I even hit him. Rounds slammed into the walls like sledgehammers or cracked through the open windows, driving me away into cover before I lost my head.

Battles are often won or lost in the first fifteen seconds of the fight. Whoever can gain the fire superiority within those first fifteen seconds can set the conditions for the rest of the battle. I may have killed a handful of thralls already, but there were still seven left on this hilltop and likely four more ready to charge in from the valley below. They didn't have night vision or thermal imaging; they weren't exactly making accurate shots. They didn't need to. Their volume of fire more than made up for their lack of accuracy, making it impossible to look out of a window or shoot back. Doing so would have made for a swift end to the fight.

This was the fifteen-second fight, and they had already won it.

*"Get up!"* the demon shouted in my ear. *"Get up and fight!"*

There was no use fighting from in there, the incoming fire was too overwhelming. But she was right. Thralls would be flooding into the blockhouse at any moment, and I had no cover to shoot from when they did. I had to find an alternative.

The blockhouses were placed on the hill in a way that somewhat resembled a right triangle, the closest of the two being directly north of me, while the other was oriented to the northwest. I drew in what little energy I could from the nexus, mostly by pure adrenaline, and tried to connect a shadow to the nearest blockhouse as I crouched. It mostly came into my vision as a blur, so I pushed what energy I could, straining my will, until I nearly tumbled inside.

I crawled into the blockhouse with stars dancing in my vision nearly blinding me from the thrall shooting out of the window. Without standing, I took an easy shot to the back of his head with his back to me. His knees gave out instantly, pitching him forward into the wall, his rifle clattering to the floor as he slid down.

Rifle shots boomed from the floor above me. I must have guessed correctly when I assumed there would only be two thralls inside. It would only be a matter of time before he realized his buddy was down, though I doubted that mattered much.

I crept up the stairs with my rifle up and at the ready, his muzzle flashes strobing with each shot he took out of the window as I approached the second floor. I caught him just as he stepped back to reload, his deft hands working the rifle. Our eyes locked, his expression blank when he brought his rifle up just as I stitched up his center line. He stiffened, falling like a plank onto his back with a thud. I was pretty sure that the fight was out of him, but I drilled him in the head when I reached the top of the stairs anyway.

The gunfire didn't exactly stop outside, but I noticed that the thralls inside the blockhouse stopped firing, and it took me a moment to realize why. The four from the village had already made it to the blockhouse I'd previously occupied and were preparing to storm inside with the other three from the hilltop. The one in the rear of the stack was limping badly, I must have hit him after all.

Lillian stood with her back to me in the circle with the table. I couldn't make out exactly what she was doing, but it was evident that she was preparing the tracker for the spell.

*"We're almost out of time,"* the demon whispered in my ear. *"We must hurry."*

"How long do we have?" I asked, sighting Lillian in through my rifle.

*"It's hard to say, but not long. Once she is finished with the tracker, the sacrifices begin."*

I carefully drew my sights to the back of her head, trying to control my breathing. *"Don't! There is no telling how much energy has been drawn into the spell already. If you kill her now, it would be catastrophic, and you are in no position to run if the spell should detonate."*

I shifted my attention back to the thralls stacking themselves by the door of the block house, snarling in frustration. With my labored breathing, it was a struggle to keep my aim steady on the thrall by the door. Forcing a steady exhale, I gently squeezed the trigger, the round punching through his neck, splattering the wall where he crumbled.

The remaining six immediately split up into teams of three, taking turns bounding to my position. One team laid down to shoot while the other ran for a couple of yards, laid down, and started shooting so the other team could move again.

The old fort once had several small buildings inside. An armory, a storage building, that sort of thing. Those buildings were long gone, and what remained were shallow pits in the ground with placards marking their spots. The thralls would frequently dive into these pits for some shallow cover after every bound. These pits made it difficult to shoot them, and their fire was accurate, though not accurate enough to hit me where I stood deep inside the room, shifting my position to engage whatever team was moving at the time.

They didn't have far to go either, maybe one hundred fifty meters before they reached my blockhouse. The first team bounded; I shifted positions and fired at one until he fell. I reloaded and shot him again to be sure, then shifted to the next team. They ran, I fired some more, another one fell. All the while, the walls thundered to my left and to my front from the thralls on the ground and inside the other blockhouse.

Four left in the field and they were soon at the walls of my little fort. It wouldn't be long before they were inside and I would lose my advantage. They would overwhelm me with numbers alone if I stayed.

The third blockhouse was still too far away for me to shadow walk, not with the energy I had left. The pits in the ground the thralls were using earlier for cover were just deep enough to form a shadow I might be able to crawl through, though, and there was one between me and the other blockhouse. It wouldn't take much for me to get there.

I crouched, pushing energy into the shadow just as the door below me crashed open from their breach. I strained myself against it, trying not to panic from the sound of footsteps coming up the stairs. My heart jumped when my hand finally touched grass, and I pulled myself onto my stomach into the pit, gasping for breath from the exhaustion.

Lying on my back, arm pressed hard against the shallow embankment, I listened for the crack of rounds that never came. They must not have noticed me in my little hiding spot, but that wouldn't last long. There was no way I could gather enough energy to shadow walk again before they spotted me. I would be a sitting duck here if they did. My body felt like lead when I rolled over to peek over the side. Still, no rounds came. The pit I was in lay a little off to the side of the next blockhouse, just inside the fort's perimeter. The thralls inside were probably looking past me, into the blockhouse I just came from.

*"Kyle, please don't —"*

Sprawling to my feet, I sprinted to the blockhouse. The sprint that took seconds felt like hours when I crossed the open ground, expecting a lethal rifle round would drill me at any moment, planting me into the ground for good.

The shots came from behind me. Rounds cracked by my head in the last couple of yards of my approach, slamming into the walls of the blockhouse when I was close.

Nearly barreling into a wall at full speed, I slowed to a walk, crouching under the port holes before taking a knee at a corner of the building to avoid the incoming fire. Gasping for breath, I watched Lillian, with chalice in hand, using a brush to paint symbols onto Amber's exposed chest with my blood.

*"That's the first sacrifice. We must hurry."*

"Shit," I cursed, rising to peek through a porthole with rifle up and at the ready.

A thrall looked panicked, snapping his head from porthole to porthole like a parrot with his mouth open. Our eyes locked just as I pulled the trigger, brain matter blowing out of the back of his head.

The door stood facing the circle encompassing the spell, though it only took a moment to expose myself to get inside. The thrall upstairs must have known something was wrong and started racing down the staircase. He must not have realized that his buddy was already dead, down the stairs nearly as fast as he could. I shot him repeatedly in the legs as soon as I saw them, which gave out from under him, pitching him forward into a tumble. My rifle thundered in the enclosed space, drowning out the cacophony of noise he made as he fell. Once at the bottom, I walked in close and planted a round into his temple.

Peeking through a porthole, I felt like time seemed to crawl when Lillian, with dagger in hand, plunged the blade into Amber's exposed stomach. With shoulders lifted off the table, Amber choked a cough, gawking breathlessly into the sky above. It punched the breath out of me when Lillian sank the blade down to the hilt, Amber going limp and unconscious with the weight of it.

My mind raced. *It's a stomach wound. I can stabilize her. This isn't over. I can still save her.*

*"The second sacrifice,"* the demon whispered breathlessly in my ear.

Lillian pulled the blade out slowly, and I fired by reflex. Three shots rang out, running my magazine dry. Lillian stumbled, dropping the dagger with the rounds punching into her chest, doubling her over onto the table.

*"Kyle, Stop! If you* disrupt *the spell now, you will kill us all!"*

Lillian glared up at me from the table, pushing herself up with one hand, and snapped.

The rifle clicked after the magazine change. Manipulating the rifle, I attempted to clear the malfunction.

Click.

I dropped the rifle, taking another off a dead thrall.

Click.

Taking from the other thrall, I leveled the rifle onto her.

Click.

"Damn it!" I snarled, throwing the ruined rifle to the ground.

Rounds slammed into the walls from the other blockhouse. I could see the muzzle flash sparkling from the second floor. I screamed my rage at the thralls in the building, knowing that I was virtually trapped here until they were dealt with.

I'd had enough.

For a moment, all awareness of the rain-soaked clothes and the frigid cold left me. The wariness and fatigue meant nothing. All I wanted was to rip this hilltop apart.

My hands seemed to move with a mind of their own, drawing my pistol when the door to the blockhouse opened. I could hear my voice above the incoming gunfire, but I was beside myself. Pushing energy into the pistol, I ignited the blue runes along the slide when the first thrall stepped outside. The pistol lurched in my hand, blowing the wall on the first floor apart, the thrall along with it. I fired again, collapsing the blockhouse completely, crushing any remaining thralls beneath its crumpled mass.

Lillian stood fully erect above the table, towering above Amber, dagger in hand with arms spread. I leveled my sights onto her, gritting my teeth, pushing what little energy I had left into the pistol.

I carefully aligned the sights, pausing on the exhale…

She brought her hands together, dagger pointing down, mumbling words of power into the night sky above…

A gentle application of force…

The dagger rose…

The sere broke…

The dagger dropped…

The slide locked to the rear…

My heart stopped…

Lillian disappeared from behind the table where she fell, her left arm tumbling along the ground at the foot of the table. I hardly noticed though. I only saw the dagger sticking hilt deep in Amber's chest, right where her heart was.

The rain stopped, drowning the hilltop in an eerie quiet.

*"Kyle, the spell! It's broken!"*

A flash of light nearly blinded me without a sound, the earth lurching beneath my feet, sending me toppling to the ground.

*"Run! Hurry!"*

The little fort groaned, wood snapping around me with its gradual lean. It may have been designed to hold up against an assault, but it apparently wasn't suitable to withstand the shaking of the earth beneath it.

Daylight seemed to shine outside the open doorway, so I sprinted from the ground outside, sliding to a halt at the sight of a giant pillar of light encompassing both the inner circles, reaching through an opening in the clouds above. The wind whipped around the hilltop in a vortex, churning the thick gray clouds around the pillar like a tornado above.

Energy flooded into the pillar from the nexus beneath my feet, threatening to draw me in with it. Half mesmerized by the light, I held my ground against the crackling of its gathering energy and the force of the wind that threatened to topple me.

I wanted to weep, watching in silence when a dark shadow floated slowly toward the clouds above, arms and legs limply spread, slowly disintegrating within the energy field.

*"Kyle, I'm sorry."*

I wanted to pull her out. I wanted to cradle her in my arms, to brush her hair out of her face. I wanted to hold her close. I wanted to tell her everything would be okay.

I wanted to take her from this wretched place.

*"She's* gone, *we have* to *go."*

Another shadow drifted up below her, Lillian's ruined corpse disintegrating as she rose, breaking me out of my trance.

It called to me.

It was reassuring, beckoning me softly to the toppled podium nearby. Its gold-and-silver inlay sparkled in the light of the pillar, the brown leather cover a contrast to the wet grass it lay in. I ran to the grimoire, plucking it off the ground that rumbled beneath my feet.

A detonation behind me broke my stride near the edge of the plateau. Stumbling off the edge, I felt the earth beneath me crack with a lurch before I could recover my stride.

*"The spell is collapsing,* you *must run faster."*

A scant tree line stood between me and the Custer house, sprouting from within another draw. Fueled with adrenaline, I ran down the hill with everything I had, sliding in some spots from the slick grass beneath my feet.

*"The tree line won't be* enough. *The hilltop is about to explode."*

"I'm not aiming for the trees," I said, sliding into the shadow within the tree line. Even here, the influx of energy crackled around me. I barely had to concentrate to take from the air around me when I connected the shadow of the tree to one within the house nearly two hundred meters away.

Pushing into the shadow, I crawled into the living room, scrambling to take cover behind a wall making up a hallway when the ground beneath me shook, taking me off of my feet. I hit the wall bodily within the chaos and the noise, broken glass cutting into me when I finally hit the ground. Debris crashed into the house, crashing into open windows, threatening to cave in the roof above me until everything fell into silence.

Cradled the book in my arms in the stillness of the hallway, heaving in gasping breaths from the fatigue. A smoky cloud crept into the house, tinting the gray of night with the smell of earth from the explosion outside. I pushed myself upright from the floor, and curled myself around the grimoire against the wall, trying to gain some semblance of comfort from its rigid frame.

Blood from fresh cuts along my arm unlocked the book with a click.

I held it close to my chest, and wept.

# Chapter 35

The shallow layer of soil wasn't enough to hold the crosses upright in some places. I had to move them when I hit the rock below, but I was determined. I didn't walk these steep trails over rocky terrain with crosses in hand, only to be deterred from planting them by some pile of rock.

My hand grew stiff around the handle that sent shock waves up my arm, my forearm growing tighter with each swing of the mallet. You would think that I was well conditioned to hammer spikes in the ground from my years working construction, but that was a long time ago, and these weren't your typical spikes.

Authorities labeled Amber a missing person soon after the fight at Fort Abraham Lincoln. I couldn't exactly tell the authorities she had been murdered by a succubus, not without raising suspicions that I might have been involved somehow or winding up in a psych ward for my efforts. It would be some time before any kind of funeral service would be held for her, if there would be any at all. It didn't seem appropriate to hold one if I were to convey the idea that she was only a missing person, after all. What message would it send if the grieving fiancée gave up so soon before a body was even found? A white wooden cross would have to do, at least for now.

The cross stood defiantly in the ground, stubbornly refusing to descend any further when the mallet pinned it against the rock once more. I cursed when I stood, glaring at the top of the cross that begun to mushroom while I rubbed the tension out of my forearm.

"That'll have to do," I said to the demon standing like a silent sentinel, staring forlornly into the valley below.

"They should hold," she said, looking down at the pair of crosses, then back up to me.

"Yeah," I said, pulling Amber's claddagh out of my pocket, feeling the weight of it in my hand. I found the ring over a mile outside the park grounds a day or so after the battle, using magic to connect it to my own. It was the only piece of Amber that I ever found.

The ensuing explosion from the collapsed spell all but obliterated the hilltop the old infantry fort stood on, leaving virtually no evidence anything was ever there in the first place. The damage to the surrounding structures from the falling debris closed the park entirely, creating a statewide debate as to whether the park was even worth saving.

I doubted it would ever open again.

The light from the pillar could be seen as far as the capital and beyond, while the explosion rocked the foundations of buildings for miles around. The incident nearly caused a panic, though it would eventually be explained away as some sort of meteor strike. Surprisingly, this explanation would be generally accepted, though some of the resulting conspiracy theories were fairly impressive. I assumed The Freemasons fabricated the story after they took my statement and accepted my request for sanctuary. That seemed to be their modus operandi, but I never found out for sure.

Clasping a silver chain through the loop of the ring, I hung the claddagh over the wooden cross and stood. "She would have loved it up here," I said, taking in the view of the wind-swept valley below Killdeer Mountain.

Autumn had already crept in, kissing the vast array of trees in the valley below with vibrant shades of red and yellow. The grasslands danced with waves of green in the wind, stretching out into the painted cliffs of the Badlands beyond.

I'd yearned to bring her up here in the weeks leading to her death. I could almost see her with me then, the crisp breeze playing along the red curls in her hair, her parted lips gifting her breath to the wonder of the landscape. Her warmth in the light would have made her a living art form on this canvas. Her vestige, a wonder set within the fall landscape.

She would have loved it here.

"I'm sorry for your loss," Asmodeus said, interrupting my musing. "She was lovely." She let her words hang, waiting for me to fill in the silence.

"She was, thank you," I said, pulling the claddagh I wore off my finger. "She was the best part of me." I could practically feel her eyes fall on me, searching for me with her lethal gaze. I was too ashamed to allow myself to meet it. I spent the days after the battle wrestling with the could-haves and should-haves of what had happened, silently lambasting myself for the myriad of things that I could have done differently. What if I had accepted her offer? Even if it meant losing myself to the demon, could that have changed things? Could I have saved Amber?

"I know some people like to give a sort of eulogy in moments like this," she said, looking mournfully down at the crosses. "Would you like to say anything?"

"No," I said, slipping a chain through the loop in the ring. "I think I've said enough." I hung the chain around the second cross planted by Amber's, watching the ring softly clicking against its stem. "I think it's time to move on now."

"To do what?"

I met her eyes, a little surprised to see a hint of genuine sadness. "I never asked for this fight, I wanted none of this."

"I know," she said softly.

"There are few things I'm particularly good at. But warfare… now, that is something I've always been good at." A flash of confusion marked her expression. "Unfortunately for the Magistrate, they wanted me to fight in their little war, so I will.

I gestured to the crosses as I spoke. "I will hunt down every one of the bastards that did this to her, I will burn their little club house down with them inside of it if I have to. I will become their living nightmare. And you" – my voice hitching in my sorrow – "you will have your chaos."

A raven took flight from a nearby tree, its throaty cry echoing along the valley as it took to the sky.

"We're being watched," the demon said, gesturing to the bird with a scowl.

"By whom?" I asked, searching after the raven disappearing into the distance.

"It's impossible to say."

My mind flashed to an old woman washing clothes in the river near Lillian's house. "The Society? The Magistrate?"

"Neither is likely." She turned to me with a worried expression. "Whatever we do, we'll need to tread lightly."

"Let them watch, then." I turned to leave, sparing another glance into the valley before making my way down the trail.

"You never told me their name," she called to me, stopping me in my tracks. When I turned to face her, she was standing right where I left her near the edge of the cliff. "Did the two of you ever choose a name?"

The pair of crosses stood next to each other, knee-high near the demon's feet. The chains glistened in the sunlight next to each other, and I wondered, for a moment, if they would find each other on the other side.

She would have been a wonderful mother.

"Lyra," I said, turning to leave.

"Her name was Lyra."

# Acknowledgement

My original beta readers, investors, and long-time friends **Doug and Leah Schermetzler.**

My original beta readers who took it upon themselves to suffer through the original edits.

- **Amy Tichy**
- **Elba Gotay**
- **Ana Zacheus**

The artists who helped bring this story to life.

- My cover **design** artists **Gene Mollica** and **Sasha Almazan** at **G&S Cover Design Studio.**
- **Whitney Law**
- **Kamraan Allibhaye**
- **Adrienne Renick**

To the editors.

- **Joe Nassise**
- **Tammy Salyer.**

Of course, this publication wouldn't have been possible without the support of my Kickstarter backers. Thank you for taking a chance on this brand-new author. Your support means the world to me, and I couldn't thank you enough.

**Matthew Kitajo, Valerie Anne Sizemore, Annie Kavanagh, Eddie Joo, Florentina, Adrienne Renick, Morgan G., Caitlin Jane Hughes, Melissa T., Jose Davila, Kelly McMahon, Amy Tichy, Preston Taylor, Jaimie, Brandy, Kolton, Joe, Jessica Worgo, Javier Vega, Rebecca O'Neill, R. Allen, Cathy Jo Shehorn, Shelli, Ciara Keket, Ali, Nico Hall, Tanvir Khan, Daniel Durm, Jarryd P., Kerry Grestinger, Jonathan Samuels.**

# About The Author

Originally from the Wind River Reservation in Wyoming, Timothy Sizemore is a former U.S Army Airborne Infantryman and Iraq War veteran who wore many hats both inside and out of the military. After a decade-long break, he currently serves as a helicopter mechanic and can otherwise be found raising his two daughters with his wife at home.

Good reviews are vital for Indie authors. The importance of reviews in helping readers find and take a chance on an Indie author cannot be overstated.

**If you've enjoyed this story, would you help me get it in front of more people by leaving an honest review on Amazon and Goodreads?**

I would truly appreciate it if you would. Just follow the link below.

### Amazon

### Goodreads